Amanda Cockrell, writing as Damion Hunter, is the author of seven previous Roman novels: the four-volume series The Centurions, concluding with *The Border Wolves*; and *The Legions of the Mist* and its sequel *The Wall at the Edge of the World*. *Shadow of the Eagle* is the first in The Borderlands, a new Roman series. She grew up in Ojai, California, and developed a fascination with the Romans when a college friend gave her Rosemary Sutcliff's books to read. After a checkered career as a newspaper feature writer and a copywriter for a rock radio station, she taught literature and creative writing for many years at Hollins University in Roanoke, Virginia, where she now lives.

www.amandacockrell.com

Also by Amanda Cockrell writing as Damion Hunter

AMANDA COCKRELL WRITING AS
DAMION HUNTER
EMPIRE'S EDGE

CANELO

First published in the United Kingdom in 2023 by

Canelo
Unit 9, 5th Floor
Cargo Works, 1–2 Hatfields
London SE1 9PG
United Kingdom

A CIP catalogue record for this book is available from the British Library.

Print ISBN 978 1 80032 669 9
Ebook ISBN 978 1 80032 668 2

Cover design by Mark Swan

Look for more great books at www.canelo.co

Printed and bound in Great Britain by Clays Ltd, Elcograf S.p.A.

I

For Liz and Therry

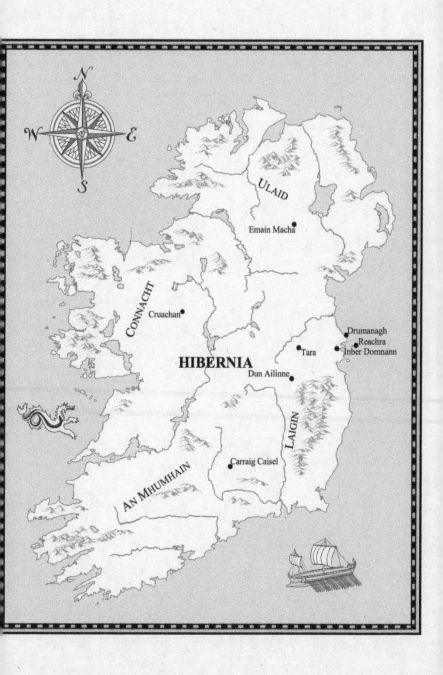

Characters

Romans

Agricola Gnaeus Julius Agricola, former governor of Britain
Ansgarius Faustus's optio in the First Batavians
Arrius Laenas legate of the Second Augusta
Caecilius tribune on Sallustius Lucullus's staff
Constantia daughter of Silanus
Diulius Naso Constantia's husband
Faustus Faustus Silvius Valerianus
Gaia Valeriani (Guennola) Faustus's mother; deceased
Indus soldier of First Batavians
Lartius Lartius Marena the younger, tribune formerly attached to Second Augusta
Lartius Marena Lartius Marena senior, father of Lartius
Lascius surgeon with the First Batavians
Lucius Lucius Manlius the younger, son of Silvia
Lucullus Sallustius Lucullus, governor of Britain
Manlius Lucius Manlius senior, husband of Silvia, father of Lucius
Marcus Silvius Marcus Silvius Valerianus, father of Faustus; deceased
Marcus Silvius Minor Marcus Silvius Valerianus Minor, older brother of Faustus; deceased
Paullus Faustus's slave
Silus ex-army surgeon
Silvia sister of Faustus
Silanus senior surgeon of the Second Augusta

Gaels and others in Inis Fáil (Hibernia)

Aíbinn a Druid
Ailill eldest son of Elim and king of Ulaid
Baine daughter of Elim
Beric one of Faustus's captains
Cassan Tuathal's father's man
Cennétig chief of the brehons
Conrach mac Derg heir to Sanb of Connacht
Dai one of Faustus's captains
Elim Elim mac Conrach, High King
Elwyn man of Tuathal's army
Eochaid king of Laigin
Eochu Eochaid's nephew
Fiachra Tuathal's father's man
Finmall Tuathal's father's man
Foirbre king of An Mhumhain
Llwyd one of Faustus's captains
Morcant Elim's second son
Olwenna Baine's maid
Owain one of Faustus's captains
Riderch Laigin landholder
Sanb king of Connacht
Sechnal Chief Druid of Connacht
Tuathal Techtmar exiled claimant to throne of Inis Fáil

Britons

Aelwen wife of Calgacos
Calgacos former leader of united Caledones
Cadman Epidii chief
Celyn one of Calgacos's Kindred, killed in battle
Ceridwen daughter of Calgacos
Coran Harper harper and one of Calgacos's Kindred
Cuno a trader
Curlew Old One of the sidhe of Llanmelin
Drust hound in Aelwen's household

Efa Rhion's wife

Eirian Orkney woman

Emrys overchief of the Caledones

Guennola original name of Faustus's mother

Gwladus Dobunni woman hired to take care of Silvia and Lucius

Hafren wife of Emrys

Idgual spear brother of Piran

Magpie one of the Old Ones, of the sidhe of Tarvo Dubron

Matauc young chief of the mainland Cornovii

Nall chieftain of the mainland Cornovii

Piran Caledone lord

Rhion one of Calgacos's Kindred, husband of Efa

Rotri a trader

Salmon Curlew's brother, of the sidhe of Llanmelin

Starling one of the highland Old Ones

Swyddog younger Druid of Rhion's household

Vellaunos Chief Druid of Calgacos's clan

I. OWAIN

The men from Hibernia were a bright ring around Tuathal where he sat in the great chair by the hearth. And where had that chair come from, Faustus wondered. It was just enough like a throne to make a statement.

Cassan, the youngest of the three, wore enough gold to sink a small boat and a woolen cloak of bright red and green like a parrot. His pale hair fell over his shoulders as he leaned forward. Fiachra was older, no less showily dressed, with a formidable dark mustache and bright blue cloak over a scarlet shirt. Finmall was brown-haired and lanky, with a lazy way of moving that made Faustus think of Galerius, in Isca Silurum with the Second Legion Augusta where theoretically Faustus should be also. The assignment to help Tuathal Techtmar train his motley war band to retake his father's throne in Hibernia was strictly unofficial.

Finmall was doing the talking. All three of them spoke British with a soft overlay of the tongue of the island they called Inis Fáil and the Roman's Hibernia. "Eochaid Ainchenn of Laigin will come to your banner when you land."

"What surety of that?" Tuathal asked. He was tall and lankier than Finmall now, some seven years since Faustus had first met him as a boy of fourteen with his father's sword and a single-minded purpose. His dark hair was bound with a gold fillet, and he sat at ease in the great carved chair, his boots to the fire. It was summer but the coastal villages of the Epidii were chill at night when a sea mist rolled over them like a cold blanket.

I

"His word, and because Laigin is in your path to Elim mac Conrach and Eochaid does not find Elim mac Conrach worth Laigin's blood," Finmall said. "Not anymore."

Tuathal nodded. He and Faustus were both inclined to take Finmall's assessment as truth. Finmall and Cassan and Fiachra had been his father's men before Elim mac Conrach of Ulaid had usurped the throne by murder, which as far as Faustus could tell seemed to be the way that the High Kingship generally changed hands. It was at any rate the way that Tuathal's father had acquired it from the king of Ulaid who had succeeded Tuathal's grandfather. The lesser kings of Ulaid, Laigin, Connacht, and An Mhumhain were bound to the High King only so long as he could hold the throne, and clan ties counted for more than political ones. Fiachra, Cassan and Finmall, lordless after Elim's victory, had attached themselves instead to the merchants who traded across the water to Britain and Gaul and whose caravans were tempting targets, supplemented by raids on those who declined their services. They had had twenty-one years to go where the merchants went, which was everywhere, and to listen.

"What of Foirbre of An Mhumhain?" Tuathal asked and Finmall shook his head. "Elim has been dangling a marriage with his daughter Baine before Foirbre and Sanb of Connacht both. Foirbre will back Elim."

"And Sanb of Connacht?"

"Sanb will wait and see." Sanb was second or third cousin to Tuathal in some leftwise manner that Faustus couldn't follow. It meant that he might be either more or less inclined to back him.

"Elim has hinted that he favors Sanb," Cassan said. "But if he gives Baine to Sanb he loses his best hold on Foirbre."

"Sanb will likely send an emissary," Fiachra said. "As will Eochaid."

"They will need gifts," Finmall said. "Just slightly more valuable than those they bring you. But only slightly."

"And Elim will send an emissary in response to yours," Fiachra said. "Who must be sent now, before you sail. He'll get no good answer but it must be done in proper fashion if you want the others to follow you."

"Which of you three?" Tuathal asked and Faustus watched with interest as they sorted out who might best have the upper hand in Elim's hall. The Hibernian clans were small kinship bands that aligned themselves according to marriage ties or land holdings and occasionally according to whoever had given an insult that offered the excuse to fight. Elim would never bow to Tuathal but he could be made uneasy with the right approach, and uneasy kings made mistakes in battle.

You are not in command, Faustus reminded himself, as he had regularly since they had sailed from Isca for the Epidii's islands on the western coast where Tuathal's mother had been born. Tuathal, even as an exile, knew his people best, and was a born commander. Faustus's job was to drill Tuathal's war band into the precision of a Roman legion. They had been well on their way when the legate at Isca had suggested that the governor was growing uneasy over his decision to allow that many men not under Roman command to be trained in Roman tactics and that it might be best to be out from under his nose. The chieftain of the Epidii was content to have them in his territory where Rome had very little presence, because Tuathal had an open hand with which he had paid for ships to be built and sent south for his war band. Like the Roman governor, Cadman of the Epidii had been unaware of the size of the war chest which Tuathal's mother had spirited out of Hibernia along with her infant until it was too late to appropriate it. In compensation, having his nephew on the High King's throne in Hibernia would be politically useful and would give him the advantage in trade between there and Britain.

It would be well to sail soon, Faustus thought, both to give them as long a campaigning season as possible, and because the war band camped outside the wall on the landward side of Cadman's hold was growing restless. They wanted to fight someone. He left Tuathal and the Hibernians and wandered out of the hall through the warren of buildings, threading his way between the guest hall, the dairy, and the women's weaving

3

house. From the seaward side of the surrounding village, perched on a promontory above the water, he could look out to the westward islands that rose humpbacked above gray water. Landward stretched Cadman's fields and outlying farmsteads and Faustus's army arrayed amid its tents and wagons in the orderly geometry of a Roman marching camp. Beside the camp was the drill field, targets for archery, straw men for sword practice, and the posts which every man learned to hit with a slingstone.

It had not been an easy thing to instill in them the habits of a professional army, particularly the sons of wealthy southern houses with a taste for adventure, who arrived in shirts and breeches of fine wool, their throats heavy with gold torques, attended by armor-bearers and grooms and indignant at the expectation that they carry their own shields and armor on the march. There were flax-haired farm boys, muscular and efficient-looking as young bulls, and dark-haired Silures armed with bows and spears, their chests tattooed with the clan marks of their houses. There were men of no recognizable tribe or city, armed with serviceable long swords and clad in ring mail and iron helmets, and men from the highlands who had probably been fighting the Romans the year before, when Julius Agricola had taken Roman control of the island clear to the northern shores. There were a handful of ex-legionaries and a few that Faustus thought might be and weren't admitting it, since there were not many other ways to leave the legions other than honorable discharge.

And there was the tall blond man with a right arm that hung immobile at his side and a sword belt slung to be drawn with the left hand, who had appeared looking for Centurion Valerianus not long after they had come to the Epidii camp. He had the accent and the tribal tattooing of the highlands but unlike most of the Britons, who cultivated luxurious mustaches, he was clean-shaven.

Faustus had given him a long thoughtful look and said only, "Can you fight?"

"Try me."

4

Faustus had settled his helmet on his head and picked up his shield, its legionary insignia painted over with the sunburst emblem adopted by Tuathal. "Paullus! Get me my sword!"

Paullus stuck his head around the tent flap. "Here. Wait and I'll get your hauberk."

Faustus shook his head. He had adopted a shirt of ring mail like the one the stranger wore in place of the instantly recognizable plates of a legionary lorica, it weighed more than he cared for and he was reasonably sure this man didn't actually want to kill him.

The stranger put a nondescript iron helmet over his cropped hair and strapped a round shield to his useless right arm with the fingers of his left hand. Faustus could see that he could only swing it side to side. Faustus took his sword, raised his shield, and advanced on the blond man. The mobility of his shield arm gave him an unfair advantage but that was the point. Everyone else this man would have to fight would have a working shield arm too. The blond man hefted a long sword heavy enough, Faustus knew, to break bone, but less useful in close quarters than the short legionary gladius. They circled each other carefully, watchful. Faustus shoved his shield at his opponent, hard, trying to put him off-balance, get his blade in past the other's guard. The heavy long sword came down on the shield with staggering force, slicing through its edge, jerking it almost out of Faustus's grip. He recovered, stepped back, took stock. They were attracting a crowd of spectators and he saw men placing bets.

The blond man swung and Faustus jumped into the blow, pushing hard against the other man again, trying to get his short sword under the shield or around it. The blond man took a step back. He clearly knew the danger of letting a man with a short sword get too close, under the effective range of the slashing long sword. He kept it well out, holding Faustus at bay. It was when he drew back to strike that his defenses would be in danger.

Faustus feinted, and the stranger seemed to anticipate him. They circled each other, each taking the other man's measure. The man swung again and this time Faustus slid past the blow and got his sword under the other's battered shield and felt the point nick through the ring mail. He backed off before the man could retaliate and stood panting. "What are you called?"

"Owain."

Faustus got his breath back. "You can fight. Get that seen to. I drew blood."

Owain grimaced. "You did. I have no one to see to it."

He was alone then; not even a slave. "Our surgeon is in the tent under the alders over there, behind the field ovens. Paullus will take you." Faustus pointed at his own slave.

The man followed Paullus toward Silus's warren of tents and supply wagons. Silus had come to Faustus in Isca, where he had served until he had been invalided out with a twisted leg, a gift from an encounter with an iron-bound wagon wheel. He had the wheat-colored hair of a Gaul and was, like Faustus, a provincial Roman citizen from a farming family. Faustus had been relieved to acquire a battlefield surgeon; they were going to need one. He nodded at the men settling their bets and went to his tent to think about the advisability of taking Owain into the war band.

He was still thinking about it now, leaning against Cadman's gatepost while Tuathal negotiated with the Hibernians. There was a skull set into the gate just above his head, some ancient enemy of Cadman or Cadman's ancestors. It shone eerily in the long summer twilight that was only now giving over to full dark.

–

The man who called himself Owain noted the Roman's figure silhouetted in the gate, backlit by the village fires. He had been face to face with him, asking for a place in the war band, before he had recognized him and almost certainly seen recognition dawn in the Roman's face as well. If the Roman knew where he had seen Owain before, why he hadn't said so was a matter to puzzle over before Owain decided whether or not to run again. The governor that Centurion Valerianus had fought for in the highlands had been called back to Rome. Given leave to train a ragtag army for Tuathal Techtmar, what did the centurion owe the new Roman

6

governor, if anything? He would think on it, Owain decided, and watch his back, if only for a few more nights in the warmth of a fire and the company of spear brothers again. He wondered if there would be more who had made their way last autumn out of the chaos of the final battle, through the wild mountains of the north and the western coast to find refuge and purpose here. He found himself scanning the faces around other fires, the men he now drilled with in the formations the Roman had taught them. He had seen only one, and he had shied from him. Dai might not forgive that the man who was now Owain had been in command when Celyn died. Celyn had been Dai's spear brother, lover, other half. Looking at Dai now, you could almost see the gaping wound that was Celyn's absence.

—

In the morning Fiachra sailed for Hibernia with a message from Tuathal politely inviting Elim mac Conrach to cede the High King's throne to its rightful heir. Fiachra was the eldest of the three and had been fostered in Elim's household as a boy. The ties of fosterage did not preclude being on opposing sides in a war, but they did serve to remind Elim that Fiachra might know him better than was comfortable. An embarrassment here and there for the poets to get their teeth into would be useful.

Faustus found himself bemused by the power that poets appeared to hold in Hibernia. Satirists like Martial could infuriate the powerful in Rome, but Hibernian poets were held to be able to raise welts on the skin and even shift the tide of battle.

Fiachra would land where Tuathal intended to, on the coast along Inber Domnann where the trading port was, and ride from there to Tara. The guard he would take was strictly to ward off the bandits who preyed on travelers ("other bandits," Tuathal said) along the road. Elim would do him no harm. Elim's own emissary, if he sent one, would not trouble to go to Britain with a response but would meet Tuathal on the coast to tell him what he might do with his father's sword. Then, the niceties having been observed, they would fight.

In the meantime, Faustus found his charges things to do to ward off the boredom that could take the edge off an army's restlessness. Tuathal had gathered some three thousand men, less than the strength of the single legion with which Agricola claimed he could conquer the island, but sufficient enough with the addition of Eochaid of Laigin's men to install Tuathal at Tara where he would have the legitimacy of a rightful king. Eochaid's men worried Faustus. The Hibernians fought the way the Britons did, recklessly, screaming like fiends, and utterly without discipline. Once loosed on the enemy they were uncontrollable. Eochaid's men, he decided, would be expendable.

He set the rest to a mock battle with wooden training weapons and a prize of good wine for the winning side. Faustus had broken them into six cohorts in the Roman style and they advanced in formation, the rear ranks holding back as the spearmen attacked, and then moving up in lockstep to batter the opposing line. The cavalry closed with each other on both flanks, tumbling their opponents from the saddle with wooden spear shafts while the loose horses tangled with the spearmen on foot. The infantry fighters closed a shield wall and the horses balked and scattered. The "dead," under orders to retire if unhorsed or struck a solid blow, limped to the sidelines to cheer for their side where Cadman's villagers had come from their fields to see the show.

Faustus and Tuathal watched from the slope below Cadman's wall, with Cadman, Cassan, and Finmall. "They will send Elim mac Conrach and his sons to Annwn for me," Tuathal said approvingly. "I am glad now for the Roman governor's reluctance. Rome will have had no hand in it and I will not have to figure out how to make them leave again."

"What are you going to do with them afterward?" Faustus asked. Three thousand men could eat even a king's hall bare, and eventually grow restless and make trouble. Cadman was already eager for them to sail. The young lords who had come for adventure would go home again to boast to their kin, if they lived. But the rest…

"I have been thinking on that," Tuathal said.

"And?" The two sides battling below them were locked, neither willing to give ground. With luck, none of them would actually kill each other. A cloud of dust rose from them, carried on the wind, and a loose horse galloped out of the fray and into the camp, tearing out tent pegs as it went.

"Inis Fáil is fertile and there is uninhabited land enough for grants of household to men who will swear to me for it," Tuathal said. "And Elim's widows to marry."

Cassan and Finmall nodded.

"You are ruthless enough to be High King," Faustus said.

"I am practical."

"So was Agricola. It's the same thing."

"No doubt, and the reason it is best to do this thing without him. You told me yourself that Rome would want a price, even for your services."

"Rome always wants a price," Cadman said, "and for that reason we prefer to be ignored by Rome. You may bide in these islands only so long as you do not trouble Rome."

"For my services, all Rome will want is assurance that you won't ally with rebellious Britons," Faustus said to Tuathal.

"Easily enough granted since I have no intention of it. I am not a fool." Tuathal turned to the trumpeter at his side. "Halt them before they batter each other further, we will award wine to both sides in a draw."

–

Owain sat outside his tent nursing a bruise on his shin as the Inis Fáil men went around with jars of wine. The sky was a rare bright blue, full of wheeling gulls, and the mud flats on the seaward side were crowded with wading birds probing the sand at low tide. A shadow fell across Owain's lap and stayed there as he looked up. Dai. He had known Dai would find him since they had come helmet to helmet across the shield line in the mock war. Dai had fought furiously, viciously, but that had always been his way. Dai would fight anything that offered him the chance.

After a long moment Dai sat, folding his legs under him and pushing his brown hair out of his eyes. His arms were bare, the clan marks spiraling down them overlaid with dirt and runnels of sweat. "What do you call yourself?" he asked finally.

"Owain."

"We were told you died." Dai's voice was bitter with anger at the lie. "Aelwen brought your sword to Emrys to prove it."

Owain pulled his shirt away from the twisted red knot of scar tissue that was his right shoulder. "Aelwen did my bidding. A warlord must be whole. Could Emrys have held the clans together long enough to make peace if I had gone back, even just as headman of our own?"

"I don't know. I didn't stay. Only long enough to bury Celyn."

Owain closed his eyes. He had a brief memory, sharp as glass, of Dai standing over Celyn's body beating the oncoming Romans off it until Owain had pulled him forcibly away to carry the word that would bring the women into the chariot line, a desperate last resort. "Do you blame me for Celyn too?"

Dai's face was bleak, anger cooling into sorrow. "I blame myself because I couldn't keep him alive."

"It was not your task to keep him alive. Nor he you."

"Nor was it yours. I was angry that you left us."

"Why have you come here?"

"I am thinking for the same reason you have," Dai said. "To fight someone."

Owain laughed, a short bark that was not quite amused. "The Old Ones said I was not to die and so I haven't. I tended pigs for a swineherd and sowed barley for a farmwife before I heard of the war band gathering here. You could have stayed among the Kindred and been headman."

"Not without Celyn."

While they waited for Fiachra to return with Elim's refusal, Faustus made his final choice of captains from among the war band, with Tuathal's assent: a Silure horseman named Llwyd to command the cavalry; Beric, the son of a Catuvellauni lord in the south; Owain, Dai, Cassan, and Finmall. They were an oddly assorted lot. Llwyd seemed to speak mainly to horses but the cavalry learned to pivot on a spearpoint under his command. Beric had arrived with two slaves, a string of five good horses, and a silvered cuirass that would have done a tribune proud. But he carried his own shield on the march without complaint, paid close attention to Faustus's instructions and example, and brought his cohort into shape with the easygoing geniality of someone used to being obeyed. In contrast, Owain and Dai in patched and worn breeches and cloaks, with battered shields and dented helmets, exuded an air of grim efficiency that their men strove to imitate. Cassan and Finmall were gaudy as an emperor's favorite and lethal as adders.

They would fight under Tuathal's command with Faustus as his second, an optio in the Roman fashion to be the commander's voice, to carry orders, to sort out the string of people wanting to speak with the commander, to give advice, and to take command if the commander fell. Faustus had no illusions about what would happen if that occurred. He had freed Paullus in his will some time ago during the campaign for the north, and left instructions to send his back pay to his sister in Narbo Martius. He knew that he should have written to Silvia and at least told her what he was doing, but she would only worry over it. Constantia, the surgeon's daughter at Isca who was a friend of several years, had said cheerfully that she supposed he knew what he was doing and counted on him to come back to Isca with his head still attached. Silvia on the other hand... Conveniently, there was no military post handy and he couldn't spare a rider to take a letter to Isca. He pulled her last letter from his camp desk and read it again, guiltily.

My dear brother,

*Now that Julius Agricola has retired I don't see why
you cannot retire as well. Your nephew is six now and
really should know his uncle. Manlius says there are several
promising posts in his office where you could start a career.
And he has a cousin who is old enough to marry now
and Manlius believes her father would welcome the match.
None of us think her condition is serious enough to be an
impediment.*

What horrible thing was wrong with the child, Faustus wondered
again.

*Britain sounds like a dreadful country, nothing but rain. I
can't help feeling that Mother must have been glad to be
taken from there, even under the circumstances.*

The circumstances had included the slave market during Rome's
first attempts to pacify West Britain. Faustus's father had bought
her for a housekeeper and subsequently married her. Faustus
decided that Silvia didn't know what she was talking about, or
didn't want to.

*...living among barbarians with skulls on their walls and
paint all over their faces, and the women half-naked from
what I hear and the men in breeches instead of tunics
like civilized countries. Father always said that Britain
was uncivilized, even the language, all spluttery and just
incomprehensible. Do come home. If you will only send
word, Manlius will find you a good post and talk to little
Livilla's father.*

Faustus would have drowned himself before he did so, and would
have to repeat that when he got within reach of the imperial post.
Why Silvia thought he wanted to marry some infant with an
unspecified "condition" – consumption? fits? – he had no idea.

He had pointed out to her several times that he didn't want to marry at all. Less so now than ever while the girl he had known in the Orcades islands to the north still troubled his dreams. He had known from the start that he couldn't stay with Eirian or take her with him, but his nighttime mind had been slow in grasping it. Even his father's shade appeared less often than Eirian in his dreams. Silvius Valerianus, like his daughter, had had things to say ever since Faustus had sold the family farm and joined the army, and being dead had not stopped him. Since Paullus occasionally saw him too, Faustus had come to the conclusion, almost with relief, that the visitations were not entirely in his head. Being haunted seemed preferable to being insane. Paullus had even seen him pat Pandora once. Pandora was the wolfhound bitch who ostensibly belonged to Faustus, but in truth she was Paullus's dog. The two of them slept in a pile on Paullus's pallet in Faustus's quarters and Paullus kept records of her breeding history like a king's councillor arranging marriages of state. He had put away a considerable amount of money from the sale of her pups. Just now she was being guarded like a marriageable princess against unseemly suitors, since pups would be a nuisance on the coming adventure. She was in heat again and Paullus had her on a lead when he came to find Faustus.

"Fiachra's back," Paullus said.

Faustus stood. "And I suspect Elim mac Conrach hasn't offered to hand over the throne."

"No. Elim mac Conrach appears to have told Fiachra that he will see Tuathal and all his war band dead with their entrails torn out by the Morrigan's ravens and their eyes in the bellies of crows. Something like that."

"Well, we were expecting that."

"The impending High King of Inis Fáil has sent me to find you and call a council," Paullus informed him.

Faustus raised his eyebrows at Paullus since that bordered on impertinent. On the other hand, Paullus was probably entitled to it. Faustus put Silvia's letter away and pulled his cloak around him, not military scarlet but a dark brown and blue, reflecting his entirely unofficial status and the opportunity to pass for a Briton if he needed to. Paullus, he noted, had been letting his hair grow and was now tying a short, pale horse's tail back with a strip of leather. *We're all going native*, he thought. "Cassan and Finmall will have word already. Find the other four and send them to us. Is he in Cadman's hall?"

"He is, and in a fine mood. Apparently, among his people the greater the threat the higher the status you have been accorded."

Fiachra said much the same thing when they had gathered with Tuathal and the captains. A slave went around with cups of Cadman's mead, which Faustus took to be a celebration of their imminent departure. Mead, brewed from honey, was more precious than beer. Fiachra raised his cup. "To consternation for Elim mac Conrach, may twenty-one years of accumulated ill fortune now come down upon him."

Tuathal drank from his cup and the rest raised theirs. His eyes rested on each of them in turn. "Before we sail you will give me your oath to fight for me and for us all, in exchange for land and gold when we gain our victory."

"We have sworn to that already," Llwyd said.

"You have. But you will swear again now, in the name of whatever god you hold most holy, and I will swear also, on my father's sword." He drew it. The scabbard was fine bronze, bound in strips of red leather that had darkened with age. The leaf-shaped blade was old as well, dark and polished. The hilt formed a crowned face with staring gold eyes, and in the dim hall the fire made them flicker as if they were alive. There was a little whispered intake of breath as they looked at it. It exuded some old power, possibly holy, possibly not.

"By the Dagda, the good god, I will swear," Fiachra said.

"And I," Finmall said. "And by Brigid, patron of poets. I will make a song to raise weeping pustules on Elim mac Conrach's treacherous skin."

"By the Dagda," Cassan said. "And by Manannan mac Lir of the waters we must cross."

14

"Very well," Llwyd said. "By Lleu and Epona of the horses."

"By Lugh Brightspear whom my fathers worshipped," Beric said. "This being a matter for the old gods." These days Beric's father was priest of the Temple of the Deified Claudius in Camulodunum.

"By Mithras, god of soldiers," Faustus said. He looked at Llwyd. "And by Lleu who my mother's people worshipped." He gave it the pronunciation that Llwyd had.

They looked at him with interest. That was something that only Tuathal had known.

"By Lugh," Owain said, and Dai echoed him, "By Lugh."

–

A white cow and a red one awaited sacrifice to the Sun Lord in all his forms. Tuathal would offer them himself at the altar on the hold's seaward side. Reading of the omens would wait until they had crossed the water since the Druids of the highlands had flown to Inis Fáil after the battle in the north. Druids were proscribed in any province under Roman control for their constant incitement of rebellion. Cadman no doubt had Druids in his household, but they were not there now so long as a Roman officer was.

Two quick strokes of Tuathal's knife dropped the cattle soundlessly in their tracks, even before the second could react to the smell of blood, in itself a favorable omen. Faustus breathed a little more easily after that. He knew that some of his men were uneasy at the lack of sufficient signs of victory with no priests to read them. The Druids could see patterns in the organs of sacrificed beasts or in the schooling of fish and the starlings wheeling like a banner in the wind. Faustus just saw birds in the air and what omens were spoken in the shape of their flight he had no idea.

For himself he dug a makeshift altar in the bank of the little creek that traversed Cadman's barley fields and set a stone above it for a roof with a channel below so that the water flowed in and out. Water was holy. He put a piece of the meat on the stone while the scent of the roasting carcasses blew down on the breeze from the altar on the hilltop. He knelt before it in the river mud to pray.

"Mithras, lord of armies, god of soldiers, guide me. Grant us victory." The wild things would steal the meat as soon as he was gone, but that wasn't the point. The point was the gift. If the foxes ate it, then they might prosper too.

—

In the guest hall the captains knelt by the hearth while Fiachra sketched the landscape of Inis Fáil in the ashes and Cadman's hounds nosed among the rushes on the floor for the leavings from their meal.

"Here is Ulaid," Fiachra said. "And then Laigin to the south, where Eochaid is king, and Sanb of Connacht to the west." He drew a finger through the ashes. "And in the far south Foirbre of An Mhumhain. With Tara here, where the High King has his throne." He put his thumb midway up.

"And the High King rules the other kings?" Beric asked.

"Not as such," Finmall said. "It's complicated. Except for Ulaid maybe, which Elim gave over to his son. The High King can command tribute, and fighting men if he has a quarrel to settle. The lesser kings otherwise do as they please – within the limits of the law. The brehons rule even kings."

"What are they?"

"Judges. The brehons make the law and interpret it. Even a king cannot go against their decision."

"Then why does Tuathal Techtmar raise an expensive war band for a kingship that comes with such constraints?"

"If you were not practically a Roman, Beric, you would know this," Llwyd said, and Finmall laughed.

"The High King holds the power to call up a war band and put a different man on the throne in place of a lesser king," Finmall said. "It is all a matter of power. And in Inis Fáil power rests in gold and cattle."

"Indeed." Cassan leaned past Dai's shoulder to tap his finger on the thumbprint of Tara. "And that is a holy thing in itself and marks the gods' favor on him. Most wars start over cattle and tribute."

"The brehons do not interfere with that?" Dai asked him.

"Brehons rule on matters such as insult or theft or killing between individuals, and set the price to be paid. Or on issues of marriage and divorce. Wars are not their business, no more than that of the Druids."

"Not even this one?"

"If Tuathal's Roman were leading Romans, and not Tuathal's hired men, yes," Cassan said, "as I have heard that the Druids in the northern highlands took a stand. But clan against clan, no."

"The Druids of the north were late in deciding," Dai said quietly.

"I expect they may have thought on that," Cassan said. "Since then."

"Those that are left."

Cassan said, "Best you look westward, not back."

Owain had been silent, listening, but he stood now and stretched, pulling his bad arm with his left to keep it from stiffening more. Outside the guest hall, outside the houses and byres and kitchen gardens of Cadman's promontory hold, outside its stone walls and ring ditch and beyond the sea cliffs where it perched, lay an unknown land, a new country that he might fight for a place in with no old ghosts to cling to him. A place in which to either live or die.

II. BRAN AND THE FINMAN

"That will no doubt grow to your fingers," Emrys said. "Put it down and eat."

Aelwen laid the spindle and distaff in her lap. It never left her now, nor any of the other women, if they were to have enough wool to pay the Roman taxes. Emrys's wife Hafren sat across the fire from them with her own spindle. She motioned to a slave and the woman brought bowls of soup, heavy bread, and a cheese. At least Hafren was well settled since Emrys's eye had lighted on her, Aelwen thought. Emrys and Calcagos had been old enemies before they had joined against the Romans, but that didn't matter now. Too many of the Caledone women were widows or would go unmarried all their lives for want of men. Calgacos might be alive or he might not. He had gone with the Old Ones inside the hills and from there, no one knew. Officially, he was dead.

"You should marry," Emrys said, as if reading that thought, although it was a subject that he had broached before. "The Druids would release you."

"Only if you find me a man who can spin," Aelwen said, spinning just now being more useful than the male pursuits of fighting and cattle raiding. "And the Druids are not thick on the ground just now, with the Romans watching." She was aware that Emrys wanted Calgacos's widow wed to solidify his hold on the chieftainship that now, after the war with the Romans, bound all the Caledone tribes together, at least in theory, despite the fact that the new landholders were mostly old men and boys barely past their spear-taking.

"I will find you a man who can manage your hold," Emrys said.

"My brother does well enough," Aelwen said. "Leave off, Emrys, I am not of your Kindred." Of her own clan's Kindred, only Dai, Coran Harper, and her brother Rhion had survived, Dai possibly because he didn't care after Celyn was killed. Afterward Dai had shaved his face and gone with the women to find Celyn's body and bring it back, risking death or the slave market to do it. He had seen him buried and then vanished, whether into the southern lands or into Annwn with Celyn no one knew. Rhion had a healing wound in his calf that had cut the muscle and left him limping. The clan had elected him headman nonetheless, a departure from the belief that a headman must be whole or ill luck would follow. They had had the ill luck already and Rhion had the respect of the clan.

"Better we talk of whether the grain will stretch to feed us all through the winter," Aelwen said, trying to divert the conversation. She had not ridden four days from Bryn Caledon to make herself heartsore fighting Emrys on the matter of marriage.

Half the cattle and sheep had gone to feed the Roman army as it flowed over their lands like a bloody tide, and the hides and wool sent south. The ruined fields had been brought back under the plow this spring, but the hands to work them were few when most of the slaves had been sold or simply taken by the Romans. What was planted ran to weeds or was torn up by wild pigs. The hounds, boys fostered in the lords' households, worked alongside the other children, some too young to be at the task, with any adult who could be spared from other work.

Aelwen put her spoon in the bowl that Hafren's woman had brought her and set herself to come to an agreement on grain distribution with Emrys. His northern lands were in somewhat better condition than hers to the south and that meant that she needed his goodwill.

-

Bryn Caledon had suffered from lack of hands to maintain it, despite what Rhion could do. Aelwen surveyed it from the chariot track that wound up the slope with simultaneous relief at homecoming and despair at the damage. The small hound driving stood proudly at the reins. To him it still looked very fine. But the roof needed thatch and the pony shed doors hung like drunkards on their hinges where the doorframe was rotting. The disrepair didn't show yet to a hound of twelve, and Drust was proud to be fostered by the headman's sister.

"Visitors," he said now, interested.

Another chariot sat in the courtyard, its ponies unhitched. Aelwen eyed the driver walking them dry. Piran's man. Which meant Piran, no doubt.

It was. He was sitting by the fire in the hall, feet on the hearth and a cup of beer in his hand. The other hand rested on the carved arm of the chair that had been Calgacos's. Aelwen gritted her teeth, exasperated. The slave who had brought the beer looked at her apologetically. It was required to offer hospitality and was not for a slave to deny it to a Caledone lord.

Piran was very fine, in a bright cloak of red and black, no doubt part of the new weaving from his hold that should have gone to pay the Roman taxes, Aelwen thought, irritated. He had not sent his full share yet. The gold torque at his throat caught her eye. Like all the other Caledone women she wore thin bronze wires twisted through her ears to keep open the holes where her gold ear drops had been before the war.

Piran rose, beaming at her. Aelwen was aware that she was still beautiful, with little gray as yet in her fox-colored hair, but Piran's gaze made her think of young stags in rut, chasing any doe.

"Bring us some bread and cheese," Aelwen said to the slave. "While Piran tells me where he came by that gold torque."

Piran laughed. "A Roman had no need for it anymore."

Aelwen looked more closely. The fine hairs along her arms rose. "That is a thing they give the Roman soldiers for bravery. They wear them on their chest. What have you done?"

"Only what we should all be doing," Piran said. "It was a very great fight," he added, his eyes dancing.

"You will have them down on our heads!"

"No. We buried them. There were only four of them, out hunting, like fools, in my hunting runs. All their commanders will know is that they did not come home."

The slave came back with a wheel of cheese and a loaf of warm bread. She set it beside the chair that Piran had been occupying and he sat back down.

Aelwen sat, automatically pulling wool from the distaff between her fingers. Emrys was right. It would grow into them soon. "I am not a fool, Piran. If a Roman sees that thing, you endanger the treaty."

"I will sell it then," Piran said, "to buy you a bride gift."

"I have told you no before now," Aelwen snapped. "You are half my age." Not even Emrys would have chosen Piran, who was as unreliable as a cat. She debated telling Emrys that Piran had been raiding the Roman outposts. Piran had followers, other young fools, and it might make a division that would be hard to heal.

"I do not yet grow old and timorous," Piran said. "Are we to be Rome's lap dogs forever? There is talk of a war band sailing for Inis Fáil to put a new king on the throne there."

"And what has that to do with us?" Piran just wanted a war, any war. Aelwen was sick to her core of war, and she came of a warlike people. Before the Romans, raiding other clans for gold and cattle had been a grand contest to see who could amass the most. The Romans' inevitable, unstoppable advance had made war, and its aftermath, into a desperate battle for survival.

"If we ally with the new king in Inis Fáil, we will have a base from which to strike Rome." Piran spoke as if that was obvious. The gold torque gleamed at his throat, red in the reflected light from the hearth fire.

Aelwen held out her hand. "Let me see that."

Piran pulled it off, grinning. She turned it over in her fingers, holding it at an angle to the light. As she had thought, there was writing inside. Like most of her people, Aelwen did not read, either her own language or Latin. The letters were run together around the inside. It would be the name of the man who had been awarded it, and possibly his legion or the battle in which he had earned it. It was as identifiable as the clan patterns tattooed in blue woad on her own arms to a man who could read it.

She handed it back. "File those marks away, and sell it."

"That will lessen its weight," Piran protested.

"The loss of your head will lessen yours!" Aelwen said.

Piran grinned at her again. "Will you wed me if I do?"

"I will tell Emrys if you don't."

"Emrys! Now we follow Emrys, and we were Calgacos's lords. There are some who don't like that."

Piran might as well have been a half-grown ram, butting everything with new horns. "You only took your holding after Calgacos died," Aelwen said furiously. "If your father had lived, and your uncle, you would not have that holding. Rhion gave it to you because there was no one else. Remember that while you are sitting in Calgacos's chair. Now go away and rid yourself of that torque." She rose and clapped her hands for the slave. "Tell Lord Piran's driver to hitch his ponies."

When she had heard Piran's chariot retreating down the track she sat by the hearth again, willing the anger to leave her. She was so angry most of the time that it made her head ache.

–

"Did I not say she wouldn't have you?" Piran's driver asked. Idgual was spear brother to Piran and could see no reason to court a woman who could have been his mother.

"I want that one. If we're to push the Romans out again I will need her influence, even though she is a woman."

"She doesn't want you," Idgual observed.

"When a woman is that angry at a man it means she wants him," Piran said. "You'll see."

Idgual looked dubious. That had not been his experience, but better to concentrate just now on navigating the winding track that crouched atop the mountainside. Below, a lake of dark water reflected back the late sun and the pine forest at its edge, mirrored in the water like a kingdom of the Otherworld. He had watched the Druids throw the last of the clan's gold, two bowls old and sacred, into that Otherworld before the last battle. Then the war band had marched and left behind Idgual and Piran and the other boys on the edge of manhood, and most had not come back.

How much gold was in that lake, Idgual wondered, given to the gods for victories that had not come? He shook that thought from him. It was unlucky at best and sacrilegious at worst. The back of his neck itched and he said a quick prayer of apology to Lugh Brightspear and to the Mother, to whom it was unwise to deny their due.

–

Piran was not to be shifted, and so Idgual followed, as he always had, when Piran took his news to Emrys.

Emrys raised one eyebrow. The old scar on his cheekbone, memory of a long-ago cattle raid, was whiter even than his pale skin and lime-bleached hair and mustache, like a vein of quartz in stone. He asked Piran, "And where heard you this news out of Inis Fáil?"

"It was a trader from the Epidii. The claimant to the High Kingship there is Cadman's kin through his mother's line."

"Let me understand," Emrys said, and Idgual shifted his feet uneasily. "You would draw off the few fighting-age men we have left to ally with a man who has been living in the Romans' laps for seven years – did you know that part of the tale? – and then come back here and fight the Romans again."

"They are in our land!" Piran said, fists clenched. "Taking anything their eye lights on, marching lordly-wise up and down their roads – which they force us to build for them through our own lands!"

Emrys nodded. "They are. And it chafes me as it does you. But I have learned a thing that you have not, being young and greener than unripe barley, and until you have learned it, do not come and lecture me!"

Piran subsided and Hafren, Emrys's new young wife, came out from the women's quarters with a bundle of blankets in her arms. "Take these to the guesthouse," she said, giving them to Piran, "and make yourselves beds there. There are traders come from the islands in the north and maybe they will have new tales to tell if you ask."

It was a plain and expert dismissal and Emrys watched it with amused respect. She was barely older than Piran, and had been taken in a raid on the Damnonii to the south in revenge for treating with Rome. In the aftermath of the war, Emrys, several years widowed, had seen the resilient core and the quick mind beneath the surface.

Now she said, "There is not enough meat for even a thin stew. I have told them to kill the black hen that's stopped laying and the cock that chased the pig boy yesterday, although I expect we'll need to boil him with a stone until the stone grows tender to get any good of him."

"An evil bird," Emrys said. "Set it on Piran. And see that those blankets are collected in the morning as soon as he is out of them. One night is sufficient hospitality in fair weather."

"One night is more than he deserves," Hafren muttered, but there were rules about that. And in any case, the only others in the guesthouse were the traders come from the Orcades, and traders were always wise enough to keep their hands out of other people's quarrels.

There was no telling what tribe, if any, these belonged to. They had no clan marks and their clothes were nondescript breeches and woolen shirts, serviceable cloaks. Their hair was cropped and they wore substantial mustaches in the British fashion. Traders were travelers, often for generations. They had a Cornovii pilot with them, no doubt hired in the islands to navigate the treacherous local currents and the strait between the islands and the northern mainland. Since the Romans had come to the north one effect had been to increase trade among the Caledone tribes in the east and the Cornovii and other peoples of the northwest. With Rome on their doorstep, the mainland Cornovii had been part of the peace treaty at the war's end. Only the Cornovii of the Orcades had kept clear of the war, and the Romans had sent an army to winter there despite that.

–

Piran had thought better of wearing the gold torque in front of Emrys and he sold it to one of the traders in the guesthouse.

The trader waited until he had turned away, pocketing his coin, before he nudged his fellow and held the torque out to show him. The other man raised his eyebrows but neither said anything.

They had spread their wares on a rug by the hearth for the people of Lyn Emrys to see, after giving the lord and his wife first look. There was a box of carefully cushioned Roman glass cups and a blue glass vase with gold spirals curling around its midsection; jewelry, some of it very likely among the gold sold to buy grain in the last years of the war; knives and pony trappings, bronze and clay cook pots, amulets and small fairings like ribbon and spools of silver wire. Emrys's people had come to buy what they could and to listen to the traders' pilot, who surprisingly was a woman despite her breeches, and had a great store of tales to tell concerning ancient battles and talking fish.

The pilot for her part noted the young man with sleek brown hair who made her think of an otter, and the gold torque, because certain things were beginning to occur to her. On the other hand, if they were true, that was Cuno and Rotri's business and not hers. Likely they would send her back to High Isle if they thought she knew more than she should.

High Isle had grown small since the Romans had come and gone. Cuno and Rotri had come to the Orcades to sell their wares and buy wool, leather, metalwork, and salt fish, and their helmsman had been killed in a drunken brawl. Because he had started it there was no blood price. But because he was dead,

Catumanus the priest had declared that Cuno and Rotri were due pilotage across the firth. Eirian had offered to go and had simply kept going. She was aware that if her suspicions were correct, eventually they would send her back anyway and that was probably as well.

In the meantime, the only harm done was to deprive her father and brothers of a housekeeper and surely they would not die of that despite their protests.

"If you go with traders no man will have you afterward!" Faelan had snapped.

"No man will have me now!" Eirian had retorted.

"You should have stayed away from the Roman!"

"You should have told me about my mother!" She still didn't know. Her mother had vanished when she was less than a year old, back to the sea it was said, or the seals from which she had magically transformed. Or she had come with traders and left again with them like her daughter, having had enough of Faelan. If anything made Eirian unmarriageable, it was that and not the Roman.

She had thought that, half seal or no, her bones were rooted to the seal rocks of High Isle. But when Faustus had come and gone, it had seemed not. So she would see what other wanderers saw, maybe even what her mother had seen.

At first it was not very different. She had piloted the *Mercurius*, a fat merchant craft with bright black eyes painted on its prow, through the islands' tricky currents and across the Bowl to the northern Orcades and back, and then across the firth to the mainland. The northern mainland had seemed much the same as the islands and the war had left little mark there. But further west and south when they docked at coastal settlements or followed navigable rivers inland, she saw the Romans' path in ruined fields and burned steadings.

From there they loaded their goods on a wagon and traveled the new Roman roads to visit inland holds. The roads were mainly graveled tracks as yet but already ditched to either side for drainage. Cuno told her that eventually they would be paved with stone and level earthen paths laid to either side for horse traffic. Their small cavalcade halted at checkpoints along the way to have their goods inspected and to pay tolls. The Romans, Rotri said, taxed everything that moved. At each stop they emptied out every pack. No weapons beyond dagger length were allowed to be sold to the highland clans.

"You won't sell much else to this lot either," one of the soldiers at a checkpoint said, inspecting the wooden tablet Rotri presented for the proper seals. "They can barely feed themselves."

"And whose fault is that then?" Rotri retorted. "They'll have goods to sell to us instead, whatever *your* lot haven't taken from them."

The soldier seemed unoffended. "Watch your back then." He handed back the tablet and said something else in a low voice, too quietly for Eirian to catch.

"*That* will have been a mistake," Rotri said in answer, and they moved on.

Now in Emrys's guesthouse, Eirian wondered if "*that*" was the gold torque. She might have asked the seals if they had not been so far inland. They had always spoken to her, forming words with their cries that no one else could distinguish. Catumanus said it was a gift that some islanders had always had, but no one in these days did and it made everyone else uneasy. She had learned not to talk about what the seals said. The gold torque looked familiar to her too. Faustus had worn a pair of them when he dressed for parade in all his awards. Surely not Faustus… He was in Inis Fáil. There were plenty of Romans to have owned that torque in the garrisons they had passed, but she noted that Cuno had not asked Piran where he had come by it. She also noticed that Rotri was sliding the hearth talk to local matters as they broached a barrel of beer that Cuno had offloaded from the wagon.

"We couldn't travel two paces without meeting another Roman patrol," Rotri said disgustedly. "Romans at the docks, Romans at each crossroad, Roman watchtowers like great mushrooms everywhere, stone mileposts along every road with Caesar's name on them, and a Roman at every fucking one with his hand out."

There was a general aggrieved muttering.

"They are like fleas on a dog. Bite one and they move to the other leg."

"We pay their taxes and we starve."

"It may be that Emrys has made us a bad bargain," Piran suggested.

At that Emrys's horsemaster snapped his head around to glare at him. He had a bright scar down one cheek. "It is only because Emrys made a peace that you have your holding at all! And what are you doing here so far from it?"

"Speaking with Emrys concerning certain matters," Piran said loftily.

"You are a puppy!" the horsemaster said. "And not even our puppy, but one of Calgacos's. Go home to your clan and tell your new headman to mend your manners for you."

"There is discord over the treaty?" Cuno asked. "We of the road have not heard that and we hear most things."

"The only discord is this fool," the horsemaster said.

"There was very little choice in the matter," one of Hafren's women said quietly.

"The Druids say the Romans will leave if we can but wait them out," another man said.

"The Druids! Pah!" Piran said. "The Druids fled to Inis Fáil when the Romans won the last battle. Only now do they come creeping back. And we are to listen?"

The horsemaster gave him a long look. "You have too much beer in you." It was never a good idea to disparage the Druids, whether they were present or not.

Piran realized that and said quickly, "Of course they are wise. I only thought—"

"You didn't," the horsemaster said.

"So there are some who would break the treaty?" Cuno asked. He rested his chin in his hand, rubbing the underside with his thumb, a habit Eirian had noted when he was intent on some matter. She watched him thoughtfully. Ordinarily he and Rotri would smooth over quarrels if they could, as they were never good for trade. Instead Cuno seemed to be poking at this one like a man encouraging a new fire.

"A great war band is forming in the south," Piran said. "To take the throne of Inis Fáil for the old king's son. They recruit fighting men and promise them land and gold in Inis Fáil. If we join with them we could have all the men we need at our backs when we return. Some of our men have likely gone to them already."

"Ah. We have heard of that," Rotri said. "He is kin to the Epidii chieftain through his mother's blood, and he has spent the last seven years in the Roman general Agricola's camps."

The horsemaster grinned and then winced as the scar pained him. He said to Piran, "So you will go to him and say, 'we will fight for you if you will fight Rome for us afterward. And call Rome down on your own head'? When you are not drunk you will see the difficulty in that."

"He is young," Cuno said, grinning back.

"Too young to have fought with his betters in the war he wishes to start again."

Piran glared at both of them and Rotri seemed to decide that it was best to end it. "Eirian, tell us a tale to suit the night."

That could be taken a number of ways and Eirian thought he knew it. "Well then," she said, thinking. "I will tell you of the man who hired himself out to the finfolk, who live in the waters of the Orcades."

Piran looked angry but they settled themselves to listen. Storytellers were as valuable an entertainment as harpers.

"Now most men have sense enough to run when they see a finman on the shore," Eirian said, "much less a finwoman, for if you are male she will take you down with her to the bottom of the sea, and whether it is to wed you or eat you no one has ever known. But this man, his name was Bran, was young and cocky and when one autumn day a tall dark man said he would pay to

29

have Bran ferry his cow to one of the northern isles, Bran did not ask him uncomfortable questions. He just set to rowing, even though the man had brought the cow aboard by carrying it in his arms, which is a bit unusual and might have made Bran think for a moment.

"Each island they came to, Bran asked the dark man if he should put ashore and the dark man told him to keep going, passing east of that island to the next one, and the next. Finally, when they had passed the northernmost of the islands, Bran asked him their destination. The dark man said nothing and a fog came down on the boat. When it had cleared, Bran saw that they had sailed clear into the next summer, or so it seemed. The sun shone on an enchanted land and shining silver women in the breakers on the shore sang a song that transfixed him with its loveliness.

"'Are you married then?' one of the silver women asked, and Bran said he was because it had come to him what they were and he had no wish to marry one of them, or whatever else she might want to do with him. They began then to shriek and wail and Bran put into shore to unload the cow in a hurry. He held out his hand for his payment and the finman, for that is what he was, said to him, 'You know that we cannot touch silver. I will pay you in copper coin or give you this horse, whichever you like.' He whistled and a horse came trotting along the beach. It was a fine tall horse, a gray roan beast with a foam-colored mane and tail. Bran knew that even the copper coins of finfolk are often enchanted, so he said, 'The horse.'

"He began to lead it onto the boat and the finman said, 'You'll have to mount or it will not board.' 'Very well,' said Bran, and swung up onto its back. Instead of going into the boat the horse whirled and leaped into the sea with Bran clinging to its mane, and that was when Bran began to think ill of his decisions. The horse plunged under the waves, turned around and gripped Bran with its teeth, by the leg of his breeches. It was a water horse, of course, which only the finfolk can ride, and they eat human flesh. The water horse's teeth sank through the cloth into his calf and Bran got his head above the waves and shouted that he had changed his mind.

"'It's too late for that,' the finman said. Bran thought frantically. 'I never said I would take it,' he shouted. 'I only named it. I will not take it!' The finman hesitated, but there are rules, even for magical folk. 'Very well.' He whistled again and the horse let go of Bran's breeches and disappeared into the sea. Bran got in his boat, where he found a handful of copper coins, and rowed as hard as he could for home."

"And did he get there safely?" one of the women asked.

Eirian smiled. "He did. But the coins were a puddle of foul-smelling stuff in the bottom of the boat when he got there. He was careful who he hired out to after that, no matter what pay was offered."

III. CASTING THE DICE

The Hibernian coast was already visible when thirty ships slipped past the headland at the southernmost tip of the Epidii peninsula and into open water. Across the channel the rocky cliffs that guarded most of the island rose up as they approached, thronged with seabird colonies nesting noisily on the ledges. The dark, dog-like heads of seals bobbed in the water, watching their passage. They would come ashore at Inber Domnann on the next day and the die would be cast, Faustus thought, and remembered that Julius Caesar was reputed to have said that as he crossed the Rubicon river into Italy with an army behind him, in defiance of the Senate.

There was no way to land three thousand men without warning and so Tuathal had decided to make as much noise about it as possible. The trading colony around Inber Domnann and on the island of Reachra just offshore was populated by merchants and middlemen, whose only interest in the coming war would be in staying on the right side of the winner. They would neither help nor hinder. The fortified promontory of Drumanagh no doubt held Elim mac Conrach's garrison, but it too would be circumspect unless Elim had sent his entire war band to its aid, which was unlikely. Elim would approach cautiously, testing his footing and trying for the best advantage, negotiating alliances and seeing who of Tuathal's men could perhaps be pulled away, and whether Eochaid of Laigin could be turned the other way.

In the afternoon of the next day the fleet passed the green knoll of Reachra and the merchant harbor, and ran their ships onto the wide flat shore of the estuary above the tide line. Faustus could see a cluster of tents and banners snapping in the coastal wind from a camp some distance away and looked uneasily at Finmall, who seemed unconcerned.

"That's Eochaid of Laigin's banner," Finmall said.

"Are you positive that Elim mac Conrach isn't sitting under it?"

"If he was, those would be in their burrows." Finmall swept a hand at the crowd of market-goers, shopkeepers and traders who had clustered along the dock on the other side of the estuary to watch. A shower of rain, blown in and out again on the ocean winds, had not deterred them. Rain and sun chased each other forever through the skies over Inis Fáil, dark clouds sailing with the sun on their tails as swiftly as boats.

As Faustus watched, still suspicious, a tall man in a green cloak strode across the wet stony sand, with two others following to carry his stag's-head banner and a wooden chest bound at the corners with gold.

Tuathal walked out to meet him with Cassan and Fiachra. Cassan carried a box as well, its silver lid embossed with Tuathal's sunburst ensign. On the shore the war band was off-loading from the ships, a seemingly endless stream of men and tents and horses and wagons with the oxen to pull them. Finmall followed Tuathal, and Faustus detached himself from the ordering of the camp to follow Finmall. He wanted to hear what the emissary said; the speech of Hibernia was close enough to that of his native Gaul that after a time with the Inis Fáil men he understood it reasonably well.

Eochaid of Laigin was red-haired and red-faced, with a bushy mustache and hair tied back in a plume like a fox's brush. His neck and arms were heavy with gold. He said, "Tuathal Techtmar who would be High King, I have brought my men as agreed. And a gift to seal the compact." His man brought forward the gold-bound box.

"Tell me why you back my claim," Tuathal said. "I would hear it from your own mouth."

"My father helped Elim mac Conrach overthrow yours," Eochaid said. "For that he received gold and cattle that Elim has taken back year by year in tribute while he grows fat and Laigin grows lean. Eleven bad years of the last twenty-one, with corn stunted and trees bearing only green fruit. The gods have left Elim mac Conrach and withered the land while he is High King. I will undo the mistake my father made."

Tuathal nodded his acceptance of that. There was no need to mention that Laigin lay in Tuathal's path and he had three thousand men to Eochaid's eight hundred. The carefully chosen presents were now exchanged, the silver box housing a small golden bowl, and the gold-bound box a knife in a silver scabbard. In the diplomacy of gifts, the knife signified service to an overlord, and the bowl a life of plenty under Tuathal's kingship.

"We will make camp here with the ships," Tuathal said now. "And send word to Elim mac Conrach."

"And if he does not return word?" Eochaid asked.

"Then we will speak to him at spearpoint," Tuathal said. "It will come to that anyway. But he will come. He will pay us to go away if he can."

"And can he?" Eochaid asked.

"No. I am not unfaithful to those who swear to me."

"He will try," Fiachra said. "Thinking that everyone possesses the morals of a stoat as he does."

"He will send an emissary," Tuathal said, "for whom we will wait three days while we put defenses around the fleet."

"Sanb of Connacht will likely send one as well," Fiachra said. "And it would be well to wait and see what he will say."

"Sanb of Connacht will go to the side he thinks will win," Eochaid said.

"Which one that is will become clear to Sanb of Connacht shortly," Tuathal said. "It would be best for him if it is clear before he sides with Elim."

"Elim has offered Sanb his daughter Baine," Eochaid said.

"Whom he has also offered to Foirbre of An Mhumhain," Fiachra commented. "And there is only one of her."

"Sanb of Connacht will be here by morning," Fiachra said. "I would bet my best belt knife on it. His spies will have seen our ships yesterday."

Faustus wondered how many of the lesser kings had spies in each other's halls. All of them probably, and spies in Elim's hall as well. "Best we finish our defenses tonight," he said. "As Sanb is undecided."

Eochaid gave him a long look. "I heard that Tuathal Techtmar had hired a Roman to command his war band."

"To train them, yes," Tuathal snapped. "To command them, no. I command. You will remember that."

"Nor am I hired," Faustus said quietly and Eochaid let the subject go, but Faustus thought again that Eochaid's men were probably going to be expendable. Eochaid did not look like a man to follow anyone's orders, even Tuathal's, once a battle started. The freemen of Inis Fáil were defined by the *fine*, the family in the male line for five generations, and the families of a kingdom, its *tuath*, elected their king from among them. They all called themselves Gaels, the children of Goidel Glas, legendary conqueror of the island, but *fine* and *tuath* loyalties were paramount and allegiance was personal. If Eochaid fell, his warriors would most likely go home. Faustus left Tuathal and Eochaid to conclude their negotiations and went back to supervising the camp and the defenses of the beached ships, in case that proved to be more immediately important.

He found the process proceeding with Roman efficiency and was congratulating himself on that when Owain came to him.

"I don't think we're likely to see trouble just now," Faustus said, assuming he had come for orders. "But I want a strong watch set for tonight nevertheless."

"That's been done. The watchword is 'red cow.' We need to speak to each other. I am weary of looking sideways."

Faustus raised his eyebrows. "I thought you might prefer that."

"If you were going to hand me over to your governor, you would have done it in Britain," Owain said.

"I would," Faustus said. "But it seemed late for that, and pointless." He thought of what had happened to Vercingetorix, who had gone willingly to the Romans to save as many of his men as possible. Julius Caesar had executed him after parading him in a triumph.

"Would it not have meant a promotion or some award?" Owain asked. "I am trying to understand Romans."

"Maybe, but don't start with me. I am in disgrace. I annoyed a tribune. That's why they've sent me here."

Owain gave a short bark of laughter. It was the first time Faustus had heard him do that.

"I have some decent wine in my tent," Faustus said. "A small hoard I have kept from Tuathal's bandits. We should drink it before they find it."

"A Roman decadence I never thought to acquire a taste for," Owain said. He followed Faustus when he motioned toward his tent.

Paullus was grooming Arion, Faustus's big bay troop horse. Faustus jerked his head in a gesture that meant "elsewhere" and Paullus disappeared with Pandora padding at his heels.

The wine was decent only by British standards, but they each drank a cup.

"We looked for your body," Faustus said when he was halfway through his. "Very thoroughly." As one of the few who had seen the Caledones' warlord up close, Faustus had been detailed to inspect an endless line of corpses.

Owain nodded. The glow from the iron brazier that warmed the tent cast a sheen like blood on the tent floor.

"And it occurred to me that there was maybe only one folk who could have got you out from under our noses."

Owain nodded again.

"I knew a family of the little hill people in the south, at Llanmelin near Isca," Faustus said. "My mother was Silure. I am told there is sidhe blood in the Silures. The Old One at Llanmelin said so at any rate." He touched the little blue stone around his throat that she had given him when he said goodbye; a part of them to go with him, she had said. He would offer something of his own story in exchange for Owain's.

"They found me half-dead," Owain said finally, "and my wife with a wound in her arm, trying to drag a chariot herself, with me on it. They brought us to one of their holds in the mountain."

"Do you know where?"

"No. They called it the sidhe of Bryn Dan. When I began to heal they took me…" He paused. "Somewhere else."

"To the Orcades?" Faustus asked. "Just a guess, but I spent the winter there, being diplomatic with the islanders on the old governor's behalf. Certain things…" He filled Owain's cup again.

Owain stared into the cup. Whatever he saw was darker than the wine.

"Aelwen…" Owain said finally but he didn't continue.

"She is well," Faustus said. "She came with Emrys and made peace and assured us that you were dead. We didn't believe her."

Owain drained the cup. "I sent her to Emrys with my sword to prove it."

"Does she know where you have gone?"

"How could I? I have no home to give her. And she is needed to hold our people together under Emrys and let him make a peace with yours. I thought then that would not be possible with me slinking home maimed to give the warlord's place to Emrys and then to hover like a shadow at his elbow, with our people likely coming to me and not him. Even if the Romans let me live. I still think it. And our own clan fighting among themselves over who should be headman."

He was silent then, and Faustus was quiet too, thinking. They were all trying to find some new life to overlay the old. Dai, who had clearly been one of Owain's men; Fiachra and Finmall and Cassan with twenty-one years of waiting behind them; Beric who had found life in Camulodunum too easy for his restless nature; Llwyd who had watched his old king die in ritual battle to seal the new king in his place and keep the Romans from setting up a puppet queen. Faustus had heard that story from soldiers of the Second Augusta who had been in Britain then. Small wonder Llwyd chafed at living under Rome.

And what about himself, Faustus thought, brooding now over the places he couldn't go back to and the places he didn't want to, which were unfortunately not the same. There was a grand adventure to be had in the Hibernian campaign. He had teased himself with that all last winter and spring, and now it was well launched. If his troubles were only an annoyed tribune and a woman he couldn't have, then he was well off.

–

In the morning Sanb's emissary arrived in a four-wheeled chariot with a green awning, its sides painted with the white bull of Connacht. He had forty men with him on horseback and in lighter two-wheeled chariots, enough for a guard along the road but not enough to be a threat to a nervous commander. It had rained again but the sun was out now, glittering on the grass and the water of the bay and the estuary that fed it, and on the emissary's silver-mounted chariot.

The emissary sat with arms folded, unmoving while the horses fidgeted and the driver whispered to them. Tuathal emerged from the camp gates and waited. Fiachra, Finmall, and Cassan ranged themselves beside him.

The other captains had come out to see what would happen. The elaborate theatrics produced a snort of annoyance from Owain. "Do they sit there until one falls over or someone has to piss?"

"Cassan says they will wait until Eochaid's Druids read the omens for a council," Dai said, "and then they will meet halfway. Sanb's man will come just a little farther," he added, and as he spoke an old man in a white gown padded onto the sand from Eochaid's camp and raised a staff with a gold sun wheel at the top.

"I thought Druids didn't interfere?" Faustus said.

"They don't," Owain said. "They will read the omens but they won't say what to do with them. If the omens say the council will end in disaster, the Druid will say so. But he won't stop anyone who wants to meet anyway."

There was something unsettling about that, an echo of old stories of ill omens disregarded, setting in place the inevitable chain of sorrow and death. Faustus watched the Druid uneasily, but the omens appeared to be fair. The old man thumped the staff twice in the sand and marched away to Eochaid's camp again. Sanb's man dismounted from his chariot and Tuathal walked to meet him. As Dai had said, not quite halfway.

This time Faustus couldn't hear what was said, and fidgeted unhappily, watching the emissary's escort, and for any motion from Eochaid's camp. The exchange of gifts looked perfunctory, as did the exchange of words. Sanb's man shook his head once. And then he turned and strode back to his chariot, spoke to the driver, and the entourage wheeled around and set off again in the way they had come.

–

Tuathal summoned his captains to a council while a small retinue of slaves unfolded Roman-style camp chairs in his tent and set them on the thick rugs that covered the floor. An iron brazier with wolf's-head legs warmed the interior. Tuathal said, "Elim mac Conrach is dangling his daughter Baine over Sanb's head like a mayfly over a trout."

"Elim has promised her before to anyone he's sought alliance with," Fiachra said. "He has yet to actually give her to anyone."

"He won't do it now if he can help it," Finmall said. "She's far more use to him unwed. Sanb should know that. Once Elim actually marries her to someone he hasn't anything left to offer. After Baine, the queen had two stillbirths that nearly killed her, and there won't be any more, poor woman."

"What about sons?" Faustus asked.

"There's no guarantee a son will succeed his father so sons make less valuable marriage prospects," Finmall said. "Elim has two. Ailill is king in Ulaid, but there are rumblings there and crops have failed."

"Elim would have divorced to marry again and get a daughter," Fiachra said, "but the queen would have taken her property with her and he couldn't afford it. So he tried to force the issue this spring and got her with child again after the Druids told him not to, and she died of it. Now her property has gone back to her family and it will not be easy to find a woman in Inis Fáil to marry Elim, High King or no."

"What good would an infant girl have done him?" Faustus asked.

Finmall snorted. "He's been promising Baine since the day she was born."

"It seems that Elim mac Conrach has done little to make people love him," Beric said. "Perhaps that will open doors for us."

"They will open or we will open them," Tuathal said. "Eochaid's Druids say that Elim's envoy will arrive by the morning."

"How do they know that?" Beric asked suspiciously.

"Druids all talk to each other like a tree full of birds," Dai said.

Tuathal touched the hilt of his father's sword. "After that there will be no more diplomacy. Sanb can decide to cast his lot with us or go down."

When his captains had left and the slaves had cooked his dinner and served it, Tuathal stood and looked out the tent flap at the surrounding camp, glowing now with cooking fires and field ovens in the dusk. The shapes of the great ships rose up on the seaward side like sleeping dragons, or the ancient beasts whose monstrous bones surfaced sometimes from the earth. This was the venture he had been born for, an infant bundled into a basket and rowed from Inis Fáil to Britain by his mother as Elim mac Conrach's men overran the High King's hall at Tara. His mother

Eithne had been a royal woman of the Epidii. When she knew she was dying, Tuathal had been fourteen. She had sent him to the Roman governor Julius Agricola with his father's sword, the war chest she had stolen hidden among his belongings until the day it could be used to put him on his father's throne. Tuathal still thought of her now and then, mostly at night, although the first great crushing grief had faded years ago. His not having been there when she actually died had given her an elusive quality in his mind as if she might still come back alive. Cadman had shown him her barrow, a green mound outside the stone walls, but he still felt her presence sometimes, a weary, determined ghost. She would rest, he thought, when he sat on the throne at Tara.

–

In the morning, under a sullen sky and a pelting rain, the envoy from Elim arrived on horseback at the head of a cavalcade of riders with the red hand of Ulaid on their banners. The lead rider wore a cloak of checkered red and blue wool, its hood pulled up against the rain, and sat atop a black horse fitted with a silver-trimmed bridle and saddle on a scarlet saddle cloth. The feet that hung beside the pony's flanks were shod in scarlet boots. A tall figure muffled in a dark cloak rode a roan pony a pace behind, with the staff of a gold sun wheel in one hand, resting on a booted toe.

Tuathal strode to meet them with his captains behind him. The sky cleared as he did and the lead rider threw back the checkered hood and shook the water away from a fall of black hair. Above the red boots she wore men's clothing with a gold-hilted knife at her belt. Her face was pale with dark straight brows over blue eyes and an aquiline nose. Her expression was imperious.

"Baine," Fiachra whispered. "That's Baine."

"My father the High King," Baine said, "sends to tell the would-be usurper Tuathal Techtmar that he has one day to take ship again for Britain. After that there will be no mercy."

She stayed astride her silver-mounted saddle looking down at Tuathal who perforce must look up at her. He planted his feet in the sandy earth and lifted his chin. In some ways they were much alike, both tall and dark-haired, lean and lordly looking, like a pair of black wolfhounds.

"I have heard that your father the High King has promised your marriage to so many men the brehons have lost count," Tuathal said. "He had best make up his mind before I ride into Tara and give you to the pig boy."

The rider at her side kicked the roan pony forward. The Druid was a woman as well, with a fall of pale hair and a heavy flat sun disk around her neck over a black gown bunched around her knees. She said, "Tuathal Techtmar, be certain of what you want and how high the price."

Tuathal chose his words carefully. Insulting a Druid was never a good idea. "I have paid much of the price already. Therefore my destiny is to go forward."

The Druid nodded. Baine gave her a dark look, which she ignored.

"When the crows are eating your eyes you may count the rest of the cost," Baine said. She raised a hand to the men behind her and they wheeled their horses about.

—

Elim mac Conrach waited until his daughter had stripped off her sodden cloak and stood drying herself by the fire before he spoke. The High King was much like her in height but where she was dark, he was sandy-haired, with a mustache that tinged toward red. They had the same straight brows and nose, an angular face, and a shared explosive temperament. The slave who had just refilled his cup with mead and the ones carrying baskets of fresh herbs to sweeten the cavernous hall edged out of reach as Elim and his daughter regarded each other across the hearth at its center. As often as not, such encounters escalated swiftly into shouting and thrown objects and it was as well to be ready to duck. The fighting men of Elim's immediate household watched warily too, pausing in their spear practice, and the women spinning by the fireside gathered up their wool and spindles and retreated to the second floor.

The Great Hall of Tara capped a mound surrounded by four concentric rings where the ancient lords of Inis Fáil lay sleeping in their barrows. The hall, built by the new lords who had succeeded the Bronze People and the yet older ones, rose to three stories with a stairwell between its outer and inner walls. Within, the council hall occupied the first floor, and the sleeping chambers the second. It was always crowded with someone doing something, carrying something, cooking something, the household warriors who had been Elim's hounds in their boyhood, the women of the house, the slaves, physicians, priests, thatchers mending the roof, poets, harpers, and anyone passing through and thus due hospitality. There was no privacy and Elim didn't care.

"What answer did he give?" he demanded.

Baine spread her wet cloak on a drying rack, shooing a sleeping dog from its place by the fire. "He threatened to wed me to the swineherd when he has taken Tara."

Elim glared at her. "You are to wed Sanb of Connacht and Tuathal Techtmar's head will watch from a spike on the wall."

Baine regarded him from the other side of the fire, the heated air making her face waver as if she too were emanating from the flames. "He will win."

The household stilled on a collective indrawn breath. Speaking a thing might make it so, particularly when the speaker was a royal woman.

"The Druids say he will not," Elim snapped.

"The Druids say there will be a great battle and the false king will fall," Baine said. "That may be interpreted in several ways, as with most matters having to do with Druids." Tuathal's father had himself acquired the throne at spearpoint from the king who had taken it following Tuathal's grandfather. The exact identity of the false king was therefore unclear. She had pressed Aíbinn on that most of the way home and Aíbinn had simply repeated her comment that everything had a price. If there was anything that Baine already knew in her bones, it was that.

"Go and put on a gown. And the gold collar that was your mother's. Sanb will be here for the handfasting."

"I am not your cow to show off to Sanb. And the gold collar went to my mother's uncle in Connacht with the rest of her possessions when she died."

"Sanb will take it back and give it to you again once he's got between your legs."

"Sanb can fuck a pig! And so can you!"

Elim raised his hand and the cup sailed across the hearth. It landed on the stones on the other side and shattered, sending a spray of mead hissing into the flames.

"You will do as you are bid or I will beat you!"

"Beat me and I will curse you." A royal woman's curse was nearly as dangerous as a Druid's. It was why Elim had not tried to beat her since her mother had died. She had cursed him then, for getting her mother with child, and he had vomited for a ten-day.

Elim's fists clenched on the carved arms of his chair. Still, he did not mean to marry her to Sanb just yet, if indeed he finally had to this time. He might. But the handfasting alone should keep Sanb and his men in Elim's war band.

"Get dressed. And find Morcant for me. I want him to take a message to Ailill."

"Morcant is drunk. I saw him as I rode in, he can barely walk. He's staggering around the cow byre bothering the women at the milking."

"Then have someone throw him in the trough." Elim looked around him for a slave. "Bring me drink."

Baine strode out, still in her breeches, calling to two of her father's men to follow. They threw Morcant in the trough as instructed and when he surfaced spluttering she said, "Father wants you." She didn't look to see if he obeyed. She picked her way through the cow dung and churned mud outside the byre – she was fond of those red boots – and went out the causeway gate to where the Five Roads joined.

From the Hill of Tara you could see whatever was coming a long way off, even the Great Barrow of the Old Ones to the north.

There was no sign of Sanb of Connacht or his men. He wouldn't come, despite what Elim thought, not until he saw which way the wind blew between Tuathal Techtmar and the High King. Aíbinn had said so, and Druids generally knew. Tara was not merely a royal residence, it was a holy site; the giant wooden ring built from trees felled in the sacred grove loomed over everything and the ancient ridgeway tracks fanned out from Tara like the spokes of a wheel. Tara had always been sacred. The Druids controlled life there from the great festivals to the small daily observances. When he no longer felt need of the power that emanated from Tara, Elim would go back to Ulaid and Ailill's hold at Emain Macha. Baine walked a way down the Ulaid road now, lifting a hand to the sentries in the outpost house along the way.

"Take an escort, lady!" one shouted but she shook her head. She could reach the gates again before anyone could gallop across the empty green expanse of the river valley. The only movement came from the white clouds of sheep that drifted across the turf beyond stone-walled fields, and a line of cattle coming into their byre. Birds were settling for the night, squabbling for roosts in the hedgerows. Baine took a deep breath of the clean air and sat down on one of the white boundary stones that marked either side of the road. The earlier rain had brought out the scent of wet earth and the pungent stems of henbane and woundwort that grew on the verge. After a while Morcant rode past with a handful of their father's men for escort; and to keep him from falling off his horse, Baine thought contemptuously. Their mounts churned up a splatter of wet earth and she threw a rock after Morcant. They wouldn't get far by dark, even at this time of year, but she thought her father was worried. They would come back with Ailill's men behind them for all of Elim's stated intent of beating Tuathal's war band with only the men of An Mhumhain and Connacht. *If* the men of Connacht came. She wondered if he was beginning to suspect they wouldn't.

Three mornings later, the High King's men rode out without waiting for Ailill. Elim had his own warriors behind him, and the war band of Foirbre of An Mhumhain that had mustered on the border of Laigin and Connacht a ten-day earlier in preparation were now eating their camp and the surrounding countryside bare with an appetite that could have emptied the Dagda's cauldron. He would have to use them quickly and give them a chance to plunder Laigin, or risk the possibility of Sanb's switching sides. Sanb had not come to Tara despite Elim's command, nor had he sent his war band. So far neither had he gone to Tuathal Techtmar. Both sides had given up waiting for Sanb to decide. Tuathal's war band was marching inland to Tara with Eochaid of Laigin. Elim would meet him and come home with his head, and Eochaid of Laigin would regret his faithlessness.

Tara had grown suddenly empty at their leaving. Only the women of the king's house remained, and the farmers and shepherds in the little village on the outskirts. The Druids, poets, and harpers had all gone with the king. Druids were healers, and the poets and harpers would declaim the history of Elim mac Conrach's line and describe in bloody detail the fine fierce vengeance they would impose on Tuathal Techtmar for his impudence, to the inspiration of Elim's men in battle and the terror of the enemy.

–

"All they make is noise," Faustus said dismissively. "If you have ever known a man slain by poetry, I would hear of it." The war band arrayed on the ridge before them caught the morning light on their banners and spearpoints, shouting threats and insults.

"If we do not respond in kind we will be marked for lesser men," Eochaid said. "This is tradition, the way of war among men in Inis Fáil."

Tuathal shook his head. "We will meet them with silence and let them worry that we are not human."

Eochaid looked doubtful but his arguments and his poets had been refused. His own men mostly went half-naked in a show of bravado, armed with spears and axes and battle fury. Tuathal Techtmar's men wore as much armor as he had been able to provide to those who lacked it. They were formed up in five cohorts of infantry and a cavalry wing across a valley sodden with rain, each under their own commander and standard, each commander looking to Tuathal and the Roman. The Roman was mounted on a bigger horse than the native ponies and armed with a spear and a long cavalry sword. A second spear and a short infantry sword hung from his saddle and the face under his iron helmet was watchful. They all stood silently, waiting, each shield in perfect alignment with its neighbor. To Eochaid, they might have been Fomorians come from the Underworld, deadly and unspeaking. It was no doubt best to be on their side but they made him uneasy.

"Keep his men back as best you can," Faustus said quietly to Tuathal. "You know you'll not get them under control once they're let fight."

Nor could they. Unnerved by the silent ranks waiting for them, Elim's men threw themselves down the ridge without waiting for Tuathal to come to them, and Eochaid's war band began to shout and slam their spears against their shields, screaming insults, the whole line shivering like a beast on an unreliable chain. Elim's chariots hurled themselves across the gap between them, their hoofbeats churning up clods of mud and shaking the valley floor until Faustus felt it through Arion's saddle. Tuathal had sent half of his men forward, under Owain, Finmall, and Llwyd, with the cavalry splitting to come around the flanks of Elim's force. They flung throwing spears at the oncoming chariots, and closed shields to make a solid wall to force the horses to balk. The screaming foot warriors poured down the slope behind the chariot line, battering at the shield wall.

"Now!" Eochaid shouted. "Now we will fight like men and not like Roman lapdogs!"

They wouldn't hold but a moment more, and so Tuathal loosed them and they ran screaming at Elim's army, axe and spearpoint flashing in the sun, with Eochaid at their head.

47

"Take the front line and pull them together," Tuathal said to Faustus. "If Eochaid's head ends on a spear he will no doubt be feasted in the Otherworld."

Faustus kicked Arion down the slope, merging with Owain's cohort while behind him a trumpet sounded the *Advance*. One of Faustus's ex-legionaries had spent months teaching them to heed the Roman trumpet calls that could speak to the whole war band at once over the deafening sounds of battle. Elim's chariots were beginning to drop their warriors to fight on foot while the drivers took their teams to the rear. The Gaels fought much as the Britons did, the way that Dai and Owain had first learned to fight, and also learned the disadvantages of in the face of Roman formation. Faustus noted Owain holding his position at the left end of his front line where the shield next to him gave some cover. Elim's men hacked and clawed at them like demons, shrieking furious taunts, swinging the wicked blades of battle-axes, stabbing with their war spears. They were undisciplined but their fury gave them a power that for a while was overwhelming. Like Eochaid's men, most fought shirtless or even naked. They did not paint themselves as the Britons did but their throats were ringed with gold torques and their war chariots hung with gold fittings. Eochaid and the Laigin warriors had got in front of the disciplined cohorts of Faustus's army and where they clashed with Elim's men was an unreadable chaos of blood and bodies.

"Hold the line," Faustus said to Owain. The men of Laigin were faltering now, outnumbered by Elim's men backed by Foirbre's. "Be ready to let them in." If the Laigin men broke, Elim's would pursue them into any gaps between Tuathal's cohorts and then the cohorts would close around them. That was how it was done, how Rome had done it for centuries. He wondered briefly how painful it might be for Owain to take commands from him, and then had no more time for thinking of anything but the fight as it roared around him. A slingstone went by his head like a hornet and another ticked his helmet, making his ears ring.

He put his shield up. Slingstones that hit their mark were deadly. From Arion's back he could see that the Laigin men were scattering outward instead of falling back, and he cursed them.

Owain, locked in his cohort's shield wall, gritted his teeth and forced himself to fight as Faustus had ordered. A Caledone warlord rode at the head of his men, the first to charge the enemy, the first to make a kill. The Roman insisted there was more honor in holding his cohort together than in drawing first blood. It felt wrong to Owain down to his bones not to let battle fury drive him through the enemy spearmen, and instead to feed the cold, dogged determination that advanced him step by step in line with his cohort while a screaming Gael came at him with a flashing axe; to block it with his shield, swing the heavy long sword with precision, take another step with the rest of the line. A few minutes into the battle the line grew somewhat ragged but it formed again and reformed, always pulling back into formation as Elim's men battered at it. The line was moving faster now because Elim's men were outnumbered and had no experience with Roman tactics, as Owain once had not. Elim would likely pull back and change his tactics and wait for more men. It was what Owain had done until the last desperate battle when that had no longer been a choice. A spearman came at him, driving the blade hard into their line, sinking it into Owain's shield. He wrenched his bad arm sideways to dislodge it and discovered with satisfaction that though it hurt like fire it didn't matter. The man he had been slipped a little further away, and the man he was now swung the shield the other way, pulling the spear shaft from its owner's grip and catching him under the chin with it. The man on his right slid a sword through the gap and drove it in.

The rest of Tuathal's army was moving to spread around the front lines of Elim's men. A screaming An Mhumhain warrior with a blood-splashed shield swung an axe at Faustus's right leg. Faustus blocked the blow with his sword blade but the hilt was knocked from his grip. The man swung the axe again and Faustus brought his spear to hand and his shield across Arion's withers barely in time, feeling the blade bite into the edge of his shield,

49

pulling him nearly from the saddle. He wrenched it back, stabbed downward past the other's shield before he could swing the axe again, and felt the spear go in. He looked for the next man and saw instead, surprised, that Elim's men were pulling back.

Faustus halted Arion to watch, mistrustful. Finmall's cohort had begun to pursue them but Elim's retreat was suspiciously orderly, keeping together, making themselves a dangerous target for pursuers. Faustus put his heels to Arion's flanks and shouted at Finmall, "Don't chase them!"

"I'm not yet such a fool!" Finmall shouted back. A horn sounded the *Halt Pursuit* as he spoke. "There's bog ahead, I can see it. Elim isn't as bright as he thinks he is, but he knows the ground and he's smart enough to try to pull us into it once he was fool enough not to wait for Ailill to bring Ulaid up."

Faustus looked at the army spread across the valley behind him. "You argued that we should push him hard now and see what happened. You were right."

Finmall grinned. "He's probably in a temper over Connacht and couldn't wait to go kill somebody. That whole family has the temper of fiends."

—

"Elim is a better strategist than Eochaid," Tuathal said disgustedly, looking at the body of Laigin's king laid out in ceremony with his weapons at his side.

The carrion birds, reivers of the skies, had begun to circle overhead. When Tuathal's men had stripped Elim's dead, they let Elim's men come under a green branch and take them. Eventually Tuathal would rule the widows and children of those dead so it was best not to leave their men's bones to be scattered by the wolves. Elim had realized his mistake in not waiting for Ailill and the men of Ulaid, and also in underestimating Tuathal, and so losses on both sides were slight, but the next battle would be another matter.

In the meantime there was the issue of the men of Laigin. Eochu, who was Eochaid's nephew and possible heir, had ridden in Eochaid's war band, but nothing was guaranteed, not Eochu's succession as king of Laigin nor his alliance with Tuathal if he was elected. Eochu would have to ride the ten miles to Dun Ailinne, seat of the Laigin kings, and make his case. Most of the Laigin war band, members of the *tuath* that would elect the new king, would go with him.

Elim wouldn't confront Tuathal again until he had the men of Ulaid behind him. That might give them time to await an answer from Dun Ailinne. In addition, Eochu had demanded to take Eochaid's body to Reachra, the traditional burial site of the great lords of Ulaid and Laigin.

"You could have bought a villa in Britain with that war chest, more splendid than Tara and with fewer inconveniences," Faustus informed Tuathal. He scratched his head where the helmet liner had made it itch. "It could have had a bath house."

"And you could have stayed on your father's farm in Gaul and been a provincial magistrate," Tuathal retorted.

"Instead I am fool enough to play adventurer here." Faustus scratched some more. He was filthy and everything itched. "I can't advise you on the succession of lesser kings. That's Fiachra's business. I am going to go wash in the river."

On the way back, wrapped in his cloak and trailing his filthy tunic in his hand, he went to the supply wagons and stopped to see how much wine they had – or beer, he supposed, would do – and for a barrel to hold Eochaid's body until they could take it to Reachra. Otherwise it would stink long before that and be an ill omen.

He took the dirty tunic to his tent where Paullus gave him a clean one and a bowl of stew. The smell of baking camp bread filled the air. The natural world, frozen to stillness by the battles of men, woke again and the long summer dusk filled with the chirring of insects. Cassan and Dai had acquired two sheep, now roasting on spits. Faustus decided not to ask where they had come from. His ill-assorted army had fought as one and a bonding not possible during drills had taken place as a result. Most had acquired enough language in common to form a rough mutual vernacular. He noted that Dai and Cassan were playing wisdom with the set of stones that Cassan kept in a pouch. Dai's dark head bent over the board, scratched out in the dirt by the firepit. It was the first time Faustus had seen him do anything when the day ended but sit and stare into the night.

In the morning the camp woke with the early light, stretching stiff muscles and making morning prayers to a host of gods who inhabited the trees, the sky, or the small bronze statues carried wrapped in wool in soldiers' packs. Faustus turned toward Rome, missing the morning prayers at the chapel of the standards, the invocation to Jupiter Best and Greatest, to Juno and Minerva, with the gold Eagle of the legion lifted over their heads. He had always given the Empire's official gods their due, but there was something about the prayers at the standards that went deeper. This campaign, "adventuring" he had called it, had left him adrift from the army that had been home for seven years.

Faustus splashed water on his face and waited while Paullus laced his boots. Someone outside, one of the ex-legionaries, was singing a cheerful song about a girl in Puteoli who hadn't loved him.

Paullus set porridge to heating over a clay brazier, pushing Pandora's nose out of it. "I saved you some mutton," he told her.

Faustus glared at him. "The dog gets the mutton?"

"The Centurion has not had puppies."

"Neither has she lately, and mind your manners."

"She needs to keep her strength up. This is very good porridge." Paullus looked hurt.

Faustus, who loathed porridge, went to the surgeon's tent to see how the wounded were faring and whether Silus's slave had something more palatable to offer. Silus offered him bread spread with mutton fat, which was only marginally better, and they made the rounds of those whom Silus had decreed should be watched overnight rather than sent back to be tended by their fellows. Silus, with a pair of orderlies who were learning their business as they went, had spent a good part of the night cleaning and stitching sword cuts and spear wounds, picking out the splinters of a shield driven clean through its owner's leather hauberk by an axe, and setting the broken arm of a man who would have to be sent back to the ships.

"He can go in a wagon with the king of Laigin's body," Faustus said. He was not going to cart a king's corpse with them on the march. Eochaid could go to Inber Domnann and wait there for his final passage to the Otherworld. Faustus planned to send him off before Eochu could come back and complain. "And anyone else who's not fit to fight," he added.

"There are not many." Silus limped to the surgery desk and produced a list.

Faustus scanned it, grateful for Silus's Roman competence at record-keeping. The Gaels, like the old-fashioned among the native Britons, never wrote anything down. Tuathal Techtmar would be an anomaly as High King for the ability to read Latin.

"Be as generous as you can in their last pay," Silus said. *Better than I got* was implicit. The money for a soldier invalided out of Rome's army was notoriously little. Silus's pale hair was still cut short in a military crop, his body muscular despite the twisted leg. The stone roadway had left its mark on his face as well, a white scar across the cheekbone. He was only twenty-four and his career had been overturned by a wagon wheel.

Faustus tucked the list into his tunic, considering what he could persuade Tuathal to stand for. A babble of conversation outside caught his attention.

"You! Where's the Roman?"

"He came by just now. He's with the surgeon."

"Fetch him out! Tuathal Techtmar wants him. He wasn't looking like he wanted to wait."

What in the name of Mithras could have boiled up in the last hour?

Beric was outside grinning and buckling his sword belt. "A rider's come from Sanb of Connacht!"

IV. THE BLACK PIG'S DYKE

Elim mac Conrach looked about him for something to throw, his eyes narrowed under sandy red brows. He looked dangerous.

"I will hang Sanb's eyeless head on a tree!" Elim pounded on the table beside him, scattering game pieces in the rushes on the floor.

The hounds nosed the pieces and decided they weren't food and Foirbre of An Mhumhain motioned to a slave to pick them up. He was gray-haired and in his fifties, and the temper of the High King had long since ceased to impress him. It was a given, like the weather or the eccentricities of the gods. The war band had withdrawn to Tara to wait for Morcant and Ailill and the men of Ulaid, knowing that the death of Eochaid would stall Tuathal's march for a few days.

"*Where's my daughter?*"

A slave scurried toward the stairs.

The high lords had filled the hall and the guesthouse, drinking and making poems about the coming battle and drinking some more, until the women had mostly retreated to the sleeping quarters upstairs and Baine had put a guard on their door. She took some time now to answer her father's summons.

"He is shouting," the maid said, frightened.

"He always shouts," Baine said. "Bring me my blue gown and my jewel box. And the red belt." She pulled off the rough brown tunic she had worn to boil herbs for wound salve. Olwenna dropped the blue gown over Baine's linen undershift, arranged its folds, and knelt to fasten the belt. She hung Baine's keys, silver spoon, and knife from it while Baine picked through the jewel box and selected a pair of carnelian ear drops, a gold collar hung with pearls, and three rings, all of them gifts from previous suitors who had thought that Elim might actually marry her to them. He was still shouting in the hall below.

"Comb my hair out."

Olwenna undid the dark braids and brushed them out so that they hung in waves over Baine's shoulders. Baine picked a gold fillet from the jewel box and settled it on her hair. The maid held up a polished silver mirror and Baine nodded.

"Very well. I will go down now before he shouts himself into an apoplexy."

Olwenna thought that might happen if the gods listened. She had not been in the High King's household long, only since he had bought her in the spring for his bed and to serve his daughter, from a trader who had bought her from another who had taken her in a raid on the west coast of Britain. Olwenna had been a slave there too and the High King's house offered more comforts than her old one, but the High King made her think of a rabid fox she had seen once, biting everything in its path. She couldn't be the only one praying for his death.

"*Where is my daughter?*"

Baine stood in the stairwell and looked disdainfully at him. "The High King wishes my presence?"

Elim thrust himself out of his chair and took her by the wrist. "Foirbre!"

Foirbre stood.

Elim pulled Baine across the hall to Foirbre. "Where are the Druids? Where is Aíbinn?"

"The Druids are not to be shouted for." Aíbinn was suddenly standing beside him. Elim had not seen her come and he glared at her.

"Witness the handfasting of my daughter Baine to Foirbre of An Mhumhain," he said. He put Baine's hand in Foirbre's.

"It is witnessed," Aíbinn said.

Baine slid a glance at Foirbre. He had a look of satisfaction, a man who had waited out the rest, playing his game with skill.

For all the many times Elim had promised her, it had never yet come to a handfasting. This time she might be wed. She gritted her teeth. If it came to it, she would not be able to stop it. She might as well be Olwenna.

"Witness also," Elim said, "that I put the king's curse on Sanb of Connacht and a price of thirty cows on his head."

Aíbinn gave him a long look. Her pale hair hung beside her pale face like mist and bone over her black gown. "Is the High King certain?" She waited to see if he would change his mind. The king's curse brought death, always to the one who was cursed and sometimes to the king who had set it if it was wrongfully done.

"He is cursed," Elim said. "Witness it."

"It is witnessed," Aíbinn said.

-

Sanb of Connacht was thin and ascetic-looking, like a hermit mystic. He sat among Tuathal's captains, long-fingered hands folded in his lap. Sanb was a Druid in his own right and like all of them he bore the look of one who considered every pathway before stepping from his threshold. Beside him sat Eochu, with the red-gold diadem of the king of Laigin on his head. It was understood that Eochu's election as the new king had rested on his vow to regain the gold and cattle taxed away by Elim mac Conrach. No one knew whether Sanb had come because he distrusted Elim, because he had seen that Tuathal would win, or for some other vision or reason. It did not matter. With Sanb's men they would sweep south through An Mhumhain and force Foirbre to follow to defend it, and Elim perforce to follow Foirbre or lose him.

"The farther we draw Elim from Tara," Tuathal said, "and from Ulaid, the longer his supply lines. Laigin has already been stripped bare. If Elim goes west toward Connacht he will waste days while we fall on An Mhumhain."

"And our own?" Fiachra asked. "What we brought on the ships is draining out by the hour, even with the stores bought here in Laigin."

"That is a matter that we will mend in An Mhumhain," Tuathal said.

They would have to, Faustus thought. The logistics of an army on the march over several hundred miles of open land were complex and it was not only human fodder that must be found. There was graze available in this lush countryside, but the horses and the oxen that pulled the wagons required grain for the work being asked of them. Hunting parties went foraging, to catch up in the evening with the main column, slowed by its baggage train, but oxen couldn't eat deer or for that matter pilfered sheep. The aggrieved owners of the sheep had appeared not long after Sanb's rider, threatening the entire war band with the brehons. Knowing that they could make good on it, and that the brehons would be obeyed, Faustus had paid for the sheep from Tuathal's war chest and bought three more – a ram who was refusing his obligations and two elderly ewes that were probably more useful as shoe leather. An Mhumhain's cattle would provide a promised feast and serve the double purpose of insulting Foirbre.

Faustus was acquiring an increasing admiration for his old commander, Julius Agricola, who had taken an army from West Britain to the Caledones' highland fortresses in the northern mountains, coordinating re-supply by ship and by land, laying down outposts along the way that would later serve as supply depots, bribing and taxing the tribes whose territory they passed through for sacks of grain and sides of beef, and building roads on which to transport them. The roads in Hibernia were ancient routes along gravel ridges, widened and leveled for wheeled traffic in some places, but mostly still trackways. The five great roads that led to Tara were roads only in the sense that you could follow them and get somewhere.

After full dark he lay in his tent on the cot that was a Roman luxury while the rest of the war band settled to the night. Above him a harvestman explored the crevice between tent pole and leather, eight threadlike legs feeling delicately for things to eat. An owl uttered a bloodcurdling screech from its roost in the tree line behind the camp. The horses were snuffling for stray grain left from their evening feed and Paullus was polishing both Faustus's helmet and the bronze cooking pot with a goathair cloth, Pandora snoring at his feet. It took a moment before Faustus was aware of the translucent shape that wavered in the light of Paullus's lamp. He closed his eyes but it was still there when he opened them. Paullus put down the pot and the polishing rag and whistled Pandora to his heel. They went out into the night. Faustus never knew whether Paullus saw it or not but he mostly found a reason to leave when the shade of Silvius Valerianus appeared.

"Hibernia is an ill-omened place of barbarian gods," the shade said. "You disgrace my name."

"Only two thirds of it," Faustus retorted. Marcus Silvius Valerianus the Younger had been his older brother, the one who would have been the perfect son. Faustus Silvius Valerianus had proved to be lacking in perfection. He softened his tone. "I thought you had deserted me." He hadn't seen his father's shade since he had left Britain and he had learned by now that the old man, or what was left of him, existed in some kind of undefined misery that penned him this side of the Styx.

"I tried to." The shade sounded perplexed.

"What do you want? Do you know that? Besides to tell me that I am a disappointment."

Silvius Valerianus twisted the ring on his finger. Sometimes he wore his toga, the image of the paterfamilias. Tonight, he was dressed in a tunic and sandals as if he had just come from the field. "I suppose I should be glad you have left the army."

"I have not left the army," Faustus said. "I am on leave because we failed young Tuathal in our promise to put him back on his throne here. I am to make good on Rome's word."

"You angered Lartius Marena."

"Well, if you know that, then you know why I'm here. And in any case, I have orders from the governor. I will go back to my legion when we have won here."

"Lartius Marena has a long arm," the shade said.

Lartius Marena the Elder had a finger in nearly every stew pot in Rome, and an unpleasant reputation. He had grown rich from various court cases that always seemed to be decided in his favor by judges about whom he knew something. Lartius the Younger had been a broad-stripe tribune with political ambitions whose nose Faustus had broken over Constantia when Lartius had courted her publicly and then called her a provincial diversion. That both Faustus and the tribune had been drunk had not made the tribune more understanding. And his father was an *amicus* of the emperor.

"I can't do anything about him," Faustus said. "I can do something about this campaign. That is what I am doing."

A moth whispered through the outline of his father's shoulder, courting death at the oil lamp. Silvius Valerianus shimmered and vanished. The owl screeched again and Faustus got up. He might as well make the rounds of the camp. They weren't going to like that owl. As he stepped through the tent flap its white shape drifted silently overhead, a mouse in its talons.

–

They were on the march in the morning, along the track south toward An Mhumhain and Foirbre's stronghold at Caisel. Once their direction was clear, the High King's war band would be in pursuit and they would need to position themselves carefully between it and whatever defenses Foirbre had left behind him in An Mhumhain. According to Finmall and Fiachra, that was likely to be no more than plowmen with sickles and hay forks and a handful of Foirbre's spear band.

They marched south past the fields around Dun Ailinne and the low green hills dotted with red cattle, and prepared to ford the river that formed the southern border of Laigin. The current was passable here but barely, cold and swift-running. Faustus rode out to sound the depth and ordered the heaviest of Llwyd's cavalry into the water in lines above and below the ford. The upstream line would break the force of the flow for men and wagons crossing below them and the lower line would capture anything snatched by the current. It was chancy, Faustus thought. The current was just deep and strong enough to be worrisome. If the infantry began to flounder in it they would have to try to draw some depth away by ditching trenches through the banks to let water into the surrounding plain. He thought wistfully of Agricola's engineers and pile-driving machinery and the small boats that with an adequate supply of planks and nails could be made to support a bridge in an afternoon.

When the first of Llwyd's horsemen reached the far bank, the lines following turned their noses to face the column and the first two cohorts under Cassan and Dai began to make the crossing. By the time they came spluttering to the western bank, the next contingent had begun to cross.

Dai shook himself off and watched a man who had lost his footing mid-river being handed horse to horse by the lower cavalry line and deposited on the bank. He promptly fell in again, behind the last horse, and Dai swore and started to run.

The downriver line was struggling to halt an overturned wagon and the floundering oxen being towed into the current by its weight. Below them Dai's man, weighed down by a mail shirt, fought the water, snatching at overhanging branches. On the bank, Dai stumbled through stones and undergrowth. His foot skidded in the steep, slick mud of an otter slide and he nearly went into the river himself. He reached out a hand as he came even with his man and felt another hand grasp his belt.

"Pull!" Cassan said. "I've got you."

The man in the water scrabbled at the bank until Dai caught his hand. With Cassan bracing him, Dai reached out his other hand, closing his fingers around a wrist slick with water weeds and mud.

"Steady," Cassan said behind him. "I'm going to try to back up slowly and bring you with me. And you in the water, stop flopping like a fish and be still!"

Dai dug his boots into the slick bank, inching back carefully, and together they pulled. Shouting from upriver told them that someone else had fallen in, but Dai could see through the hanging branches that the cavalry had caught him. The oxcart was righted and being towed slowly across. They heaved and brought Dai's man up onto the bank just past the otter slide. When he got to his feet, they started cautiously back toward the ford.

Faustus had crossed with Cassan's cohort and was counting heads on the bank as the last of the column came out of the water, followed by the hospital wagons. Tuathal, Sanb, and Eochu came last with a rearguard escort.

Cassan watched Faustus tally the stragglers. "He was cursing for not having Roman engineers to build him a bridge," he said to Dai. "As if they could magic one up in a day before Elim mac Conrach gets to us."

"They could," Dai said. "I have watched them build an entire city from earth and felled trees in an afternoon."

Cassan noted the healing scar that cut through the clan markings on Dai's sword arm. "You fought them in the north," he said.

Dai was silent.

"And lost something, I'm thinking," Cassan said quietly.

A rider from Tuathal bent from his horse between them. "Form them up. We've need to put more space between us and Elim mac Conrach if we're to draw him further south."

It began to rain, which made little difference since they were already wet and would be wet again no doubt very soon. They marched along smartly, cheered at the prospect of loot from Foirbre's holds. Eochu's poet began to declaim rude verses about Elim mac Conrach and the opposing virtues of Laigin and its king, and Sanb's poet countered with his own.

—

Carraig Caisel, stronghold of the An Mhumhain kings, rose like a great ship from a wide rolling vale. Banks of stratified limestone climbed stair-step up its green heights to the hold at its summit. Faustus, eyeing it at a distance, thought wistfully of siege engines, but in fact they did not need to take the hold, only to entice Elim far enough south to keep his men unfed and force him to ravage the countryside here after Tuathal's army had done the same.

They had set about as soon as they crossed out of Laigin, marching through outlying villages, rounding up cattle from the hillsides, and looting what appealed to each man. As Fiachra had suspected, the defenders amounted only to forty or so spearmen and a rabble of angry farmers. Tuathal gave orders that the farmers were not to be harmed, other than by thievery. The spearmen retreated back into their hold atop Carraig Caisel.

Tuathal's army settled into a camp just out of sling and arrow shot of the fortress and waited for Elim mac Conrach. He was not long in coming. They heard him before they saw him, a rumble in the ground of hooves and marching feet, and then out of the morning mist a line of chariots and shouting spearmen.

Finmall pointed out Ailill of Ulaid and Elim's other son Morcant with a snort. "Morcant keeps his head in a beer barrel but he might not if Elim treated him as anything other than a spare horse. If Ailill dies it will be too late to make much of Morcant, to my thinking."

The war band halted and a rider in the lead chariot began to scream invectives at the invaders. Faustus couldn't understand all of it, but the diatribe had a cadence and a martial sound to it, like a kind of battle hymn.

"It's a poem," Finmall said. "A fierce one, enough to blister skin."

"You will note that I am unblistered," Faustus said.

"And Tuathal Techtmar himself," Finmall said. "Having been brought up in Britain. It will make him appear invulnerable."

Faustus snorted.

"For us of Inis Fáil," Finmall said seriously, "this is a grave matter. I myself have seen satire and poetry raise welts."

Faustus was willing to believe it. He had found that the gods of a place, and the magic as well, were local, intrinsic to something in the blood of the people grown on that particular soil.

Two drivers brought their teams to the front of the battle line. Atop them, Sanb's poet and Eochu's raised their arms to the morning sky and began to chant a rival music: Not only would they slaughter the illegitimate, usurping lord of Ulaid, they would lay waste to the lands of An Mhumhain where they now stood, and the ground would run with blood, the crops wither and die, the cattle sicken. There was a viciousness to it, sharp as a poisoned spearpoint and it raised the hair on Faustus's arms. He could well imagine welts if you were a child of this particular magic.

Tuathal raised his arm. He had no intention of waiting while Elim's army worked itself to a frenzy. He pointed left and right and the banners of Laigin and Connacht rose and swept forward toward either flank. Eochu had learned something from Eochaid's straining at the tether to be first in the front line as they had always done. Tuathal's Roman had brought a new battle line, and while it was foreign, it might well work, but only if the Inis Fáil men followed his orders. Eochu was prepared to do that now. Sanb, having given his alliance, would heed Tuathal's word. Tuathal nodded to Faustus and the gold sunburst of his personal standard rose in the center. The trumpet commands clashed with the war horns of Elim's battle line.

The invading army drove forward, Owain, Dai, and Finmall in the front lines, Cassan and Beric in reserve, and Llwyd's horsemen on either wing.

Owain found it easier this time to be absorbed by the great multi-headed beast that was Faustus's Roman-trained army. He saw Dai fighting as furiously as he always had but also holding his own cohort in formation with a word, a signal, a runner up and down the line, moving as another part of a single steel-clad beast.

Faustus watched with Tuathal from a stony rise that gave a view of the field. Elim's line was battering holes in the front ranks, and the front ranks closed around each of them, never losing formation. But something odd was happening. Faustus pointed.

"Look."

Tuathal narrowed his eyes. The men that breached the front lines were not trying to fight their way out – they were clawing their way farther in, seemingly more determined to drive through Tuathal's army than to fight with it. Where they could, they pushed their way through to either flank, only trying to dodge Sanb's men and Eochu's. More were peeling away from the line on either side, skirting the flanks entirely. "Those are Foirbre's men."

"They can't be trying to come at our rear. Not like that."

"They're trying to come between us and their villages," Tuathal said. "Foirbre won't hold them now. They're on their home ground and those are their wives and home farms in our path."

Faustus remembered the poets' harangue. That had been a direct threat and Foirbre's men had taken it seriously. They would fight their way to their home holds, having no doubt already marched past the destruction of the outlying lands. They would defend those; Elim mac Conrach and Foirbre himself might fight Tuathal's army without them.

The diversion of the An Mhumhain men turned the battle line to chaos as they watched. Foirbre tried to rally them to the raven banner that wavered on its pole above his head, but they didn't heed him. A king in Inis Fáil only ruled with the consent of the lords below him. Whether Foirbre lived or died, there would now be a new king in An Mhumhain. The garrison in the fortress emerged to meet those who had marched with Elim, and together they formed a shield wall between Carraig Caisel and Tuathal's reserves. Elim's line crumpled with none but Ulaid behind him.

"They are pulling back," Faustus said. In another moment, they were in full retreat with Tuathal's army howling on their heels. Faustus cast a look backward at the An Mhumhain men. Better maybe to be certain of their intent before chasing Elim. He suggested as much and Tuathal nodded. A trumpet sounded *Halt Pursuit* and Faustus hoped they would heed it. Owain, Dai, and Finmall's cohorts halted and began to form up, and Llwyd's horsemen slowed their pursuit, circling back. The question was whether Eochu and Sanb would obey. Tuathal's ultimate claim to the High Kingship might rest on that question. As he watched, the Connacht and Laigin men also slowed, pulled back, began to collect their dead. Faustus let his breath out.

In an hour, the lords of An Mhumhain came with a green branch. "Foirbre is dead," the leader of them said. "None would stand with him in this. Nor will we stand with Elim mac Conrach, nor with you."

Tuathal considered. He let his dark gaze rest on the An Mhumhain lord until the man began to fidget. "When there is a new king in An Mhumhain," Tuathal said, "he must stand somewhere, if he wishes to remain in this world."

"We must bury the old king," the An Mhumhain lord protested. "The election of a new king is a matter for every man of the *tuath*. There will be deliberation."

For as long as they could manage, Faustus thought. An Mhumhain was the farthest province from Ulaid and from Tara. They would be content to watch the claimants to the High Kingship tear each other's throats out like stoats fighting for the same den until they were exhausted. The dubious advantage of a marriage to Elim mac Conrach's daughter would not be enough anymore.

In the morning word came from the scouts dispatched to follow Elim that he had abandoned An Mhumhain and was moving north toward Connacht to exact his revenge on Sanb.

"Ever a man with no idea of his own," Finmall said, scornful. "He must use *our* tactics!"

"We are better supplied," Fiachra said. "He will regret it." The peace with An Mhumhain had included a substantial tribute of grain and cattle, now being driven in the wake of Tuathal's army.

"We'll drive the bastard north into Ulaid and from there off the sea cliffs," Finmall said with satisfaction. "He robbed me of twenty years of my life, and my hold and my wife, and I will have it back tenfold from him."

"May that come to pass," Owain said. *What would it be like to go back if you could?*

They reversed course to dog Elim's heels, biting at his rearguard as they went, waiting for him to turn at bay. The country seemed to be made of water. If it wasn't raining, they were knee-deep in another river. Sometimes both. They halted at a ford where Elim's war band had fought the current the day before, lost two wagons and drowned four men mid-river. By the time Tuathal's army approached, the level was higher yet and flowing swiftly. Faustus ordered the riverbank cut with trenches above the ford.

The warriors of Laigin and Connacht protested that they were fighting men and not farm slaves. Tuathal shamed them by putting his own foot to a shovel and they ceased to grumble. Faustus marked the line of each trench, hacking a path for the ditchers to follow through marsh fern and blackthorn, each captain and his cohort working along the same cut. As they went and the cuts deepened, the water followed.

Cassan watched Dai digging with his men, all of them blackened with mud, and called to him cheerfully, "You look like the boar that dug the Black Pig's Dyke."

"And what is that then?" Dai called back.

"We'll be crossing it no doubt," Cassan said.

The water began to flow faster, rising around his ankles, and Cassan gave his attention back to the ditch. Faustus rode into the river again, declared the level satisfactory, and they crossed by nightfall.

"Those channels will silt up again eventually," Faustus told Eochu, into whose meadow the river had flowed, while the army cooked its evening meal on the far side in the twilight. The captains had settled around the commander's fire with a stew made of An Mhumhain beef and were passing a jug of An Mhumhain beer from cup to cup.

"After they turn the land to marsh," Eochu said, eyeing the sheet of water that was forming.

"Sooner," Faustus said.

"Have you done this before?"

"As it happens, no," Faustus admitted. "It is a tactic recommended by our engineers."

Eochu gave his opinion of foreign engineers and Cassan said, "Engineers are what we have in these sad days when there is no magic left."

"Tell me about your boar and the Black Pig's Dyke," Dai said to him.

"It is a very ancient tale," Cassan said. "The dyke was gouged out by a great black pig, so they say, in the days of the Old Ones, when it fell into a fit of rage and ran between Connacht and Ulaid with its tusks to the ground, cutting a great ditch that can still be seen."

"What angered it so?"

"Who asks the wild boar why he is angry?" Cassan said. "He just is."

"True enough," Dai said, smiling a little. "I have hunted boar and their temper, as you say, is precarious."

"We will hunt them again when this war is done," Cassan said softly. "You will like this land."

Dai stood. "It is a good land," he said, "for a man who can make a home here." He gathered up his bowl and spoon and set off toward his tent. Cassan watched him until he was out of sight in the shadows and the scattered flicker of fires that stretched across the river valley.

Finmall chortled. "Cassan is lovelorn. He sighs. He melts. He woos with promises of pigs."

Cassan eyed him across the fire. "Finmall will close his braying mouth or Cassan will put a boot in it."

Faustus wondered how likely it was that they would start a fight but Finmall just grinned. "Cassan was my fosterling in the days when I had a hold of my own. Cassan will mind his manners."

"Finmall will mind his own business."

"My commanders will mind *my* business, which is Elim mac Conrach," Tuathal said, standing over them. He had developed an unsettling way of appearing when you didn't see him coming. There was not much left of the adolescent boy Faustus had first met in a tavern in Isca Silurum with his father's sword at his belt. There was a certain mythic quality to the High Kingship, an aura of old magic and old gods, and it was settling around Tuathal's shoulders like a cloak. Faustus thought that it would be sliding from Elim's back at the same time, as that kind of thing came to only one man at a time.

—

Baine glared at the mud-spattered messenger who had ridden up the Connacht road to Tara in the rain to summon the High King's daughter to him. "I will come when my woman has gathered my things. In the meantime, go to the kitchen and ask for a meal for yourself and your men. And a fire to dry by."

"The king gave an order for speed, Princess," the messenger said.

"I have no doubt. The king is always in a hurry. I am not." And to whom did he intend to offer her this time, she wondered. Not Foirbre, at least.

She delayed as long as she could, mostly out of vindictiveness, but in the morning she and Olwenna rode out with the escort that had come to bring her to Elim.

"What does he want with me?" she asked Aíbinn, who had been sent with the messenger, for reasons Baine was uncertain of. The Druids always carried power around them in the same way a snail did its shell, and for that reason Elim had been keeping them by him.

"He doesn't know," Aíbinn said. "These days he only wants."

"Tuathal Techtmar will win," Baine said. "You have known it but not spoken clearly."

"Clearly enough had he been listening."

Whatever the Druids read in the skies or the water would come about, although it might come in some sideways fashion that not even they expected. Baine was silent after that as they rode to meet the war band in the Connacht lowlands around Cruachan, stronghold of the Connacht kings. Aíbinn said that Sanb of Connacht, riding with Tuathal Techtmar, was also hard on her father's heels, and Baine remembered the High King's curse.

—

The armies came together again on stony ground on the border of Connacht. Elim was outnumbered but it was still possible to lose the war to him. Tuathal and Faustus had inspected the terrain beforehand and chosen a place where Elim would have to come to them over a stretch of rocky outcropping, or go around and be caught between Tuathal's waiting cohorts and a lake framed by steep cliffs.

Elim was growing ever more angry and it did not make him a better commander, but his curse flew true. Sanb of Connacht rode into the tangle of men and chariots at the front of Elim's line and did not ride out again. His driver brought his body out and swore that a great black bird had sat on his helmet crest as he fell.

It was possible that he had known. Sanb had given orders that on his death his men were to give their loyalty to Tuathal Techtmar, and no man crowned king of Connacht after him who went against his word.

Faustus gathered the Connacht men and set them at Elim's flank, shouting "For Sanb! For your king!" They followed him with a howl.

Elim's men were nearly as angry as the High King was, hungry, weary, and with no path other than to follow Elim wherever he led them, and that had been nowhere good so far. Faustus recognized one of the gold-decked lords as Morcant, at the front of Elim's line with an ill-assorted band of spearmen and axe- and sword-wielders. They were on Connacht land and Faustus took advantage to drive the Connacht men into their midst with all the fury of the invaded for the invader. Morcant urged his men forward to meet them, shouting orders that were ignored by men who knew he was expendable.

-

Baine met her father's war band riding hard northeast into Ulaid. Sanb of Connacht was dead but the battle had gone to Tuathal Techtmar, and Elim's army bore her brother Morcant's body with them. She should mourn him, she supposed, but he had never given her reason to, any more than her father or Ailill, her elder brother, had. It seemed that Elim did not mourn greatly either, as they were to raise a barrow for Morcant in Ulaid rather than taking him to Reachra. Elim flung his anger at anyone near him, boasting that his curse had brought death to Sanb in Connacht. He tried to call the same curse on Tuathal Techtmar but no Druid would witness it. His anger at them vibrated like a wasp in a box but not even Elim would challenge the Druids. He called the war band to him and shouted that he would give his daughter to the man who brought him Tuathal Techtmar's head.

At night in the muddy marching camp Baine listened to the war band drink and boast. Olwenna stood guard outside her tent with a knife in her hand. Toward dawn they fell silent and the night gave way to the midsummer whirr of insects and the rustle of small creatures in the bracken, the yip of a fox in the distance, the noise of the natural world getting on with its business outside the world of men. The women slept then and stumbled awake at first light when Elim went shouting through the camp, cursing his men from their beds.

On the border of Ulaid, the army of Tuathal Techtmar caught up with them. Elim's band marched out to meet them, but they had barely engaged when a fog came down that covered both armies and made fighting impossible. The Druids, assuming credit for it, announced that the final conflict would be fought at Tara. Any battle begun elsewhere would end in defeat, but the Morrigan herself would come to Tara.

"I don't doubt it," Baine said wearily. "She likes death."

–

Tuathal's army too had been growing smaller, although still outnumbering Elim's. The men of Connacht had stayed at Cruachan to elect a new king. The rest had made their way in pursuit of Elim, crossing several times, as Cassan had predicted, the old ditch and earthwork, now overgrown with bracken and blackthorn, that had made the Black Pig's Dyke.

"And we have the sorry faithless bastard now!" Finmall whooped joyously as they came upon Elim's army under a gray cloud bank that had already begun to descend. The poets of Laigin began to declaim the sacred lineage of Tuathal Techtmar, son of Fíacha Finnolach, and the revenge he would wreak upon the usurper. Finmall's cohort was in the front line, beside Cassan and Beric. Faustus felt his heart pounding. This was it surely. This would be the battle to bring Inis Fáil under Tuathal's kingship, the reason Faustus was here in this sodden land and not with his legion. A story, and a fine one, to take back to the legate and the governor, and earn a plum posting, maybe even a higher cohort than the Ninth to command. If he brought this off, the emperor would be pleased enough with the governor who had sent him that Lartius Marena would be no trouble to him.

He moved Arion into the battle line beside Finmall, but the fog was thickening quickly. Elim's chariots thundered out of it, already barely visible. Helmets and sword blades came and went in the gray mist, a horse's head appeared and vanished, a spear thrown blindly caught him in the thigh, streaking a bloody gash across it. No standards could be seen and the battle sounds were muffled and distorted by the mist. Faustus bumbled his way through the chaos with no idea who he was fighting until the trumpets called *Pull Back*. War horns brayed and Elim's men began to draw off too.

When the mist had cleared an hour later, dissipating as swiftly as it had come, Elim's army was not to be found, although their passage to the south was obvious in the wet, trampled earth. Casualties were few but Faustus, looking for wounded, found Cassan weeping over Finmall's still body.

-

They buried Finmall beside the Black Pig's Dyke with his sword and his gold, and raised a barrow with a cairn of stones atop it so that anyone passing would know that a battle had been fought there and a hero had died. The other captains stood solemnly in the rain that had begun again, and took it in turns to heap earth atop the grave.

Cassan dug his shovel into the bank of the dyke, adding to the mound of muddy soil. "I had only just come to him for fostering when the king was killed," he said miserably. "My father and mother died and his wife too and he kept me by him through all the roving years. He was finally to have had his own hold and house again. Maybe a wife again."

Dai put a hand on Cassan's shoulder, and took the shovel from him for his turn.

Finmall's cohort were paraded along the edge of the dyke, grim-faced and uneasy. The fog had felt too full of magic, like a malign wet shroud. Faustus watched as Finmall's second-in-command spoke quietly to them but they shuffled their feet and their eyes slid sideways to the forest and the tangles of blackthorn as if something baleful lurked there.

V. THE HILL OF ACHALL

MIDSUMMER

Elim mac Conrach turned to fight on the Hill of Achall. It rose up across the valley from Tara, a limestone outcrop higher than Tara's slope and shrouded with old magic, the legendary death site of an ancient princess. Achall overlooked both Tara and the Ulaid road that ran along a gravel ridge between them.

It should be easy, but Faustus knew that it would not be. Tuathal had his own war band and the men of Laigin behind him. The men of Connacht, having chosen their new king, were marching vengefully on Elim as well, so said a courier from Cruachan. Elim had only the men of Ulaid. The men of Connacht would never follow him now, in retribution for the death of their king, any more than the men of An Mhumhain would willingly shed more blood for him. All of which should have assured victory. But Elim was not sane, something that Sanb of Connacht had said more than once. Faustus had seen Sanb go down, surrounded by warriors of Ulaid who had driven straight toward him, clearly with no goal but Sanb. More than half of them had died doing it. Fiachra's spies said that Elim had put the king's curse on Sanb and a price of thirty cows on his head, and had tried to put the same curse on Tuathal but no Druid would witness it. That argued desperation, and desperate commanders did not surrender. They would have to fight their way through a river of blood until all of Elim's men were dead.

The fog that had come down around them in the last encounter had left Tuathal's men with the feeling that something more than human agency was abroad and now they made the sign of horns every time a twig cracked. Finmall's cohort was the worst. Faustus took reluctant command of them and his self-drawn line between military advisor and officer in Tuathal's army grew hazier. The fog was followed by rain and the kind of wind that howls with inhuman voices, and Finmall's second-in-command said frankly that they were uneasy enough to be unstable.

"Some of them think Elim's Druids let loose spirits with that fog, and some come from countries where the Dark Ones ride wind and water. The rest think that the frightened ones will buckle when it comes to a fight. Now they are at odds with each other."

Faustus paraded Finmall's cohort under a sopping sky. "This country is nothing but water," he informed them. "If there was a spirit in every fog and rain shower we wouldn't be able to move for them. Whatever you were before you came under my command, you are now an army, not a band of undisciplined peasants seeing hobgoblins in the soup."

They muttered uncomfortably and he glared at them. "You follow the orders of your century-commander who follows the orders of his captain, which right now is myself. The captains follow the orders of the High King's captain, which is also myself, and I follow the king's orders. Thus are great battles won. Remember who you are now, and the oath you swore. That is all you need to be thinking about, other than the share of gold and land you'll be given when the High King takes back his throne."

They brightened at that as he thought they would do, but also that he couldn't give them back to Finmall's second. The second was an ex-auxiliaryman, a seasoned soldier who had been a low-level decurion, but he hadn't the experience of high command, or the learned ability to look down his nose and pull rank. Eirian had called it speaking lordly-wise, he remembered wistfully.

When the scouts reported that Elim had halted his army at the Hill of Achall, Faustus sat with Tuathal and Fiachra and sketched the landscape on a tablet whose wax was wearing thin with erasures. A country with no writing materials was driving him mad. If he ever ventured away from Roman supply lines again, he would bring a trunk filled with rolls of blank papyrus, pristine wax and wooden tablets, and bottomless bottles of ink.

Fiachra scraped a line with his fingernail. "There is a shallow brook that drains into the River Bhóinn here. It is not deep but it will slow us. If there is any more rain, it will be worse."

"And the ground around it?" Tuathal asked.

"Flat excepting the Ulaid road that runs along the ridge. Elim has the high ground and he is unlikely to give it up, so we will likely cross unhindered but we will have the water and wet ground at our backs."

"How many men has he now?" Faustus asked.

"The scouts count no more than two thousand," Fiachra said. "Half our number when Connacht catches up to us."

"We may not be able to wait," Faustus said. "This is Elim's country and his men will have stripped it bare already. Our supplies are short from chasing them back and forth like dogs after a hare. We can't halt for Connacht very long."

"We will halt for one day," Tuathal said. "The gods have favored us thus far. We will wait one day for them to bring Connacht to us. Tomorrow is Lughnasa, and if we have a cow left we will pay the god his due and see what comes."

In the morning they slaughtered the cow and the meat went afterward into cook pots to hearten a stew of barley and greens and the last withered turnips, while the scent of the burning bones rose skyward for the god. Pandora prowled wistfully about the fire until the Druids drove her off with sticks and Paullus tied her up. At sunset the Druids consulted the omens and pronounced them good.

The field where they were camped was a short enough march from Elim mac Conrach's men that Faustus posted sentries all around the perimeter. At midsummer sunset came late and the sky lightened again early, a pale sheen like shells, becoming paler and brighter as the birdsong called it into daybreak. When it did, the men of Connacht had not come.

A scout reported sighting Connacht a half day's march away in the west. Tuathal gave the order to form up. "They will come," he said. "With luck we will drive Elim's men into them."

Given the terrain, Faustus thought that was possible but chancy. *You are not in command*, he told himself one more time. He was finding that an uncomfortable bridle to wear. As they crossed the shallow brook that Fiachra had spoken of, he saw Tuathal helmetless with a gold fillet on his dark hair. Faustus wanted to tell him to put his helmet on, but knew the force of Tuathal's men seeing him thus, regal and instantly identifiable.

The sky cleared to an almost unnatural blue. The ground around the brook was damp and yellow with buttercups, the hill in the distance purple with heather. Elim mac Conrach's men were arrayed across the hilltop under white banners that bore the red hand of Ulaid, and a golden standard marked Elim's place in the battle line. At the base of the hill a ridge of sand and gravel humped up from the valley floor. The Ulaid road that ran partway along it was no more than a broad cow track and Tuathal's army overflowed it on either side.

Elim's men began to shriek their battle chants and threats as soon as Tuathal's men came in sight. Under Tuathal's orders, and to the disapproval of the Druids and fury of the poets, his own band stayed silent as they marched. Even Fiachra and Cassan had to admit that there was something terrifying in that silence.

They formed a long, deep front, curved on either flank: Faustus, Cassan, and Dai forward, Owain and Beric to the rear, with Llwyd's cavalry forming wings on either side, intermingled with the Laigin men on the left to push any retreat into the path of the Connacht war band. Faustus went on foot with his cohort, Tuathal riding at their head. Tuathal drew his father's sword and raised it to that unnatural sky under the sunburst banner. The light caught the ancient blade and it flashed like a beacon. The sun made an aureole of light around Tuathal's head and the gold fillet glowed.

Tuathal raised his shield in his other hand, dropped it, and his army flowed behind him toward Elim's line. This time he would ride before them into the battle that would end the matter, one way or the other. If he was to rule as High King there was no other way. Faustus had argued with him and Tuathal had said only, "I cannot govern Inis Fáil if I command like a Roman."

Faustus could see the truth in that. And also that if Tuathal died, the whole purpose of the war died with him, and then what would Faustus do with a band of mercenaries, adventurers, and men who most likely could not go back to wherever they had come from? It was probably as well not to dwell on that.

War horns bellowed from the slope above them and Tuathal's trumpets sounded their own calls. The front lines tilted their shields to cover their heads as a death-dealing rain of slingstones thundered down on them followed by thrown spears and a shower of arrows.

"Push up the slope!" Faustus shouted to his second, tucking his own head down. Arrows and sling bullets from their own men whined overhead, homing on the war band on the hill. Faustus had had the bullets cast with holes through the center so they whistled as they went over, a message to the enemy that something unseen and deadly was coming. The bean-sidhe, the hag of the hollow hills, had a voice like that, Finmall had said when he heard them.

The Hill of Achall wasn't steep, but the ground was rough with limestone boulders jutting from the heather, thick, wiry grass, and tangled scrubs and briars. The horsemen had harder going there and swung around the lower slopes to hold the flanks when Elim's men began to pour down the hill to meet them.

Elim rode in a chariot at the head of their onslaught, his war band a ragged, shrieking torrent behind him. The fury with which they fought came partly from the blind rush to battle, the tension built up by the theatrics beforehand, and the wild surge of blood that washed caution out of any head. It was counterpoint to the stolid discipline of Roman lines and at a certain point capable of overwhelming it.

"Hold formation!" Faustus shouted. All along the front line the other captains were positioning their men to meet the flood of screaming warriors: chariots and then spearmen and men armed with axes and long swords. The men of Laigin on the left flank broke their silence to scream back but they held formation, this time under Eochu's command.

A chariot drove straight at Faustus, its driver urging the horses on, its rider hurling spear after spear. The horses reared as they came against the shield line and Faustus got under the deadly hooves with his short sword and one went down. It kicked his helmet against his skull as it did. Faustus always hated killing horses but they were vulnerable and an unhorsed rider or charioteer was more so. He straightened, his head ringing, as the rider leapt down and came at him. He drove at Faustus with his spear, staying out of range of Faustus's sword, thrusting, prodding for an opening. The driver, weaponless, was trying to cut the other pony from the traces. To either side, Faustus's cohort battled their way through the onslaught, taking one step and then another up the hill. Faustus saw Elim's standard and Tuathal's swaying over the battle line but there was no time to give them more than a glance. The spearpoint went past the cheekpiece of Faustus's dented helmet and the man behind it lost his balance for an instant on the uneven ground. Faustus swung his sword hard, fast, at the spearman's bare head before he could recover and nearly took it off. He stepped over the body through a shower of spurting blood, gagging, and pushed on, Finmall's cohort solidly behind him now.

Just here another thin brook ran down the slope, curving between the outcroppings to join the one below, and the ground was soft. The hooves and chariot wheels of Elim's army had churned it to mud. Both sides slipped and staggered, but Tuathal's army slowly pushed Elim's backward up the slope and Tuathal's rear ranks began to clamber over bodies as they climbed. Riding or marching to battle unarmored was a point of bravery and pride among the warriors of Inis Fáil but it was costing them dearly against the mail and plate of Tuathal's band. The warrior of Ulaid swinging an axe at Faustus's head went down before he could finish the blow, with a shaft through his ribs from the spearmen Faustus had interspersed among his ranks like a spiked wall. Unarmored, any blow that came past a shield would sink into muscle and bone. Faustus had argued that point with the men of Laigin who mostly went bare like the men of Ulaid, and had not been listened to. Nor likely would the men of Connacht. It was why Tuathal had ridden out helmetless, although he at least had a shirt of mail.

"They have always fought each other for amusement," Owain had said grimly. "When that is the case and a man expects to be as happy drinking with the gods in the Otherworld as here, then it is little matter and shows bravery."

"And when the stakes change?" Faustus had asked.

"Then it matters." Owain in another life had bought as much mail and as many helmets as he could find the gold for, to hold off Rome. It had not been enough but it had made the victory harder.

Elim mac Conrach, like Tuathal, went bare-headed into this fight, as did most of his warriors who counted on battle frenzy to armor them. And it might even be enough, Faustus thought, still battling desperately against a howling torrent of them, who kept running, kept fighting, eyes glazed with fury, kept raging even as they bled to death. They had nothing to lose now. If Elim went down they would have no place under Tuathal. The frontline cohorts were beginning to flag. Tuathal saw and ordered them to the rear and Owain's and Beric's men forward.

"Take them back and rest them," Faustus told his second. "Keep them together. They may have to come up again. And if you can find my slave tell him to bring my horse up." He straightened his battered helmet and tightened the chin strap. When Paullus came from the rear with Arion, he mounted and surveyed the moving tide of men, looking for soft spots, for holes to patch, for any century getting too far out from its comrades. He could see Tuathal's standard above the front line with Beric's cohort, and Llwyd's cavalry on both flanks, but he couldn't find Llwyd.

Beric's men had opened ranks to let the flagging cohorts through and closed again with a precision that would have done the legions proud. Newly brought up from the reserves, they were fresh and were now pushing Elim's tiring men steadily backward. Even the fever of battle could only last so long, and when it wore off it left the body nearly empty.

Elim could see his men giving ground. He stood in his chariot, shield in hand, red in the face and venomous with fury. "Are you nothing but women? Drive them out!"

His driver was his son Ailill, king of Ulaid, who raised his arms, spear and shield in hand. "Men of Ulaid! Follow your king!"

They rallied, the ones who could not hear over the chaos of the battle catching a second wind from those who could. Their line stiffened and when one man went down, another screaming warrior filled his place, bloody axe in hand.

Tuathal was in the thick of it, swinging a long sword from his horse's back, both his spears gone. Faustus pushed Arion up beside him, giving him cover from the Ulaid men, keeping them both visible to the cohorts beside them steadily pushing Elim's war band back up the slope.

Ailill drove Elim's chariot straight at Tuathal, forcing the horses to the advancing line when they began to balk. Tuathal's horse spun to the side and Tuathal slashed at Elim with his sword, holding off a spear with the shield in his other hand. His horse's reins were knotted around its neck now and he guided it with his knees. Faustus followed, blessing Paullus for having tied two fresh spears to his saddle. He drove one of them at Ailill. It slid off the edge of Ailill's shield and Faustus fought it back into his grip and lunged again, lifting his shield against Ailill's spear. Elim and his son were both bareheaded, gold fillets of their rank crowning sandy hair, but they were clad in hauberks of gilded scale. The scale caught the sun like the skins of great armored fish. With their gold torques and armbands and the gold and silver chariot fittings, they made an excellent target and Faustus heard a sling bullet whistle overhead. He ducked reflexively but it had been carefully aimed and it took Ailill in the chest. He lost the reins and the horses began to bolt. Elim jumped from the chariot.

A man on horseback had both advantages and disadvantages in fighting a man on foot. Faustus began to dismount to hold Elim from Tuathal.

"No!" Tuathal slid from his own horse. "He is mine. Mine and my father's!"

Elim lunged at him with his spear and Tuathal caught it on his shield. The point stuck and Tuathal wrenched it out before Elim could pull it back. Tuathal snapped the staff under his foot and drew his sword. Faustus and Beric's cohort fought Elim's men back as the two circled each other. The dark head and the sandy one looked to Faustus like an image distorted in water, one true, one altered by the depths beneath the surface. Tuathal wore a hauberk of dark mail, his gold jewelry and fillet a counterpoint to the mail and the dark breeches and boots. Elim's breeches and cloak were gaudy and fine, red checked with blue and bordered with yellow. Tuathal had dressed deliberately, Faustus thought, to make Elim think of ravens. An advantage of the mind, he had called it once and said he had learned it from Agricola.

Faustus fought off any of Elim's men who got near and Beric's cohort battered at Elim's front line. Farther to the left, Owain's cohort had driven a wedge into the Ulaid line and was beginning to push them sideways along the hill into the cavalry on the flank. Elim's men were failing but that wouldn't matter if Tuathal went down. Beric came at Elim as he struck at Tuathal and Tuathal shouted him away too.

"Mine! Mine and my father's!" Tuathal's father's sword swung wide, feinted, sliced sideways like a striking snake and came past Elim's guard. Elim staggered, a long gash opened in his hauberk.

"Elim mac Conrach, you bought your death when you killed the king and drove my mother to Britain!" Tuathal raised his sword again, looking for another opening.

"It is the way of the kingship," Elim grunted. "Your father too bought it with blood." He swung his sword, caught it on the edge of Tuathal's shield, and pulled it to the side.

Tuathal shook free, slammed his shield into Elim's, trying to drive him back onto a broken wheel lying in the grass. Elim kept his feet and an Ulaid man snatched the wheel with both hands and sent it whirling overhead into Tuathal's ranks.

Faustus swung Arion around to drive his spear at an Ulaid man who clambered over the body of his fellow to come at him with an already bloody axe. Faustus's spearpoint drove hard into the shield and knocked its bearer off-balance and Beric thrust his sword into the man's bare ribs. Another came behind him and Faustus was too late to block the blow that caught Beric in the throat. He fell and one of his men pulled him from under trampling feet, but Faustus knew he was dead. There was no time for the mourning that would come down on him after the battle, as it always did. All around them the line was wavering and the men of Ulaid were being driven back save for the ones surrounding Elim, his household spears. If Elim went down they would flow away like water. If Tuathal did…

Faustus saw Fiachra, dismounted and sword in hand. He was bleeding steadily from his shield arm. "Take my horse," Faustus said, swinging down. "Get to the rear and get that bleeding stopped."

Fiachra shook his head. "Give me your scarf. I will see that bastard dead with my own eyes. I have waited twenty years."

Faustus pulled the scarf that padded the neck of his hauberk and tied it as tightly as he could around Fiachra's arm. He looked at Tuathal and Elim encircled by a ring of men of both sides.

"He's tiring," Faustus said, drawing his sword again.

"No. You are still thinking of him as you first knew him, as a boy. He is not and he must do this himself if he is to be High King."

Faustus halted but he waited, watchful and unconvinced, sword in hand, for other attackers to come out of Elim's retreating line. One of Elim's spearmen lunged at Tuathal and Elim too warned him away.

"This is between us!" Elim spat, his breath coming more rapidly and increasingly ragged.

Tuathal's eye was caught by the spearman for an instant. Elim swung his sword, hard, and it slid a fraction past Tuathal's guard, raking down his sword arm. Tuathal stepped back out of reach and came again at Elim, facing sideways to the hillside, each man off balance with the slope. An outcropping of rock lifted its teeth from the ground just there, half-hidden by a tangle of briars. Tuathal's sword arm was seeping blood. The cut wasn't deep and he could still use it; Faustus saw that with relief, thinking of Owain. But blood loss would take a toll.

Elim, bleeding from the gash in his hauberk, knew that too. He closed with Tuathal fast and hard while Tuathal was still assessing the strength in his arm. Tuathal put his foot between Elim's legs and slammed Elim's shield with his own, reckless of Elim's sword. Elim swung at Tuathal's head but he stumbled and the blow went barely wide. Tuathal feinted as Elim tried to right himself, swung his sword the other way and drove it downward, hard, into Elim's throat.

A howl of fury went up from the Ulaid men but there was no one now for them to follow. Some threw themselves at the cohort around Tuathal in a last fury and went down. The rest, uncertain and leaderless, fled down the hillside pursued by Llwyd's cavalry.

Faustus grabbed the first man he saw. "Go and get Silus!"

–

Silus poured vinegar into the gash in Tuathal's sword arm and stitched it there in the field while Tuathal sat on one of the limestone outcroppings and listened to his scouts' reports. The Hill of Achall was empty of all but his men and the dead, Beric and Llwyd among them. The remnants of Elim's war band had scattered. Ailill's bolting horses had dragged his chariot in the wake of the retreat, finally throwing him from it. His men had found him on the ground and picked him up to carry with them in retreat, but with Llwyd's vengeful cavalry on their heels, they had met the war band of Connacht coming from the west. Ailill had been taken prisoner but he was dead or would be shortly.

The stone had caused deep internal damage in his chest and he was bubbling blood from his lips.

"That's likely killed him by now," Silus said, giving his professional opinion. "Keep this clean, High King, and I will send you some more salve for it. I have others to see to now."

Tuathal stood and motioned to Faustus and together they said the legionary Prayer for the Slain for Beric and Llwyd. Then Tuathal ordered the field combed for the rest of their dead. The Morrigan's birds had already begun to come, circling the Hill of Achall in a black cloud. Faustus followed Silus to his hospital tent to count their wounded.

He found Dai there, with Cassan standing over him. Cassan's pale hair, loosed from his helmet, was sweat-soaked, his hauberk smeared with mud and blood that must have been someone else's. He was furiously fending off an orderly.

"You wait for the surgeon! You're a half-trained pup."

"And you aren't in command!"

The hospital was full of those who had been coming in throughout the battle and the floor was littered with bloody bandages and shreds of tunics and breeches. A line of lesser wounded still waited for the orderlies going down their rows. Silus bent over Dai where he sat on a bench, the shaft of an arrow protruding from his shoulder through the ring mail of his hauberk.

"It's not deep," the orderly said. "But we think it's barbed." He gave Cassan an insulted glare.

"We know it is," Cassan said. "And you aren't going to be the one to pull it."

Silus prodded gently at the shaft. Dai grimaced, mouth twisting under his dark mustache.

"Get metal cutters. And poppy tears."

"Already brought them," the orderly said, with another black look at Cassan.

"I can be still," Dai gasped. "I don't need poppy to cloud my head."

"No, you can't, and yes, you do," Silus said wearily. He held a cup to Dai's lips. "Drink this, I have others to see to." Dai swallowed. Poppy was tricky and used sparingly. Too much could kill a patient, especially a weakened one. In a cautious dose it wouldn't block pain completely, but took the edge off enough to keep a man still while a surgeon tried to save him.

Silus carefully clipped the rings of mail around the arrow shaft, pulling each away from the wound while the poppy tears took effect. When he had opened what he judged to be a sufficient gap in the mail, he said, "All right, lie down, it will be easier for me to get at it that way." To the orderly he said, "Hand me the spoon. And wound dressing. This is going to bleed like Bellona's fountain when we pull it."

The orderly handed him a deep, cup-shaped instrument with a hole in the bottom, and Dai lay flat and clenched his teeth. Silus worked the spoon down the shaft until he felt it catch the barbed point. He pulled it back and Dai grunted as the arrow came out in a gush of blood. Silus pressed a heavy dressing against the hole it left. The orderly handed him a pot of vinegar and Silus pulled the dressing back long enough to pour it into the wound. Dai jerked under his hand and his fingers clenched the edge of the bench. When the vinegar had run out again on a fresh flow of blood, Silus put another dressing to it.

"Hold this there until the bleeding slows," he told Cassan. "Then we'll get him out of that mail and I'll wrap a bandage over it. It's best not to stitch these but to let them close on their own."

Dai began to sit up and caught his breath. Cassan pushed him down.

Silus handed the orderly a clay jar stoppered with a cork. "Take this to the High King and say he is to put it on his arm twice a day. Tell him I will rebandage it tomorrow."

Dai raised his head at that. "Then we have won?"

"Even for you I would not be here else," Cassan said. "Yes, we have won."

-

The Druids came to Tuathal the next morning at Tara. Tuathal sat in the great chair recently occupied by Elim mac Conrach with his surviving captains arrayed in a half circle to either side of him. He wore a fine red cloak, blue breeches, and a blue and green checked shirt. His arms were encircled with gold bands, his throat with a gold torque. The red-gold crown of the High King, fallen from Elim mac Conrach's head, sat on his dark hair. Elim's head itself topped a pole in the courtyard.

After breakfast the new king had begun dictating orders and decisions in the presence of the brehons who had appeared out of the morning mist from all four provinces to supervise. Kings might rise and fall and kill each other in the rising and falling, but the brehons sat in judgment on what was lawful thereafter. Faustus watched the process with interest.

Cennétig, chief of them, listened to Tuathal's division of the lands that had lately belonged to Elim and to Ailill and the Ulaid lords. "And their women?" he asked Tuathal. A steady line of weeping women had come that morning and been sent away again.

"No new lord may dispossess a widow," Tuathal said. "They may marry if she is willing."

The brehons nodded. That was reasonable.

"If not, he must give her a house."

The brehons nodded again. To make peace with the women was wise.

Fiachra came from the outer court and stepped carefully through the lawyers. "The Druids have come, High King."

"Whose Druids?" Tuathal asked, not moving.

"We belong to no king," the old man in the doorway said. Faustus recognized him as one of the Druids of Laigin. He had not seen the two men with him, but the fourth was a woman, the pale one who had come with Elim's daughter Baine when Tuathal had made landfall at Inber Domnann. The daughter who, with her women, was still occupying the upstairs quarters of the High King's hall.

The Druids swept through the brehons and stood facing Tuathal. The heavy gold disks about their throats proclaimed that they spoke for the Sun Lord, but they were otherwise unadorned, their gowns plain black or white, only a spray of wheat tucked through their belts.

"We have spoken to the stars," the old man said.

"And what have they said to you?" Tuathal asked suspiciously.

"To seal your right to the kingship, you must marry the daughter of Ulaid."

There was a stirring and then silence as everyone eyed the High King with some unease.

Faustus remembered her, tall and imperious, threatening to feed his eyes to the ravens that were now at work on her father's.

"As to the princess of Ulaid," Tuathal said after a long moment, "I had not thought to seek a wife so soon." And most particularly not that one.

The old man said, "The High King weds the Goddess at Samhain each year. The seventh year is of particular import and this is a seventh year."

"I am aware of that," Tuathal said. And of the fact that in the ancient days, there was a new king, chosen by the queen, to slay the old one each seventh year. He gave the Druids a long look to indicate that he knew that too. "I will marry the Goddess as is appropriate and her due. That is all that is required."

The Druids were unmoved.

"And was her mother not from Connacht?" Tuathal demanded. "As was my father. Likely we are kin and would bring ill luck instead."

"You are not," one of the others said flatly. Between them the Druids knew the lineage of each *tuath*. "Only in the fifth degree which makes no barrier."

"That is unfortunate," Tuathal said, "because I still will not marry her."

The pale woman spoke now. "A royal woman is the body of the Goddess on earth. Your marriage with the princess of Ulaid, daughter of the old king, will unite Inis Fáil. We have had enough of war."

Fiachra bent to whisper in Tuathal's ear, and Cassan leaned forward too.

"Inheritance is often matrilineal. Marriage to Elim's daughter will give your sons their best claim to come after you."

"She will be a danger to you else, High King, if she marries a man with ambition," Cassan added.

"Unless you kill her," Fiachra said.

Tuathal looked at the Druid in the black gown and at the staircase that led to the chambers upstairs, and at the half-open door of the king's hall, outside which Elim mac Conrach's head sat on a pole. He closed his eyes for a moment, and then spoke. "Holy mother – tell me what you are called?"

"Aíbinn."

"Aíbinn, bring her to me here tonight."

Faustus thought he saw some last piece of the kingship settle on the High King's shoulders.

—

Olwenna had washed Baine's hair in a bucket, dried it by the fire in her chamber, and shaken out a clean gown from the clothes chest. They had come road-weary and bedraggled to Tara when the tide of the battle had turned, because there was nowhere else to go. Now she set the gold collar with its cascade of gold drops over Baine's shoulders and pulled the red boots onto her feet. Aíbinn waited in the doorway and there was no point in refusing to go. Olwenna said a quick prayer to the Mother and to the Dagda both. What happened tonight would set the course of both their lives.

Baine set the gold fillet on her hair because she was still a king's daughter, and nodded at Aíbinn. The ancient skulls in the walls that enclosed the stairs watched her passage from their niches as she descended, long-dead kings and heroes and enemies familiar to her since her childhood, part of the power that made Tara a place of the gods.

The great hall was cavernous when it was empty, like some ancient barrow deep in the earth. Torches lined the walls and the hearth fire was lit, but the only human in it was the new High King, sitting in her father's chair. Another chair was drawn next to it and there was food and drink on a table beside them. Outside, Baine could hear the shouting and revelry of a victorious army. They would be in the feasting hall drinking down her father's store of mead and listening to their poets and harpers recount the battles that would grow in the telling until the man who sat by the hearth had killed ten thousand with his own sword.

The High King had been staring into the fire but now he turned to look at her. "Come and sit down, Princess."

"Leave us," Baine said to Aíbinn.

Aíbinn hesitated.

"Leave us!"

"Which of us is it you distrust?" Tuathal asked the Druid.

Aíbinn didn't answer, but she went out the great doors at the hall's end into the twilit courtyard.

"She will wait outside," Baine said. "And no doubt listen at the door."

Tuathal poured mead from a pitcher into a gold cup and offered it to her. A lean gold hound pursued a boar around its midsection.

"My father took these cups in a raid on An Mhumhain when they were slow to pay their taxes," Baine said, turning it in her hand. She didn't drink from it.

"It's Inis Fáil goldwork, I believe," Tuathal said. "Very fine." He was silent for a long moment and then he said abruptly, "The Druids have told you what they wish."

She nodded. Her father's crown was a glowing ring above his dark hair. His face was slightly wolfish, high cheekbones and a long jaw.

"Could you wed me?" he asked her bluntly. "When I have brought about his death?" Tuathal's shield and sword hung on the

90

wall beyond the hearth, firelight glinting red from the gold eyes on the hilt. "The Druids say it is foreordained, but I will not take an unwilling woman." He could wed her whether she liked it or not, and they both knew that. If he wanted to chance a knife in his back one night.

"The Druids spend their time translating signs that no one else can read," Baine said, "and reciting the history of dead kings. They do not understand living people or care for their wishes."

"No," he admitted.

"Nevertheless, I will wed you."

"For what reason?"

She drank from her cup then. "For the reason that my father promised me to any man he wanted alliance with. For the reason that he got my mother with child and killed her to provide him another daughter to sell. I am not Achall, to die of grief at the sight of his head, when he offered me to any man who brought me yours. Or over my brothers, who were no different."

"Your mother was from Connacht, was she not?" Tuathal asked.

"Yes."

"So was my father. It may be we are kin in some leftwise way, but the Druids say it is not close enough to matter. I asked, in hope that there was some way out of this."

"Did you have another woman in mind for wife?" *That would be a bad start.*

"No. I had it in mind to claim my father's throne. That only, since I have been old enough to hear the tale."

"And now the Druids have decided that you shall have me," Baine said, "and I you. I am not a bad bargain. I have all my teeth. I know how to weave and make cheese and doctor cattle. What virtues can *you* offer to make you preferable to the pig boy?"

Tuathal's mouth twitched at the corner and she saw it with swift relief.

"I am sorry I said that," he told her. "I am as yet unacquainted with the pig boy so I can only speak for myself. I have been told

91

that I am a considerate lover. Also, I am a patient man who can spend a morning with the brehons and not slay any of them."

"That would be most unwise, and argues restraint," Baine agreed, "although understandable. A brehon's honor price is high."

"I can also play latrunculi with the Roman frontier scouts and win. Latrunculi is like wisdom but more complicated, and the frontier scouts cheat."

"That seems less useful."

"That means I recognize a Roman scout when I encounter one," Tuathal said.

"And what of your tame Roman?" Baine was curious about him. "I am told the Romans have an acquisitive eye."

"Precisely why it is useful to recognize their spies."

"Would Rome look to Inis Fáil?"

"Anything is possible. My old general thought he could take it with one legion, and I have done nearly that. But the Romans just now will have trouble enough holding the land they have taken in Britain. There is rebellion on their frontiers elsewhere and they move their legions around like men on a wisdom board, afraid to leave too many under one general for too long, lest he become yet another sword-made emperor."

"We have fought wars among ourselves for so long," Baine said. "King after sword-made king. If that ceases with you, I would find it reason enough to wed you. I am weary of death."

He took a ring from his finger then, heavy gold set with a bull's head carved in green chalcedony. He put it on hers, a gesture from which there was no going back, even before the Druids came to witness the matter.

—

"Will you go or stay?" Faustus had asked the question endlessly all morning of the men lined up outside the feasting hall to be paid off or else shunted to the great hall where those who would make a new life in Inis Fáil waited to be allotted their land.

"I will go," Silus said. "I'm not fit to farm, and I'm not likely to find a living as a physician here." The Druids guarded that work as their own. "I'm grateful for the chance at one last field service. Now I'll take my pay and be a country doctor in some village in the provinces, and pot up face cream for the magistrates' wives."

"You'll be welcome, no doubt," Faustus said. "It's rare that they have anyone who can do more than that. The village at Isca brings its hunting accidents and knife-fight survivors to our surgeons at the fort."

"I remember," Silus said. "At Eburacum too, where I was posted before." There was a wistful note in his voice that wasn't lost on Faustus. The army had been Silus's home. Discharge had left him centerless and wandering until he had come to Tuathal's camp. Silus gave Faustus a formal army salute, took his pay, and moved on.

Faustus scanned the waiting line. All morning each came in his turn, spoke his decision, and was paid or sent to the great hall. Most would stay. Only a few, with something to return to, would not. Llwyd would have stayed, he thought, if he had lived. Beric would have gone home to Britain and Faustus had even wondered if there was a way to wangle citizenship for him, a ticket into the Centuriate. He closed his eyes and said a small prayer to Mithras for each of them. The High King's throne had been dearly bought.

Dai was near the end of the line, with Owain behind him. It had taken him all morning to think on it, and his face was paler than usual against his dark hair and mustache, his eyes bright with unease and a kind of desperate hope. Faustus had heard him speaking softly with Cassan when the captains had gathered one last time as a command over a breakfast of beer and porridge.

"There is always loss. No man is proof against it." Cassan's pale head bent near Dai's dark one. "Look at you, Dai, it is only that possibility that allows for joy."

"And pain," Dai had said, but now he said, "I will stay," to Faustus.

"Go and speak with Fiachra and the brehons then," Faustus said, relieved. He would as soon not have Dai in Britain, or anyone else who had fought in the north. He looked past Dai at Owain.

"I will settle here," Owain said. "As I think you know. There is nothing I can go back to without attracting Rome's eye."

"Wise, perhaps," Faustus said. Owain had begun to grow his mustache out again, he saw, and his barley-colored hair hung over his ears. It was darkening a bit in the way of pale hair over the years, but he would be recognizable to anyone who had seen him before. If Owain was in Hibernia, neither of them would have to worry about Faustus's conscience and what he owed to Rome in the way of information.

"The High King has given me cattle and a piece of good land," Owain said. "And offered a wife," he added, "but there are no doubt men enough to marry widows without me."

Dai turned. "You are wed already." He flicked an eye at Faustus. "The Druids have said that the Romans will not stay long."

When Faustus went back to the army, he would be required to notice a number of things, particularly Druids. But just now he could say blandly, "The predictions of seers are open to inter- pretation and the Druids are unreliable about matters of time. A Druid's definition of 'tomorrow' is likely to involve your great- grandchildren."

"I have this day to think of," Owain said. "At one time I did not care to live longer, but the Old Ones said differently and now I have found that I do. But I would leave my people in peace. Take what you are given, Dai, and do not try to send me home in your place."

VI. PATERFAMILIAS

AUTUMN

Back in regulation uniform, in lorica, crested helmet, and scarlet military cloak, Faustus parted with Silus on the dock at Isca Silurum. He sent Paullus with Pandora and the horses to the fort and went first into the vicus, the civilian village that surrounded it. He had a message to deliver before he was waylaid by the army, which would be inevitable the moment he set foot in the Isca fortress.

Abudia's house was where it had been before the campaign, brightly painted yellow with a purple door and a bronze phallus for a knocker. The steward who opened the door was a burly ex-legionary.

"Is Clio about?"

The steward held out his hand.

Faustus put a piece of silver in it. There was no point in saying he had just stopped by for a chat. The steward wouldn't believe him anyway, and neither would Abudia. Chats cost the same as any other service.

Clio was in her chamber, a tiny room with a bed, a dressing table, and a cushioned chair, hung with bright scarves and draperies. Faustus had known her in his first posting at Isca, and with the rest of Abudia's girls she had followed the column for most of Agricola's campaign. She was a welcome sight after a year among Tuathal's motley army.

"Faustus!" She hopped up from the chair, dislodging a ginger cat. "I was sure you were dead in Hibernia!" She put her arm through his and looked genuinely glad to see him.

"I am not, as it happens." Faustus reached into the pouch at his belt. "I have brought you something from Tuathal Techtmar, who now sits on his father's throne."

"From Tuathal? Is he really king in Hibernia now?" Clio's eyes widened.

"He is. He sent this for you." Faustus held out his hand and Clio's eyes widened further.

"He says that he promised you a house with lions on the floor. Mithras knows why, but this might be enough. Don't let Abudia know you have it."

"Oh, Juno! I never thought he meant it." Clio's hand closed around the gold coins. "Men always say things like that."

Faustus grinned. "He's going to be married. He says you taught him some things."

"Not this much." Clio opened her hand and looked at the coins again. "Oh, Faustus. I'm going to cry."

She did, and the kohl around her eyes began to run. Faustus rubbed at it with his fingertip. "Here, now."

"You don't know what this means."

"Did you want out of here so badly?" Faustus felt mildly guilty now. "You could have married, I know three men who would have paid off Abudia and married you."

"I don't want to marry! And follow some man around and put up with him and do everything he says all day and all night, not just for an hour."

"What will you do?"

Clio pulled a box from under the bed and opened it with a key that hung around her neck beside a silver lunula. She tucked the gold in and locked it. "I don't know. I could do anything now! I could go to Aquae Sulis and have a silk shop for the rich wives. All those lovely fabrics." She gave Faustus a dreamy look. "Or open a tavern, with a little business in the back, very selective." He laughed and she held her arms out. "Take off your lorica so I can thank you properly."

"I didn't come for that," he protested, but only half-heartedly. He still ached for Eirian, but Eirian wasn't there.

"For old times' sake," she said. "I know you paid for it already. Corso wouldn't have let you in otherwise."

–

When he left Clio, the sun was shining and a whirl of autumn leaves did a little joyous dance about his boots. He dodged a street sweeper's cart full of malodorous rubbish and a wagonload of roof tiles to thread his way through the narrow streets to the fort. Unlike the orderly layout of a fortress, a vicus tended simply to accrete, its thoroughfares evolving from cow paths and lined with a jumble of shops selling hot food, leather goods, weapons, charms, and cookware. A butcher's stall offered a side of venison hanging from hooks. A small boy stood beside it, occasionally brushing flies away with a leafy branch while his mother argued with an officer's wife over the price of a hare.

Isca fortress loomed above it all, an imposing edifice of timber and stone, roofed with red tile. Faustus felt a sharper stab of feeling than he would have admitted as he crossed the ditch and saluted the sentries at the gates, gave his name and rank, and was passed through into the Via Praetoria. Hibernia had been an adventure, a substitute both for the expected campaign that had been abandoned on Agricola's recall to Rome, and for Eirian. But the army, in the form just now of the Isca fortress, was home.

He would report to the legate straightaway, Faustus decided, and see how his cohort had done in his absence and praise his second century commander, because he had no doubt kept them in good order. Then he would have a proper bath and soak for hours in the hot pool. He still had gold in his pouch, his pay from Tuathal – not strictly part of the bargain since the army was still paying him, but Faustus had not been inclined to turn it down. Life was more promising than it had been in some time.

He waited only long enough to blow the dust off his desk in his old quarters, where Paullus was sweeping the floors and chasing beetles out of the bedding. He wrote up a proper report for the legate, with a copy for the governor, and presented both to the headquarters optio since the legate was not there after all.

"He's gone to Viroconium to try to swindle the commander there out of a surgeon," the optio said. "We're down to nothing but one junior since Silanus died, and no one's posting replacements to Britain right now."

"Silanus is dead?" Faustus was startled out of his cheerful mood.

"A week ago," the optio said. "Died of an apoplexy or something like. Just fell over. There was some friend of his from Eburacum there, another surgeon, and he and the junior worked on him, so I heard, but he was gone."

"Where's his daughter?" The death of Silanus was bound to upend life for Constantia and the old aunt who was the only other family she had.

"Gone into the vicus, she and the aunt."

"Where?" Faustus glared at the optio. They couldn't have let Constantia stay on in the fortress surgeon's house, but they might have given her more than a week.

"She's married," the optio said, startling him again.

"*What?*"

"She married the old surgeon that came to visit her pa. They're all at that inn beside the Epona shrine, if they haven't left. We sent their trunks there day before yesterday."

Epona's Inn, run by an ex-cavalryman, was a plastered timber house, two stories and rectangular in the Roman fashion. Faustus stalked through the herd of baaing sheep that clogged the lane outside under the care of a small boy and dog, and demanded Constantia's whereabouts of the slave who answered the door.

She greeted him in the inn's dining room, in a gown of dark mourning gray, a black shawl pulled around her shoulders. Her gold hair was dressed in fashionably crimped curls but her eyes were red and she looked weary.

"You've heard," she said. "Did you just come back?"

"From Hibernia, yes," Faustus said. "What have you done?"

"That's a fine greeting."

"I'm sorry. And I'm sorry about Silanus. How could you marry someone old enough to be your father?"

"Grandfather," she murmured.

He stared at her. "You can get a divorce, you know, if you say you were mad with grief." She must have been.

"I don't want to. Faustus, I had to do something. It was marry Diulius or go live in Antium with Aunt Popillia and I couldn't face it. We're only here until we get her on a ship. If I went with her, they'd find me some distant uncle or cousin to be my guardian and he'd make me marry somebody. This way I'll have some freedom."

"Some man you've just met? *I* would have married you before I let you do that."

"Don't be ridiculous. You weren't here and I'm not fool enough to marry you anyway. And you're still pining for that girl in the Orcades."

"That isn't your business." Faustus glanced around the room. The only other occupants were a pair of men with another herd dog at their feet, no doubt the owners of the sheep. They appeared uninterested. "How do you know about her?"

Constantia rolled her eyes. "Demetrius told me. You weren't exactly discreet. People probably know about it in Egypt."

Demetrius of Tarsus, scholar and gossip, had followed Agricola's campaign to study the religions of the native Britons; a letter from the emperor had prevented Agricola from objecting to that. Constantia had befriended him but he had driven most of his other minders mad.

"That was an extremely unsuitable thing to tell an innocent young woman," Faustus said and Constantia managed a small laugh.

"Demetrius is a scholar. He also told me some things about ancient Sumerian love poetry. His mind is on facts, not suitability.

And he told me that if anything happened to Father, I should marry someone here and not go back to Rome. I've grown up following the army. It would be like being in a cage and he saw that."

"There must have been something else you could do," Faustus said. He had no idea what.

Constantia put a hand on his arm and he noted the little gold ring on it. "I made a bargain with Diulius and I am content with it. Don't fuss at me. Diulius is a good man but he's not young and his health is frail. He needs someone to care for him and I'll be able to practice medicine beside him and learn from him. He has a private clinic in Eburacum. He'll leave me that estate if I'm widowed."

"When you're widowed," Faustus said.

"Well yes, probably. We are both clear on that."

"Practical of you."

"Stop it! What did you expect me to do? I wish the gods would make you a woman for a year and teach you what it's like."

"Centurion Valerianus!" Constantia's Aunt Popillia bustled out of the inn's private quarters with a gray-haired man behind her. "How nice to see you!" She looked less than certain.

"And you." Faustus smiled to indicate that he would upset no applecarts. "I came to offer my sympathy on your loss. And to congratulate Constantia on her marriage."

Constantia tucked her arm through her husband's. "My dear, this is Centurion Silvius Valerianus of the Second Augusta."

"Diulius Naso," the gray-haired man said. "I served with Silanus rather more years ago than I like to remember."

"Father was a junior surgeon with Diulius," Constantia said.

Diulius smiled. "Just out of his training year. He had such promise even then. I've told Constantia I will welcome her in my surgery if she was trained by Silanus."

Faustus began to relax his gritted teeth. It was hard not to like Diulius, a rangy man with slate-colored hair that looked as if he still kept up a military cut, and the knobby hands of someone who had used them over decades for fine work.

"Will you stay and dine with us?" Constantia asked. "I want to hear your tale. You aren't the only adventurer back from Hibernia. There's another surgeon staying here who's just come from there. Diulius knows him. Tuathal has actually done it?"

"He has," Faustus said. "He is sitting on the High King's throne and Elim mac Conrach's head is sitting on a pole, or was." Aunt Popillia looked horrified and he murmured an apology. He turned to Diulius. "Do all surgeons know each other?" He had always thought of them as a secret brotherhood with arcane knowledge of the human interior.

"Often," Diulius said. "Juniors on their way up bounce from post to post the way Centuriate officers do. Silus was my apprentice the year before I retired. It's a shame about his leg, he had great promise too."

"I'm afraid you'll have to get the tale from him, at least for tonight," Faustus said. If he stayed he was certain to say something unfortunate. "I have a neglected cohort to see to."

He threaded his way back through the sheep, convinced now that there was no telling what might have gone on since the spring. He didn't know quite why he had expected people to stay where he had left them, but he had, and they had not. Now he thought that anything might have happened. In his absence the Ninth Cohort might have fallen into a bog, or Circe might have come from Aeaea and turned them all to pigs.

He stopped short of the fort to look for Silanus's stone among the graves that lay along the road between Isca and Venta Silurum. He found it easily, a temporary wooden marker above the newly dug earth that covered his ashes. Faustus stood a moment over it and said a prayer for a man he had liked and whose absence had cut a hole in the life of a woman he also liked.

It was twilight now and he found his father's shade at his shoulder, draped in a dark gray mourning toga. "Why did you think that other people simply stopped being when you weren't watching them?" the shade inquired.

"Learned it from you!" Faustus snapped.

The shade looked affronted. "We've just buried your mother," he said.

"We buried her seven years ago. Before we buried you. At least she's stayed that way."

"She's gone," the shade said mournfully. "I can't find her."

That might be a relief to her, Faustus thought, wherever she was. His father had insisted on knowing her whereabouts at every moment. He could be heard shouting "Gaia!" any time he lost track of her, dragging her from the dairy or her weaving or the garden. "Gaia!" That was the name he had given her at her manumission before their marriage. He never called her Guennola, the old name that only the few other British slaves on the farm would use. When she got sick he had hovered over her bedside as if insisting she stay in this world.

Faustus remembered her slipping from them. It was not long after his father had lost most of their fortune, such as it had been, through bad investments. She had been furious at him over that, but had had no voice in his decisions. She left no deathbed wishes, but pulled Faustus and his sister Silvia close and kissed them both. When they washed her body the old tribal tattoo, a mark like a six-petaled flower between her breasts, was stark against the paper-thin skin and seemed to have darkened again from the faded blue-gray that Faustus remembered from his babyhood.

It was almost Samhain now, when the Britons believed the veil between the worlds was thin and the dead came back on the Samhain wind. Would she come if he invited her, Faustus wondered. If he went out on Samhain night – when anyone with any sense stayed home – would she visit him? She had been Silure and this was the Silures' country. What would he say to her if she came? Maybe that he wished he had paid more attention. His father had been a presence to be obeyed and often feared. His mother had simply been Mother.

The shade at his elbow sighed, a little breath like the closing of a door. "Why are you still looking for her?" Faustus demanded. "Did you ever think of just letting her be?"

"Why would I do that?"

The answer Faustus gave would have been more than unfilial but the presence at his side had whispered away on another little wordless breath and he was alone. He stalked back to the fort, passing the stone he had paid for when he had first come to Isca, dedicated to his father's memory in the hope of settling the old man into his own grave in Gaul. It did not appear to have worked.

–

His cohort did not appear to have been enchanted into pigs either and he found with relief that they were actually in the excellent shape he had expected, although a junior centurion had been promoted to a higher century in a Rhenus legion cohort, to Faustus's annoyance. He remembered the optio's gloomy comment about the lack of new postings to Britain and decided to recommend Septimus, his first century optio, for promotion from the ranks.

When he had taken Septimus's report and that of the second century's centurion, he hunted down Galerius, commander of the Augusta's Seventh Cohort, and took him off to the Capricorn to trade news over the proprietor's second-best wine and a bowl of mutton stew.

"We'll be lucky to keep what we've got," Galerius said of the dearth of new postings. "It's always the way," he added when Faustus ground his teeth. "If Domitian didn't trust Agricola with four legions, he certainly won't trust Sallustius Lucullus."

Faustus raised his eyebrows.

"Lucullus hasn't got Agricola's lack of political ambition," Galerius said. He lowered his voice a bit. The Capricorn was run by Ingenuus, an ex-legionary, and was a favorite haunt of the Augusta's officers. "The old general just wanted to enlarge the Empire. Lucullus is more interested in enlarging his own position. But never mind him and things we can't change, I want to hear the tale of Tuathal in Hibernia. Leaving out no instance of your own heroism, of course."

Faustus obliged, neglecting only certain things to do with Owain. It was fine to be back to the army, to friends like Galerius, to the routine of drill and patrol and even the winter occupations of producing roof tile and drainpipe. They commiserated at one remove with Constantia and agreed, over the third cup of wine, that she really couldn't have done anything else, although it was a pity. By the time he made his way back to his quarters, Paullus and Pandora were both snoring and Faustus knew he would have a sore head in the morning, but it had been worth it to chase away the sense of having little control over anything.

In the morning the legate returned and summoned Faustus to his office. It was drizzling rain and Faustus stamped off as much water as possible in the portico of the Principia. His helmet was channeling a small rivulet down the back of his neck.

"An excellent report," Arrius Laenas said, tapping the stack of tablets on his desk. "An excellent job of informal diplomacy, Centurion. It will be greatly to our benefit to have a stable Hibernia under a ruler who owes Rome something, even in sidelong fashion. I will forward it to Governor Lucullus."

"Thank you, sir."

Laenas picked up a different tablet, this one unexpectedly stamped with an imperial cipher. He offered it to Faustus and watched while Faustus hesitantly slid his thumbnail through the seal.

"New orders, Centurion Valerianus. You are returning to the Batavian cohort you handled so well in the last battle. As prefect this time."

"Thank you, sir," Faustus said, startled. It was a substantial promotion. The Batavians were a military double cohort eight hundred strong, at least on the enlistment rolls. Faustus's headache disappeared.

"Congratulations, Centurion, although I am less than happy to lose you," Laenas said. "How solid is your current second century commander? Is he ready for cohort command? With postings to Britain halted I feel as if I am plugging wine jars with not enough

104

corks, and this hasn't helped. We just keep balancing the ones least likely to topple and spill. I gave Flaminius Arvina at Viroconium my last draft of troop horses to transfer a junior surgeon. Horses are easier to come by than surgeons."

"Are all postings stopped?" *After all that Agricola did? After all we did over six years?*

"With what seems to be permanent trouble on the Rhenus and things looking uneasy on the Danuvius, yes, effectively," Laenas said. "Governor Lucullus has made it clear. Who in your cohort could move up?"

Faustus recommended his second century commander for cohort rank, and Septimus to replace the junior centurion already missing. The legate could move the other junior commanders up a century each and find another man from the ranks for the lowest one.

"That will do," Laenas said. "The Batavians are quartered with us for the winter so you'll find them waiting for you. After that, Governor Lucullus has informed me that the Adiutrix is likely to be transferred out of Britain in the spring and the auxiliaries shifted about to cover the gaps, particularly critical posts in the north."

"Critical posts, sir?" Faustus suspected that all the northern posts would be critical now.

"Your cohort is assigned to Castra Borea."

Faustus grew suddenly suspicious. Castra Borea was one of the footholds established by Agricola after the final battle with the Caledones, and as far north as the army could send him without dropping him into the northern ocean. "I was under the impression, sir, that that one was to be a temporary camp."

"It may well be. In the meantime, the governor would like to keep a presence there as long as possible."

"Is this posting because I failed to get killed in Hibernia?" Faustus demanded. That bordered dangerously on insubordination, but if he was right he thought the legate wouldn't deny it since Faustus knew, which he was not supposed to, that the governor had lent him to Tuathal in the first place because Lartius Marena had suggested that it would be a favor if something happened to him. One did not break a Marena's nose without consequences.

The legate rubbed his knuckles, which pained him in wet weather. "I may be overly cautious but Marena the Elder is leaning on Governor Lucullus in a number of ways. I am not sure how much he actually cares about his son's nose by now, but I don't want you to be a bone to throw to him."

"I don't either, sir. I am sorry if I have put you in an unpleasant position," Faustus said stiffly.

"The governor has put me in an unpleasant position," the legate said. "A matter which will remain between the two of us. However, you are an excellent choice for the posting, any other reasons aside. You will be the senior officer among the northern fort commanders and as such responsible for general oversight among them. Your job and theirs is to keep the peace we have established. I've read your report from the Orcades expedition and you have a knack for diplomacy, which many military men lack." The legate paused. "There is another other issue, however, that requires your attention currently."

"Yes, sir?" Faustus asked, wary. He supposed it couldn't be too dreadful, not when he had been given an impressive promotion, even for suspicious reasons. One of his men dragged home at dawn by the Watch, no doubt, from some girl's bed in the vicus. Or her aggrieved father.

"Your sister is here."

"*Who?*" Faustus looked wildly around the legate's office.

"Your sister. She arrived this morning. She's in the Praetorium with my wife."

"My sister Silvia?"

"Do you have another?"

"No, sir." Faustus's headache reappeared.

"You'll want to see her, of course."

No, I don't. He couldn't say that. If Silvia was here, something ghastly had happened. "Of course."

The Isca Praetorium, the fortress commander's house, was a lavish residence behind the Principia, screened by juniper and box hedge from the workshops on either side and from the barracks behind. A gardener, shielded from the drizzle by a large hat, was trimming the box hedge with shears.

Laenas's steward met Faustus in the portico where he tried again to shake off as much water as possible, feeling like an inconvenient dog who had come to call after getting in the garden. The steward handed him a towel to dry his lorica and harness skirt and held out his hands for the helmet. Faustus handed it over and dried his neck.

The steward tucked the helmet under his arm. "The ladies are in the atrium, Centurion."

The legate's wife looked up – with some relief, Faustus thought – as he entered. She was tall, her head adorned with the elaborate beehive of curls made fashionable by the current empress. "There now, dear," she said to Silvia. "I told you he would come straightaway."

Silvia was wrapped in a plain dark gray gown and a black mantle that made her look even smaller, telling Faustus everything he needed to know. A little boy playing with a wheeled wooden horse by the edge of the atrium pool looked with interest at the stranger in the steel plate and military scarlet.

"I wrote to you!" Silvia wailed. "But no one was expecting me this morning when we docked."

"I never got a letter," Faustus said, thanking Jupiter he had got to Isca before she did. It was probably waylaid in the baggage of whatever traveler she had given it to. The military post was not for civilians although Constantia regularly charmed her letters into its bags. "What has happened? Is it Manlius?" It had to be. He held out his arms to her and she hugged him, gingerly.

"I'll leave you to speak in private," the legate's wife said, departing with relief.

"It was a fever," Silvia said, sniffling. "Just like the one that took Father." She put her mantle to her face and sobbed.

"I am so sorry," Faustus said. "Do you need me to help settle his affairs? I could have come to Gaul."

Silvia emerged from the folds of the mantle. "Since you haven't come to Gaul in seven years, I didn't imagine you would," she said. "And there aren't any affairs. Manlius had debts. We have nowhere to go, Faustus. We must live with you."

"With *me*? What about your father-in-law?" A reasonably decent man, as Faustus recalled, and in any case he would have been obliged to take them in.

"He's dead," Silvia said. "And his uncles have been very unkind." Silvia pulled her mantle over her face again.

Meaning that they would not take in a penniless widow who had a brother who could support her. "Manlius was well off," he protested. "And you had a dowry. I sold the farm to provide it. What did Manlius *do* with it?"

"I don't know," Silvia wailed. "I told you, he had debts. It's just like Father all over again and if you hadn't sold the farm, we would not be brought to this."

He ignored the illogic of that. What in Vesta's name was he going to do with her? And with a six-year-old? He'd have to find a house in the vicus. "I don't suppose you brought any servants?"

"Of course not! I told you. Everything went! His horrid uncles bought most of the slaves, and my *cook*! And the carriage horses, and Manlius's chariot team."

Chariot team. Chariot racing was a rich man's pursuit. Rich as in much wealthier than Manlius. Some things began to become clear.

"Lucius," Silvia said to the child. "Come and meet your Uncle Faustus. He is going to be your father now."

The child stood up politely, clutching the horse. He wore a dark mourning tunic and sandals not nearly sturdy enough for Britain. "Good morning, Uncle," he said shyly.

"Good morning, Lucius," Faustus said. His *father*? He wondered frantically how quickly he could get Silvia married again.

"Will we live here?" Lucius asked. "With the soldiers?"

"No," Faustus and Silvia said at the same time. Lucius looked disappointed. "This is a cavalry horse," he said, exhibiting the wooden toy.

"It is not," Silvia said.

"It *is*," Lucius said. The silver *fascinus* that Faustus had sent as a baby present hung around his neck with his *bulla*, the protective amulet that Roman boys wore throughout their childhood. Neither seemed to have done its work.

The legate's wife poked her head back in. "All settled?" she inquired.

"Yes, thank you," Faustus said hastily. "I will send my slave for my sister's baggage as soon as we find a suitable inn. It was kind of you to look after her."

"Oh, no trouble at all. She's had a dreadful time. I'm so glad she has you, Centurion, to rely on."

Faustus noted that she didn't suggest that Silvia stay longer with her. He suspected it had been a long morning already.

The steward met them at the door with Faustus's helmet, dried and its scarlet crest brushed into a proper fan, and he settled it on his head to Lucius's obvious admiration. Epona's Inn, Faustus thought. It was respectable and Constantia was there, at least temporarily. Silvia would have another woman to talk to. Silvia clung to his arm, holding up her hem as they made their way through the rainy streets of the fort, and out through the Praetorian Gate to the village beyond. Her shoes were already mud-covered. Faustus couldn't help regarding her as yet another thing that had refused to stay where he had left it. Everything he had run from had come marching after him. Had his father known about Silvia when he had reappeared wearing mourning two days ago? Faustus thought that time might be as unreliable in the Underworld as among the Druids, but that would have been when Silvia was taking ship for Britain.

The rain was falling harder and Faustus put his heavy cloak around both of them. "I'm sorry," he said again.

Silvia sniffled. "We gave him a proper funeral, with mourners and flute-players and a sow for Ceres. His uncles at least paid for that and a proper monument, horrid old men. Now my son has nothing."

There was no point yet in suggesting that she might remarry. For some reason she had loved Lucius Manlius the Elder, who had seemed to Faustus as interesting as a block of cheese. He concentrated on arranging a room at Epona's Inn and introducing Silvia to Constantia, and to Aunt Popillia who clucked about her like a concerned hen and took her off to her new room to lie down and put a cold cloth on her head, despite the fact that she was already wet.

"Juno!" Constantia said, when Aunt Popillia had bustled off with Silvia and Lucius. "Now aren't you glad I didn't marry you?"

"I have to find her a house for the winter," Faustus said gloomily. "And a slave, I suppose. And then I'm to be posted to Castra Borea in the spring with the Batavians to replace a cohort that's being drained off to uphold the Empire on the Danuvius. The boy will need school or a tutor – nothing he'll learn in a frontier camp will be fit for his mother to hear."

"Castra Borea? Isn't that practically off the edge of the world?"

"Why, yes," Faustus said pointedly. "I failed to get myself killed in Hibernia to please certain people, thus Castra Borea."

"Oh, no. It's Lartius, isn't it? Faustus, I'm sorry."

"And I'm posted to the back side of the butt of Boreas himself. With Silvia. I can't leave her here."

"No, you can't," Constantia agreed on the basis of their short acquaintance.

"Maybe she could go to Eburacum with—"

"She could not. I am apologetic, Faustus, I really am, but no. We're already taking Silus with us."

"I will trade you. Why are you taking Silus?"

"My husband's taking him under his wing. He's an excellent surgeon, you saw him in the field, and Diulius remembers him.

Eburacum's growing and we'll have enough custom for another physician."

Faustus thought of Silus, who was amusing and attractive despite his leg... and young. He wondered if Diulius knew what he was doing.

—

At dinner two nights later, Faustus decided that Diulius knew exactly what he was doing. The meal was a farewell of sorts. Aunt Popillia's ship would sail for Antium in the morning and then Constantia and her new household would take passage with a merchant bound for Eburacum. Silvia and Lucius would move to the lodgings that Faustus had found in the vicus, a tiny apartment above a vegetable stall and, to Silvia's horror, next to a fish market. Faustus said firmly that it was all that was available except for the one next to the whorehouse and Silvia said faintly that she would no doubt be dead soon so it did not matter. Tonight she was dry-eyed and dignified but Faustus knew she was angry. Diulius rose to the occasion and guided the conversation in hopeful channels. Faustus saw that he was frailer than he had seemed on first meeting. Even in the warm light of the oil lamps, his skin had a pallor that made Faustus think of cloth dried and faded by the sun. His hands shook as he lifted his wine cup and as he picked a meat pie from a platter on the table.

"Plain tavern fare," Diulius assured Silvia. "Not fancy but the wife here is an excellent cook."

Silvia regarded the small pie dubiously. Faustus bit into one. It might be horsemeat but it probably wasn't rat, and the heavy addition of herbs disguised any shortcomings.

"It's lovely," Constantia said firmly and Diulius gave her a glance of avuncular approval. Faustus began to understand that Diulius had rescued an old friend's daughter with the only means at his disposal. If he had wanted a wife otherwise he would have had one by now.

If Diulius knew what he was doing, Faustus was increasingly, alarmingly aware that he himself did not. If he did, he would know how to get rid of Father and what to do with Silvia. And what purpose the gods had for him in this life, he supposed, although the philosophers said that the man who knew that was rare. It was Faustus's opinion that the gods didn't particularly care unless you annoyed one of them.

In the morning, supervising the unloading of Silvia's trunk ("My only possessions!") in the vicus, he asked her tentatively if she ever thought about Father.

"Of course! And," she added severely, "of what was due to his memory that was not done. I am sure he cannot rest in his grave."

"If I hadn't sold the farm before," Faustus said, "I would have to do it now to pay for Manlius's chariot ponies. I suppose he bet on them and I don't imagine they ever won." He regretted it instantly when Silvia's face crumpled.

"They were nice ponies," Lucius said with the obvious intention of smoothing things over. "They had soft, whiskery noses."

"You know this is the country that Mother came from," Faustus said, repentant, trying to change the subject. "The Silures were her people."

"These natives?" Silvia looked disapprovingly at a tattooed tribesman driving a pair of pigs down the road. He wore checked breeches and shirt, and wolfskin boots. A worn brown cloak showed every indication of being bed as well as clothing.

"Do you remember her name? Her real name?"

"I do not," Silvia said repressively.

"Guennola," Faustus snapped, good intentions eluding him again.

The wind sent a flurry of dry leaves careening about them. Silvia batted at them as if they were insects. The Samhain wind. The dying of the year, the hinge between light and darkness. In two days the Britons would light the need-fires in the village and in the tribal holds in the hills.

"There will be a great bonfire by the river overmorrow night," Faustus said. "I'll take you and Lucius to it and you can see something of the local people."

"Certainly not," Silvia said. "That's no place for Lucius. That we must have lodgings among them is bad enough." She looked with distaste at a girl unloading a bucket of mussels for the fish market.

"Lucius needs to know where his grandmother came from if he's going to live with me," Faustus said. He would take a stand on that. "Since I am now paterfamilias." Silvia glared at him but Silvia could card that wool and spin it whether she liked it or not, and so could the old man.

VII. SAMHAIN

Cruachan, hereditary hold of the kings of Connacht, was holy to the Goddess, especially at Samhain, and therefore even though the High King had made his residence at Tara, he would come to Cruachan to be wed.

Connacht made ready to welcome him with a great bustle of baking and brewing and slaughter of pigs and the best of the young cattle. The feast hall was decorated with sheaves of wheat and boughs of holly and yew. The guest hall was swept, fresh herbs strewn on the floors, armloads of blankets hung to air and then folded neatly on the beds. Druids, brehons, and lords would come from all of Inis Fáil, including defeated Ulaid where a new king ruled, to take home a spark of the need-fire and see the High King wed to the old king's daughter.

Baine had been here among her mother's people since the handfasting, in the household of Conrach mac Derg, new king of Connacht and successor to Sanb. The Druids had ruled her life since then; Aíbinn followed her everywhere. An endless parade of holy men and women from the Druids' school that had existed at Cruachan for centuries dictated the rituals that encircled the Goddess on earth like a thorn hedge. Once wed she would be able to shed most of their restrictions. In the meantime, she became something not entirely human but a vessel for the powers of the Goddess in all her aspects. At Samhain, and in the wake of war, Baine felt the Morrigan's cloak most closely about her shoulders, like a growth of dark feathers, but there was the Mother as well, seeing to the seed buried in the earth for the winter, quickening the children conceived by women with husbands returned from war or with the new lords of the High King's victorious army.

As Samhain approached she tried to remember Tuathal as a man and not as the High King, a role that shrouded its inhabitant in the same power her father had held. In two more days he would ride from Tara and they would descend into the Morrigan's Cave and come out changed.

–

The High King rode into Cruachan on the morning of Samhain before a wet wind, the skies alternately clear and cloudy, spattered with birds on their autumn routes. Fiachra and the king's captains, Owain, Cassan, and Dai, rode with him, come from their new holdings in a flurry of banners and gold chariot fittings.

"A fine showing and lacking only an elephant," Fiachra pronounced.

Beric had described for them the great beast that the victorious Emperor Claudius had ridden into Camulodunum over forty years ago. His father had seen it as a small boy, Beric had said, like a mountain on legs. There was a moment of silence for Beric, who lay under a cairn of stones on the Hill of Achall, and then Tuathal laughed. The High King himself, although not an elephant, was very fine. His dark hair was freshly washed and under the gold crown it rippled in the wind like a black silk banner. His shirt and breeches and cloak were embroidered over nearly every inch, with gold thread and red, blue, and green silks.

Greenery decked the wagons that accompanied him and the oxen that pulled them. Before them young hounds newly fostered to Tara drove thirty head of cattle, the High King's gift to the lord of Cruachan. A four-wheeled chariot bore the bride gift in a gold-bound box lined with green silk – a girdle of gold and silver bells that chimed with each movement, interspersed with carnelian beads and pearls. He had sent Fiachra to buy it in the jewelry markets of Gaul although there were many beautiful things in the spoils from Ulaid. He would not give her something tainted by war.

There was no sign of her as they drove through the great gates of Cruachan's timber palisade and then its double ring of stone walls. Slaves came to take the horses, and Conrach's wife to welcome the visitors. The High King's entourage were taken to settle in the best quarters of the guesthouse while the household hounds of Conrach brought them a pleasant and apparently unending supply of mead.

Tuathal himself was met by the Chief Druid of Connacht, Sechnal, a man in middle age with a graying reddish beard that covered most of his chest.

"The High King will come with us," Sechnal said.

Tuathal obeyed. He had known he would have to. Behind Sechnal two other white-robed Druids carried a heavy bronze box between them. The air grew thicker as he followed them in a procession to somewhere. They passed through the great gates again, on foot this time, and diverged from the Connacht road that led back to Tara in the east onto a path barely discernible in the grass. A grove of ancient ash trees appeared at the end, the path disappearing into it beneath a tangle of bare, contorted limbs. The morning seemed to shift to afternoon without his noticing. The grove smelled of water; a spring at its heart bubbled between outcropping stones half-hidden in vines and fern and blackening stalks of wolfsbane. At their approach a mouse or some other small forest creature hurried away in a frantic rustle through the fallen leaves.

It was cold, and colder still when Sechnal ordered him to strip and wash in the icy water of the spring. Tuathal obeyed, teeth chattering, although he said, "If I die of an ague on my wedding night, then what will you do?"

"You will not die," Sechnal said. "The High King must stand still now."

The attendant Druids opened the bronze box and took out two vials of some unguent and a clay pot stoppered with wax. They touched Tuathal with the unguent on heart and loins and both sides of his neck and Sechnal dipped a finger in the clay pot. It left blue lines where he traced it on Tuathal's forehead and chest, slanting marks that crossed and recrossed in some meaning that only the Druids knew. The unguent had the sharp scent of vervain and the paint smelled of rotting leaves and earth. Tuathal shivered in the cold wind.

"The High King may dress now," Sechnal told him.

Tuathal did, gratefully. He saw, startled, that the sky above the grove had begun to darken. They had spent the day here somehow. The smell of roasting meat drifted from Cruachan on the hilltop. They walked back and midway there a small hound met them with a bowl of meat and hot bread and a cup of mead.

"Eat and drink here," Sechnal said. "You may not go under a roof again until afterward."

The Druids had set down the bronze box with their unguents and paint and Tuathal sat down on it, daring them to tell him not to. He reached out his hands for the bowl and wolfed down the meat and bread. He drank cautiously from the cup. It tasted odd and he looked up at Sechnal.

"The High King must drink it," Sechnal said.

Tuathal hesitated, but if they wished to kill him, it could have been done long ago. Whatever the potion was, he might see visions, but the Druids were skilled herbalists and unlikely to poison him by mistake. He drank.

–

The cave was an open mouth in the earth. He had not seen it until they were nearly on it, despite the dark bulk of the mound above it and the torches that lit their way. Behind, streamed a procession of Druids, lords, and all the common folk of the villages with the ability to travel and say that once they had seen a High King wed. Torches, lit from the need-fire that now burned in the meadow below Cruachan, dotted the darkness, a shifting tide of flame and shadow. The thorn bush that grew over the cave's entrance had been recently cut back, revealing the opening, a dark triangular gap narrowing at the bottom where it descended steeply into blackness.

Tuathal had to crouch – there was not enough headroom for a child. He let himself slip downward, feeling the ground shift under his hands and knees. Whatever had been in the Druids' potion made him feel as if they were not quite solid on the stone beneath them, a sensation of inhabiting some other world simultaneously with his own. At the shaft's end he found he could stand and he stopped to let his eyes adjust to the dim light still filtering from above. He carried no light himself but he could see far below him a faint glow from the heart of the cave. He was in a small chamber from which two passages descended again, to the right and the left. He was to take the right, the Druids had said. They both led to the same chamber but Tuathal wondered if he would find something different within it if he took the left.

The air grew colder as he made his way down. The whispers of the Samhain wind at the cave entrance murmured like the breath of some great beast and the shadowed walls seemed to move in and out to either side of him. At first he had to go on hands and knees again, but then the narrow passage opened overhead and he could walk upright, following the dim glow until he could see the end of the passage limned by its faint light, and the cave that opened from it and receded into darkness beyond.

She was waiting for him, sitting on a stool, a hooded figure in a dark cloak, with an oil lamp at her feet. By its small flame he could see a pallet of furs and blankets on the cave floor. He stood before her and she rose, shedding the cloak, her face sharp-angled in the flickering light, her hair as dark as the blackness of the cave. The green chalcedony ring glinted on her finger.

"The High King comes to the Goddess," she said, "in her body on earth."

He put his hands on her shoulders and saw on the wall behind her the dim shadow of a monstrous bird. Her eyes glistened like lake water with the lamplight and something else. No doubt the Druids had given her the potion as well. The drug was the doorway that opened the Otherworld, that gave the Goddess entrance into her body and gave him the power to lie with her and not be killed by it.

He unbuckled his belt, laid sword and dagger on the stone floor, and pulled off his shirt and then his breeches so that she need not be the first to stand naked. She nodded at that and undid her own girdle and then slid the dark gown over her head. He touched her shoulders again and drew off her shift as well. She was as tall as he was, pale and lean. He could just see in the near darkness that her skin too had been painted, from her breasts across her belly to the black triangle between her legs, a mirror of the cave opening he had already crossed. He put his hands on her hips and then on her breasts. He felt her skin quiver under his hands, whether from desire or fear or the cold, he couldn't know. He led her to the pallet and they lay down among the blankets and furs, drawing them over themselves, huddling together warm body to warm body. He slid his hand between her legs and she put her mouth to his and opened to let him in.

Whatever he was making love to, goddess or woman, met him with a fierce desire that surprised him. Most of the girls he had tumbled, in hay barns or brothels, had been compliant, or like Clio enthusiastically inventive, but none had pulled him to them with such *wanting*. It sparked from her, insistent and consuming. For himself, he felt detached from the urgency of his own desire. She wrapped her legs around his back and her hands in his hair and his body responded hungrily but beneath the hunger was the knowledge that he was making – or was himself – some offering, some promise that might have to be redeemed.

–

Afterward, they lay entwined in the furs and blankets, still unspeaking but spent, the sensation of being inhabited by some otherworldly power fading. When he woke again, the oil lamp was guttering out and he shook her.

"We must go up before the lamp burns out."

"If we don't they will come for us," she protested, but she sat up and reached for her shift.

When they could see daylight from the cave mouth they left the oil lamp behind and crawled up the narrow passage. Tuathal, hearing her curse in un-Goddesslike fashion when she barked her shins, remembered a tale that Constantia had told him about the Greek hero Orpheus who was allowed to bring his dead wife back from the Underworld so long as he did not look at her on the journey. Orpheus looked, of course, heroes always being such fools, and she disappeared underground again. As they reached the cave mouth, Tuathal scrambled into the light and turned to reach out his hand. The woman behind him did not disappear, nor did she now wear, as the back of his mind had kept suggesting with unwelcome insistence, the face of the Morrigan. It was only Baine, inky hair a tangle down her back, gown shredded from the climb.

The Druids were waiting for them at the cave mouth. Everyone else had spent the night feasting and drinking to the bridal couple who would be wed today in human fashion. As they came to the gates of Cruachan, Baine's women and Tuathal's captains bore them off to their separate lodgings one last time. There they washed themselves clean of the Druids' paint and dressed in bridal finery, Baine in the bride gift girdle that was waiting in her chamber.

Olwenna fastened it around Baine's hips, flicking the little bells to make them ring. She looked at Baine sideways, pretending not to, to see how things had gone.

"Last night is not your business," Baine said. "But I saw his driver looking at you. If you like Ultan, I will speak to the king about it. It's time you were wed yourself before someone gets you with child." Olwenna was too pretty for that not to happen eventually.

"You would let me pick?" Olwenna sounded startled.

"There are some freedoms even a slave may possess that a royal woman does not," Baine said. She gave a last look at her face in the mirror that Olwenna held up and for an instant saw Tuathal's behind it. The daylight wedding was a formality. She was joined to the High King now in ways that not even brehons or priests could undo.

—

In the north of Britain, Cuno and Rotri had spent the summer and early autumn trading among the coastwise villages, going as far south as the Roman fort at Trimontium where Eirian marveled at its turf ramparts and great defensive ditches. At Samhain they had come to the highlands again and the clan whose headman had once been the warlord of the Caledones. He was gone – his body taken into the hills by the Old Ones, it was whispered, a story that Cuno and Rotri noted with interest. The new headman Rhion hoped to sell them the last of the summer's wool and hides. It was a well-timed visit since the clan's Kindred and lesser holders would be gathering, and after a summer's good crop might be more inclined to buy luxuries than they had been. At Samhain no traveler was left unsheltered, even without goods to sell, and the headman's wife gave them places in the guesthouse and at the table for the feasting that would follow the kindling of the need-fire.

As dusk fell, all fires in the hold were doused, Rhion's hounds running from hall to outbuildings to make certain every spark was out. In the growing darkness, Eirian felt the Samhain wind down her neck and noted again, as she had in hold after hold in the highlands, how few men of fighting age there were. Had they come home on that wind, the dead torn from their lives in the fight with Rome? She imagined them overhead like a vast skein of birds, yearning toward the living.

With hearth and cookfire doused, Rhion and his holders took it in turns to work the drill that would raise a spark to kindle the need-fire. The headman was tall and red-haired, with a slight limp in his stride, tattooed with the spirals and sunrays that also marked the arms of his sister, the old headman's widow. Across hers ran a fading scar that cut through the pattern on her right arm. Her sword arm, Eirian thought. The women had fought in that war too.

The widow, Aelwen, saw her looking, and looked at Eirian's own arms where her cloak hung loosely about her shoulders. "Cornovii, are you not?"

"Yes, lady."

"And a long way from home."

"Yes." Eirian thought that short answer might be rude, and added, "I never thought to be a wanderer, but I find that the road suits me."

"A dangerous place for a woman," one of the holders said, overhearing. "Even in breeches." He gave her an appraising look that made Eirian draw her cloak around her. She had put on a gown tonight, when everyone dressed in their best, her light brown hair loose down her shoulders.

"Go and take your turn with the fire drill, Piran!" Aelwen snapped.

Eirian remembered that sleek cap of brown hair. "No more than when I saw you in Lyn Emrys in the summer," she said to Piran, "and as you see, I can defend myself." She laid a hand on the knife at her belt and wondered what he had been doing there if he was one of Rhion's holders.

"You were in Emrys's hold?" Aelwen demanded.

"To speak with him about matters of mutual concern," Piran said loftily, "and not the concerns of women."

"You insult me," Aelwen said between her teeth.

"When we are wed, I will value your counsel," Piran said hastily. "I meant only that we should not discuss the clan's affairs with strangers, nor mix them with courtship."

Eirian thought that Aelwen was about to hit him but then she stalked away, fury in every stride. Piran seemed undisturbed. A shout went up from the crowd around the fire drill and Eirian edged away to see the need-fire spark. Slowly the wavering little flame grew as Rhion and an old priest in a white gown fed it wisps of grass and then small twigs. Eirian looked curiously at the priest. Druids were a priesthood of the mainland. Priests of the Orcades like Catumanus spoke to the watery gods of the sea and the holy springs; the Druids spoke to the sun and the stars. Proscribed by Rome, most of them had fled to Inis Fáil at the end of the war and had begun only slowly to return, quietly and out of Rome's sight.

When the need-fire was well alight, the old priest and the headman kindled the waiting bonfire with it and the people of Rhion's hold pressed around it, warming their hands at proof that darkness could be driven off, that the coming black cold of the winter would turn to light again. Hounds from each household stuck torches in the fire and ran to their dark hearths, sparks streaming behind them. Later each outlying holder would take coals home in a pot to kindle his own cold hearth.

When the fire in Rhion's hall had been relit and the lords and their wives gone inside to feast, the villagers crowded the courtyard where whole pigs and cattle had roasted all day on spits. The highlands had stayed on the edge of hunger for most of the summer, but sheep and cattle left to them had lambed and calved. The pigs had fattened on the acorn crop of a mast year, and the fall harvest had come in plentifully enough to have grain even after the Roman taxes had been paid. They were not wealthy, not with the portion that Rome demanded, but no longer starving, the children no longer bone thin. The old Druid stood up before them in the feasting hall to remind them that the Sun Lord had given them all this through the agency of the Druids.

Cuno snorted. "Druids told Calgacos he could beat Rome," he told Eirian under his breath.

Eirian wondered again what gods Cuno and Rotri worshipped. She had never asked.

The old priest helped himself to the best cut from the roasted meat before him. His gown was disheveled, streaked with soot from the fire, and his hands shook.

"That one's gone odd, if you ask me," Rotri said quietly. "I was talking to the harper, who's a kind of Druid too but they don't mention that so much these days, and he says the old man made himself a hut in the woods and never leaves it. Coran Harper brings him food. This is the first time he's been out of the trees in months."

Cuno shrugged. "All Druids are odd."

"Not like this."

Was it another thing to lay at Rome's feet, Eirian wondered, that even a man who spoke to the gods was losing his mind? Or maybe it was speaking to the gods for too long that did that.

When the meal ended, Coran Harper sang for them, tales of the gods at the beginning of the world, triumphant cattle raids, and the wooing of fated lovers. Rhion's dogs and the visitors' squabbled over bones on the floor and then settled to sleep under the table. Nearly everyone was growing drunk on beer and the precious cask of mead that Rhion's wife Efa had been hoarding for Samhain. The hall was thick with the smell of woodsmoke and bodies who had last had a bath in the summer. Eirian set her cup down and slipped outside, taking deep breaths of the cold, clean air. The courtyard was empty, the bonfire banked to embers and the village folk gone to their beds. The chill would drive her back inside soon enough, but for now she was content to stare at the sky and its wash of stars like foam on dark water. If there were ghosts in the air she felt no threat from them, only the old deep portent of the turning of the year, something ending, something coming.

The rustling in the shadows at her side was not ghosts. She felt him before he moved again and when the hand closed around her face and mouth, she already had her knife out. They struggled in the dark and his other hand grasped her wrist and twisted it until she let go the knife. The hand came away then and grabbed her breast, pinning her against the stone wall under the overhang of the roof thatch. She fought him, the noise of singing and drunken laughter from the hall drowning the sound of their struggle. He pulled her gown up, prodded beneath it, pushing against her. The hand covering her mouth slipped enough that she got a finger between her teeth and bit down. He took his hand from under her gown to hit her and she brought her knee up sharply between his legs and felt him stagger. She bit him again and he pulled his hand back. She reached for her boot and stood facing him, a little bright blade in her hand. He cursed her, reached for her again and she raked the blade across his arm. He reached for his own knife.

Eirian stepped back, wondering exactly how drunk he was. "You might get away with rape, Piran, but if you kill a guest you will be exiled. They will turn you out into the dark on Samhain and let the night ghouls have you."

"Parading around in breeches like a whore," Piran spat. "Why shouldn't you have me? I expect you have your masters often enough."

"They are not my masters." Eirian edged closer to the hall door. She felt her belt knife with her foot and bent swiftly to pick it up.

One of Rhion's men came out to piss in the courtyard and she said to Piran between her teeth, "Now I will go back inside and tell Cuno and Rotri, and if anything else happens to me they will find you and kill you." She was reasonably certain that they could do both things without being seen. She could accuse him publicly now and shame him, but she thought that Cuno and Rotri would not care to entangle themselves between headman and holder. The threat would likely be enough. They were leaving in the morning anyway, to winter in one of the coastal towns and put ship and wagons under cover. She turned her back on him and went into the hall, daring him to stop her.

Aelwen saw her come in, saw her bend to put a small blade back into the sheath in her boot, and when Piran followed looking sulky, drew her own accurate conclusion. She spoke to Rhion when the last of the guests had staggered from the hall to sleep and the slaves were sweeping their leavings from the floor.

"He is a danger. He should never have been allowed that holding."

"He is young," Rhion said wearily. "And the girl wasn't harmed."

"If a man tried to do the same to Efa," Aelwen demanded, "would you say no harm because he did not succeed? And it is not for the girl's sake anyway. He killed a Roman and hid the body. We are lucky he did not have them down on us for that. And he has been in Emrys's hold, urging a pact with the new king in Inis Fáil for a war with Rome, when the new king is in Rome's debt. He will be the end of us."

"Did Emrys listen?"

"I imagine not. But fools like Idgual will follow him."

"Idgual is his spear brother. Name another who will follow him."

"I don't know."

"You are angry because he won't stop courting you," Rhion suggested.

"He brought me a wren in a cage. I let the poor thing go." Before she had opened the door, it had sat miserably on its perch, refusing to eat. "I am old enough to be his mother. I know exactly why he wants to marry me."

"Tell him I forbid the marriage," Rhion said sleepily. "He will have to listen to that."

"Rhion, that is not the problem!"

Rhion considered. "I have a head full of mead. I need to stick it in the rain barrel and then sleep. But are you sure that he is not right about the other thing?"

Aelwen balanced her dislike of Piran against that possibility. She had no reason to love Rome and four excellent ones for her hatred. "I am sure." All she knew with certainty was that they would end like the southern tribes, like wrens in cages, if they fought Rome again.

–

Lucius gripped his uncle's fingers tightly as Faustus's small household joined the crowd flowing out of the Isca vicus and along the bridge to the open field where the Samhain fire would be lit. Lights still spilled from the walls of the Roman fort and perhaps a quarter of the houses in the village, but the rest were dark, residents with a foot in both worlds. Silvia marched angrily beside them, followed by Paullus and Pandora. Paullus had not said much about the arrival of his master's sister but Faustus suspected that Paullus was as alarmed as he was at the prospect of her accompanying them to a northern garrison. Even in Isca she regarded the native population with a mixture of disdain and fear.

Lucius, on the other hand, was wide-eyed with interest and asked constant questions. "What if they can't light the fire again?"

"It always lights eventually, but it's bad luck if it takes too long."

"What if the wind blows it out?"

"That's worse luck."

"What do they do afterward?"

"Eat and drink." There was already a crowd of food sellers offering sausages on sticks and apples dipped stickily in honey. Faustus bought Lucius a slice of apple to Silvia's annoyance.

"Silvia, stop it. He can be washed."

"It will probably disagree with him." Silvia looked suspiciously at the apple seller.

"Come and watch the fire spark. It's good luck to see the first ember." He edged them through to a place where she could see the fire drill. A little wisp of smoke rose as it spun. Faustus put Lucius on his shoulders and whispered, "Watch."

To spark a fire as their most distant ancestors must have done, by the friction of wood on wood rather than with flint and steel, he told Lucius, was a thread that stretched down the eons of mankind – farther back even than the great kings of Mesopotamia or the people who set the standing stones across Gaul and Britain. Even the little dark people who wouldn't touch iron used flint and stone. To bring fire from the wood itself was an old, deep magic.

Lucius watched wide-eyed, and even Silvia seemed momentarily ensnared. Faustus had bought sweet buns from another of the food sellers and she paused, staring, with hers halfway to her mouth as the fire sparked and caught. Two priestesses of the Epona shrine bent to feed it wisps of dried grass. Samhain was the time of year when the horse herds, along with the last of the cattle and sheep, were brought down from the high pastures to winter in the milder lowlands. Isca Silurum folk had given up those ways for town life, but in the Silure Hills to the north and west they would be driving the pregnant mares between twin fires to bring healthy foals in the summer.

Faustus saw Silvia let her breath out as the tiny flame caught in the grass. It was impossible not to be touched by that old power, he thought, whether you would or no. "These are your people," he whispered in her ear. "Our mother's people. Half our blood is in their veins."

Silvia twisted her mantle around her hands, a habit when she was anxious. "I don't like that. Mother was Roman."

"Mother was Silure under the skin. And on it." He tapped his own chest where the many-petaled mark had been between her breasts.

"Well, I'm not," Silvia said irritably.

"More than you know," Faustus said. "There is old blood in the Silures, and we carry that too."

"I don't know what you mean."

"The little dark people who live in the hills. We have a grandmother from them somewhere."

"I don't believe you." Silvia bit into her bun as if it might argue. "And I am really outdone with you, Faustus, for telling Lucius about them. They don't even exist. The vegetable seller's wife said so."

"And then she made the sign of horns and told you to stay away from them, I expect," Faustus said. "I will prove it to you. I am to go to Llanmelin, most unofficially, and gauge how much trouble they might be if we pull a cohort or two out of Isca. I'll take you with me."

"I am not going to see some old witch in the hills," Silvia said. "And you are not taking Lucius either, filling his head with nonsense."

The Old One could prove it to her, Faustus thought, if the Old One was willing. He still remembered her showing him their mother's face in her mirror, winged dark brows, pointed chin, superimposed on his own. But maybe Isca Silurum was as much as Silvia could stand just now.

Silvia turned away from him to watch the fire blaze up and light the faces of the crowd around it, throwing their shadows across the meadow. The Old One's people would be lighting their own fires, he expected, well out of sight of the invaders and the Britons both.

Silvia didn't change her mind the next day when he mounted Arion, a bag of apples tied to the saddle, and she demanded that he not go either.

"You can't leave us alone here!"

Faustus considered explaining what should be obvious, that he did not have license to ignore an order. The legate had found his acquaintance with the people of the sidhe useful before now. "Stop fussing at me," he said. "I'm leaving Paullus with you and I'll only be gone a few days. We'll be sent north as soon as spring comes. It is important that I pay my respects."

"What if something happens to you?"

Faustus ground his teeth. The loss of Lucius Manlius the Elder had left Silvia convinced that anyone she took her eye off could die. "I'm in the army. Something could always happen to me."

That had not been the right response. Silvia burst into tears and Faustus rode away wishing that Constantia was still in Isca. She might have been able to tell him how to deal with Silvia. Maybe the Old One could.

He came to Llanmelin at midday and tethered Arion on the edge of an oak grove at the foot of the hill. The old Silure stronghold, abandoned in the war with Julius Frontinus's legions over a decade ago, was now overgrown by briars and young trees rooting in the mulch made by fallen roof thatch. The little dark people did not actually live at Llanmelin but named their habitations by the nearest landmark. Faustus thought that he could probably find their dwelling by himself, but he would not try. It was best to wait in the grove for permission. He checked himself for any iron besides his dagger and sword, both tied to Arion's saddle with his helmet and lorica. His belt buckle and cloak pin were bronze, his boots devoid of hobnails. He went into the dim light of the grove and sat down beside the spring at its center. The oaks still wore their leaves, rustling in the autumn wind, and the sound of the spring burbling from an outcrop of rock was like a faint voice, murmuring back to them as it filled the stone bowl below and spilled over into a stream running to join the myriad other streams that flowed south from Llanmelin into the tidal estuary of the Sabrina. Faustus put a silver coin in the water, an offering to the Mother, who was the hill people's primary deity. Then he settled himself to wait.

For once he saw the little dark man before he was standing at his side, despite the fact that he had moved through the trees like a whisper of wind. Faustus rose to meet him.

"I grow careless," Salmon said. "No doubt it is because it gives me pleasure to see you." He was barefoot, dressed in a wool shirt and wildcat skins, his black hair loose down his back, his face and arms tattooed with spiraling patterns like vines.

"And I you," Faustus said. "I have brought a gift since I remember that your sister is fond of apples."

"We all are," Salmon said. "The Old One sent me to you when my brothers heard you on the road. Come."

Faustus mounted and followed Salmon along a path that was still indistinguishable to him, although in a remembered direction, toward a particular notch in the ragged line of hills to the north. Salmon moved silently through the drying bracken and scrub brush with a skill that the border wolves, the elite of Rome's frontier scouts, would have envied.

In a while Faustus caught the faint smell of peat smoke and knew that they were near. There was the hawthorn thicket and the wind-twisted trees on the hillside, and this time he saw, behind the clump of wild briars that screened it, the door itself.

He dismounted before Salmon told him to, and Salmon said, "You have learned to see things."

Faustus tied Arion to the bare branches of a hawthorn and put the bag of apples over his shoulder. He pushed past the briars to the wood-framed doorway and followed Salmon through its low opening. Even Salmon had to duck to enter, but inside Faustus could stand upright, barely.

When his eyes had adjusted to the darkness and he could make out more than the glow of the hearth fire, he saw a woman sitting beside it. Salmon dropped to one knee the way he had done before the Old One, but this woman was young. Her black hair fell about her shoulders over a rough woolen gown, and her face and upper arms were marked like Salmon's, her eyes the same startling blue. It took Faustus a moment to realize that it was Curlew. She was only months older than when he had last seen her but some change had come upon her, both indefinable and unmistakable.

Faustus knelt too. "You are the Old One now?" he asked. A small child played on a rug by the hearth, no doubt the baby he had seen at her breast in the spring.

She nodded. "It is not a matter of age but lineage. My grandmother was young too when she became the Old One."

Faustus felt a stab of sorrow. As Curlew she had been a friend; as the Old One she was something beyond that.

She seemed to know what he was thinking and smiled. "You have brought me apples and I am not yet too dignified to love apples. Nor to be glad that you have come back from Inis Fáil, Faustus. There is a stool there. Sit down and tell me how you have fared."

Faustus touched the little bead on the cord around his throat, the blue stone with the small white eye. "And the Old One your grandmother is gone? I am sorry."

"Thank you. I did not wish to follow her at first, but I am daughter to her daughter's daughter, and so..."

"And so we do as we must," Faustus said.

She cocked her head at him. "What troubles you is not your war in Inis Fáil, I think."

"Am I so plainly troubled?"

She chuckled. The child at her feet began to fuss and a woman came from the passage behind her and scooped it up. "Thank you," Curlew said. "And bring us something to drink, please, and to eat."

Faustus hoped they could spare it. The hill people often went on the thin edge of hunger, but hospitality could neither be withheld nor refused. "I am to be posted north again," he said, "which is not the source of my troubles either. My sister has come to live with me and I do not know what to do with her."

The other woman brought a plate of small, flat barley cakes and a clay cup. She offered them to Faustus and he drank, the same strange brew as on earlier visits, spiced with something unfamiliar but not unpleasant.

Curlew asked him, "Why has your sister come to you?"

"Her husband died and I am all she has. What do your people do when a woman is widowed?"

"We do not marry," Curlew said. "It is much simpler that way."

Faustus thought that it might be, although not for Silvia. "She is kin to you as I am. I wanted to bring her here with me. I thought... I don't know what I thought. That you could make her less afraid maybe, but she wouldn't come."

"She is afraid?"

"She is afraid of everything. Afraid of Britain and Isca, afraid of the Silures, afraid of being alone. And now afraid of a distant grandmother out of a sidhe, because like a fool I told her."

"Then it is best she not come." Curlew's face was serious now. "People who are afraid are dangerous."

"I know. I am sorry now that I told her. I will not bring her."

Curlew nodded. "Will you take her north with you?"

"I will have to. No doubt she will hate the north even more than Isca."

"When do you leave?"

"In the spring. We are to replace a legion likely being sent to the Danuvius to fight a war there. That is in Moesia," he added when she looked questioning. "Beyond Germany."

"Overwater," Curlew said. "If all your legions went overwater, it would not displease us."

"I know," Faustus said. "But you would still have the Silures here and the other Sun People to trouble you. Are we worse?"

"No. You are just more."

"And if we are fewer than we have been when some of us march north? Will the rest find little bronze arrows in their backs if they are careless?"

"If you step on an adder you will likely be bitten," Curlew said. "If we are not stepped on, then no."

Often enough the legions did not look where they stepped. "I am sorry that my people are a trouble to yours. I would not have it that way."

"Nor would we," Curlew said with a small smile. "But you yourself are welcome here. Tell your Eagle commander that if he wants to make sure, he can leave a load of grain at Llanmelin."

"I will," Faustus said. It was a small enough price. The ones most likely to make trouble if Isca was undermanned were the Silures. There might be sidhe blood in the Silures but they and the little dark people were still wary of each other and the Silures hunted them for slaves. If a load of grain would see to it that they did not make common cause, it was more than worth it. "Thank you for your hospitality."

"I will ask the Goddess to watch over you. And your sister, too. I am sorry that she fears us, but it may be as well."

Outside again, Faustus decided that he must make it clear that whoever delivered the grain should leave it in the ruins of Llanmelin and not go looking elsewhere. The first time he had visited Curlew's people he had been somewhat afraid that he would emerge from the hillside afterward to find what many of the Britons believed: a thousand years gone by, Llanmelin vanished entirely and Isca only a pile of stones. Now he thought that any danger lay in the other direction. He could find Curlew's people again unaided, but he would not, not ever, no more than he would think of Owain by any other name that that. He mounted Arion, wondering how many such secrets a man might end up with, bottled in his head like bees in a jar.

VIII. CASTRA BOREA

SPRING, 839 ab urbe condita

In spring the Second Adiutrix was indeed pulled from Britain, bound for the emperor's war in Moesia, which drove worry over things he shouldn't know about in the first place from Faustus's mind in the chaos of shepherding cohort and household north. There had been little leisure over the winter either for worries that were not immediate, with the necessity of getting the Batavian troops reaccustomed to him and he to them, keeping them occupied with marches and drills when weather permitted, and when it did not, trying to keep bored soldiers from brawling for sport in the taverns or Abudia's house. Batavians considered war to be their national pastime, the only provincials whose tax to the Empire was paid solely with military recruits. Their previous commander had kept them in good order, however, and Faustus found that Indus, who had been both a pain in the backside and the recipient of a silver phalera at Faustus's recommendation after the last battle, now held the exalted rank of watch commander of the second century. Amused at this transformation, Faustus took the opportunity to swap Indus into his own command when his first century watch commander retired to open a cobbler's shop in the vicus at the end of winter. Indus was only a pain when there was no one to fight, and that was unlikely to be a problem. Paullus unearthed the ring-mail hauberk again and the horsetail-crested helmet that Faustus had worn in his last command of the Batavians, and polished them up, whistling. Mail was infinitely easier to keep clean than a legionary lorica's overlapping plates.

There was also the matter of Silvia. Faustus found a Dobunni woman, Gwladus, the unofficial wife of a man in his cohort, and hired her to look after Silvia and Lucius, keep them fed, and clean the apartment. The woman was happy to go north with them since her man would be at Castra Borea and ordinarily not allowed to take his household with him. That was the privilege of officers.

Faustus had considered whether he could leave Silvia in Isca but she was afraid to be alone and she had never had to manage her own funds. She had no idea of the cost of anything and would be in debt in a month. But taking her with him raised the question of what to do with Lucius. Over the winter Lucius had gone to a school in the vicus run by a Greek freedman who had once belonged to a tribune at Isca and taught the tribune's children until they outgrew his limited knowledge.

"You can teach him for a while," Faustus said hopefully to Silvia. "At his age all he needs is sums and to practice his Greek."

Silvia sniffled. "This horrible wet country has given me a cold. He needs to be exposed to *civilization*, Faustus! Not to the sort of men under your command."

"The Batavians are one of the best cohorts in the auxiliaries," Faustus said, stung, and ignoring the pair he had written up that morning, with a smack of the vine staff for good measure, for smuggling two of Abudia's girls into the fortress baths at midnight.

"They are not a good influence for a child."

Faustus thought of Constantia, who had followed the column with her surgeon father from the time she was born. "The other officers' families have survived," he snapped, and then wished he hadn't. Silvia had made tentative friendships with a few officers' wives, although her loathing of the army had not lessened. They could commiserate over the climate and the lack of good wine and dress goods, but they were all staunchly loyal to their husbands' service.

Silvia raised her eyebrows. "*Their* children will no doubt follow a military career. That is not what we were bred to."

"No, we were bred to dig turnips on a provincial farm," Faustus said and she glared at him. His growing acquaintance with Lucius was beginning to suggest that his nephew was no more suited to that life than Faustus had been.

By the time their transport sailed, Silvia had abandoned the subject and instead adopted an attitude of long-suffering sanctity; she boarded the ship in an excellent imitation of someone going to their execution. Lucius, on the other hand, boosted onto Faustus's shoulders, watched excitedly while the First Batavians marched smartly aboard and saluted their commander.

The transport fleet sailed down the Sabrina channel, skirted the southern coast, and put into port at Rutupiae to pick up the military post along with various supplies and messages from Rome for the governor in Eburacum. From there they sailed north along the coast and upriver to Eburacum to empty the hold of the jars of Gaulish wine destined for the governor's house, and collect two centurions and a cavalry officer posted up from the south to Trimontium.

Constantia met them on the crowded dock, a bright figure in a blue mantle among the dock workers loading and unloading grain sacks and barrels of oysters from the ships along the wharf. She waved at him and he made his way to her.

"Come into the vicus with us. We have room for you overnight and we don't smell nearly this bad." She wrinkled her nose at the stench of rotting fish and nameless other scents.

Faustus handed off command to his second and collected his household.

"I thought you were bound to stop here," she said with satisfaction. "Practically all the ships do when the governor's here. I've been ruining my reputation coming down to meet all the transports." She didn't sound worried about it.

They followed her through the crowded harbor district, dodging an ox-drawn cart loaded with oil jars that had somehow got wedged across a narrow street and was trying to extricate itself amid the advice of a gathering crowd.

"It gets worse every day," Constantia said cheerfully. "With the governor in residence, everyone wants to set up shop here.

We even had a theater troupe come though. They were dreadful, but everyone came out to see them." She tucked her arm through Silvia's and beckoned Paullus and Gwladus to come along.

Silvia took Lucius's hand in her other one, pulling him close to her side, but she seemed to relax a little around Constantia. Faustus looked carefully at Constantia and saw that the gray circles were gone from her eyes, although she looked older than she had before her father's death. She had written to him over the winter, apparently still with the ability to charm her messages into the military post: the practice was growing, Silus was settling in well, Aunt Popillia was happily ensconced in Antium. Faustus suspected that it was having followed the army that had given Constantia the resilience to cope with the overturning of her life. He wondered if she could teach that to Silvia.

The house in the Eburacum vicus held both clinic and private quarters. It was a Roman-style complex, built around a court-yard and an herb bed abuzz with bees. Inside, a local artist with reasonable skill had painted scenes of the gods dining in a garden. Diulius welcomed them, leaning on a cane, with an apron tied over his tunic, indication of a patient with something messy the matter with them.

"I'm afraid it's Higuel and that suppurating arm again," he said to Constantia. "He won't keep it clean. I've told his wife he'll die of it if he won't stay out of the pigsty." He kissed her cheek. "I've just sent him off. I shall wash and be right back." He disappeared into the clinic again.

"Can I see the pigs?" Lucius asked.

"Certainly not," Silvia said.

Constantia smiled at him. "We don't have any. It's Higuel's pig and she's an evil old sow."

Lucius looked disappointed, but at dinner Constantia produced a tame hedgehog, a little bristly thing like a scrubbing brush. "Silus found her. She mostly lives in the garden but she likes to come in the kitchen." She held the creature out and Lucius stroked its spiny back.

Diulius said, "Cook is not overly fond of that. They're nocturnal and she rattles around in the cook pots looking for insects."

"Is that what she eats?"

"That and worms and snails, little frogs, birds' eggs."

"Can I have one?"

"No," Faustus and Silvia said together.

"An army camp isn't a good place for a hedgehog," Constantia told him.

"I could practice my Greek on it," he said hopefully. Greek seemed to be important to his mother.

"This is why he needs a tutor!" Silvia said, exasperated.

"I had a tutor in Narbo Martius," Lucius offered. "I didn't like him."

"What is Eburacum like since the new governor's come?" Faustus asked his hosts before that went any further.

"Life is more formal than under Agricola," Constantia said. "More attention to protocol." She handed the hedgehog to the slave who had brought the dinner dishes. "Put her in the garden, please."

"Less willingness to let the fort surgeons treat the local populace," Diulius said as they gathered around the table, a family dinner with Lucius tucked on a couch next to his mother. "A mistake, I think, because it builds goodwill."

"Now they mostly come to us," Constantia said, "except for the hostage children. The governor takes a personal interest in them." The slave returned with ewers of water and wine and she held out her cup. "Two parts water, please."

Agricola had demanded hostages from the northern tribes and many of those sent had been children. It had been Agricola's opinion that children would best serve Rome's ultimate purpose – they would be Roman by the time they were grown. Faustus remembered Aelwen suggesting to Agricola that he would not succeed in turning wolf cubs into lap dogs. "How are they faring?" he asked.

"Governor Lucullus lines them up once a month to pat them on the head and ask them questions in Greek and Latin and award prizes for the best answers. The fort surgeon makes them stick out their tongues and prods them in the stomach and asks them about their bowels. If I were one of them I would run away."

"I don't imagine you'd get the chance," Diulius said. "They have a good deal of liberty but they're closely watched."

"And only Janus knows what they'll be when they're grown."

Faustus said, "Something not quite Briton and not quite Roman, I imagine."

"I expect the ones who were practically babies when they came to us will never be able to go home," Constantia said. "It's the ones who were ten or so that will be... I don't know what... like those wobbling toys that don't ever settle. One touch spins them round again."

"And we have lost the Second Adiutrix," Diulius said, to Faustus's ear a not entirely unconnected comment.

"For all practical purposes," Faustus said. "It takes time to shift a whole legion and not leave garrisons unmanned. We're part of the shift. They'll all be gone by late summer, I expect. How has the governor taken that news?"

"With as good a grace as possible," Constantia said. "He can hardly complain, or he'll look like he has plans. No doubt the emperor finds four legions a dangerous excess for a province this size."

"Not for a province that wants to keep its northern territory," Faustus said grumpily. "Six years! Six years with Agricola to take the whole of the island and now we lose a legion!"

The slave with wine and water paused by Silvia's couch and Silvia directed a minute amount of wine into Lucius's cup. "These are lovely," she said to Constantia, ignoring Faustus and turning the silver cup in her hand.

"They were my mother's," Constantia said. "She carted them about with her for a dozen years from post to post. Father always said they made him think of her, after she died."

"I can't imagine a life like that." Silvia gave an unfortunately obvious shudder. Faustus started to retort and she said repressively, "Yes, I know I shall be obliged to."

"Have some of this," Constantia said, pointing to a patina of spring herbs. "It's very good."

"The governor has invented a new kind of lance," Diulius said.

Faustus laughed. "My sister ordinarily has very good manners. I have been a trial to her. A new kind of lance?"

"Yes, they're calling it the Lucullian," Constantia said. "I don't know if it's any good or not."

"Most likely not," Diulius said.

"He should probably hope it isn't," Faustus said. Emperors did not take well to that sort of personal aggrandizement by their generals. He was curious enough to hope for a demonstration though – it would entertain Lucius.

In the morning, however, Faustus found that he had lost track of the days and the Ninth Hispana, the fortress garrison, was paraded for the *Rosaliae signorum* instead, the garlanding of the standards. By the time they boarded ship again, Lucius was chattering happily about the gold and silver honors that adorned the standards, the scarlet garlands of flowers, the splendidness of the great gold Eagle of the Ninth Legion.

"The standards are the heart of a legion," Faustus told him. "We honor them and the shades of the legion's dead the way you honor your ancestors and household gods."

"Mother says you didn't honor Grandfather properly because you joined the army," Lucius said.

"*Lucius!*"

Faustus eyed his sister. "Your mother doesn't know the half of it." The Rosaliae overlapped, not coincidentally, the Lemuria, days on which to propitiate restless shades. "Go and find Gwladus, because you need a nap and I need to talk to your mother."

"Go," Silvia said. "Your uncle is right." She waited until he was out of earshot, in the cramped quarters that Faustus had bribed the captain to allot them. "Faustus, I won't have you filling his head with glorified talk about the army."

"And I would appreciate it if you didn't speak as if you were in direct communication with Father."

"I know what he must be thinking," Silvia said stiffly.

"Have you ever seen his shade? Talked to him?"

"Certainly not. I'm not insane."

"Well, then. You don't know, do you?" He was half hoping she would say she had.

"I am going to go lie down as well. I have a headache coming on."

She turned on her heel, an indignant figure bundled in layers like an onion against the wind and salt spray. After a few steps, she turned back. "Faustus?"

"Yes?"

"What is it going to be like? Castra Borea?"

Faustus sighed. "Cold. Cramped. Uncomfortable but safe." He hoped he was right about that.

—

The transports took them north around the rocky headland of the Taexali, minor kin of the Caledones, and west to where a fishing village sat at the mouth of a shallow, sandy estuary that emptied into the firth lying between the two great hands of the highland mountains. Castra Borea itself lay a few miles upriver and although local fishing boats could handle the estuary's depth, the transports' captain was disinclined to try, even at high tide. A crowd gathered on the shore and small dock to watch the Batavians come in and disembark. No one seemed inclined to greet them. Faustus wondered how tentative the relationship was between fort and village.

The current garrison commander had sent carts to load their supplies, and Faustus put Silvia on one with Lucius and Gwladus, among the grain sacks and oil jars. When he swung onto the saddle, Arion danced under him, ecstatic to be on solid ground.

The road to Castra Borea ran along the south bank of the river, several miles of packed earth that looked as if it had been professionally leveled under the eye of a Roman overseer, but not paved or even graveled. A dipper waiting to spot a fish rose up from its rock on the bank in an indignant flap of feathers as they tramped by. Overhead Faustus could hear the long, mournful, bubbling call of a curlew. To the south the great ragged mountains of the highlands rose into the sky. The land that he had described to Constantia as the backside of the god of the north was starkly beautiful, but the sense of loneliness as they passed out of sight of the village was overwhelming. His men swiveled their heads as they marched as if they felt the breath of some northern monster on their necks until Faustus snapped at them to straighten up before they walked into the river.

"Good hunting country," Paullus said, edging his horse up beside his master's, with Faustus's spare mount by the lead and Pandora padding at his side.

"Very likely," Faustus said. "Don't go out alone."

"Jupiter, no," Paullus said.

They rounded a clump of willow and alder growing out from the riverbank and their destination came into view. Castra Borea was turf-built, with a single ditch and turf wall in front of a sharp-toothed timber palisade, a temporary marching camp put to use as a border outpost. A second ring of ditch was half-dug and looked to have been worked on only the day before. No doubt the garrison's scouts had noted their arrival and passed along the happy news to down tools. Faustus supposed he should be glad they had dug half of it.

The fort held timber-built barracks, latrines, a small hospital, the Principia, a granary, two workshops, a cistern, and a rudimentary bath house situated outside the walls for fear of fire from the furnace. All but the bath house and cistern were wood- or dirt-floored and only the bath had a hypocaust for heat. Beyond the bath, a wooden bridge crossed the river into the wild land beyond.

The garrison they were replacing was a cohort of Dalmatian auxiliaries, leaving to fill the empty spots in outposts further

south that were in turn being emptied by cohorts of the Second
Adiutrix bound for the Danuvius. Faustus sat down with their
commander in the drafty Principia, which was not much more
elegant than the barracks, and doubled as the commander's house
since there was no Praetorium.

"We're supposedly at peace up here," the Dalmatian prefect
said. "Emrys, who is the Caledones' new warlord, seems to be
enforcing that among his people, but there have been some incid-
ents. A hunting party that didn't come back – don't go out with
less than a half century is my advice. Or the usual annoyances
of trees felled across our roads or water fouled in any number of
disgusting ways. And we're undermanned up here."

"How badly?" Faustus asked him.

"This is the largest garrison until you get to the new legionary
fort they're building to the south at Castra Pinnata, and Mithras
knows what legion they plan to put in it. The Ninth supposedly,
what there is of it. So, essentially, you're in charge of the highlands.
The border wolves say that Emrys may be hard put to keep his
people under control, and that's if he even wants to."

The border wolves were often closer to spies than scouts. They
were known for their ability to go into enemy territory, root
around there undetected, and generally come out again. They had
the longest leash of any of the frontier scouts and often operated
independently for months at a time.

"I have no idea where they are now but they'll appear in a day
or so," the prefect said. "If you see a pair of Britons looking like
ragpickers and trying to sell you dubious wine or whatever else
they've picked up, that will be them."

–

As predicted, the scouts appeared two days later and presented
themselves at the gates as Prefect Decius Cuno of the ala Petriana
and Centurion Aurelius Rotri of the Twentieth Valeria Victrix,
detached for special assignment. Their command of Latin and of
several specifically military curses convinced the guard at the gate

that they were genuine, despite their braided hair and exuberant mustaches.

"You look appalling, if authentically native," Faustus said.

"We are native," Cuno said. "Or mostly."

"Native born, anyway," Rotri said.

Faustus wondered if that gave them the same sense of inhabiting two skins at once that it gave him. Probably not. They had been raised here and it was their profession to switch skins. They reported on the purchase of the gold torque and showed it to him.

Faustus stiffened at the sight. "And you identified the tribesman who had it?"

"Piran, one of Calgacos's holders," Cuno said. "Or Rhion's to be precise. Rhion's the new headman, brother of Calgacos's widow. Piran is courting her, by the way, but she looks more likely to stick a spear in him."

Faustus absorbed that. "You're posing as traders?" It was the most common guise for a man who wanted certain entrance to any hold.

"Not so much posing," Rotri said cheerfully. "We've made a fair profit. Something to retire on if we live."

Faustus was aware that if they were identified the chances of that would be greatly diminished. He said, "Ask my optio for ink and papyrus and write out your report. Only one sheet, please. It has to be shipped up from the south." There was no vicus attached to Castra Borea — no temples, no taverns, and to the cohort's annoyance, no women. Women and beer might be found in the fishing village downriver, but no one there could write or had need for anything like ink.

Cuno held out the torque. "You take this, Prefect. It makes my skin itch."

Faustus put it in the desk that constituted most of the furniture in the commander's office. It made his skin itch too. The scouts saluted and left, and he took up a wax tablet and began to make a list: Finish the ditch. Dig cellars for decent furnaces under the barracks and particularly under the Principia. Clean the fort latrines, find out where the smell in the granary was coming from and hope it wasn't the latrines. Add a private latrine for Silvia. (Faustus underlined that entry twice.) Finish the ditch first.

"Faustus!" Silvia stood in the doorway, shaking with fury.

Faustus jerked his head up. "What?"

Silvia burst into tears. "He wants to join the army! I can't bear it!"

"He's seven," Faustus said. "He can't."

"He follows the soldiers around when he isn't following you and he learned a filthy song and they're making a pet of him, and I won't have it!"

Gwladus appeared and put her arm around Silvia. "Come now, lady, you'll make yourself sick." She shook her head at Faustus. "No, let me see to her."

Gwladus led her away to the one bedchamber in the Principia. Faustus himself was reduced to sleeping on a pallet in a storeroom with Paullus and Pandora. He opened the desk and took out the torque again and looked at it for a long time.

SUMMER

Lucius loved Castra Borea. There was always something to do when he ran away from his mother's lessons, or she took to her bed with a weepy headache. He felt sorry for her, but Gwladus said she just needed to rest and learn what could be changed and what couldn't. He made pretend forts in the mud by the bridge, where there were frogs and snails and little fat dipper birds diving for fish from stones on the bank, water striders in the shallows, and dragonflies hovering over them.

Lascius the cohort surgeon let him grind things up for medicines and come with him to look for useful plants. Paullus let him pat the horses and sometimes ride one. The trumpeter let him try to blow a trumpet and the signifer gave him a rag and let him help polish the silver spearpoint at the top of the cohort standard, and try on his fox-skin hood. Once the latrine caught fire because his uncle said the old garrison hadn't mucked it out properly.

It scorched the wooden seats so that they had to be replaced. His uncle showed him how the drains worked and said clean drains were the most important part of a commander's job. Rather than dampening Lucius's enthusiasm for the army as intended, it impressed him with the weight of his uncle's responsibilities. All in all, Castra Borea was the most exciting place Lucius had ever been.

Faustus kept up regular patrols between Castra Borea and every outlying fort, and worked his way doggedly through his list. In late July he took his sister and nephew on the several days' journey to Lughnasa Fair, with a substantial escort. Here, the scattered clans of the highlands gathered yearly to sacrifice to the Sun Lord, to trade with each other, make matches, and exchange news. A horse fair went on all day. It was good for the natives to see the commander taking an interest, he told Silvia. By that time, Silvia was so bored that she would have gone to see sheep sheared, and Lucius was ecstatic.

Wagons and tents dotted the great meadow under the midsummer sun and a cloudless sky. Traders displayed their wares from carts and rugs spread on the grass beside a row of chariots gleaming with bronze fittings, a few with silver. Aside from the cattle herds, such wealth as the Caledones possessed even now was displayed on their bodies or their horses.

Faustus recognized the tall fair man running a team of roan ponies through their paces and he went to watch. Emrys took note of him but he didn't draw rein. He drove the ponies through an ever-more complicated series of turns until he was apparently satisfied before he stepped down, handed the reins to their owner, and strode toward Faustus.

They took stock of each other warily. Their only previous meeting had been when peace was made between Agricola and the Caledones and Faustus had been the general's translator. Emrys's pale hair was cropped short and lime-bleached to near white and an old scar ran down his cheekbone into the flowing ends of a thick pale mustache. He wore breeches and a shirt of good wool and a bronze torque at his throat. His only weapon was the knife in his belt, all that Rome allowed. Swords and war spears had been confiscated, although Faustus was certain they had not got them all. In any case, it was not possible to completely disarm a rural population when axes and hunting spears were tools of survival. The peace depended on the Caledones finding it too expensive to break it.

"Prefect," Emrys said, nodding to Faustus. "Have you come to see the horse fair and buy a pair of ponies, or to sniff out rebellion?"

"Only to bring my household to the fair," Faustus said carefully. He pointed to Silvia and Lucius wandering among the traders' carts, trailed by two of his escort. "My sister and her son. She is recently widowed."

"My condolences."

There was no need to mention how many widows there were in Lyn Emrys. Faustus knew. "Also to pay my respects to the chief of the Caledones," he said.

"That is polite of you. How do you find our country now that you have spent a season here?"

"It is a very beautiful land. Not without its dangers." Faustus paused. He had a point to make and he wanted to see Emrys's reaction. "We have lost a few men in odd circumstances. Men who did not come back from hunting, or otherwise disappeared."

"There are always bogs," Emrys said. "A man who doesn't know the ground..."

"Or is dead when he goes in. I bought a gold torque from a trader who was passing through. He didn't know what he had, or I doubt he would have touched it. It was a Roman military decoration. Inscribed on the inside to a man who had served locally."

"I expect the man sold it himself." Emrys's voice was even, but Faustus thought he was angry and possibly surprised. He saw the scar on Emrys's cheek twitch.

"A Roman soldier does not sell a thing like that," Faustus said. "Particularly not if he is dead. The man who owned it was among those who did not come back from a hunt."

148

"That is unfortunate." Emrys's expression was grim now, but whether his anger was at Faustus or at someone else, Faustus wasn't sure. Both, most likely.

"There is also the matter of blocked roads and fouled water," Faustus said. "And no one in the nearest village ever knows who has done such a thing."

Emrys said, "Prefect, I have kept the truce, as have my household and my holders. I have seen to it that the other clans have done so to the best of my ability. I am not Caesar who may command as he wishes. Our people do not yoke themselves easily to one lord, and now that the war is ended, they remind me that they are free people still. And I will remind you that if Rome retaliates indiscriminately for blocked roads or bad water, Rome will start a fire you may not be able to put out."

"Your point is taken," Faustus said. He would have to ignore a certain amount of that kind of thing or resort to wholesale brutality. "However, dead soldiers are another matter. If anyone just happens not to come back from hunting again, I will track the men responsible and they will die unpleasantly. Do I make myself clear?"

Emrys looked away from him at the tents and wagons spread across the meadow. A group of girls were dancing around a great stone at the meadow's center while the young men turned from their talk of horses to watch them. A swarm of shrieking children chased each other in and out of the dance while the girls swatted at them. Where the trees marched along the meadow's edge two men were tying green sprigs into a white horse's mane before he was given to the god. At Lughnasa Fair the quarrelsome, unwieldy clans of the highlands came together and one might almost think them one people again, as they had been, finally, in the fight with Rome. But when the fair was over, they would go back to raiding each other's cattle, to old blood feuds and new ones, to all the things he could not control. "Yes, Prefect," Emrys said finally. "You are clear." He walked away.

Faustus saw Lucius, escaped from his mother, among the group of children teasing the dancing girls, wondered if he ought to collect him, and then decided to let him be. Paullus and the escort had put up the tents, Faustus's a splotch of officer's scarlet against the green of the trees behind it, with one to each side for Silvia and the escort. No Briton had pitched a tent nearby, or would, and an empty space like an invisible ditch enclosed them. When the children tired of teasing the dancers, Faustus saw them approach the tents, taunting each other to some dare. Lucius went into his mother's tent, came out with a bowl of dried figs, and they ran off in a herd across the grass, carrying the figs.

"Children stand always with one foot into some other world, Prefect," a voice said at his side, and he turned to see Aelwen beside him. The anger he had seen in her face when she came with Emrys to make the peace had been replaced with weariness and he slammed his mind closed on the thing that he knew and should not. The red hair that fell nearly to her waist was a bit duller than he remembered and beginning to be ticked with gray. A fillet of twisted bronze encircled her forehead and there were bronze drops in her ears, and she wore them both with the same air that she had worn gold before the war.

Faustus recalled again what she had said to Agricola about wolf cubs. "It may be that they grow into what that other world requires," he said.

"I hope so, Prefect." He could see that she wanted to say something else and he flinched, waiting for it.

"I lost both of mine to this war," she said finally. "My son and then my daughter."

"Your daughter? I am sorry." He knew the women had fought beside their men. Aelwen had a scar on her right arm, her sword arm, from that last desperate stand.

"My son to death, my daughter to the hostages that Rome took," she said quietly.

"You sent your own daughter?"

"We drew lots. It was the only way to do it honorably." She seemed surprised that he would question it. "And who would have heeded me if I had kept back my own child?"

150

"And Emrys needed you to bind the clans to him," Faustus said. "I see. It must have been hard, to send the children."

"They were most easily spared," Aelwen said. "We can have more children. We cannot magic up those old enough to tend herds and drive the plow when so many of them were lost." She turned to watch the swarm of small ones darting across the meadow like a school of fish. "But I would ask you – if you know how they are faring?"

"I was in Eburacum on my way north in the spring," Faustus said. "I did not see them but I am told that they are in the governor's particular care."

"And he will send them back as Romans when they are grown. Or keep them, I suppose. By that time it won't matter."

"That may not be true," Faustus said. "They will still be Caledone." He knew that was a facile thing to say, a cheap comfort that like as not was false.

"Your mother was British, was she not?" Aelwen asked him.

"Yes. She was Silure."

"And how came she to Rome?"

"To Gaul," Faustus said. "But that is much the same. She was taken when Claudius Caesar conquered the south of Britain. My father bought her for a housekeeper, and then wed her."

"And she gave him children."

"Yes."

"And lived as a Roman in all ways. Could she have gone back to her people, after that?"

Faustus had wondered the same thing. How many small changes, how many new habits would overlie the old longing and the fading clan mark? How alien would she seem to the tribe that had been hers? How tainted with the scent of Rome? "I don't know," he said finally.

"There are some things that cannot be undone, Prefect," Aelwen said. She too walked away, in the opposite direction from the one Emrys had taken. A brown-haired man, young with a swaggering walk, approached her and she faced him with an anger that Faustus could see even at a distance. Piran, perhaps, he thought, remembering what Cuno had said. He took a long look so as to remember the face.

–

"There are Cornovii here!" Aelwen said furiously to Piran.

"It is Lughnasa. Should they not come and sacrifice with their allies?"

"The Cornovii have never traveled this distance before, except to raid cattle." Their home territory was in the far northwest across the northern firth from their kin in the Orcades. Only the threat of Rome had forced them into alliance with the eastern Caledone clans. Aelwen stared at Piran until he fidgeted. "You have something to do with this."

"And they see what you do not, that with a base in their lands and another in Inis Fáil we may take the Romans by surprise and drive them out, maybe even from Britain."

"You have gone too far, Piran. You may be my brother's holder, but I will go to Emrys with this."

Piran shrugged. "Emrys knows. He made veiled threats to me that he cannot make good on. Now he is drinking with the Cornovii chief."

"You are a fool, and you make my head ache." She looked back at the Roman prefect. "How many of the Cornovii does this chief command?"

"Not all," Piran admitted. "Nall is old and may yet die of the wounds he took, but he will not give over to another yet. So because Nall is an old fool, the young ones set themselves up as chiefs, each over his own clan."

Aelwen saw the Roman watching her and said, "When you find yourself riding Epona's mare with a Roman spear through your throat, no doubt you will think on your mistakes. And if you bring them down on us, I will do it myself."

"If Emrys – and you – wish to hold your place among us, *you* should think on what I have said!" Piran retorted and found himself speaking to her retreating back, hair flaming in the sun now like a small angry fire.

Idgual unfolded himself from his wagon where he had been sitting with a horn of beer. He stretched and grinned at Piran as Aelwen stalked away. "Still no handfasting?"

"She will change her mind," Piran said. "She will get lonely and her bed will get cold."

Idgual didn't think he was right about that, but no doubt the Romans could be driven away without her agreement and then there would be younger, more compliant women to wed. Idgual would as soon have wed Epona's mare herself as Aelwen. But Piran was his spear brother and had been the leader in most things since their training days. It was just the way it was. Piran led and Idgual followed. After Lughnasa he would follow him west and north with the Cornovii chief and then they would sail for Inis Fáil together.

IX. TARA

The great hall at Tara had been re-roofed over the winter and scrubbed down to the floorboards on the orders of the new Queen. The windows were left open to the soft air of summer and outside was the bustle of building; carts laden with stone and timber, thatchers with bundles on their backs, surveyors marking out the footings of new halls and stables. Since his marriage, the High King had made Tara his principal residence, carving a piece of land from each of the four surrounding kingdoms to make Midhe, the middle kingdom from which he intended to rule. If the lesser kings had objections to that, they had found it best not to voice them. Indeed, Ulaid and An Mhumhain were under the joint rule of men Tuathal had chosen.

With the High King's coronation Inis Fáil had shaken itself like a dog shaking water and resettled. Eochaid of Laigin's body had been sent to Reachra for burial, escorted by Eochu his heir and the High King himself in tribute to Laigin's loyalty. The nearby trading port at Drumanagh had taken the change in overlords with equanimity. Kings rose and fell but business was business. The new governor of Britain dispatched an emissary to ensure easy trade between the islands and profess the governor's pleasure in the High King's ascension to his throne. The governor was no doubt particularly interested in stability on Britain's borders, with the emperor campaigning on the Danuvius frontier and drawing one of Britain's legions after him. This last was according to a tin merchant from West Britain, who also reported that the governor was occupying himself with enlarging a villa on Britain's southern coast, formerly the property of a local chieftain. The work now covered more than four and a half hectares.

"Flaming thing's going to be bigger than Nero's old palace in Rome," the tin merchant had said wonderingly. "Don't know what he's going to do with it all unless he's got a harem like a Parthian."

Tuathal voiced his opinion in private that the governor would get himself in trouble with that kind of ambition. "Agricola would have known better," he said.

"Better the Roman governor play with his new palace than look across the water," was Baine's opinion. "Your Agricola would have made you a client king if he could. So would your tame Roman."

Tuathal agreed. "He would. If he could. But all the same I do not want to see Britain come apart. Falling kingdoms have a way of shedding stones on onlookers."

Since Samhain they had developed a tentative companionship, coming slowly to know each other's small oddities and desires. It was Baine who had insisted on the cleaning of the Great Hall until, she said, she could no longer feel her father in it like fleas in a blanket. Her father's crown on Tuathal's head, however, did not seem to trouble her, and when he ordered Tara's metal-workers to fashion her one to match it she studied her reflection with satisfaction. She proved to be a willing, even joyous bed partner, but never again displayed the consuming hunger, the terrifying *wanting* of her incarnation as Goddess on earth. Tuathal was relieved by that when on the night after their aboveground wedding they lay wrapped in furs beside a warm hearth with the sound of their people's revelry outside. He did not ask her about it. That was women's business and unhealthy for men to pry too closely into.

Olwenna was married to Tuathal's driver, Ultan, at Lughnasa with the blessing of the High King who gave her a gold ring for a bride gift. Since he did not drag her from her bed into his at night as the old king had done, Olwenna had accorded him a devotion whose example to the rest of the household smoothed its running in a way that no amount of discipline from the top could have done.

In late summer, Tuathal convened a court with Baine beside him to hear the complaints and petitions of his new people and rule on such matters as did not require the judgment of the brehons. Fiachra consulted with Baine as each approached, settling who should address the High King, who should go straight to the brehons, and who should be sent off to sort out their own troubles.

"Elwyn wishes to marry a sheepherder's daughter and not the widow of his new holding," Baine said to Tuathal. "The sheepherder's daughter is very beautiful, and also half his age."

"And so he may," Tuathal said, "although I suspect the more fool he. But he will still build the widow a house of her own."

"The widow does not want to wed him either now, but she is insulted and wants silver for the slight. That must go to the brehons."

"Are there any of the matches we made that have held together?" Tuathal asked her. This was the third rearrangement so far.

"Most of them," Baine said. "People are generally practical. Elwyn was sensible until the girl's mother, who is clever, arranged to have him see her washing in the brook."

Tuathal wondered if it was only that same practicality that bound Baine to him, but he was beginning to think not, and that pleased him.

Fiachra sent Elwyn to the brehons with the widow marching adamantly behind him, and consulted the queen on the next petitioner in line.

"Riderch holds land in Laigin that was fought over in the summer and the crop spoiled, and he petitions for a remission of his taxes," Fiachra said.

Baine asked, "Has Riderch a tally of how many spoiled fields to argue an amount?"

Fiachra nodded and she spoke to Tuathal. The two reposed like brightly dressed ravens, gold-crowned and black-haired, on the thrones of the Great Hall. Fiachra was struck again by how much they resembled each other, tall and lean and imperious.

"Send me Riderch," Tuathal said, and Fiachra prodded him forward, taking note of the length of the line still waiting. Even the ones with need to speak to the king directly would take up the better part of the day. He would have to put a stop to it at noon and let people eat or tempers would flare. He beckoned one of the King's household hounds to him with orders to see to beer and meat. They would begin again in the afternoon and finish, with luck, by nightfall. The High King's household wasn't the Dagda's cauldron; they could take themselves home to feed after that.

–

Naturally the later petitioners could not be expected to begin their homeward journey by moonlight, and so they stayed on until morning, drinking the High King's beer, grumbling or boasting of the verdicts handed down, crowding the guest hall and quarreling over dice and poetry.

In the royal chamber above the Great Hall, Baine pulled the blankets up around her shoulders and leaned on her elbows over Tuathal. "My father used to storm out in his nightshift with a cow whip in one hand and a cudgel in the other, roaring, when he had had enough," she told him. "Have you thought of that?"

Tuathal laughed, looking up at her inside the curtain of her hair. "They will be gone by morning, and then something else will arrive to trouble me. Dragons, maybe." Kings did not sit on their thrones unmolested. If there was no war, there were petitioners, and Druids who read signs in the sky that required new sacrifices or new temples, and people for whom the caprice of human desire and the tits of sheepherder's daughters had overruled reason.

A roar of laughter and then angry shouting came through the walls from the guesthouse. Baine cocked her head to the sound. Tuathal pulled her down to him. "Fiachra will deal with it. Unless you would like to get a cow whip?" He pictured her in her nightshift, barefoot, hair wild around her.

"No." She rolled over so that he was on top of her, settling herself under him with a contented sound. "I like you much better than the pig boy," she whispered after a moment, sliding warm hands down his back.

"And I like you better than the sheepherder's daughter, even though I have never seen her." His own hands explored between her thighs.

"Are you sure you don't want to look at her first?"

"And anger Elwyn? That is how one gets entangled with brehons. I would sooner have fleas."

She gave a snorting laugh and he covered her mouth with his and they rolled in the blankets while whoever was roaring inside the guest hall fell suddenly to silence as Fiachra outshouted them.

—

The morning failed to produce dragons. Instead it brought a trio of riders coming up the road from Drumanagh. Sentries barred the way when the riders reached the green barrows where the unknown lords of old guarded Tara in their sleep. After a while, an outpost rider trotted up the gravel track.

The High King sat in a pool of sun in the courtyard, content until now with the small domestic business of the morning, watching his wife spin and a line of dairy maids taking cheese to the cellar. He gave an irritable look at the visitors as a sentry rider dismounted and knelt before him. Three figures, antlike seen from the top of Tara's mound, but purposeful in their stance.

"Britons, King," the rider said. "Their language tangles in my head, but they want audience with you. They were plain enough about that."

Baine laid her distaff and spindle across her lap. "Our guests have left," she murmured to Tuathal. "I sent Olwenna to see to cleaning the guest hall to hurry them on." There was nothing like a woman who wanted to clean to prod a man from his bed.

Tuathal read her unspoken thought. The visitors could be kept there, apart from the High King's lords, until he knew why they had come. "What tribe?" he asked the sentry.

"Northerners, by the look of them. Big men with clan marks, and they wear their cloaks pinned the way Lord Owain does."

Tuathal bent to the small hound who sat at his feet waiting to see what the king might need. "Go find me Lord Fiachra." To the sentry he said, "Bring them up. Straight to the guest hall and set a guard to see that they stay there."

The sentry nodded and rode away down the hill. When Fiachra came, Tuathal told him, "Send for Owain and Dai. If these are their people, I want no surprises. For me or for them."

"Not dragons then," Baine said, watching as Fiachra's riders crossed paths with the visitors coming the other way where the Five Roads met. "But who?"

–

The guest hall was freshly swept and there were sweet herbs on the floor. A hound brought jugs of beer and plates of meat, bread, and early apples. The beds were fine, spread with furs and heavy woolen blankets. And there was a guard on the door.

"We did not expect to be treated as prisoners!" Piran protested.

"You are guests," the guard said blandly. "The High King will see you tomorrow. Or the day after."

–

"They are your people, I think," Tuathal said.

Owain stood in the shadow of the Great Hall's stairwell observing the three men on the other side of the hearth. "Two of them," he said. "The other is Cornovii, most likely. I don't recognize him. Piran and Idgual were of my clan and not yet old enough to take their spears two years ago."

"Do you know what they want?"

"Piran is too young for Emrys or Rhion to have sent him as emissary for anything they might propose," Owain said.

Dai said to Owain, "Piran's father was ready to follow Idris when Idris challenged you as headman. You had to kill Idris. Remember that."

"I am not headman now."

"Do you want them to see you?" Tuathal asked. "I would have you hear whatever it is, but you may listen from a distance if you wish."

"I am Owain now," Owain said and Tuathal noted that he had shaved his face again and cropped his hair, no doubt when Fiachra's rider had said there were men come from Britain.

"Very well. Sit with the rest then and we will see what they want." He nodded to the circle of lords and lesser kings seated before the visitors: Conrach mac Derg of Connacht and Eochu of Laigin, Cassan, and Fiachra. Owain and Dai took their chairs with the rest and Tuathal saw the visitors' eyes fasten on them.

Only the chairs of the High King and the Queen were empty now. Baine followed Tuathal across the hall and they seated themselves facing the visitors and the lords of Inis Fáil. They were regal, crowned with gold, necks and arms encircled with more gold. The three from across the water stood and bowed to them, stiffly because it was not a highland custom but the instructions from Fiachra had been explicit.

"Why have you come to Inis Fáil?" Tuathal asked them. He pointed at their chairs. "You may sit down again."

Piran sat and leaned forward, eager. "The Eagles are faltering. We of the north have seen it. We come to ask you for a gathering place where we may build a war band that will push Rome from our lands again."

Tuathal saw Owain stiffen and Dai mutter under his breath to Cassan.

"We come to make alliance." Piran looked at Dai and Owain and his eyes narrowed. He nudged Idgual.

Tuathal said, "I thought it might be that, and so I have called my lords here to listen and have their say."

"Who are you that we should go to Britain to fight Rome for you?" Conrach mac Derg asked.

"I am Matauc, chieftain of the Cornovii," the third man said. He was young, like Piran and Idgual, with a carefully cultivated brush of a mustache and bronze pins fastening his red hair.

"Is Nall dead then?" Dai asked him.

"Nall is old," Matauc said. "He will give over soon and in the meantime—"

"In the meantime you would turn Rome's eyes on us?" Cassan asked. "We are not such fools."

"You were a landless bandit before the High King came," Piran said. "Or so I am told. No doubt you grew used to bowing to any master who fed you."

Cassan and Dai both put their hands on their knives and Tuathal shook his head. They subsided, grudgingly.

"But you," Piran said, looking at Dai, who had made no effort to alter his appearance. "You will understand, who lost all you had to the Romans when they came." His eyes slid to Owain. He was almost certain. "And if the warlord returns to lead us, we will drive the Romans south from our lands entirely. We did not know you were here or we would have come sooner."

Owain did not answer.

"I know you, lord," Piran said.

"You do not."

"I am of your clan!"

"You mistake me for someone else," Owain said.

Piran looked at Dai. "Do you tell me you are not who you seem as well?" he demanded.

"I tell you that you are a puppy who lived while better puppies died when Rome came," Dai said between his teeth.

"This is a quarrel between yourselves and Rome, it seems," Eochu of Laigin said. "For what reason do you seek to involve Inis Fáil? Why do you not gather a war band in your own lands if the Romans have so slight a grip?"

"That we will do," Matauc said. "But with your help we could drive the Romans from Britain entirely, never to trouble either of our lands again."

"Pah!" Cassan looked disgusted. "I said you were fools, and you have proved it. Do you not think that if the southern tribes there could have driven Rome away, they would have? Those people paid a dear price for trying. Go home to your mothers."

"Rome does not trouble Inis Fáil," Tuathal said. "Nor shall we trouble Rome."

"All we ask is leave to muster our war band here," Piran said.

"I forbid it," Tuathal said.

"I have been told," Piran said carefully, "that the High King does not command all things in Inis Fáil, and may be gainsaid if his lords so vote."

Tuathal's expression was dangerous. "My lords voted not a year ago with bloody swords. Be careful about asking them to vote again. Take your leave in the morning before I have a collar put on you and set you to work in the cow byre."

Piran's face flamed but he held his tongue. He stood, beckoning Idgual and Matauc to him.

—

"It is him," Piran said. It was only a little past dawn and already the High King's men had roused them, none too gently, to be on their way. Piran returned to the subject of the day before as soon as his eyes opened.

Matauc shrugged. "I never saw him close to. Are you sure?"

"He was our headman," Idgual said, pulling on his boots. "Of course we're sure."

"Then why is he here?"

Idgual thought of the tales that had spread after the last defeat, that the warlord had gone away with the Old Ones inside the hills and slept there until he should rise and lead the Caledones again. Or that he had been secretly buried in a cave where the Romans could never find his body to desecrate it. Neither seemed likely now.

"Waiting to come and lead us," Piran said.

"He didn't sound like it," Idgual said.

"He is maimed," Matauc said. "I watched him. He can barely lift anything with his right hand and that shoulder is twisted. He wears his sword on his left side."

"That is ill luck," Idgual said, uneasy.

"And ill luck likely will follow him," Matauc said.

"It may be that he is different," Piran said stubbornly. "Touched by the gods maybe, by the Morrigan herself. Otherwise why does he still live?"

"Look," Matauc said as they came from the guest hall. "Watch him." He pointed at the tall figure in the courtyard fastening the traces of a pair of red ponies, reaching awkwardly for the headstall with his right hand. It was clear that he could lift the arm only a little. His driver came to help and Owain brushed him away.

Piran pushed past Matauc to stand stubbornly beside the ponies.

"You should be on the road," Owain told him. "The High King has limited patience."

"As do I," Piran said. "Why do you deny what I can see?"

"What you see deceives you." Owain tightened the pony's traces.

"What if the Kindred knew of you? Knew that Calgacos is alive in Inis Fáil?"

"The Kindred know that Calgacos is dead in Britain." He tugged at the trace to test it.

"Ha!" Piran pounced. "And how do *you* know that?"

Owain gave him a long look, long enough for Piran to almost begin to doubt himself. The clean-shaven face was grim beneath shorn pale hair that was going gray – a thing that startled Piran. But his shirt was tied closed at the throat and his arms were covered by the long sleeves of his linen shirt.

"Show me your arms," Piran said softly.

Owain drew his belt knife so quickly that Piran did not have time to step back before its point was at his throat. "Go home. Do not meddle here. And do not meddle with Rome. If you call them down on your own head, you endanger what is left of your people and the peace that has been made."

"So says Aelwen." Piran threw the name at him despite the knife pricking at his throat. He felt the blade shiver and ducked backward quickly, keeping his distance now. "She follows Emrys now, foolish as women are."

Owain took a step after him.

"I am the High King's guest," Piran said hastily. To harm a guest was to invite the gods' vengeance as well as the King's.

"Go back to Britain, Piran, before you find out how little I have to lose. I have no use of my right arm, but I can kill you with my left."

--

"It is him though," Matauc said as they rode back down the gravel track to the coast, trailed by a dozen of the High King's men to see that they kept going. The day was overcast, spitting rain now and then. He pulled his cloak over his head. "You proved that. Will you tell his clan?"

Piran thought it unlikely to be useful while the warlord still refused. Better to give him time to think and come around, if he was going to. And there was Aelwen. Nor would she come around if she knew. "No, we will not speak of him. We will build our war band in Cornovii lands and the Caledones will come to us then. And if Matauc is right and the maimed arm has taken power from him along with the right to chieftainship, then best he be let alone." But it seemed to Piran an unreasonable thing for a man to pass up that kind of power; surely he had a plan he was keeping hidden. Piran would keep the secret too for now, until he could find some way to use it.

The rain began to pelt them, churning the track to mud, and they looked wistfully at a farmhouse with smoke rising through the rain above its comfortably thatched roof. A glance over his shoulder told Piran that the High King's escort still trailed them. As they reached a rutted path that ran from the road past stone-fenced sheep pens to the farmyard, the lead rider behind them raised his spear and pointed down the road. They kept going.

A constant stream of visitors came to the High King's court at Tara, looking for favor or opportunity: representatives of the trading ports along the British and Gaulish coasts; wool buyers and dealers in hides; merchants with gold torques and armbands to offer, enameled silver pony harnesses and Gaulish glass packed in straw; others with fine steel blades from Hispania, or eastern silks; horse traders; traveling physicians with potted cures for every ailment; tinkers making the rounds of farmsteads for pots to mend and wanting just to see the new king and the marvels being built at Tara.

A British trader with collyrium sticks and other salves for eye disease caught the High King's attention. Eye infections were common and a crowd had gathered while the visitor laid out his wares and showed how to scrape a thumbnail's worth of powder from the stick and mix it with water. Tuathal watched him silently, waiting for memory to surface, and when it did, he sent Fiachra to fetch him.

Fiachra, who likely would not have known his own grandmother in the wrong circumstances, was aware that the king, on the other hand, did not forget faces, ever. Thus he was not overly surprised when Tuathal waited until the man standing before him began to fidget and then asked quietly, "Do you report to the governor from Rome or to some lower commander?"

"I do not understand you, King. I sell eye wash." The man looked hopeful of this being a suitable explanation.

Tuathal raised his eyebrows. "Come close to me."

The man stepped forward, gingerly, and the king's hand shot out and clenched its fingers around his chin. The other hand ran a fingertip beneath it. The man's eyes widened but he did not speak.

Tuathal let him go. "That is the gall mark of a chin strap. How long did you serve in the line before you joined the border wolves?" He used the Latin term for that, the army vernacular of men who served the Eagles.

"I do not understand you."

"Of course you do. Also I can tell by the way you walk that you have been drilled."

At this the man looked insulted. "You cannot!" he blurted. It was a matter of pride with the frontier scouts that they could lose that telltale carriage at will.

Tuathal knew that. And in truth nothing in the man's bearing other than his face betrayed him. Tuathal had simply seen him before, years since, in Agricola's camp. "You will take a message to Britain for me, to a prefect of the auxiliaries there," he told him now. "He was posted to Isca Silurum last autumn but my own spies tell me he has gone to a command in the north."

"I am not a spy!"

"I have played latrunculi with your brother wolves, and I know one when I meet one because it is the business of the High King to know. Also, I expected the governor to send spies. Is it the governor you report to?"

The man gave up. "He only wishes to know how things fare here, and that the men you recruited in Britain are well settled in Inis Fáil."

"Having so recently taken my throne in Inis Fáil, I would be a fool to leave them landless and at a loose end, and I am not a fool. Is your governor?"

"No."

Tuathal thought his expression said, *not exactly*.

"What is the message?"

"I will write it out under my seal."

The border wolf kept a noncommittal countenance now. It would be rude to exhibit surprise that the High King could write, but this one had lived among Romans.

"You may put it in the military post when you return to Britain if that will serve," Tuathal said. "I only wish to be certain that he receives it."

"You are trusting, High King." If he could write, then he also knew how easily a seal could be removed.

"There will be nothing in it that I do not wish the governor to know," Tuathal said. "I will have it for you in the morning. In the meantime you may sell your eye wash to my villagers. I assume it is genuine?"

"Of course it is. I am not a charlatan." The guise of a dealer in cures reasserted itself. "It comes from a compounder in Londinium, only the best ingredients. The governor uses it himself."

"Very well." It would be the same ingredients, zinc and herbs, that the Druids compounded for the same ailment, but anything foreign was held to have superior powers.

–

Tuathal took a flask of ink and a sheet of papyrus from the chest where he kept a small store of them. He laid the papyrus on a table in his chamber while Baine watched with a curiosity tinged with unease. To her, the marks left by the pen looked ominous and indecipherable, a spell that only another sorcerer could unravel. The spoken word, committed to memory, was how her people transmitted information. History was memorized by the Druids, short messages by the messengers.

"How is it that you know how to do this?" she asked Tuathal. "Did your Roman teach you?" The Romans, she knew, put their symbols on everything, on those flat sheets made from a plant that Tuathal said came from Egypt, on tablets of wood or wax, on buildings, even on posts set at every interval along their roads, marking who had built the road and how far it was to the next village. Dai had described them for her.

"I lived among them for seven years. I like to learn things. I can write in Greek as well." Tuathal dipped his pen in the ink.

"There is different writing for different languages?" Baine was startled. A spell was a spell, or should be.

"The letters make sounds," Tuathal said, realizing that she didn't know that. "Look, this one sounds like 'ahhh' and this one 'ffff'." He wrote out a few more letters, making their sounds for her.

"But they make different noises if it is Greek?"

"Greek uses different letters altogether. They have their own sounds."

Baine considered this, and returned to the fact that the lesson made obvious to her. "If you send a message to your tame Roman with these letters, then anyone else can read it. Any Roman. Couldn't they?"

"Governor Lucullus's spy has suggested that to me already. I have no intention of writing anything I do not want the governor to know. Faustus will read what else he needs to from it." Tuathal took a clean sheet of papyrus.

"Aíbinn says that the Druids do not like this." Baine watched the letters forming, blooming magically on the blank surface. She was intrigued now, but she had a healthy respect for the Druids.

"The Druids do not like that I can do something they cannot," Tuathal said.

"Will not," Baine said. "Sechnal Chief Druid says it is forbidden by the gods."

Tuathal put the pen to his message again. "The Druids also say that the gods approve that which benefits the land. Keeping that fool and his followers out of Inis Fáil should please them, however it is done."

X. AMONG THE CORNOVII

AUTUMN

> *To Faustus Silvius Valerianus, prefect of the First Batavian*
> *Cohort, from Tuathal Techtmar, High King of Hibernia,*
> *greetings*

> *Faustus my friend,*
>   *I was pleased to hear that you have been given command*
> *of the northern garrisons.*

And how did he know that, Faustus wondered, although Tuathal's ability to know things was startling and his spies were no doubt excellent. He scanned the unfolded sheet which had come in the bags of the military post. Faustus also wondered how Tuathal had managed that.

> *We make our court at Tara, greatly enlarged now with new*
> *building...*

We? He must have wed Elim mac Conrach's daughter and survived the experience.

> *...and received in August a delegation of three lords from*
> *the tribes of your highlands.*

The purpose of the message began to be clear.

It was not a sanctioned visit, as I believe that Emrys still abides by the treaty he made with Julius Agricola. But there was much large talk of a new war band which these men propose to assemble in my kingdom.

Typhon take them, whoever they were. Faustus gritted his teeth.

Please assure your governor that I have allowed no such thing, nor will I. I have sent them home again with the threat of acquiring an iron collar if they return. All the same, since I have given them no leave, they will look elsewhere, and in Britain the land most out of Rome's reach is among the Cornovii, so I thought it best to send this to you.

To make certain that he knew about it, Faustus thought. Did he think the governor would ignore it? Or not recognize the danger? There was something between the lines there.

Piran and Idgual are of the home clan of Calgacos, but Matauc is Cornovii. Matauc is unofficial in his claim to the chieftainship since the old chief still lives, or did, but Matauc, who is some sort of sister's son to him, appears to consider that a formality.

Nall was still alive, Faustus knew, but barely; a festering wound from the war refused to heal and continued to damage both tissue and Nall's grip on the chieftainship.

What Matauc's actual influence among his people may be, I do not know. Piran and Idgual were plainly here without the permission of their current headman. Piran was ill advised enough to suggest that one of my own captains should lead them.

Owain. Tuathal would not name him but it was obvious. The things that Faustus should not know and did collided with the things he did not know and urgently needed to. He cursed Piran.

The suggestion was not well received, by the man himself
or by other of my lords, but what wild tales they may return
to tell in Britain I cannot say.

Faustus read the letter again, trying to decide how much Emrys
might know about this and what he might be planning to do
about it. What Piran might or might not have said. Whether it
was better to descend on Emrys's hold or Rhion's with the full
weight of the cohort behind him and demand that the culprits
be handed over – and risk their refusing – or to assume them
to be building their war band among the Cornovii, farther from
Emrys's reach.

A commotion outside the Principia window drew his attention from the letter. With most of his original list accomplished,
Faustus had ordered a small house built to serve as Praetorium.
It was to have private quarters for his sister and her household
and Silvia had changed her requirements thirteen times by his last
count and driven the centurion in charge to drink. Now for some
reason she was weeping noisily into her mantle while Gwladus
pulled at her arm to come away while the hapless crew stood
staring at their boots.

Faustus cursed and put Tuathal's letter in his desk with the gold
torque. He went out through the Principia's portico, dodging the
water that sluiced from its roof. It was raining again.

"What is it?"

Silvia went on weeping and the centurion of the building crew
looked at him helplessly.

Faustus put his arm around his sister's sodden shoulders and
dragged her into the Principia. "Silvia, stop it!" Once in his office
she buried her face in his shoulder and howled, hiccupping loudly.
"Stop it!" he said again.

She backed away a little, mostly because he was wearing his
lorica and its hinges scratched her face. He took her dripping
cloak off, pulled up a chair and sat her in it. Her wet hair, combed
into a bedraggled knot at the back of her head, was coming out of
its pins. She went on weeping loudly, with a strangled snort every

time she caught her breath. Faustus was beginning to wonder if he ought to send for Lascius, the cohort surgeon, a very junior medical officer who would be horrified at having to examine the commander's sister. The howling finally slowed and then quieted to small sobs.

Faustus pulled his chair up to hers so that their knees touched. He put his hands on the hands balled in her lap. "Silvia, what is it?"

She lifted a red, tear-slicked face. Her eyes were puffy, her cheeks mottled, and she gasped for breath. "I can't bear it," she said, more distinctly than he expected.

"Castra Borea?"

"My entire life. Britain. The army. The rain. The bugs in my wine. Mice. I would kill myself, Faustus, but I can't leave Lucius."

Juno. He thought she had been settling in. Apparently he hadn't been paying attention.

"All my nice things are gone. I sold my *clothes* to pay them off, just when I'd thought all the debts were settled."

"Who?"

"Lartius Marena and his son. Manlius borrowed from them too, and he said I would be a fair trade for the last of the debt!" She put her face in her hands.

"Who said?"

"Lartius Marena, the younger one. He wanted me to—"

"I can imagine what he wanted," Faustus said grimly. "But you paid him off?"

"The uncles paid the last bit, to avoid a scandal, but they blamed me for it, as if I'd invited him, and packed me off to you."

"But he didn't hurt you?"

Silvia narrowed her reddened eyes. "If you think that was pleasant—"

"Of course not. Silvia, I am so sorry." He searched wildly for something to offer. What did women like to do? Shop and drink wine with their friends? Those had been Silvia's occupations in Isca, lacking as they had been. What had his mother done? What

172

had Silvia done in Narbo Martius? Looked after their households, he supposed. "I had hoped you'd be happy keeping house for me," he ventured.

Silvia glared at him. "There is no house to keep. No servants to direct, no cook. We eat whatever Paullus throws in a pot. The only garden is a patch by the hospital, such as it is. Venus knows what's growing in it. It certainly isn't mine. There is only so much of my day that I can spend spinning and teaching Lucius his sums before we both go mad. There are no other women here except Gwladus and whatever village whore your men smuggle upriver for the night. I can't even bathe in peace without a dozen men outside the bath house grumbling until I finish. The drains back up every time it rains. Did I mention that it rains all the time?"

"You could go into the village," Faustus said. "I could send a few men to escort you."

"There is nothing to buy there but salt fish," Silvia said dismally. "And more wool to spin. And no one to talk to except fish wives who look at me as if I were a gorgon."

"You could write to your friends in Narbo Martius," Faustus suggested, cursing Manlius's uncles for the eightieth time.

"I did that in Isca," Silvia said. "They don't write back."

Faustus cursed them too, for shallow brats. Impoverished widows packed off to live on the frontier were plainly not useful to know, particularly with the hint of scandal trailing after them. He pulled off his scarf and wiped her face with it. "I'll try to make it better. If you'll just let them get on with it, we'll have a house for you. I know you brought your Lares. I'll make sure you have a niche to set them up in and maybe you can paint it for them. You used to paint."

"I used to do a lot of things," Silvia said miserably. "I just don't know what I'm going to do now."

"Not anything stupid, please," Faustus said uneasily.

Silvia sighed. "No. I have Lucius to think of."

"Let him run wild for a while," Faustus said. "Remember when we were small?" They had had the run of the farm and the surrounding woods and streams. They had explored them all with Marcus, the elder brother who should have inherited the farm that Faustus had abandoned. Silvia had been more adventurous before their brother Marcus died.

"There were no wild natives in the woods," Silvia said. "All our dangers were imaginary."

"He never goes past the sentries," Faustus said. "I've been very clear with him on that, and they have no reason to steal a child anyway. He's in no danger."

"Only of growing up to be like you!" Silvia said icily. She stood abruptly and stalked off.

"Go and dry out!" Faustus shouted after her. "It might improve your temper." It infuriated him that Manlius's extravagances and Silvia's resulting banishment to the hinterlands had apparently become his fault for being there to receive her in the first place. He was uncomfortably aware that Lartius Marena's proposition probably *was* his fault, assuming the Marenas knew their relationship, and the Marenas knew most things.

He snatched a wooden tablet and a bit of string from his desk and wrote out as vicious a curse as he could think of. He pulled a silver phalera from among the decorations on his parade harness and stalked out of the fort and past the bath house while the sentries watched curiously. At the river he stood on the edge of the pool where the dippers fished and balanced the tablet and the phalera in his hands. He could have used a coin, but an offering was more effective when you gave something that mattered to you. The phalera had been his first award, given early in Agricola's campaign.

"Mithras, you who are the Unconquered Sun." He paused. "And Juno, protectress of women. Take this offering and take Lartius Marena the younger and elder from this earth for what they did to my sister." He tied the tablet to the silver disc and dropped them in the water. Eirian had always said that water was a channel to the gods' ears. Whether the gods would listen or no was up to them, but it quenched some of Faustus's flaming anger when it sank into the water.

He went back to the Principia and took Tuathal's letter out of his desk and read it again, it was a thing he could do something about, as opposed to managing his sister, which wasn't. He called to his optio, who had been going over the Fit for Duty roster in the Principia records room and pretending that he couldn't hear anything.

"Put the word out to the southern garrisons that the next time they see Cuno and Rotri I want them sent up to me immediately."

"I believe they've been in Emrys's mountains," Ansgarius said.

"They have been, because I sent them, and because we thought that was where any rebellious activity would originate."

"And now we don't?"

"Now we have no flaming idea, but something is going on in Cornovii territory." Faustus handed him the letter. "This isn't to go any further than your eyes."

"Cornovii territory is so far north it might as well be Hyperborea," Ansgarius said when he had read it.

"The Cornovii sent men to the war band two years ago," Faustus said. "Nominally they are under our jurisdiction now."

"And we haven't the men to do much about it if they decide to argue with that, have we?"

"Not just at the moment, no."

Ansgarius saluted. "I'll send a rider to the garrison at Tuesis and tell them to pass it south." He hesitated. "We have scouts attached to our cohort here, sir."

"I want those two," Faustus said. The border wolves were specialists. Nominally classed with the rest of the frontier scouts, the wolves had the best chance of going where no one sane would go and come back out alive.

He left Ansgarius to send his message on its way and went to see what he could do with Silvia. The door to the bedchamber was closed and he could hear no sounds behind it. He was about to open it and upset her again just to be sure she was breathing when he heard the small murmur of Lucius's voice, so he left them alone. He turned away to find his father's shade standing irritably beside him.

Faustus jumped. "Don't do that!" He looked down the corridor to see if anyone was coming to catch the commander talking to himself.

"Is this how you care for your sister?" The shade's face was stern, what Faustus and his siblings had called his "more disappointed than angry" face, just before he became angry as well and there was a beating.

Faustus said, "*You* chose her husband – a spendthrift with a taste for chariot racing. And let him have charge of her money."

They glared at each other.

"Do you know what the fool did?" Faustus asked. "He borrowed from Lartius Marena once he ran through his own money and Silvia's. I just got that out of her. It took the last sesterce she had to pay that debt; she sold most of her clothes. And you know the kind of thing Lartius would have wanted otherwise. He has the morals of a seagull. She's just lucky to be safe and out of his reach."

"In a mud fort in Britain among savages," his father's shade said dolefully.

Faustus gritted his teeth. Disrespecting your parents, or even your ancestors, was ill luck as well as bad manners. "Have you discussed it with her then? Had a chat?"

"No. I…" The shade's voice trailed off.

"She can't see you, can she? Then why in Hades's name can I?"

"Because you are the paterfamilias now."

The word made a lump in Faustus's belly like meat gone bad.

"And ill-suited for it," his father's shade said, and vanished.

–

The scattered farmers and fisher folk of the village along the estuary were building the Samhain bonfires by the time Cuno and Rotri docked their boat along the village wharf. It was late in the year for any more sailing, even coastal voyages. They left their crew at the town's one ramshackle inn while they went to see what the commander at Castra Borea wanted, using the ostensible errand of selling small luxuries to the bored soldiers of the fort upriver. They would have reported to Faustus about now anyway, in the normal manner of things, but the order that had reached them in the south had an ominous ring to it.

Faustus took a look at them and sent them to the bath house. They reappeared, clean and grateful, an hour later. Cuno's wet hair, longer than Silvia's, hung down over his shoulders and he was working a comb through it.

Faustus handed Rotri the High King's message. Rotri read it and raised his eyebrows, whether at the message itself or at Faustus's acquaintance with the High King of Hibernia. "Any idea how many people have read this on its way?" Rotri inquired. He passed the letter to Cuno.

"Quite a lot, I imagine, likely including some men of the governor's," Faustus said. "It was in a military postbag by the time it reached me."

"Then it won't be news to Lucullus," Cuno said, looking up from it, "although he'll expect you to handle it, being busy with his new villa and all."

"New villa?" Faustus asked, diverted.

"The tale may grow with the telling," Cuno admitted, "but it's said to be as big as the emperor's house in Rome. And handily situated on the southern coast near Vectis Water, where an enterprising man could set up a profitable port."

Faustus's first thought, like Tuathal's, was that that might be a bad idea, but it wasn't his business, and certainly not his pressing concern. "I need to know what in Jupiter's name is going on among the Cornovii. As far as I know, Nall is still alive. How much influence does this Matauc have? And are that pair of Caledones building an actual war band there? Or is it large talk? Or both? And what is Emrys doing about it, because I am not going to believe that he doesn't know."

"Of course he knows. As for Matauc, that will be tricky. What sort of relation is he to Nall?"

"Tuathal said sister's son," Faustus said.

"That's vague and could go back a few generations," Rotri said. "The Cornovii are old-fashioned."

"Druids will know," Cuno said. He seemed to have no objection to Druids. Faustus thought that the native born saw things differently. There was always some old grandfather with a stack of skulls in his hall; in the maternal line generally.

"We'll need to settle in for the winter there," Rotri told Faustus. "Bad weather is coming soon. Our pilot is practically fearless but when she says stay off the water, we listen."

"She?" Faustus asked, startled.

"Orcades girl."

Faustus froze. "Unusual," he managed to say. Surely not…

"We lost our helmsman in a brawl in a tavern on High Isle. Some old priest who seems to be the last word on things like that ruled that we weren't due a blood price because our man started it, but we should have a helmsman to get us back across the water. Then this girl volunteered. We didn't want her at first, but the old man insisted she was better with a boat than most of their men. She is, too."

"I spent a winter on High Isle," Faustus said carefully. "All of them are in boats from the time they can walk."

"We only pick up a crew when we need one," Cuno said. "We didn't think she'd stick with us but she's useful in the towns and tribal farms. The women talk to Eirian when they don't trust us. And then she talks to us."

Eirian. Faustus said the first thing that came to him. "So you recruited a woman into the wolves, a woman who did not sign on to spy for Rome, and took her away from her home!" The thing that *he* had not done and thereby afflicted himself with a year's worth of second thoughts.

"She doesn't know," Rotri said. "No more than the crew. That would defeat the purpose, now wouldn't it? And she doesn't seem to want to go home."

"She knows," Faustus said. "You are insane if you think she doesn't know." How much could he admit to them without making a fearful mess?

"How would she know?" Cuno said, insulted. The border wolves prided themselves on their authenticity. It was generally what kept them alive.

"I knew her on High Isle," Faustus said cautiously. He paused for a long moment, then, "You'll think I'm mad, but the seals tell her things."

"Not so mad," Cuno said. "My grandmother could talk to them. All the same, she doesn't know. The seals mostly talk about the fishing."

Why had she left High Isle? Had they driven her out because of him? Faustus couldn't ask but the knowledge that she was at an inn in the village... Would she even want to see him? And how insane would they both be if she did? "Tell her," he said, and hesitated while they eyed him curiously, "tell her that Prefect... that Centurion Valerianus sends his greeting."

—

"What do we tell her?" Cuno asked as they rode back downriver.

"Not that," Rotri said. "I don't care what the prefect thinks, we aren't fool enough to admit that much acquaintance with him."

"No. But she had a fling with the prefect while he was on High Isle, I'll bet my front teeth."

Rotri chuckled. "And we thought she was impervious."

"Well, he wants her to know he's here. Is it fair not to tell her?"

"Are we matchmakers?"

"Who are we to stand in the way of honest lust?"

"Men who'll need a new pilot. We can't take her north if she gets a notion that we aren't unimpeachable. And she's Cornovii – the people on High Isle are all kin to the mainland ones. If we just turn her loose, that's a bad idea too."

At the inn they found Eirian outside mending a tear in her cloak in the last of the sunlight.

Cuno said, "We sold a fine wolfskin to uh, Centurion Valerianus, the prefect at the fort upriver, so go and buy us a jar of decent wine if anyone has it to sell." He gave her a coin.

Eirian put the coin in her pouch while Rotri rolled his eyes at Cuno. Cuno shrugged. "Go before the dark settles in."

They waited but she didn't say anything else.

–

The Samhain bonfire was laid on the beach just above the tide line and they went down at dusk to see it lit. Rotri sold three amulets from the stock in their packs as defense against anything that might be riding the Samhain wind, which was salt-laden and smelled of seaweed and fish. The tide was running in, ripples of froth curled and retreated and came in again, each time a little higher, carrying bits of kelp and small creatures who burrowed their way back into the wet sand. Eirian stood a little away from the crowd around the fire drill and listened to the seals lying on their rocks out in the firth. She could pick no words from their talk except for *fish*, but fish were always on their minds.

Faustus. She had thought him gone to Inis Fáil, and for some reason that he would stay there. But of course he was a Roman, he would go where Rome sent him. The Romans signed on for twenty-five years under their Eagles, Faustus had told her.

The Samhain fire was well alight now, fiery enough to keep any but the most determined night wanderer away. A log, burned in half, settled abruptly and threw a shower of sparks into the black air, where a little whirling sea wind took it and spiraled it upward. Cuno and Rotri were drinking the good wine before anyone else got into it, talking with the innkeeper. And what had *they* signed on for? she wondered. They had decided to go north to Cornovii country, they said, to ride out the winter there and bargain for furs and woolen goods. It was something to do with Faustus, and Piran, whose name Eirian had caught when they thought she wasn't listening; Piran who came of the old warlord's clan – the warlord who had been brought to High Isle by the Old Ones after the war. Everything about that war was like a great tentacled sea creature with a different prey coiled in each arm, and all of them with Rome's shadow overhead. Best that she not know anything she shouldn't, there among her mainland kin. And that took care of what to do about Faustus, which was nothing, and would leave them both the happier no doubt. Twenty-five years, and few took their women with them.

—

"Piran has been in Inis Fáil," Aelwen said to Emrys. "Give him to Rome or kill him."

"No."

"For what reason?" Aelwen put her boots closer to Emrys's fire. She had ridden through snow and cold to come argue with him. Now it was snowing again and Drust said the track looked as if they would be stranded here for days. It was going to be a wolf winter, so the priests said, and the heavy coats on the cattle spoke the truth of that.

Emrys sent a slave to bring them a warm drink and a blanket for Aelwen's shoulders. "I have given Rome enough hostages," he said. "I will not give one voluntarily."

"He will jeopardize the peace," Aelwen said furiously. "And Rome will blame us!"

"He will jeopardize the Cornovii who have decided to follow young Matauc before Nall is even dead. If Rome marches against Matauc I will not weep."

"For Nall's sake?" Aelwen's face was set, and her hair, loosed from its hood and drying in the fire's heat, stood out around her face in a flaming cloud to match her temper. "I did not bring you Calgacos's sword for the sake of keeping Nall in his chieftainship."

"For the sake of making peace with Rome, was it not?" Emrys said. "Though it stuck in both our throats?"

"Perforce, yes."

"Then let Rome look to its peace. I will not be their servant. If they want Piran, they can take him, along with the Cornovii who are fomenting trouble."

"You will let Rome clean your house for you."

"If you choose to put it that way. I will not hand a man of ours over to Rome, however much I wish to be rid of him."

"That is a dangerous game. I have met the new commander in the north and I do not think he is witless."

"No more do I."

"What does Hafren say?"

"My wife knows better than to argue with me on this." Emrys smiled. "Also she is with child and has her mind on her belly."

Aelwen drank from the warm cup in her hands, brooding. It was burnished redware, with a raised design of vine leaves, treaty gift of the old governor, Julius Agricola.

"I will kill Piran if I have to," Emrys told her. "If it comes to it. But I will not give him to Rome."

SPRING, 840 ab urbe condita

It was a late spring, the tag end of a soaking winter, and the snow, even more than usual, still lay in drifts in the fields and woods around Nall's hold and in dirty piles where it had been shoveled away from byre and hall. Dogs and boots brought mud and slop inside with every step and the only spring pleasure so far was fresh wild greens: dandelions and nettle from the fields where they poked their heads above the snow, and watercress in the half-frozen streams.

As planned, Cuno and Rotri had burrowed in for the winter, welcomed for their goods from the cities in the south and from Gaul. The horses had been sold rather than have them eating their heads off all winter, the ship's crew had been paid off, and the *Mercurius* hauled out and put under a boat shed in one of Nall's coastal villages. Only Eirian remained.

Old Nall had made a pet of Eirian for her songs and stories. He was almost entirely bedridden, with a wound in his hip that would not heal no matter all the attentions of the Druids and a series of itinerant potion sellers. As such he could no longer command the chieftain's place, but no other chieftain had been chosen while the various factions quarreled with each other. His wife tended him solicitously and brought Eirian to him to sing and amuse him with her tales of seals and finmen and kings from the days when kings were half gods and battled each other with one foot planted on the mainland and the other in the Orcades.

Eirian watched how Piran and Idgual made free with Nall's hold with Matauc in their wake, and how Nall's wife scowled at them behind their backs. Piran kept his distance from her, and from Cuno and Rotri, perhaps remembering her threat. What he was doing here was clear now, as was the reason for Cuno and Rotri's presence. None of which, she told herself, was business of hers, watching Piran conversing with Nall's young holders and Matauc growing daily more lordly-wise. As spring came, so did men from the surrounding mountains and coastal holds that owed their allegiance, at least in part, to Nall or his successor. They seemed to have no business with Nall, but gathered with Matauc and Piran and drank and boasted and practiced with spear and shield. They fought their sham battles across the floor of the great hall and laughed when Nall's wife ordered them out.

At the lambing, which marked the start of a new season for people weary of winter, the snow and sleet had not slackened and the herders spent their days pulling lambs and ewes out of drifts. Eirian watched Nall grow weaker and Nall's wife grow despairing.

"If it were not for Nall, I would go and live with the holy women on Mona and leave them to whatever they bring on themselves," she said to Eirian as Eirian helped her card the last ragged bits of the previous year's shearing. It was mostly poor quality and discolored, but nothing was wasted and it would serve for clothing for the lowest in the household.

Eirian drew her comb through the clump of wool, holding it flat on her lap with one hand. It was clear to anyone that Nall would not be a concern for much longer. And then Matauc would fight his way to the chieftainship if he still had to. The men he was drawing around him – while their own holds went neglected, no doubt – would speak for him before Nall was laid in his barrow.

"Will you go there then, when the time comes?" Eirian asked her. She knew of the colony of priestesses who lived on Mona. Faustus had told her how his General Agricola had destroyed the Druids' hold there but left the holy women alone.

"I lost my children in the war. I came from the islands to wed Nall. I have no reason to bide here, or to go back there. I will go to the Mother and she will take me in."

Eirian nodded, but it seemed a suffocating thing to her, to mure oneself up in a household dedicated to the Goddess. Eirian suspected that the Goddess wanted too much, more than Eirian would be willing to give her.

Nall's wife laid the roving down and put her hands on Eirian's. "Come, child, and sing him a song before his hound brings his dinner. It's all he asks for lately, that and a lark outside his window. 'One more lark,' he said to me this morning. 'One more lark.'" She began to weep.

–

"Not long," Piran said to Idgual, watching the women going into Nall's chamber.

"What then?" Idgual asked.

"Then Matauc will be chieftain. Is it not unfolding as I told you it would?"

"Yes," Idgual said. That much was true. With all of the Cornovii at their backs they would have enough men to take on the northern garrisons of the Romans, as long as the Romans did not send reinforcements. And as long as Piran could bring at least some of the Caledones to his banner. He and Idgual had been just short of taking their spears when the last battle with the Romans was fought at Pap of the Mother, the peak that was held to be the breast of the Goddess herself. The boys of the year ahead had gone into the war band, fought and died, and no doubt been carried to Annwn by the Morrigan herself, to feast with the gods, so Piran said, leaving Piran and Idgual to the shame of Roman masters. Privately, Idgual suspected that Piran had no desire to go to the Otherworld just yet but a strong desire to be chieftain, which was not unreasonable.

–

The window sills were rimed with ice despite the hangings covering them. More hangings surrounded Nall's bed to keep out the cold, and the bed was piled with furs and heavy blankets. Eirian remembered Nall as he had been in her father's house when Nall had come to the islands with Calgacos to sell what gold the mainlanders had left. It would feed them through the winter, they said, until they could drive the Romans back in one last great battle. He had been a big man then, muscular, with hair the bright red of a fox in summer, his chin stubborn. He had been a wind even her father Faelan couldn't stand against. Now his face seemed to have shrunk onto his skull, and his body to its bones.

The wound in his hip was all that Nall had got from that battle and it was slowly killing him. It still would not heal. When it closed, it grew inflamed and leaked pus and burst open again. The Druids cleaned it while Nall gritted his teeth, but it went deeper each time and now they said it was so deep in the bone that nothing could be done, so Eirian sang to him while he slowly disappeared into death.

"'The Seal Wife'," Nall said to Eirian. "I like that one."

"That's a sad song," his wife protested.

"Aye. True and sad, all about what we cannot keep," Nall said.

"Very well." Eirian wasn't sure why she had ever sung him that song in the first place. There were rumors enough about her mother in the islands, but then Nall didn't know them. He just liked the wistfulness of it, of wanting something that the fates or the gods or the seals themselves were going to take away again.

So she sang it, a melody like the seals crying offshore, of how a selkie came to land and a fisherman took her to wife.

> *She's up in the morning to bake his bread,*
> *Chill her flesh at night in his bed,*
> *But children she bore him three.*

He hid her sealskin in the rafters of the house so that she could not go back to the sea, but trying to prison a selkie is like trying to prison water.

> *She's made a magic of fire and bone,*
> *Bound up her hair with a fishbone comb...*

Nall's wife laid a hand on Eirian's arm. "He's asleep."

Eirian let the song slide into silence and looked at him. "He's gone, lady."

XI. THERE IS ALWAYS A PRICE

"We of the Cornovii do not answer to Caledone men," Matauc informed Piran. He settled his bright woolen cloak about his shoulders and pinned it with the great gold stag's-head pin that had been Nall's. "When we have laid my uncle in his barrow, then I will tell you how we will come against the Romans in the south."

Matauc was losing no time in doing that, Idgual noted. Nor any time in claiming the chieftainship. Matuac had nearly snatched the pin and other goods from Nall's bedside, leaving his widow to bury with him what she could keep a grip on.

Piran glowered back at Matauc. The plan to drive Rome out had been his: he had shaped it, he had led Matauc to Inis Fáil, he had defied Emrys and Rhion at risk of his own life to keep the honor of the highland clans intact and save them from disgrace as slaves of Rome. He said so and Matauc snapped, "This is the business of the Cornovii! If you do not wish to follow me, then go back to Emrys with your tail between your legs."

Idgual thought for a moment that Piran was going to draw his knife. Matauc stood and faced him down and then Piran shrugged and turned away. "Sending Nall to the gods is also no business of mine, therefore Idgual and I will hunt the wolf that was at your lambing pens last night."

"Why are we doing that?" Idgual asked, following him across the stone-flagged courtyard to the guesthouse.

"Because I will not stand about like Matauc's hound while the others bow to him. I must be seen as separate, not a vassal of Matauc. These things matter."

Reluctantly, Idgual changed his boots for heavier ones and leggings that laced around the calves of his breeches. He took up his hunting spear. He would have preferred to follow the chieftain's household in procession to the barrow and then retire to the great hall for hot mead and the burial feast. Instead they were going to tramp through the snow looking for a wolf. But no doubt Piran was right. These things did matter. It was important, Piran said, how you made people look at something, and Piran had generally been able to show people the side of a thing that he wished them to see. Somehow the other side grew murky and the side he held toward you was shiny as a bright coin or a gold collar, something valuable that you wanted to reach for.

They whistled up one of Nall's dogs and rode down the switch-back track that descended from the hold at the hill's summit, keeping behind the procession walking Nall to his barrow. The piled dirt was stark against the slushy snow, waiting to fill the hole in the sodden earth. They would lay him there under a cairn of stones, among the graves of the ancient chieftains of the Cornovii, some so old that no one knew who they held, not even the Druids.

The Druids had never been gone from Cornovii lands, only invisible for the brief time that Rome had swept its sea patrols along their coasts. Not even the northernmost of the Roman garrisons encroached on the Cornovii's hunting runs now, but to those disinclined to stick a spear in Rome's hide, Piran and Matauc had spoken of the shame of even nominal subservience to Rome, and almost worse, to Emrys of the Caledones. The Druids had lent their voices to Matauc's almost as soon as Nall had ceased to breathe. They had a score to settle with Rome.

Piran and Idgual turned off the track before they came to the barrows at the slope's foot. They followed a footpath wide enough for their horses, but not for chariots, down to the lambing pens and the lower sheep folds. The sun had come out and melted the top crust of snow even though the air was still an icy breath on their necks. Only faint traces of the wolf's tracks remained but they followed them and the hound's nose across the moorland below Nall's hold; Matauc's hold now, Idgual supposed. Bogs, small lakes, and patches of woodland dotted the rolling landscape. The wolf seemed purposeful, no doubt headed toward a den somewhere in the woods. There was no sign of its packmates. An outcast maybe, or simply the only one left after an evil winter. The bright sun glinted off the snow, making Idgual squint. His nose dripped and despite a fur cap, his ears were freezing. He was relieved when the dog halted at a small ice-rimmed burn that flowed through a stand of willow and alder. The woods were silent; only the little burble of the river spoke from the stream bed.

The water ran past a tower of stone jutting at an angle from the earth, twice a man's height, thrust out by some old upheaval. A pair of rowan trees clung to its crest, roots prying between opposing faces of the stone like fingers. A cleft opened at its base – likely the den, since the tracks, faint now but still discernible, led into it. The hound nosed dubiously at the entrance.

They readied their spears and ordered the hound into the opening. There was no sound except a low whine and then a sharp bark. They advanced on the den but nothing emerged but the dog, looking shamefaced, with a wolf's paw in its teeth. Piran dismounted and snatched it from him.

Idgual peered at it. It was old, cut off above the pastern and sewn shut. A piece of stick protruded from it. The hair rose on the back of Idgual's neck.

The hound whined again. The light shifted on the mouth of the cleft. There was a stone just inside that was not a stone, a gray scrap of cloth, no – a wolfskin, no – a cloak, there was a hand, it was a tree root wedged between rocks, it was a hand, it was a root...

Piran's arm shot out and his fingers clenched around it and the little man came into focus suddenly. He was small and dark-skinned, dressed in gray wolf's fur, and his hand was pinned between two stones where the cave opening had shifted as the frozen water in the rock had thawed.

"Not a wolf." Piran threw the wolf's paw down. "I've heard of the little beasts doing that to throw their betters off the trail. Get up!" He prodded the small man.

"He can't," Idgual said. "His hand is caught. See?"

Piran bent cautiously. There was a small bronze knife in the man's other hand. "Were you going to kill me with that, now?" he asked, laughing.

The man didn't answer.

"Free himself with it," Idgual said. There was a gash in the trapped wrist and blood on the knife. "He was about to take his hand off when we came along."

Piran studied him. "We'll get him free," he announced. "Give us that knife and hold still," he said to the man. "I know you can understand me."

The little man opened his other hand and let the knife fall. Idgual picked it up. It had a leaf-shaped bronze blade, very lovely and very sharp, and a hilt of deer antler. He stuck it in his belt and looked curiously at the man while Piran went to fetch something to lever the stones apart. The man was small, he would come no higher than Idgual's shoulder. His skin was dark, traced with patterns like vines, and his eyes were a startling blue. His black hair was threaded with polished stone beads and red cord. One of the Old Ones. Idgual knew of them, of course, but they had always seemed more like a firelight tale to him, something out of legend, unrelated to the miserable few tied up in Caledone slave houses. It was the Old Ones who were said to have taken Calgacos from the battlefield.

It was easy enough to see what had happened. A piece of the outcrop had shifted at the top where the rowan roots were prying it apart, and fallen into the entrance. It would have killed the man if it had hit him straight on. As it was, it had pinned his hand to the stone below it and there was no way he could have shifted it with his other. If they had not come along he would have cut his own hand off to get free. He would have had to, or die long before anyone came for him. There were actual wolves about and it had been a hungry winter.

Piran came back with his hunting spear and inspected the stone. The gap beside the man's wrist offered space to jam the spear shaft a hand's breadth under. That might be enough. He wedged the shaft in as far as he could. "Pull him out when I shift it," he told Idgual. "This may not hold it long." Idgual could see the shaft bending as he spoke.

Piran put his weight on the spear and Idgual yanked the man back, dodging the point that nearly put his eye out as it snapped back up. The man screamed with pain, a shriek that cut through the silence of the woods and made the horses fling up their heads. He writhed away from Idgual.

"Hold him!"

Idgual caught him by the arm and the man thrashed in his grip and bit his ear. Idgual raised a hand and smacked him and then held him down.

"Ungrateful beast," Piran said. "I nearly broke my best spear for you."

A drop of blood fell on Idgual's arm and he put his fingers to his ear. "I'm bleeding," he complained. "Like as not their bite is poison too."

The man sat still now in Idgual's grip, moaning and cradling the ruined hand in his lap.

"Who are you?" Piran asked him. The man didn't speak and Piran kicked him. "Tell me or we'll put you back under that rock."

"Magpie." His speech was odd, as if their language was not his natural tongue.

"That is your name? Magpie?"

"Yes." His teeth were clenched, probably against the pain. The hand must be nearly unbearable now that feeling was coming back to it.

Piran looked pleased. "Very well then, Magpie, you owe me a gift now. A trade for your hand."

"We have nought that the Sun People value," Magpie said sullenly.

"There are rules," Piran said. "I know this. I have heard the tales." He grinned.

Magpie snorted. "All of which are wrong."

"But you owe return for a life, for a favor, do you not? Can you tell me that is wrong?"

"No," he said grudgingly. "That is not wrong."

"And you are bound to pay it."

Magpie's face was sheened with sweat now, even in the cold, and he shook.

"While you are thinking it over," Piran said, "you can give us back the lamb you stole."

"My brothers took that and went the other way," Magpie said. "I was only to put the wolf tracks down."

Idgual kept his grip on him. He could tell that the little man would run if he found a chance. He smelled of peat smoke and damp earth, and pain.

Piran squatted on the ground beside him. "It was your people who took the old warlord from the battlefield, after the war with the Romans, was it not?"

Magpie shook his head. "That was far from us."

"But it was your kind, wasn't it?" Piran persisted. "The old warlord made alliance with them."

Magpie was silent.

"What would you have done if we hadn't seen you?"

"You would not have if I could have shut the pain out," Magpie muttered.

"But now you have two hands when you would have had one and like as not bled to death, or been scented by the wolves," Piran said. "So there is a price for that. Do you agree you owe me a price?"

Magpie looked resentful, but finally he nodded.

Idgual waited to see what Piran would ask. Piran was clever. He knew all the old stories, although maybe you could discount the ones about hoards of gold in the Old Ones' hills. If they had hoards of gold, they wouldn't need to steal sheep. Magpie was bone thin. Idgual could see his ribs protruding where the wolfskins gapped open.

Piran stood. "Bring your people to my banner against the Romans," he said. "Mine, not Matauc's."

Magpie looked startled, or appalled. "No."

"No?" Piran prodded him with his boot.

"We do not hunt with the Sun People," Magpie said. "You stink of iron and we do not trust you. It cannot be done. No matter what *I* promise, it cannot be done."

"What if I just kill you?" Piran suggested.

"It wouldn't matter," Magpie said, resigned. "This is not in my gift."

"There is a war band assembling in Inis Fáil to fight with us," Piran said. "Together we could push the Romans and their Eagles across the water into Gaul."

"You could not," Magpie said. "And in any case, we will be here when the Romans are gone and you are gone as well."

"We could take you back to Nall's hold with us," Piran said. "In exchange for that lamb. Put a collar on you. Iron," he added.

Idgual doubted that would gain them much. The Caledones did sometimes make slaves of the little dark people but they usually died after a few months.

"You would be sorry," Magpie muttered and Piran kicked him again.

"You owe us a price," he insisted.

"Yes," Magpie admitted. He seemed to be thinking, or arguing with himself. "I will give you something that *is* in my gift," he said finally. "But you will swear first to let me go afterward." He eyed Piran knowingly. "And do not think to forswear yourself, Sun Man. You will be cursed if you do, and that is also a thing that we can do."

"What will you give me?" Piran asked.

"I can tell you a thing that you do not know. You will wish to know it."

"How can I be sure of that?"

"I will swear to it beforehand, by the Mother. I cannot break that oath or she will come for me. And for you if you break yours," he added.

Idgual thought that was probably true. The Mother, as the Old Ones worshipped her, was the most ancient incarnation of the Goddess, some force out of the earth itself.

Piran seemed less concerned. "Very well." He picked up his spear and put the blade close to Magpie's face. The little man bent his head away from it. "If this thing you tell me does not interest me, then you will not have kept your bargain and I will kill you."

"It will interest you," Magpie said. "Whether you will profit from it is in your fate, not mine."

"Agreed."

"Traders from the south overwintered in Nall's hold."

"It is not Nall's hold now. And I know this."

"It is little to us who rules you. That is a thing for the Sun People to fight over."

"Neither Nall nor Matauc rules me!" Piran snapped.

"That matters little to us either. But they are not traders. They belong to the Romans, despite they do not look it."

Piran put the spear closer to Magpie's face. "How do you know that?"

"We hear things. There is always news in the heather. My people are not many but we are more than you know. We speak from house to house."

"And why did you not warn Nall?" Piran demanded.

Magpie looked surprised. "Because we do not care. Why should we? The Cornovii trample our homes in the way of all Sun People, the same as the Romans did when they came north."

"You helped Calgacos fight them!"

"That was a sidhe to the south," Magpie said. "And the business of the Old One there, not mine."

Piran thought for a long moment, tapping his fingers on his spear shaft. The hound had gone to lie down beside the horses. Piran snapped his fingers at it and it came and nosed the small man when Piran told it to. It sat back on its haunches, head cocked as if puzzled.

"If you are lying," Piran said, "I will track you. We will break open your lair and drag you out."

"I am not lying," Magpie said, "and you cannot track me although you may try."

"We tracked you here."

"You tracked the prints I left. The dog tracked the wolf scent. If I ran now, he wouldn't find me. Are you going to let me go now or will you be forsworn?"

Idgual thought that Piran was tempted to hold him anyway, but then he shrugged and motioned to Idgual to release him, to Idgual's relief.

Magpie stood and cradled his damaged hand in his other one. One of the horses nickered at something, Idgual flicked an eye at it and then back at Magpie to find him gone. There were no tracks in the melting snow.

"Sneaking little beast," Piran said. "I shouldn't have let him go."

"Yes, you should," Idgual said with conviction.

–

"Your brothers have gone to watch what the Cornovii do now." The Old One spoke gently to distract Magpie from the bath in which she was soaking his mangled hand and the gentle fingers that probed and shifted the bones inside it. It hurt a great deal all the same.

"I had to give them something, did I not?" Magpie whispered.

"Yes. You did. That is a debt that must be paid. All the same, you have upset the balance."

Magpie had known that. Spring was a changing time anyway and a particularly bad time to shift the balance of the world. For the people of the hills the balance lay in invisibility, neither aiding nor frustrating the affairs of the Sun People. Cornovii and Romans, although at each other's throats, were nonetheless indistinguishable in their danger to Magpie's kind.

The Old One bent over Magpie, her arms brushing his cheek. Three heron's feathers, stuck like a crown into the braids on top of her head, shone in the dim glow of a rush light. She wore a necklace of blue stones and acorns with a gold disk hung from a hole drilled through it. The disk had a man's face and was older even than the current house of Magpie's clan. It had belonged to the Old One before her and would go to the one after her.

A small girl came in with a bowl of broth and the Old One held it while Magpie drank. There was meat in it, more than usual, and he was grateful.

"What should I do?" he whispered.

"You must restore the balance while you still can. Your brothers say the old lord has just been laid in his barrow, and his people drunk and sleeping because of it. The men who tracked you will hold their secret until the new lord is sober. You did not promise them anything other than the words you spoke, did you?"

"No, Grandmother."

"Good. But once they speak it will be too late."

Magpie thought of the Sun People, of the smell of them, of the iron, of his fear when he had seen that he could not hide himself from them in the rock cleft. "May my brothers go to do this?" he asked, but he knew the answer.

"No." She took his hand from the bath and dried it. She laid it on a piece of smooth wood and wrapped a clean cloth around hand and wood, binding the fingers in place. "You may take someone with you who has the use of two hands but you will do this yourself. That is also part of the debt."

—

"Run, lady." The whisper in Eirian's ear was faint as a mouse rustling but enough to snap her awake. She lay motionless, eyes half-open, adjusting to the darkness of the guest hall.

"Run, lady." A small hand touched her shoulder for an instant. "Someone knows who you are," the whisper added. "They will speak when it is light. Go now and we will cover your tracks. Go by the midden gate."

Eirian could see him now, a small brown face in the darkness under a fall of dark hair, almost not there at all save for his voice. She sat up silently and pulled her boots on, wrapped her fur-lined cloak around her. All she knew was that the little dark ones didn't come to a hold full of iron for anything but some dire emergency. She slipped off the bed and shook Cuno awake, and then Rotri, a hand over each man's mouth until he saw her motion for silence. The visiting Cornovii lords in the guesthouse were snoring and she thanked the gods of strong drink for that.

"Out," she whispered. "Now. We have to go. Someone knows who you are."

"And who would that be?" Rotri asked suspiciously.

"I don't know," she hissed. "But you've been betrayed and if you make any more noise you will likely find out who."

"Argue later," Cuno said, and they followed her, slipping through the darkness to the pony shed. She didn't see the little dark man but she knew he was there.

The hold was silent under an overcast sky. Inside the pony shed it was almost pitch black and they fumbled with the bridles and girths, whispering softly to the horses to calm them.

"The midden gate," Eirian whispered.

Cuno began to ask why and then they saw that the gate stood ajar, already unbarred. They were halfway through it, stepping across the still figure of the guard, when a shout came from behind them.

"Here! Where do you think you're going? Thieves!" One of Matauc's men stumbled toward them, no doubt come from the hall to piss.

Rotri flung himself off his saddle at him and they rolled on the ground in the shells and broken crockery of the midden. Rotri had his hands around the man's throat. The man had a knife and if Rotri took his hands away he would shout. He hacked at Rotri's fingers with the knife, his feet drumming in the dirt.

Cuno slid from his horse, his own knife in his hand. Eirian saw the hunting spear tied to Cuno's saddle and looked for some

197

place to tether the ponies. If they scattered it would likely rouse the hold. She knotted their reins loosely around a broken drying rack, praying they would not spook and drag it rattling through the courtyard. Cuno was holding the man's feet down now and Eirian stood over him with the spear. Cuno looked up at her quickly and nodded and she drove it hard into his chest, pushing it through the ribs. It came out on a river of blood. He stilled and she knew she would see him again in her mind later.

The scuffle had roused someone else. Another man ran toward them, his mouth wide to cry out. As they watched he dropped, crumpling silently to the ground. A slingstone rattled down the slight rise where he had fallen. They didn't look for the source, only snatched the reins free while the horses snorted and stepped back from the blood smell. They mounted to follow the track that switchbacked from the summit down past the smithy and the tanning vats, and then the outlying sheep folds and cattle pens, going as fast as they dared in the darkness. When they reached the woods below they halted, looking backward uneasily. No further sound came except the soft hoot of an owl. Cuno snapped his head around toward it.

"Now," Rotri growled at Eirian, "who did you tell?"

"No one! If I wanted to tell Nall who you are I would have done it long ago. And I wasn't sure. But someone knows now."

"How then?" Rotri demanded.

"The little dark people," Eirian said. "I don't know why but one of them came to me. It must be something important or he wouldn't have come inside Nall's hold, past that many of us and all that iron just to find me."

"You were nearest the door." He came out of the darkness to stand at her knee and the other two stared at him. He stared back, plainly uneasy. They saw that his hand was bandaged and held in a cloth knotted around his chest. He carried a leather sling in the other hand, and a bag of stones at his belt. "It was a debt owed," he said. "But it has unbalanced things and so to right them, we will help you run."

"We?"

"My brothers and I. We are the sidhe of Tarvo Dubron. I am Magpie," he said.

"And why should we trust you?" Rotri demanded.

"For one thing," Cuno said, "because he has told us his name."

"And told Matauc's people who we are."

"And then told us," Eirian said. "You have lived in the border-lands long enough to know that their laws are strange to us but they don't break them."

"True enough," Cuno said. "We will follow you," he told Magpie.

"Not to the harbor," Rotri said, decisive now. "They'll catch up before we can get the boat on the water."

"You take the boat," Cuno said to Eirian, fishing in the purse that never came off his belt. "They won't want you if we leave a trail in the other direction."

"It may still have been her," Rotri said.

"It wasn't," Eirian said. "And you need me. I am Cornovii, I may be able to get you through their lands."

"It was not her," the little dark man said. "And no, not to the harbor. You will have to go south through the glens."

"Why your people?" Cuno asked him. The little hill people rarely if ever meddled in the affairs of what they considered the newcomers.

"I have told you," Magpie said. "It was a debt. There is always a price attached to dealing with the Sun People," he added. "It is like stepping in a bog. We will lead you as far south as we can and try to mask your trail."

"Can you get us to the Roman outpost they call Castra Borea?" Rotri asked, giving up any pretense.

"They will hunt you along the trails through the glens," Magpie said. "You will have to go somewhat sideways. If you meet Sun People on the way, let the woman speak with them. Follow us now." He disappeared into the shadows of the trees and they heard the owl hoot again.

They followed the path he had taken, emerging from the trees onto what looked like a deer track across the moor. The owl also followed them; Magpie's brothers were abroad in the heather as well. Near dawn they doubled back on their trail and halted while Magpie daubed handfuls of herbs and mud on their horses' fetlocks and hooves. Then they set out again in a different direction.

They rode until afternoon, sometimes on an obvious trail, sometimes following Magpie cautiously through a bog or along a track into the mountains that seemed more suited to goats. When night fell again they came to an ancient barrow in the hillside, its stone lintel sagging and its entrance gaping open.

Magpie motioned them in. "Take the horses inside."

Cuno and Rotri looked as if they were about to balk, but they obeyed. Inside the hill a faint light came from a gap somewhere in the roof. The remains of a fire darkened the stone floor but otherwise it was empty, looted long ago by the Cornovii or the people of the hills themselves for whatever grave goods there might have been. Cuno and Rotri looked uncomfortable but Magpie seemed at home there. No doubt the little dark people had some understanding with whoever had built the old barrows – their own ancestors perhaps. When asked about it, they always said they didn't know, and Eirian thought perhaps they didn't. If they had been kings here once, that time was gone into the mist.

Magpie left them in the darkness under the hillside. "Stay here and rest while we see what Nall's people are doing. I will come for you at night and bring food."

"I don't trust him," Rotri said when Magpie had slipped out into the gray afternoon.

"You have no choice," Eirian snapped. "And you don't trust anyone."

"We're paid not to," Cuno said.

Eirian wrapped herself in her cloak. The stone floor was cold and the air dank. It had no smell of death left but still it felt as if something whispered in the corners, perhaps only memory. "I don't suppose we dare light a fire," she said wistfully. In the dark it was too easy to see again the man she had killed, the blackness of his blood by moonlight.

"No."

"You could still go back when he comes for us," Cuno said. "To the boat. They'll be on our trail now."

"No," Eirian said.

"Look you," Rotri said. "It will take a ten-day to get to Castra Borea minimum, likely longer and they'll hunt us the whole way. *You* aren't paid to take that on."

"You'll need me," Eirian said stubbornly.

There was opportunity to prove her use the next evening when they came down from the mountains into a glen with a village at its mouth.

"You will go alone past the Sun People there," Magpie said. "We will meet you on the other side, but we won't go near them."

"What of the ones on our trail?"

"Matauc has raised a hunt but they are to the north still. You must get past the village before anyone raises the hunt among them here."

"Slinking little weasel," Rotri muttered when Magpie had disappeared into the heather. He thought for a moment. "Very well. We left our goods behind so now we are fur traders. Cuno is from Verulamium in the south and I am from Calleva, both of which are close enough to true, and we come north every year for furs to sell. You are my Cornovii wife," he told Eirian.

"Acquired with the furs, no doubt," she said.

"Indeed."

They threaded their way down the glen, fording the little stream that ran near the ring of round houses that was the village. The ground was still slush and the stream rimed with ice. Ice clung to the heather, the brown stalks of last year's bracken, and the stubborn yellow flowers of gorse. Sheep grazed on the slope below the village with a dog in attendance and a magpie watching them from the byre roof, preening its black and white feathers. Cuno gave it a suspicious look. Two children and a cow came out to meet them.

Eirian bent from her saddle. "May the gods bless the house and its children," she said.

They smiled, plainly excited to see strangers. A man and a woman came quickly after them to inspect the newcomers. Even the cow looked interested. The woman put her hands on the children's shoulders.

"We hope for a bed in the byre tonight," Rotri said. "For my wife and I, and for my partner. And if you have furs to sell, that is our purpose here in the highlands this spring. There is a good market to the south for the furs that highland weather breeds, particularly after a winter such as this."

The man nodded, seeming pleased now. "Wolf and fox, and catskins. We will show you." Silver was rare just now. The chance to earn some to buy the small luxuries that they had gone without in the past years was welcome.

Eirian saw the woman regarding her with curiosity and smiled at her. The woman smiled back cautiously and allowed the children to squirm out of her grasp.

The man, who proved to be the headman of his village, led them to his house and sent his elder children for broth and bread and beer. The round house of timber and thatch was warm, if smoky, and Eirian huddled close to the hearth while the headman spread out his furs and Cuno and Rotri bargained for them. The wife saw Eirian's arms when she stretched them to the fire and said, "You are Cornovii, are you not, lady?" She looked dubiously at Eirian's breeches.

"I am," Eirian said. "And newly wed," she elaborated, "which angered my father. Likely he is on our trail for it."

"You wed against his wishes?" The wife looked shocked but interested.

"He would have given me to a man older than himself," Eirian said. "A man of Matauc's, he who is the new lord in Nall's hold. I would sooner a life on the trail with Rotri. Also the other man's first wife died," she added darkly.

"At his hand?" The wife's eyes were wide now, caught in the tale.

"There were rumors, but he is wealthy despite the war – there are some say he had trade with the Romans – and my father is avaricious. So I put on breeches and ran away with Rotri."

The wife patted her hand. "They will not find you here if they look," she said. "My own husband is a good man. He would never do such to his daughter."

In the morning they departed with the furs tied behind their saddles, a bag of bread and cheese to take with them, and a sleety rain coming down, half-ice, half-water. They were bid to stay another day until the weather turned, but declined.

"I fear my father and Matauc's man coming for me," Eirian whispered to the wife as they mounted. Rotri sidled his horse beside hers and put a comforting arm around her shoulders for verisimilitude, and then they put their heels to the ponies' flanks.

"Recruit that one for the border wolves," Cuno commented, grinning, as they rode.

"And was not Prefect Valerianus most wroth with us when we saw him because he thought we had done so?" Rotri retorted. He glanced at Eirian riding beside him to see her reaction.

"It was he that sent you north then," was all she said. "No doubt to spy on that fool Piran, who even I can see is going to make trouble."

"To see how much trouble he makes," Rotri said.

"The prefect sent you his greeting when we were at Castra Borea," Cuno added. "It was awkward to tell you that before."

"He wintered on High Isle two years since," Eirian said. "I was acquainted with him there."

Cuno snorted and she glared at him. If she had been going to say anything else it was forestalled by Magpie who appeared under the ponies' noses when they were out of sight of the village.

"Give me a piece of your clothing, each of you."

They didn't argue, just pulled their shirts off and tore a sleeve loose from each. They turned their backs politely while Eirian did so but she didn't hesitate.

Magpie gave her a leather bag with foul-smelling stuff inside. "Rub it on the horses' hooves and then on your own feet, twice a day. Go that way up the burn and someone will come to guide you. They are coming after you. I will set them on the wrong trail if I can."

He slipped into the heather and they went in the direction he had pointed until they saw a faint shape ahead of them. It whistled and they followed it blindly since there was no other choice. They rode until dark fell, across moorland or climbing like goats up the slopes on trails they couldn't see, through heather and bracken newly unfurling or barren scree that rattled and slid under the horses' hooves, ears always pricked for sounds of pursuit behind them. As the sun dropped below the ragged line of the mountains, the shadow resolved into a small man, dark like Magpie, with a bow and quiver of arrows on his back and a sling at his belt. He was dressed in a tattered woolen shirt and breeches, and catskin boots.

"There is a cave under that outcropping ahead and there is food for you." He pointed. "Go to earth there until someone comes for you. Give me the horses."

"The horses also need feed," Cuno said. A little sparse grass poked through the slush. Not enough.

"You will have to go on foot from here. We will not travel the Sun People's roads and if you go alone there they will catch you. Give them to me and I will drive them different ways to confuse the trail. The ones hunting you are already spreading their net. The new lord is very angry."

"We could just run for it," Cuno said to Rotri.

"That will likely kill the horses and then we won't have horses *or* a guide," Rotri said.

Eirian waited while they argued it out. The thought of being on foot in these mountains with baying hounds behind her was terrifying, but her horse was already stumbling with exhaustion and if they pushed them beyond their strength, Rotri was right, it would likely kill them.

They dismounted reluctantly and Cuno and Rotri took their spears. Cuno looked at the bundle of furs tied behind his saddle and shrugged. "Take these by way of thanks," he told the little dark man.

"This is a debt we pay to restore the balance," the man said. "But we will take them. Stay in the cave until someone comes for you."

Some animal had laired in the cave before them, leaving dung and bits of gnawed bone behind, but otherwise it was empty save for a cloth bag with hard flat loaves of bread and some strips of dried meat. They ate those ravenously and, shivering, crowded together for the warmth of other bodies. Cuno and Rotri put Eirian between them and covered all three with their cloaks.

Eirian found sleep slow to come despite her weariness, for the thoughts that chased themselves around her head. Faustus was at Castra Borea, where they were going, if they lived. A moth, the length of her thumbnail and the pale green of new leaves, fluttered through the cave mouth and lit for a moment on her shoulder, then was gone. She followed the shimmer of its flight into the dusk. In this light, everything looked like an omen.

No one came with the dawn, and they waited, fidgeting and anxious and hearing faint in the distance the sound of baying dogs. It was nearly dusk again when Magpie reappeared. He dropped to one knee beside them, breathing heavily, and they waited until he had caught his breath.

"We have turned them for now," he said. "They came to the Sun People's houses where you slept two nights ago and were told that no one had seen you. They didn't believe it and began searching and the headman's wife cursed them and chased them with a sickle. There was a fight, and Matauc's men were driven off, but they are circling around trying to pick up the trail again and they have at least three hunting parties behind you."

"The woman," Eirian said. "Is she unharmed?"

"I don't know," Magpie said. "Do you have the scent I gave you?"

"Yes."

"Rub it on your feet often, it will help turn the dogs away. We will go by night now."

He waited for them to ready themselves while Eirian thought of the man she had killed and the one lying by the gate, and the other one very likely dead from the slingstone, and now, please the Goddess, not the farmwife who had been kind to her. When they left the cave, the patches of thawed ground that dotted the snow looked black as blood in the moonlight.

XII. THE HUNT

Matauc's face was furious, his eyes narrowed at Piran. "And why did you not come to me as soon as you knew?"

"For the reason that you were soaked in funeral mead." Piran glared back at him.

Both were in foul moods. Matauc's band had been chased by an old woman with a sickle and Piran's led in circles by some enchantment that masked their prey's scent and took them into a bog. Now they were tired and filthy and waiting for the dogs to pick up the trail again.

"Drunk or sober I can kill a spy," Matauc said.

Idgual, listening to them quarrel, doubted it. They had decided to wait for the morning when it had become clear that Matauc was unlikely to retain anything said to him, or worse, would get it wrong.

"The filthy little beast warned them," Piran said.

"Now they will go to the Roman commander," Matauc said, "if we do not catch them."

"That will endanger my people, not yours," Piran said. "Yours are safe enough here in the north."

"That was not what you said when you argued for war," Matauc said. "You said that the Romans would come ever farther north."

"And so they will," Piran said. "Unless we stop them. Two spies one way or the other won't change that."

"It will give them warning," Matauc growled. "Also I want them dead."

"For making a fool of you." Piran nodded. "Yes, I don't blame you."

"I am not the only fool," Matauc growled. "You are less clever than you think."

Idgual remembered the torque that Piran had sold to Rotri in Lyn Emrys. It seemed to him that Rotri and his partner likely knew a great deal more than the count of fighting men among the Cornovii. It was probably best not to say that now.

Matauc and Piran glared at each other, prepared to argue over whose fault it was until the trackers should come back with word that the dogs had a trail again.

This time Eirian could hear them clearly. The baying echoed off the mountain pass.

Magpie had left them at dawn to sleep the daylight hours in another cave, but one of his brothers came for them at midafternoon when they heard the dogs. Eirian found it hard to tell the little dark people apart, aside from Magpie, and whether they were actual brothers or just children of the same sidhe. The people of the hills tended to count relationships differently.

"Come!" this one said urgently. "This way! We must run for a while until the others can turn them."

They followed his small dark shadow through a stand of pines and across an upland meadow, and then scrambled down a slope of jagged outcrops and loose scree that shifted underfoot and twisted ankles. Eirian could see a glint of water at the bottom. Then, ominously, the baying of the dogs came again. She closed her ears to the sound and just set herself to run as she had been told. Now two more small forms were running with them. A loose stone dislodged somewhere above them rolled past. She slipped in a patch of ice beneath a wind-bent tree that clung to the slope, and slid, scraping arms and face, before she could right herself. Small hands pulled her to her feet.

They could hear shouting now, and as they slid and scrambled to the bottom of the slope, they turned to see the hunt almost on them. The ground leveled here to the banks of a dark lake nearly encircled with trees. Cuno and Rotri pushed Eirian behind them and braced themselves, spears ready, and Eirian drew her knife.

As the hunters came nearer, one fell, tripped by the loose stone, she thought – until the low sun caught the glint of a bronze arrow tip in flight and a second man dropped. Then the rest were on them. Rotri was struggling with one of Matauc's men and Cuno had a bloody gash down his face but he had laid a deep cut in his opponent's arm. A man came at Eirian and she saw him hesitate at the realization that she was a woman. She threw her cloak at his spear and twisted it. He stumbled and she went for him with her knife as he fumbled the woolen cloak from his spear shaft. He grabbed her wrist and bent it backward and she sank her teeth in his hand. A little bronze arrow pierced his throat as he cursed her.

The dogs circled them anxiously. They were tracking dogs, not war hounds, used to bringing down four-footed game, and uncertain now of what to do. A slingstone hit one in the haunch; he yelped and they scattered. Another struck the man fighting with Rotri. None of them wore mail and it drove the wool of his shirt into torn flesh. Rotri sank his spear into the man's chest. The pursuers looked wildly around them but there was no other enemy to be seen, just the deadly little bronze arrows from nowhere and the slingstones.

"They're in the trees!" someone shouted.

The hunters began to pull back, panic-driven as a slingstone hissed overhead and another man dropped. They ran.

"This way!" Magpie appeared and beckoned them on. "My brothers will hound these away from here, but there are more of them hunting and you must run. They are too many for us to fight."

They ran, gasping for breath, following Magpie's shadow through the trees. They could see no trail but he went surefooted, hesitating only briefly as he chose their direction. He might have been the bird of his naming, only a dark flicker of wings in the trees or a shadow over the wet moorland. Eventually they halted where he told them to, another cave, stone floored and smelling like a badger's sett although it appeared empty. Water flowed in a small trickle through rocks and unfurling bracken nearby and Eirian looked at it longingly.

"We can take you no farther," Magpie said. "South of here we do not know the land."

"Are there other houses of your people who would guide us?" Eirian asked. Cuno and Rotri had traded among the coastal villages the past year but those doors might be barred to them now. Inland they would be less sure of their way.

Magpie looked dubious. "That is a matter for the Old Ones, who speak privately to each other. I don't think so."

"Your kind helped Calgacos to fight Rome," Cuno said, washing the gash in his cheek with water from the stream and a piece torn from his undertunic, one of the few even marginally clean pieces of cloth they possessed. "Why give us aid now?"

"I have told you, to restore the balance that I overset. Also because we can see that Rome's hand is loosening here in the north. That is part of the balance as well. It does not serve my kin when either Rome or the Sun People have too much power. When they do, they stop looking to fight each other, and come hunting us."

Rotri laughed. "There is diplomacy in a nutshell."

Cuno said, "Very well. We thank you for the aid you have given."

"You are perhaps three days yet from the mouth of the Great Firth," Magpie said. "Lair here for tonight while we turn them west. You are out of Cornovii lands now but that may not matter much. The other tribes west of the Great Firth have no reason to aid you and perhaps many to please the chieftain of the Cornovii. Keep your feet smeared with the salve I gave you and cross water whenever you can. From here, if you follow water it will lead you south."

He left them with a bag of bread and dried meat and they shared it in the falling dark.

"That was very close," Rotri said finally.

"It was," Eirian said.

Rotri hesitated. He looked at Eirian. "They would have taken *you* alive, I think, if they could. If they catch us, if it comes to it, would you wish me to…" He trailed off, watching for her reaction.

"Would I wish you to kill me to keep me from them?" Eirian asked bluntly.

"Some women would."

Eirian snorted. "Prefer death to rape? Only because some man told them they had no value otherwise. If you come near me, Rotri, I will cut your balls off and save the Cornovii the trouble."

Cuno laughed. "Noted. You were taught to fight, were you not?"

"All our girls are taught, along with the boys," she said. "Is it not the same with yours?"

Rotri shook his head. "Roman women are somewhat different."

"Are you actually Roman?" Eirian asked him.

"Half-Roman," Cuno said. "Native born of British mothers. Among Romans it's the father's status that matters as long as the mother's not a slave. Yes, we are Roman."

Faustus's mother had been a slave, she remembered, and his father had freed her before they married. No doubt that was why. Eirian stood. "It is dark now. I am going to risk a wash in the stream there. I itch everywhere. Stand guard for me and then I will do the same for you."

She didn't wait to see what they would do, just went outside and stripped off her clothing, spreading it on a gorse bush to keep it off the wet ground. The water was icy and she shivered as she splashed it over herself, washing away as much of the trail grime as possible and blessing the Mother that she hadn't begun to bleed yet. Another ten-day with luck, enough to get them somewhere before she gave the dogs another scent to track.

Cuno and Rotri, she noted, stood sentinel with their backs politely turned, but at this point she didn't care. There were far more uncomfortable things than being watched at a bath. She thought about Rotri's question and what it implied of Roman women, although Faustus had told her that when a Roman wished to die, they did the task themselves, women included.

She was cold to the bone when she finished, but blessedly clean. She put her filthy clothes back on because they were all she had, and took Rotri's spear to stand with an eye down the trail they had come up on, while they bathed in turns. When they had, Rotri cut a branch that suited him from the alders that grew beside the water and took it into the cave. He tore a strip from the hem of his undertunic and began to bind something to the end of it. Eirian saw that it was one of the bronze arrowheads of the dark people.

"Pulled this out of the one that nearly had you," he said when he saw Eirian watching him. He had one end of the cloth between his teeth to keep it taut and spoke through clenched jaws. "You need a better weapon than a belt knife. The blade is small but you can do some harm with it."

"Here. Let me help." She took the end of the cloth and pulled while he wrapped the other end, fixing the blade onto the shaft. The bronze was finely worked, small and razor-sharp and barbed at the base. When he had finished, she stood and hefted it, balancing it in one hand and then two. "Thank you."

"I am sorry that we pulled you into this," he said. "Valerianus spoke the truth: we had no right."

"I knew who you were," Eirian said.

"And how was that?" Cuno asked. "Since our trade is in people *not* knowing that."

"The seals told me."

"The seals can bite my arse," Cuno said. "I don't believe that."

"You came to High Isle once before. Before the war with Rome. Catumanus knew." She remembered watching their ship sail away and how they had shimmered in her vision, one layer above the other, the mustache and then the clean-shaven face, the gold torque at his neck and then the red scarf. "You tried to sell me a silver mirror. I was fourteen. And a girl," she added. "No doubt you don't remember."

"Mithras," Cuno muttered.

"Catumanus? The old priest who sent you off with us?" Rotri asked. "He knew?"

"He knew I needed to leave High Isle. That much. And yes, he knew who you were."

"Still, *we* didn't know that and we had no right."

"If we get you killed," Cuno said, "Valerianus is going to be unhappy."

"Centurion Valerianus has nothing to do with it," Eirian snapped. At least not at the moment. Eirian hefted the spear in both hands, considering it. She was very likely going to need it before she needed to worry about anything else.

—

The garrison at Castra Borea saw the beacon flowering from the watchtower on the other side of the firth at dusk, and beyond it the faint glow of another. Both towers had been built at Faustus's command, with suitable diplomatic gifts to local headmen, to watch what might be coming out of the northwest. And it looked as if something was.

Faustus ordered up the first century, which was under his direct command, with orders to keep the rest of the cohort on alert. He kissed Silvia, assured her that the barbarians were not yet at their gates, and rode out into the falling dark. The mouth of the firth was not crossable without boats and the way around it led south and then west across moorland and two river fords to swing north again on the other side. A rider from the southern watchtower met them as they marched near dawn.

"Cornovii!" he said. "And this not even their land."

"How many?" Faustus asked.

"Two dozen maybe. The north tower says they came different ways and converged just below it. They didn't attack. They are hunting something."

"Then I want whatever it is before they catch it," Faustus said. He took stock of his men. They had rested once during the night. They could go on for a while yet.

"They'll not be far," the rider said, "and whatever they are after. If they haven't caught it."

"Which way?"

"It looked as if whatever they're chasing is making for the closest crossing so likely they're headed straight for you."

"Turn back and see what you can pick up, but stay away from the Cornovii if you cross their path. It's their quarry I want."

He spread the century out with Ansgarius and two others in front, Indus and a rearguard behind. It seemed unlikely that two dozen Cornovii warriors wanted to engage with Rome, and if they did, they would have started with the watchtowers, which were garrisoned by only a handful and one scout each. But assumptions had a way of turning into pit traps under unwary boots and he ordered the century to keep their helmets on and their weapons to hand.

On the other side of the moorland a small protected offshoot of the Great Firth waters ended at a stony shoreline and mud flats where herons were prospecting. The humped shape of a crannog house rose out of the water and a handful of native huts were strung along the shore. The land was marshy, studded with tangled clumps of stunted trees before meadow gave way to higher ground and thick stands of pine. The column was well into the cover of the pines when they heard shouting and baying dogs. The forest shadows became moving figures among the trees. Faustus saw their quarry then, fleeing ahead of the hunters and looking desperately for some place to make a stand.

—

Eirian braced herself with her back to a tree, Cuno and Rotri beside her. They had seen the beacons flare up the evening before when the hunt on their trail had brought itself to the watchtower's notice. Castra Borea's garrison would answer; the question had been how soon, and how long they could hold off the pursuers they could no longer outrun. They had slipped the hunters yesterday, smearing themselves with the last of Magpie's unguent, and crossing and recrossing the small rivers that laced the countryside. But this morning the dogs had found the scent again, and the scattered bands of hunters had converged on it.

The hunters were beyond caution now. They were four-and-twenty to three, and Matauc had likely promised gold to the man who killed any of them. Matauc would be furious that they had come so far out of his own lands, and needing to bribe and explain and apologize to the local chiefs as they tramped through their hunting runs. Their numbers made them reckless, and their quarry set themselves to make use of that, with little other advantage than a grim determination to take as many of Matauc's men with them as they could.

Cuno let the first of them rush him, ducked past a furious thrust and put his own spear in the man's chest. He put his foot to him to pull it out while Rotri and Eirian held off the next.

Eirian turned the first blow with her spear shaft and thrust the little bronze blade up the man's arm, cutting a bleeding channel. Her breath was coming in gasps now – they had been running all morning – and when she saw the glint of armor in the trees below them she thought at first that her vision was going. The man came at her again, blood sheeting down his arm, cursing her, before Rotri knocked the spear from his blood-slicked grip. Eirian put her small spearpoint through his throat.

There were more of them, far too many more. A Cornovii warrior charged her as she bent to pick up the dead man's fallen spear. She ducked, letting his charge take him over her, and then rose and drove the bloody spear at his back. It sank in and slipped from her grip. She pulled it out and wiped the shaft on her breeches and stood, back to a broad tree and spear leveled at the next man to come. Rotri was beside her and Cuno on her other side as the Cornovii men pressed them, blocked from their backs by the tree, tangling in each other's way. She saw the glint of sun on armor again and heard the sound of a horn and she shouted furiously at their pursuers to run before Rome put them on crosses.

Another of Matauc's men came at Cuno and this time the blow went true. Eirian felt him drop at her side. She drove her own spear into his attacker's ribs and braced for the next but no other came. The column had caught up with the battle.

-

"Get them to the rear!" Faustus shouted to Indus as he and Ansgarius took the column up and around the besieged figures, beating back the attackers who hurled themselves howling at the Roman patrol. Then he caught a glimpse of her face and heard himself shouting, "Get them out! Get them out! *Get them out!*"

The patrol encircled the Cornovii, spears ready and shields up, while Indus and five others pulled their quarry out of the trees. They sent a flight of throwing spears into the bunched enemy and followed with the wicked Roman short sword that was designed for close quarters. Faustus rode into the fray, heart pounding, using his height to give him an advantage against men on foot, and Arion's hooves to trample any who went down before they could rise again. A Cornovii warrior aimed his spear at Arion instead. Arion, an experienced troop horse, slid sideways like a crab while Faustus brought his sword down on the man's shoulder.

The Cornovii fought viciously but they were badly outnumbered and armed for hunting rather than battle. Matauc drove them on into the Roman ranks with a dogged fury until half his men were down. Only then did he call them off.

"After them?" Ansgarius asked, sheathing a bloody sword as they pulled back into the trees.

Faustus considered that. Despite the odds, he had lost two men. And there was Eirian. He would have willingly killed them all. But, "No. I doubt there are any more behind them, and we are in treaty-bound territory. I can't go after them on friendly land if we want to keep it that way. Let them limp back to the north."

He turned to the Cornovii's quarry. Eirian knelt over Cuno's still form while the century's field medic shook his head. Rotri knelt beside them, a hand on her shoulder, head bowed. *Eirian.* She was dressed in tattered breeches and a shirt with one sleeve torn out, her hair filthy and matted with leaves, face streaked with tears and dirt. He blinked, half-expecting her to disappear again, a vision only called up by longing, but she didn't. She raised her head and met his eyes but she didn't speak. He swallowed and went to kneel beside Cuno's body.

"Decius Cuno, prefect of the ala Petriana, who served Rome on her borders, may the Manes receive you kindly," he whispered to him.

"So that's who you were." Eirian put her fingers to her lips and then to Cuno's still chest.

–

Before they moved out, Faustus had Rotri's preliminary report as to what was brewing in Cornovii land, and the satisfaction of knowing he had been right about the watchtowers. Neither was of particular comfort, but it was all the knowledge likely to be gleaned from the retreating hunters if they had chased them down, although he swore when Rotri said Matauc and Piran had been with them. Rotri was limping on blistered feet from wet boots that had stiffened as they dried. Faustus pulled off his own and traded with him.

And there was Eirian. He put her up on Arion. She didn't protest, only thanked him wearily. There were things to be said between them but he didn't know how to begin.

They made their way home by the way they had come and across the water meadows, carrying their dead. When they stopped to rest they ditched the small camp carefully, but no further attacks came. There were seals in the little firth. Faustus saw their dark shapes on the rocks and in the waters near the shore and heard their voices in the dusk that was falling again. He found Eirian sitting by a fire, drying wet hair.

"Have you been out to visit the seals?" he asked.

"I have been to wash," she said. "Not so far out as that. Did you think I would swim away?"

"I didn't know," he said honestly. "I thought you might."

"I don't know where to swim to now." He wanted desperately to say, *To me*. "Now that Cuno is dead. And Rotri won't be able to spy for you anymore."

"Was Cuno—?" He felt a sharp stab of jealousy and looked away so she wouldn't see it.

"Not like that, no."

He was still angry with them for putting her in danger, but more for the question of whether all he had thought of the harm in dispossessing her of home had been wrong after all. How big a fool had he been, and how great was the barrier that he had put between them?

–

At Castra Borea, they burned Cuno's body in a military service with the other two dead and gave Cuno's ashes to Rotri to take to his people. Rotri produced a more detailed report and a list of items abandoned in their flight because under any circumstances the army demanded lists.

Faustus gave Eirian the oldest of Silvia's few gowns. "Breeches are all very well for the trail," he said bluntly as he handed them to her, "but my men will misunderstand and I don't want to punish someone for being a fool after the fact, for either of your sakes."

"Understood. Thank your sister for me."

By unspoken mutual consent they waited until the next day to talk further. Eirian bathed and put Silvia's clothes on gratefully. Paullus brought her supper to the sleeping chamber that Faustus had hastily vacated in the new Praetorium, and Pandora sat on her feet while she ate it. Silvia, at dinner with Faustus, clearly had questions which Faustus clearly was not going to answer.

Spring made a brief appearance in the morning, with a day startling enough to make Faustus thoroughly mistrust it. Any bare patch of ground suddenly sprouted dandelions and the sky cleared to the color of a starling's egg. He had insisted that Eirian let Lascius clean and treat the cuts and abrasions acquired in their flight, and after morning prayers at the standards, he found her sitting in the sunlight in the hospital garden, watching a crow hopping along the path. The crow flew up indignantly at his arrival, and he sat down on the bench beside her. They were silent for a while.

Finally he asked her, "Was it over me that you left High Isle?" That had been his fear since Cuno and Rotri had first spoken of her, that her people had driven her out because of him.

"No," she said gently. "I found I had no place there, and if that was because of you it was only for your showing me how much more there was of the world."

"So I made your home unlivable." Faustus watched the crow returning cautiously, one eye cocked to them, one on possible things to eat in the herb beds.

"Faustus, it was unlivable before." Eirian sounded exasperated now. "I had no place there, just village chatter to follow me about and people looking sideways at my hands and my brothers making jokes. Catumanus said as much, when Cuno and Rotri came."

"Catumanus sent you to follow a pair of border wolves? And don't tell me he didn't know."

"He knew. *I* knew for that matter."

"You are lucky to be alive." Faustus too sounded exasperated. He turned to look at her directly. "This was something you could do, but not come away with me?"

"You didn't ask me."

"I thought it would be cruel, to take you from your home. And try to make a Roman of you. Like trying to put a bridle on a deer."

Eirian nodded. "That may be true."

"Would you have come?"

"I don't know."

"What will you do now? Rotri will go back to his old posting because he is known now."

"He won't like that," she said, not answering his question.

"He serves Rome," Faustus said.

She nodded.

"You could stay here," Faustus said. "For a while. While you decide what to do. My sister would like having another woman for company."

Eirian raised both eyebrows. "How certain are you of that?"

"Not very, actually," Faustus said. "But I don't care." He still thought, as he had in the Orcades, that he couldn't keep her, but he would take what he could. He could not bring himself to turn from her when she was here in the flesh and not merely a longing that came when he heard seals crying in the firth.

–

Eirian agreed because she had not thought past getting out of Cornovii lands alive. And after two years on the road with Cuno and Rotri, the bedchamber in the Praetorium was close to luxury. Native rugs covered a stone floor that felt warm beneath her feet, and the bed had a solid wooden frame and a mattress stuffed with wool and aromatics. On one wall was an unfinished painting of a sea beast with a coiled tail. Faustus's sister had started to paint it, he said, but she had let the plaster dry before she finished it. Faustus had told her that Roman buildings all had paintings on their walls, of gardens and rivers and fanciful animals, gods and legends. Eirian studied the sea beast with interest, seeing how the unfinished tail should be filled in, and the missing claws on its forelegs. Catumanus said that to draw a thing would call it, but the Romans didn't appear worried about that. Their roads and milestones and armored columns marched obliviously through the river of the invisible that flowed around Eirian's world, a tide of gods and spirits that her people navigated as they would a boat on the firth. The Romans had gods – the garrison prayed to them every morning and evening at the cohort standards, and a niche in the house held a trio of silver figures particular to Faustus's family

– but if you sacrificed to them properly, Faustus said, they left you alone.

She would see what Rotri thought, perhaps.

–

Rotri's metamorphosis was startling. Centurion Aurelius Rotri of the Twentieth Legion Valeria Victrix was bare-faced now, his long mustache vanished, his hair cut to military length. Scavenged kit from the Castra Borea storehouse was not quite regulation to his legion but marked him clearly as a man of the Eagles.

Eirian blinked at his transformation and he laughed.

"You look very fine yourself," he said, observing her in Silvia's gown. "I am glad we didn't get you killed."

They were both silent for a moment, mourning Cuno.

"You'll go south now?" Eirian asked. She knew there was no question of her going with him.

"I will. I'll take Cuno's ashes to his brother and then I have a bit of leave coming. I haven't seen my mother in five years. She won't forgive me if I don't go home."

Eirian hesitated. "You said she was British…" She let it slide into a half question. No doubt he knew what she was trying to ask.

"Not so much now," Rotri said. "Running water has brought many a woman around to Roman ways."

"In the *house*?" Eirian tried to imagine that.

"In the southern cities, yes, for those with the money. And in the big forts. My father was posted to the Twentieth before he retired, and my mother took a fancy to him, he being much better looking than myself. Her father, my grandfather, was old-fashioned and against it to start, but he came around eventually. She followed the column for ten years, to big forts and little border camps, and took us with her. It isn't a comfortable life, mind you, and only officers are allowed wives in camp. Other women have to trail along behind the baggage and they're pretty much on their own to keep up. It's discouraged because they're a liability."

"I thought the men weren't permitted to marry," Eirian said. Faustus had told her most married only on retirement.

"Not officially," Rotri said. "Anyone under decurion or centurion rank can't marry until their enlistment ends. They do it anyway though, unofficially, because they can register the marriage and legitimate the children when they retire. But if they're killed before that, it's hard on the woman. Officers now, they can marry, and drag the poor woman about with them if she'll stand for it."

Eirian turned that over in her head afterward and wondered what Faustus thought about it. There was no telling. Sometimes he looked at her with a longing she could feel on her skin, and sometimes he looked as if he expected her to conjure a sealskin from the water and put it on. She didn't know how to tell him what she wanted because she didn't know.

–

Faustus for his part felt as if he had fallen into the sort of tale his old nurse used to tell, the gist of which was always that magic didn't last. As if to point that moral up, the sun disappeared, the dandelions sank into the mud, and Castra Borea was shrouded with rain again and a general aura of misery. The makeshift bed in the storeroom gave him a backache.

Silvia made cautious overtures to Eirian, but only of necessity, and appeared to have lost interest in finishing the chamber wall. She pottered dolefully in the hospital garden and spoke sadly of her lost garden in Narbo Martius where she used to sit at twilight and watch the little bats and barn swallows flit out to feed. She said so every time she saw a bat until Faustus wanted to strangle her.

The scouts reported that the Cornovii intruders had fled north to their own lands and that it looked as if Piran had slunk south to his, where no doubt he would report the identities of the pair of traders who had been run free in Caledone holds for five years, and now the Caledones would trust no one.

Pandora, who had grown white about the muzzle, went into the garden one day after a long hunt and lay down and left them, and Paullus wept over her body with an intensity that unnerved Faustus. She was an old dog, and a big one, he reminded Paullus, and big dogs lived shorter lives, but Paullus was not comforted.

The hospital was crowded with men sniffling with coryza and hacking with lung sickness. Mushrooms grew out of the floor in the Principia. Paullus set three hares on a spit in the Praetorium kitchen and forgot them, nearly setting fire to the house.

The morning after that, Faustus sent Indus to the commander of the next fort to the south, to whom Paullus had sold one of Pandora's sons, to buy him back for three times the price and a certain amount of pulling rank. He was relieved that night to see the dog curled beside Paullus on his mattress, woolen blankets pulled over them both.

"That was kind of you," Eirian said when she saw them asleep in the alcove outside the bedchamber door. She was wrapped in a woolen cloak, and a gown of her own, bought in the village from a weaver with her pay from Rotri. She hadn't let Faustus buy her anything.

"Paullus needs dogs," Faustus said. "More than people."

Eirian smiled. "I remember." The tallow dip in her hand encircled them in its flickering light, a little bubble of gold in the dark house.

Remember. The word whispered in his ear. *Remember the sea cave on High Isle, and the new grass on the little islands in the spring, and the seals' voices in the water. Remember…*

"I remember more than that," he said, half choking on the words that tumbled so quickly out of his mouth unbidden.

"Did you think to forget?" she asked him.

"I thought it wouldn't hurt so," he said honestly.

"So did I," she murmured. "And the greater fools we proved ourselves maybe."

"What now?"

She smiled slowly. "Just now, at this moment?" She blew out the tallow dip, leaving them in the whispering darkness.

He held out his hands.

Paullus and the dog twitched as they passed by them and closed the chamber door, but a snore from beyond it said that they had gone to sleep again. There was no lamp lit, only the faint barred light of a spring moon through the shutters that covered the window. He took the cloak from her shoulders and laid his belt and boots aside, pulling his uniform tunic over his head. He put his hands on her hips and she nodded and he lifted the gown over her head, and then her undershift. The clan marks on her breasts and upper arms made dark patterns against moonlit skin. The newly built Praetorium had a hypocaust beneath its stone floors for heat, privilege of the commander, but it was cold anyway, and he pulled the furs and blankets back from the bed and they lay down on it.

She felt warm and solid in his arms, and achingly familiar, a slim and muscular body in place of the ephemeral one that had visited his dreams since leaving High Isle. Her fingers laced with his and he remembered the talk of seal children with webbed hands. Village gossip that had spoiled her childhood and her place in the village, she had said. *A selkie will break your heart*, Tuathal had said, laughing, when Faustus was posted to the Orcades. Faustus slid his other hand between her legs and kissed her. That didn't matter now, although it might matter later.

XIII. CERIDWEN IN EBURACUM

SUMMER

Faustus felt as if he was watching a leaking pool drain out through some crack in the bottom. The last of the Second Adiutrix was gone from Britain and a steady trickle of auxiliaries began to follow them. The cohorts and cavalry alae that lost men to retirement or skirmishes or the ubiquitous winter lung ailments found that they were not replaced. The First Batavians, supposedly a cohort of eight hundred, actually numbered six hundred and thirty-eight fit for duty, with three more still in hospital recovering from the encounter with the Cornovii and sixteen more with inflammation of the eyes, a perpetual ailment the surgeon blamed on the bath water.

Faustus ordered the strength of the flow from river to bath and out again increased. He put in for a hundred new recruits, hoping for fifty, and got none. He could feel the unrest that had simmered to a boil in the Cornovii lands filtering down through the glens toward the Great Firth, borne on streams that grew ever more swollen with constant rain. The Cornovii were too far to the northwest for Faustus to have any hope of dealing with them, other than to keep them from crossing the firth, but the unease grew like the mushrooms that invaded every damp corner of Castra Borea, and it took hold among the northernmost of the Caledone clans.

In the meantime there was Eirian. Eirian in the Orcades had been a dream of sorts, made half of seawater and half of magic, but the woman in his courtyard helping Gwladus make lye for washing, or cajoling Silvia to mix fresh plaster and finish the painting on her wall was something else: solid in his arms when she came to his bed in the chamber he had gratefully moved back into, cross in the morning before her breakfast, amused by the dog's habit of stealing her boots. Her command of Latin was improving daily since Silvia had acquired only a smattering of British, and that reluctantly. Nothing was settled between them. If she left, her face would be known at Lyn Emrys as well as other Caledone holds. It wasn't right to use that to keep her with him. It might be that he could speak to Emrys about it, but that would require care. And he didn't know what she actually wanted because he was afraid to ask.

—

Faustus met with Emrys again at Lughnasa Fair, and this time he took neither Silvia nor Eirian.

Emrys was not inclined toward diplomacy. "I have no power over the Cornovii," he said when Faustus edged toward the subject. "Rome has seen to that." It was raining again and he was cloaked in fur-lined checkered wool. His scarred face under the hood looked like a wolf's, or a mountain cat's. Something dangerous.

"No power over your own clans either?" Faustus inquired. "The ones who have been raiding our outposts since spring?"

"I have little power to stop those either," Emrys said, "although that is not of my ordering. When Rome took my sword from my hand, Rome stripped me of authority over the clans." He looked Faustus up and down, taking in the scarlet military cloak over a mail hauberk strung with his awards, the horsetail helmet and polished greaves, and laughed suddenly. "We are much alike, you and I. You hope to hold on until Rome sends you reinforcements. I hope to outwait you until Rome's grasp slips from our land."

Faustus nodded toward his escort, who stood twenty paces away leaning on their green and gold shields. Their fox-fur caps sat jauntily atop their helmets despite the rain, and even at rest they gripped their spears with purpose. "Rome's grasp does not slip," he said, although he knew he was lying.

Emrys said, "If your spies have told you that, they are wrong."

"Spies?" Faustus inquired. "The traders that Piran, who is of your clans, tried to kill?"

"The little dark ones knew them for what they were," Emrys said.

Now Faustus laughed. "And then helped them to get away. To restore the balance, they said. I would not rely on the little dark ones."

"Piran is Rhion's man. And the woman is still in your fort," Emrys said.

Faustus said, "She knew nothing of their business. She is a pilot and came with them from the Orcades." There was little point in denying the border wolves' purpose but also little gain in admitting it outright.

"She came with them to my hold."

"And did you no harm."

They stared at each other. Finally, Emrys said, "She is known to us so her usefulness is gone. Keep her if you will."

"Will you give that order? Your authority is greater than you claim."

"When our women went into the chariot line, they risked death and many of them found it. Your woman has done the same – why should her risk be different?"

"Because the war is over," Faustus said. "Also she is not my woman."

"Nothing is over, Prefect. It isn't going to be over. Remember that." He walked away to the sacred stone where the priests, hooded against the falling rain, were making ready the sacrifice to Lugh Brightspear, Lord of the Sun. The sun itself was veiled behind gray cloud and a wall of water.

–

It kept raining. A small river flowed down the alley between the fort gates and the Castra Borea bath, the drain down its middle inadequate for the downpour. Eirian splashed through it and tried to keep her boots from the deepest of the muddy water. Silvia clutched her cloak around her and sniffled dolefully, driven by the necessity to bathe during the limited hours allotted them. Lucius hopped behind them, splattering up a satisfactory spray of mud with every hop, followed by Paullus with a basket of bath oil and towels. The half-grown dog, now named Argos, trotted at his heels.

At the bath, Paullus drove the stragglers out and stationed himself at the outer door. "You know it's the ladies' hour – Prefect's orders."

"Lucius, go to Paullus and have him wipe your feet," Silvia said. "There isn't enough bath oil in the world to take that mud off." She inspected the water in the warm pool. Oil lingered on the surface no matter how much scraping of the skin one did before climbing in, and soldiers were, in Silvia's opinion, slapdash about it. She stripped off her gown and undershift and rubbed herself with bath oil from a pottery flask, then passed it to Eirian. Silvia scraped her skin clean with a strigil and set to work on Lucius while he bounced impatiently on the lip of the pool.

Eirian oiled and scraped her own skin, a process new to her but on the whole pleasant. She found the warm pool a luxury despite possible contaminants, although she was careful to do as the fort surgeon said and keep her eyes out of the water. She slid in, soaking up the heat while the cold rain splattered on the roof. She knotted her trailing hair and repinned it. "Faustus says that some houses in the south have their own baths," she said to Silvia. Her brothers had steadfastly refused to believe that.

"Our house had one," Lucius volunteered, standing on one foot like a heron. "In Narbo Martius. And the public bath in the city had *three* pools *and* a steam room."

"That sounds very fine," Eirian said.

"It is nothing like the ones in Rome, of course," Silvia said. "Lucius, be still!"

"Have you been to Rome?" Eirian asked. Faustus had done his training there and had tried to describe it to her. It had sounded like something out of legend.

"Once," Silvia said. She inspected Lucius. "You're done. Get in the water. And don't jump in!" She followed him into the pool. "My father took us to see Titus triumph after he took Jerusalem. And after I was married my husband took me to Puteoli on the Bay of Neapolis. Puteoli is only respectable in the daytime, but we stayed in a beautiful villa at Baiae nearby. That was a lovely trip." She paused and added sadly, "Just after we were married."

"I am sorry for your loss," Eirian said.

"Thank you." Silvia hesitated. "My husband wasn't good with money, I'm afraid. So here we are with my brother."

"He had race ponies," Lucius confided.

"*Lucius!*"

Lucius transferred his attention to Eirian. "Gwladus says you came with that man who is really a spy for the army, but you didn't know it."

"Gwladus doesn't know as much as she thinks she does," Eirian said.

"Are you going to stay with my uncle?"

"Lucius!" Silvia said again, but less forcefully. No doubt she wanted to know too.

"I don't know." Eirian said. "We don't know."

They soaked, reluctant to go back out in the rain, until Paullus called that time was running out. Eirian dragged herself regretfully from the water while Silvia took Lucius into the cold pool for their health. They emerged quickly, teeth chattering, to dry off and dress while a century of impatient soldiers grumbled outside.

–

Faustus had ridden in while they were at the bath and was warming his hands at a brazier when Paullus escorted the prefect's household back to the Praetorium. His wet hauberk lay in a heap on the floor where he had shed it, along with his greaves and a

229

helmet whose sopping feathers drooped dispiritedly. It had rained for the entire return journey. "Hypocaust's out," he muttered and Paullus went to see to stoking the fire.

"Jupiter Pluvius has turned on the tap and forgot to turn it off," Faustus said gloomily. "Maybe he'll notice when the water gets up to Olympus."

Silvia took Lucius off to their chamber to wrestle with his Greek letters and Faustus said to Eirian, "I got Emrys to agree that you were harmless and to tell his clan so. I don't know that I trust them, though."

Eirian shed her wet cloak. She hung it on a hook by the door and paused, cocking her head at the far wall where the little household gods stood in their niche. "Faustus, is there something in that corner?"

Faustus snapped his head around. "What do you see?"

"I don't know," Eirian said. "I thought I did."

Faustus glared at empty space to the left of the gods' niche. "It's my father," he said, deciding that he might as well let her think he was mad. That would simplify her decision.

Eirian narrowed her eyes as if she was trying to bring something into focus.

"Silvia doesn't see him," Faustus said. "I'm not sure whether Paullus does, he won't quite say. He's been trailing around after me since I went against his orders and sold the farm in Gaul. I don't know what he wants."

"I don't expect he does either," Eirian said. "Catumanus says that people who come back often don't know why."

"He's angry that no one did what he told them to."

"If people came back only over that they would be so thick in the air you couldn't move," Eirian said. "He needs something, I expect."

"I didn't mean to tell you about him," Faustus said. "Just another reason to entice you to stay – ghosts in the house."

"He's your ghost," Eirian said practically. "I don't think he means for me to see him."

230

"Gwladus thinks he's a cobweb and goes after him with a broom sometimes." Faustus looked at her desperately. "If you want to go back to the islands, I'll pay your passage. Or give you an escort south if you want to go there, and bypass Emrys's people. The army owes you." It felt like pressing on a half-healed wound to see if he could make it worse.

"Do you want me to?" she asked.

"I— No."

"Then?"

"If you stay with me, you'll be alone while I'm gone to wherever the army sends me for the next fifteen years, or you'll have to follow the column and it's not an easy life. How can I ask either thing of you?"

"What about your sister?"

"She didn't have a choice. Also," he muttered, "the moment I am posted somewhere possible I intend to find her a husband."

Eirian started to laugh. "I hope you aren't planning the same for me."

"It might be better," he said morosely.

"Stop that. You might consider that I followed Cuno and Rotri for two years on the road and did not die of it."

"Then you will stay?" He wanted her to so much it was nearly unbearable.

She put her hands in his. They were icy. He pulled her into his arms and she whispered, "I will stay. And we will see whether we wear on each other. I would have you free to change your mind, Faustus."

"And I you." The worry that if he got her with child it would force the matter was growing greater. She had told him she knew what was safe and he had seen her consult a little tally stick with notches in it, but nothing was certain.

He would write to Constantia, he thought. The idea of asking Constantia for advice seemed mad in itself, but Constantia had followed the column and so had her mother.

Constantia squinted at the wooden tablet. The afternoon sun slanted through the open shutters of the clinic dispensary. "He's never thought I had good sense but he's desperate enough to ask me for advice. That seems to be the gist of it. His handwriting is atrocious."

Silus paused over the brazier where he was simmering dock leaves in a pot. "What does he want advice on?"

"That girl he found in the Orcades. Apparently she has reappeared traveling with a pair of border wolves. He isn't entirely clear about it."

Silus limped across the room to peer over her shoulder. He smelled of the dock leaves and marsh mallow and she breathed deeply because it was the only intimacy allowed them.

"What will you tell him?"

"That he's an idiot," she said. She sighed and stood. "I need to take Diulius some supper. Send for me if you need me."

The slave who served as cook and housekeeper had a pot of stew on the stove. She dipped out a bowlful. "Is he no better?" She frowned, worried. Heledd had been in Diulius's household far longer than his new wife and felt that she knew a thing or two.

"Some days he's stronger, and then the next..." Constantia sniffed the stew. "This smells restorative."

"It's bound to do him good. I put thyme and parsley in and garlic and the last of the lamb. You take him some hot wine with it."

"I will, Heledd. Thank you."

Heledd paused, the wine cup in her hand. "He isn't a fool, you know."

"No. And neither am I."

"You're loyal, I'll give you that."

Constantia took the bowl and cup. "So are you, which is the reason I am going to excuse this conversation, but I do not intend to have it repeated." She left Heledd to possibly rethink things while she took Diulius his supper.

"Heledd says this will revive you," she told Diulius, offering him a spoonful. Diulius propped himself up on his elbows in the bed. He was thinner even than that morning, she thought. The bones of his skull looked very near the skin.

"Heledd is a fussy hen. I always expect her to be wearing feathers."

"She loves you." Constantia fed him another spoonful.

"Here. I can manage that myself." Diulius took the bowl from her. "She was ill-used in the house I bought her from. That was years ago, but she has seen me as her savior. I have told her that when I'm gone she will be taken care of, but I think she's afraid."

"You've made rather a habit of rescuing women," Constantia said.

Diulius smiled. "I regard it as a hobby."

"How are you this afternoon, really?"

"I hurt. Bring me some poppy in wine when I've finished this; I want to sleep. Is the clinic full up today?"

"Two cases of lung congestion, a finger sliced nearly through by a cook who filched his master's wine while chopping greens, and the potter's wife for a dose of herbs to regulate her cycle. She's afraid to go to the midwife because the midwife is her husband's sister."

Diulius sighed. "No one knows more secrets than a physician."

Heledd came to the door. "I've come to empty the pot and change his tunic. You're wanted in the surgery," she said to Constantia.

"Very well. Sit with him while he eats then."

He was worse, she thought as she went out into the colonnade and across the garden to the surgery and dispensary. The pain in his back was growing and he was losing weight steadily. He was old and it could be simple degeneration of the spine, or something more serious. Constantia and Diulius both were beginning to suspect the latter. He had had a long life, and it was clear that it was ending. She halted outside the clinic. *Aesculapius send him a quiet death.*

Constantia went in through the back door of the dispensary and found a girl of about fifteen in the clinic vestibule with a younger one beside her, holding her hand. A trio of soldiers from the fort stood at attention in the portico that shaded the street entrance. A surgeon from the Ninth Legion hospital was conferring with Silus.

Silus stepped away to speak quietly to Constantia. "He's brought us a patient. Under protest, I gather. His protest, not the patient's. She's one of the Caledone hostages, they both are, I think, and she's insisted on coming to see a woman. She won't let the military surgeons get near her and the governor wants her seen to for whatever it is. Female trouble, I expect."

Constantia looked at the fort surgeon, a bull-necked young man with a shock of straw-colored hair and an exasperated look. She didn't blame the girls. "Which of you is the patient?" she asked the two.

"She is," the older one said. "This is Tegan. And I am Ceridwen, daughter of Calgacos."

Constantia smiled. The child was plainly pulling rank. She had undoubtedly been more than a match for the governor and his surgeons. They were both blond and fair, tall like most of the Caledones. They wore Roman clothing: linen undergowns, fine woolen tunics and mantles, and leather shoes in the latest design to come to the provinces from Rome. Ceridwen's hair was fashionably curled and arranged in an elaborate beribboned knot at the back of her head, and there were amber drops in her ears. Her Latin had the accent of an educated tutor.

"Go and take Diulius some poppy in wine," she said quietly to Silus. And to the fort surgeon, "You wait here." She took Tegan's hand. "We will go in another room and talk about what troubles you. Would you like Ceridwen to come with you?"

Tegan nodded.

In the consulting room, Constantia sat her on a stool and brought another for Ceridwen. "Now then. Would it be more comfortable if we spoke your own language?"

234

Tegan nodded again. She looked miserable.

"She's afraid," Ceridwen said. "A soldier attacked her. His centurion pulled him off. I want to be sure she isn't hurt."

"Oh, poor child." Constantia put her hand on Tegan's shoulder and then took it away when the girl flinched.

"The man was drunk," Ceridwen said grimly, "or he wouldn't have been so foolish. He's been punished. I expect he'll live, but maybe not."

Punishment for assaulting a ward of the governor would be draconian. He had probably been beaten nearly to death.

"Has she seen the midwife?"

"I wouldn't let them call her," Ceridwen said. "I've heard the woman and she's a vile old gossip. It's bad enough without the whole town knowing, *and* the fort, and no doubt turning the tale sideways."

Constantia remembered her patient of that morning. She looked to Tegan. "Have you started your courses?"

Tegan shook her head.

"No," Ceridwen said.

That was a relief. "Did he...? I mean, how far—?"

"He had her underthings off," Ceridwen said. "She's not sure. She's only twelve." Ceridwen was furious. It radiated from her like heat shimmer over a hot stove. Constantia wondered what the governor's intentions were for her. Agricola had said he would raise them to be Romans. It seemed unlikely that Ceridwen was going to be a malleable woman, however Roman she grew.

"It hurts," Tegan said.

"Let me have a look, child."

Reluctantly Tegan let Constantia examine her. She found abraded skin but no torn flesh. There were bruises on the child's wrists and thighs. Constantia brought a stoppered jar of dried plantain from the dispensary. "Steep this in water and use it as a wash. It will soothe the sore spots."

"They let me watch him being beaten," Tegan whispered. "It didn't help."

"No, I don't imagine it did."

"It would have helped me," Ceridwen said frankly. "But we are different."

Calgacos's daughter indeed. "If it doesn't feel better in a day or two," Constantia told Tegan, "come see me again and I will give you something else."

Tegan nodded.

"Come anyway if you just want to talk," Constantia added. "Sometimes that does help."

"Governor Lucullus will want to know how she is," Ceridwen said. "We are valuable."

"I will write him a note and send it to the fort." Along with some plain speaking and her bill, once Constantia had a grip on her temper. Only an idiot would have tried to send Tegan to an army surgeon after something like that. She thought of several other things to say besides, none of which should probably be said to the governor, so she said them to the junior surgeon waiting in the vestibule instead.

When Diulius was sleeping she settled with pen and ink to write to Faustus.

> *My dear friend Faustus,*
>
> *If you want to know what a woman is thinking, ask the woman.*
>
> *This advice is confirmed by recent actions of the governor who is as perceptive as roof tile in that respect. As a result, I have recently met Calgacos's daughter, who is growing up to be a force someone will have to reckon with. If he truly intends to marry her to some allied kinglet, I wish him well. She is not likely to be cooperative, although Agricola might perhaps have managed her.*
>
> *His successor is instead enlarging his southern villa further, importing Italian mosaic artists and all sorts of plants that will probably wither and die here. It's nice to know he is paying attention to the province.*

Diulius is failing, I fear. Silus and I do all we can, but we will lose him soon. He has been very good to me and I hope the gods receive him gently.

As for your own problem, my mother followed the army by her choice. She worried constantly of course, but she would have worried more elsewhere, if you want to run those calculations through your abacus. My mother thrived on the life and so did I. I miss it. Maybe I should have married you after all. That was a joke, don't even think it. Not every woman would, I know, but this one sounds as if she would take to it. Two years with the border wolves? Juno, what more credentials does she need?

If you haven't asked that woman what she actually wants this time, I will give up on you. How did you know she couldn't leave her people? She apparently has. Did they give her any reason to want to stay? You are an idiot.

With best wishes from your loving friend, Constantia

Oh yes, and another detachment of the Ninth just shipped out for Germany, although to be fair, I don't know what the governor could have done about that.

XIV. A FISTFUL OF HORNETS IN A BOTTLE

"Can you not bear to have peace in the land?" Fiachra gave Riderch a black look. "And a High King not inclined to tax you into beggardom, that you must poke your nose into the Romans' business?"

"And find it sliced off, like as not," Cassan said, making a half-rude gesture with his fingers.

"It is fighting season," Riderch said stubbornly. "While we sit idle and grow fat and our young men grow purposeless."

Those at the tables in the High King's new feasting hall nodded or grumbled their assent. Under his eye the warring lords of Inis Fáil had been forbidden their customary battles among themselves and now they were bored. They had come to Tara at midsummer ten days ago and would be there for another three, feasting and drinking and arguing, while their dogs mirrored them, squabbling over leavings in the rushes on the floor. Enriched by their loyalty to the High King, the lords displayed a wealth of gold jewelry and good woolens in every color of expensive dye, but mere possessions were not enough; it was the *acquisition* of wealth that mattered. The prospect of a war band to fight the Romans in Britain had the appeal of skirting the High King's restrictions while proving the independence of free men to do as they wished.

"And when you have driven the Romans out of Caledone lands – which are *my* people's lands," Dai said, "what will you do then?"

"Return with gold!" Elwyn said. He wiped his mustache on a sleeve and his hands on his breeches. "Gold and slaves."

"And that not taken entirely from the Romans," Dai retorted. "As you looted everything that did not burn your hand when you came here to fight for the High King."

"We have always raided across the water to Britain," Eochu of Laigin said. "And they us."

"You are proposing a war band and not a raiding party," Owain said, and they turned to hear him, even the kings, as they almost always did when he spoke. "You will call Rome's attention to Inis Fáil and Rome will respond and that is why it is forbidden. The High King has said so."

A spate of argument erupted again while Owain listened to them stone-faced.

"The High King has no right to rule outside Inis Fáil nor to dictate the lives of free lords!"

"Nor to interfere in our affairs, we who are kings in our own right!"

"An attack on Rome's territory is ill thought out," Conrach mac Derg of Connacht said. "But Eochu is right. The High King may command nought of us but tribute and tax, and hospitality."

"What of the fianna whom he has forbidden to take arms?" Riderch demanded. The fianna were bands of young men, not yet married and without land of their own, who fought for a lord or lesser king to whom they contracted for the season. They were a liability when not kept occupied and their elders knew it.

"The Britons suffer greatly under the Romans. They will be glad to see us, and no doubt there is room there for our younger sons lest they go landless here."

"You are thinking the Britons will welcome *you* to rob them instead?" Dai said. "You are greater fools than I thought."

"Raiding is the warrior's way," Owain said as they started to argue again. "And that fool Piran was right that he knew me. Once I was warlord among the Caledones. And it is for that reason that I tell you not to fight Rome."

Elwyn looked at Owain over his beer cup and took a long drink before he said, "Not for the reason that you fled while another man made a craven peace?"

Dai stood up, his face furious and nearly white. Cassan watched but he didn't try to stop him. Dai was a natural fighter and he too was bored with a long peace. Let him exert himself with Elwyn who needed manners anyway.

Owain stood too, ignoring Dai. He walked to Elwyn and leaned over him, crowding him, while Elwyn reached for his knife. "I have no intention of breaking the High King's peace in his own hall," he told Elwyn. "But if you want to say that again when you are sober, which you are now not, then I will answer you." He added, without looking at him, "Dai, sit down."

Fiachra said, "Elwyn, put the knife away. Nor have you ever said where *you* hailed from, before you came to Inis Fáil. Be still before we ask you."

Owain took a step back and Elwyn slid the half-drawn blade back into its sheath at his belt.

"What then have we to do?" Riderch demanded.

"Get your harvest in," Dai told him. He clapped his hands at the slave who stood drowsing in the corner and held out his cup. "Get me more beer. Fools give me a thirst."

"My tenants bring in the harvest," Riderch said with a black look at Dai. "And my son leads a fian with no one to serve, because the High King has laid a geas upon him. Is he to stook wheat instead?"

"Sechnal Chief Druid spoke to this matter from the sacred stone three days ago," Eochu said.

"He spoke to the High King and warned him of upheaval to come," Conrach said. "The High King did not listen. He forbids the fianna whether he has the right or no. Argue his right to command that before the brehons instead."

The Druids had predicted discord from the omens of the sacrifice. The brehons might be persuaded to consider the law in the matter of the fianna if they thought the High King went too far.

"I will take this to Cennétig Brehon himself and we will see what he rules," Eochu said. "And I am not needing you to tell me."

Cassan stood. The women and the High King had long gone to their quarters, leaving these to quarrel freely in their absence and drink until there was no more beer. He would go now too, he thought, before he had a bad head in the morning, and maybe then he might have a word with the King.

Owain and Dai rose as well and they walked out into the cool, damp night. It was misting slightly and the glow of fires on the meadow below Tara's hill shone like wet paint on glass. The lesser landholders and their tenants and slaves had come with the high lords to the great festival that was Lughnasa. Here, as in Britain, marriages were arranged, horses and cattle bought and sold, and holdings rented to new tenants. Not all transactions at the horse fair were above suspicion and not all betrothals uncontested. Assignations, circumspect and otherwise, were numerous and volatile. As a rule, the blood feuds that erupted from a festival were fought out by the participants and their fianna. This year...

"They are like a fistful of hornets in a bottle," Cassan said. "They will either kill each other or chew through the stopper and—"

"Attack the Romans," Dai said. "Who will swat them and look to see where they came from."

"I will speak to the High King," Cassan said. "He must let loose the leash a bit."

"Speak to the Queen," Owain said. "She knows your people and he does not. He spent a seven-year with the Romans. She will see the need, she's Elim's daughter."

Cassan said, "The Queen frights me more than Elim did. Or the High King. I saw her shadow once, on the ground at sunset, when it had wings."

"Take Dai then," Owain said, grinning. "For protection."

Dai stumbled on loose gravel and Cassan grabbed his arm. "Dai is drunk."

"Dai is more sober than Cassan," Dai said indignantly. "There was a stone in my path." He pulled his arm free and shoved Cassan away from him.

"The path is made of stones," Cassan said. He shoved back.

"Ha! Come on then, that I may show you them close to." Dai crouched, watching Cassan as he feinted to one side and the other. In a moment they were rolling on the ground, insulting each other between blows.

Owain watched them wistfully as they rolled downhill toward the guesthouse. At the doorway they stood, dislodging a sleeping hound, and went in, arms about each other's shoulders. Owain thought to follow them and then did not. He stood for a while looking down at the fires in the meadow and listening to the rattly, churring call of a nightjar. Dai had come to Inis Fáil like a would-be ghost, waiting for death to send him after Celyn. But he hadn't died, and Cassan had waited until he didn't want to anymore. And why could Owain not do as Dai had done? He didn't want to die, hadn't wanted to since before he fought Faustus Valerianus for a place in the war band. Tuathal had offered him a wife – his choice of wives – and he had refused. There were plenty of women on his holding happy to come to his bed for a silver ring or a pair of ear drops, but it was never the same and he had seen Aelwen's face on each of them and watched it vanish again. What would happen if he went back? The sick feeling that filled his stomach every time he thought about it rose up again. He didn't know the answer to that except that it would be nothing good.

–

"You cannot rule us like a Roman province." Baine propped herself on her elbow in the bed the next night and prodded Tuathal with her finger. She had waited until they had made love and he was tired and perhaps malleable, but now he showed signs of drifting into sleep. She prodded him again.

"Us?" he inquired. He had been listening, closed eyes or not.

"You lived too long among Romans," she said. "You think you can enforce a Roman peace and stop the lesser kings from fighting each other."

"That *is* what I have done," he pointed out.

"Cassan spoke to me this morning," Baine said. "Because you will maybe listen to me if not to him. Despite that he put you on the High King's throne," she added pointedly.

"Cassan was my father's man. I am not my father to be murdered in my bed. Unless you do it."

Baine sat up and tucked the blankets around her nightshift, pulling them off Tuathal in the process.

"You will give me an ague." He was naked and he tried to tug them back.

"I will give you good advice. Sit up and listen to me."

Tuathal pulled his cloak off a chair and wrapped it around him.

Baine pushed her tangled hair back from her face. "Do you remember describing for me the wonders which the Romans have in their cities? The public latrines where everyone goes?"

"Yes," he said, laughing now. "I would not have thought it the thing that would most impress you. Not the vast marble temples and the law courts? The great map of the world carved with every known road and sea route?"

"Both of which you have never seen yourself. In any case, I am a practical woman, although I would not care to relieve myself in a communal chamber." Baine looked revolted. "But also the latrines in the soldiers' camps sometimes burst into fire when the miasma that builds up has not been drawn off, and this you have seen because you told me."

"Yes," Tuathal said again, still amused. "The camp prefect was most enraged and the centurion who should have been in charge was made to muck it out with his men."

"So will you if you do not release the geas and untether the fianna," Baine said. "And your lords."

"That is a charming comparison that my lords may not appreciate as much as I do."

"Their discontent is growing. Yesternight they argued about it until they mostly passed out and Elwyn came close to drawing a knife on Owain."

"This Cassan told you?" Tuathal looked less amused.

"Yes. There was talk of following Piran to Britain."

"Piran was sent home with an escort to see that he went."

"They are restless, Tuathal. They are bored. My people live to fight. You have been too long with the Romans. You cannot rule the kings of Inis Fáil as Roman client kings. It speaks to their manhood."

Tuathal's expression was suddenly dangerous. "And my manhood? That is in question over this?"

"No! But unless you want to be proving it daily, *and* have the fools sailing for Britain, turn the fianna loose. Rule as your father ruled, and my father."

"Over a vexatious, quarrelsome people who fight each other for boasting rights and a poet to extol their victories. I was wrong. It was an excellent comparison."

"The poets will be next," Baine said, "and you will not like what they produce. Kings have fallen entangled in a poet's words. The Druids warned you of this."

"The Druids saw something in a cow's guts that they could not quite explain."

"You knew perfectly well what they meant. You chose to ignore it. Eochu of Laigin is going to the brehons."

Tuathal was silent at that. It had been two years since the crown had been set on his head by the Druids to seal his kingship. The sacred stone had spoken then, a deep groan as of the earth beneath it shifting. But not even a High King could dispute the brehons.

"When I agreed to wed you," Baine said, "it was a compact with the men who had fought for my father as well as those who fought for you. With this land, not only with your fine self."

The oil lamp beside the bed flickered in a draft. Tuathal saw her shadow on the chamber wall and remembered the feathered shape on the cave wall at Cruachan.

Baine put a hand on his. "You will have to be the king that the land wants if you want the land. I was a part of that, but not all."

Tuathal turned his hand to take hers. This was the kingship he had fought for – this woman, his father's throne, his father's people: an unwieldy, quarrelsome people, tiresomely certain of their rights. They were not going to be denied for some vision of peace that only he wanted. He lay back down and pulled the blanket over them both.

–

In the morning the High King sent for the lesser kings, their lords, and Cassan and Fiachra. They came grudgingly, arguing already, intent on shouting their grievances.

"Be quiet!" he snapped and they settled somewhat, a low rumbling of muttered discontent. He glared at them because he had no intention of giving away the upper hand. The red-gold crown of the High Kingship, which he wore infrequently now, sat on his dark hair. He said, "I put a geas on the fianna that they might not fight battles between the sons of Inis Fáil who ought to live in peace with one another."

"And thus they go hungry because who will hire them to sit eating and giving no service?"

"Who argues with me?" Tuathal swept his gaze over the men. "Who argues before I have even finished speaking? Be silent lest I change my mind."

They stared back, but whoever had spoken was silent.

"I have taken council with my captains and also with my wife, who is often wiser than us all, and now I release the fianna from their geas."

A surprised murmur answered him.

"The geas is rescinded?"

"It is rescinded," Tuathal said. "The fianna may take service where they will and may follow the orders of those they contract with, save that there will be no fighting, for any cause, on the ground of Tara or the territory of Midhe. Take your quarrels to your own lands."

"If we venture overwater?" Riderch asked.

"Raid where you will."

"You speak most carefully, Riderch," Fiachra said. "Are you hunting a way past the High King's orders regarding the Britons who came here looking for alliance against the Romans?"

"That is still forbidden," Tuathal said flatly.

There was renewed protest.

"You have not the right!" Only the Druids could halt a war and that power had not been invoked in six generations.

"You have not the right! You cannot cast a geas across the sea!"

"I cannot cast a geas across the sea, as you say, but any who go may not come back. That I can do, and will."

"That we may take to the brehons," Eochu of Laigin said.

"You are not as crafty as you think," Fiachra snapped. "The brehons do not rule on such matters."

"And you are no more than a hound to follow the High King," Eochu said. "I will hire a poet to make a song of that."

"As are we all," Conrach mac Derg of Connacht said. "You fought for his claim to the throne as did I, and nor do I regret it. If you think otherwise, remember Elim mac Conrach and think if you would wish him back again."

"No matter," Tuathal said. "Unless Elim's head can find his body, he will not be back." He paused a moment, letting them remember. Then he said, "I have spoken. The geas on the fianna is lifted. Nor do I forbid raiding the Gaulish coast or even the Britons because that is our way, and despite what some may think, I am a son of Inis Fáil and not of Rome. But – the one thing I forbid is to take a war band to fight the Romans. I know them as you do not."

–

The next morning Dai drove homeward down the Connacht road with Cassan beside him. Cassan's driver and Dai's followed with Cassan's team, fosterlings proud to be hounds to the High King's captains. Inis Fáil was an easier land than the Caledone mountains – Dai's holding ran next to Cassan's along a river and a string of blue, fish-filled lakes, through rolling hills and vast meadows where his sheep dotted the grass like tufts of their own wool, and his dogs lazed beside them, watchful. But today the mountains around Bryn Caledon were in his head instead, called up by the quarrel over a war band, and that fool Piran. Piran had been a boy when Dai had left Britain. Was it the war that had made him so thirsty for glory, for a name he had been too young to earn before? The war that had shattered so many lives but left Piran feeling somehow wanting?

Dai voiced the matter that had been in his mind all night. "Will they make war in Britain despite the king?"

"As like as not they will go, the fools that they are," Cassan said. "Riderch and Elwyn. Eochu of Laigin will think twice. Now that he is no longer forbidden to raise a fian the idea may not seem as pressing. I think for him it was a matter of pride mostly. He won't forbid Riderch though." He paused, watching anger and a certain longing pass over Dai's face. "What of you? Are you wanting to go back?"

"I could have gone back when we first overthrew Elim," Dai said. "There is nothing left for me there."

"Except perhaps a piece of the man you were there," Cassan said.

"I can't help that, Cassan. And that piece is in its barrow."

"Don't mistake me. I am glad to have the part of you that is here."

"That part of me is blithe to be here." Dai turned and smiled at Cassan. "It's all I can manage."

"It's enough."

Dai let his eyes rest on a grazing herd of red cattle spread over the grass. A flock of rooks feeding in the field rose up in a cloud as the chariot wheels rumbled past them. Slender greenish red spikes of sorrel lined the edge of the track and sun and clouds chased each other across a bright sky. The great stone cliffs of Bryn Caledon grew dimmer in his mind, but still...

"Owain," he said after a while. "I have learned to call him easily by that name now."

"I have never heard him use any other," Cassan said. "Not even three days since, even as he acknowledged Piran spoke truth about him. But you are worried. Why?"

"How can a man simply become someone else?"

"I do not think it was simple."

"What happens when he cannot anymore?"

"That is a thing he will no doubt wrestle all his life," Cassan said. "There is no god in these times to give a man back his arm, as Dian Cecht did Nuada Silverhand. He will stay as you have done."

"His wife is not dead," Dai said.

"Nor can he go like Midir to the human court and reclaim her," Cassan said. "Look you, Dai, he has told me that the little dark ones took him from the field so that his rival could gather the clans together and make peace with the Romans. If he goes back, fools like Elwyn and Riderch will follow him. Not even for a beloved can he go back."

"Elwyn and Riderch will raise fianna and go anyway," Dai said gloomily. "As you said."

"They will bring fewer to their banner without him."

"How hard will it be for him, to watch them sail? I should have argued with the High King to keep the geas in place."

"You should not. You cannot order life arranged for him to soothe your worries."

Dai didn't answer, only shook the reins out and put the ponies to a hard gallop. When the track grew rough he drew them in lest they hurt themselves, but now a foul mood boiled around him like a cloud.

Cassan was silent after that. When this black mood came on Dai, he was not to be wrestled out of it, with either argument or love. It would dissipate when it had run its course. More important in the moment was to discourage their own men's restless sons from joining a fian that intended to adventure in Britain.

248

Under threat of dispossession by Rhion, Piran had gone home to his holding near Bryn Caledon, but a muttering of discontent arose after him wherever he went, hearthside tales of the Cornovii lords who were gathering war bands, the Cornovii who would have the honor of driving Rome out now that Rome's grip was slipping, when the Caledones would not.

The Cornovii had been clients of Rome only in the most technical sense, with a promise of taxes that would probably never be paid and a peace agreement born of the last battle that would, without an actual Roman garrison in their territory, do little more than give them time to buy new weapons and plant their denuded fields. That had become plain when Julius Agricola was recalled and his army drained to strengthen the undermanned frontier along the Danuvius. Now their raiding parties began to slip across the mouth of the Great Firth like fish through a net of holes, as Ansgarius said disgustedly to Faustus. They attacked the watchtowers across the firth mouth and those garrisons only got away by hiding in the reeds along the river while their towers burned. The local villages had given no warning. The patrol from Castra Borea found the garrison and brought them in but did not find the raiders.

Faustus gave orders that the bath house outside the walls not be occupied unless there was a guard posted around it. No one was to go into the village unarmed and with less than ten companions. Silvia grew daily more terrified despite reassurances that they were safe within the fort. They might not be, but he had nowhere to send Silvia through chancy territory when she was incapable of managing on her own. Lucius, now confined inside the fort, was restless and had to be watched lest he slip out. Eirian taught him to grind bread flour and Silvia protested that that was a chore for slaves and Eirian lost her temper.

"It kept him occupied with something other than watching you weep like a sieve full of water!"

"I have reason to weep," Silvia sniffled resentfully.

"You frighten him. He asked Paullus to make him his own sword in case the raiders come." Eirian suspected that Lucius was less frightened than eager to fight like his uncle, but that was better not said.

Faustus took note of this conversation but kept out of it. He thought that Eirian might be better equipped than he to reason with his sister. At least she was female. He had offered again to send her south, risky as the journey was, because their situation actually was dangerous and Eirian knew it, but she had shaken her head. Instead she set herself to keep the household running, ordering sawdust from the workshop for Paullus to clean the floor and seeing that it was swept out again. Lucius's mother had sewn him a pair of breeches against the British weather but Silvia had never cut breeches and they didn't fit, and in any case he was outgrowing them. Eirian picked them apart and recut them. She and Gwladus bundled up the bedding and washed it in the kitchen out of the rain and hung it by the hearth. She took the spindle and distaff that Silvia was too despondent to use and carried it under her own arm, teasing out the thread while she chatted with the armorer over a dented pot. When Indus burned his hand and wouldn't go to the surgeon, she bandaged it with honey and a strip of linen. Faustus noted that his men had begun to refer to her as the prefect's lady.

Farther south there were more frequent ambushes of Roman patrols and occasional raids on villages held to be too friendly with the occupiers. Another detachment was posted out of Britain, clearly not to come back, and Governor Lucullus made his decision.

Faustus was not entirely surprised when the orders came to take the cohort south, and genuinely relieved. The incremental loss of what they had fought for could not be halted with anything except the men they didn't have. No doubt the same situation had precipitated the crisis on the Danuvius. No emperor was ever willing to leave an efficient general commanding too many legions in the same province for very long. So they stabilized one frontier and then took away the men who had done it to mend the next hole in the net. Domitian's father Vespasian had been the fourth of a series of sword-made emperors to come out of the civil war that followed Nero's death and Domitian no doubt remembered that.

It was raining when they left Castra Borea to shore up the defenses along the glen mouth forts to the south. The village watched them go as it had watched them arrive, an imposition like bad weather that would depart eventually. Faustus looked back at the rain-spattered estuary and the road that skirted it while the troop ships put out on the tide. The road would survive their absence because the natives used it, but Castra Borea would disappear into the wild, overgrown with saplings and scrub, its few stone floors and walls taken for use in dairy and hearth and hog pen. The wild would take Castra Borea as it had taken Llanmelin.

–

The new fort was Vacomagorum, the northernmost of a string planted by Julius Agricola to guard Castra Pinnata, the legionary fortress still under construction to the south. Vacomagorum, called for the sub-tribe of the Caledones who inhabited the territory, sat on a headland near the confluence of three rivers, facing northwest into the Caledone mountains. It was timber-built, with more amenities than Castra Borea, if little change in the weather. The hospital and Principia were stone-floored and the barracks floors, although beaten earth, were hard-surfaced enough to keep washed. Outside the walls an annex held a bath house and beside it a former commander had built a small stone altar to Mithras, barely a temple, only a niche with a roof, with the god and his torchbearers carved on the rock face below.

The Praetorium had three sleeping chambers, a cubbyhole by the kitchen with a private latrine for which Faustus blessed his predecessor, slave quarters, and even a small garden with an outdoor oven within its colonnaded walls. Eirian, exploring on a rare dry day, found garlic and tarragon growing in it, along with various medicinals and a patch of blackberries which she set Argos to guard against the birds that were just beginning to raid the ripe fruit. In the relative safety of Vacomagorum – relative being a chancy word – she gave no indication of wanting to leave.

Vacomagorum was considerably closer to Lyn Emrys than Castra Borea had been, and the governor's orders included a diplomatic visit by Faustus, with presents, to remind Emrys of the advantage of keeping the treaty he had made with Julius Agricola. Governor Lucullus sent a scalloped silver bowl and spoon and his confidence that Prefect Valerianus would use his previous acquaintance to Rome's advantage.

–

Lyn Emrys was an impressive hold, even after its gates had been broken and the walls of its five terraces opened in accordance with Roman orders. Rising from the surrounding moorland, it commanded a view of any approaching visitors and Faustus was not surprised to be met by a dozen of Emrys's men, their chariot wheels churning up the wet track. A switchback road led past the slighted walls, first earth and then dry-stacked stone, enclosing the four levels below the upper court. The forge and dairy, storehouses, and granary looked in good repair but of the round thatched houses nearly a third were unoccupied, their thatch disintegrating, their doors sagging, reminders of the population of Lyn Emrys that had gone to war with Rome and not returned.

"Have you lost another hunting party, Prefect?" Emrys inquired when he came out of the wool shed to meet them. "Or have you come to be sure we send our taxes?" Behind him an oxcart sat loaded with bales of hides and woolen cloth. His expression was irritated, his mouth a straight line framed by the trailing ends of his pale mustache. The scar on his cheek twitched. It was plain that Faustus was an unwelcome nuisance.

Faustus dismounted and beckoned to two of his escort to take down the leather box strapped behind his saddle. "I bring greetings from Governor Sallustius Lucullus," he said formally, "who sends you a gift in token of our alliance."

"Bring your greeting and your token to the hall," Emrys said. "Leave your men here. There is water in the well if they are thirsty."

Emrys strode away through the open gate to the top terrace and Faustus put the leather box under his arm and followed with no particular hope of having good news for the governor. To offer no drink but water was a clear statement that they were unwelcome.

The great hall of Lyn Emrys was circular stone with a second story that overlooked the first, a staircase at one end and a hearth at the center. A small hound jumped up from the warm hearth and shooed away the dogs that had been lounging there with him. He pulled two chairs forward and swiped their seat cushions with his hand. A young woman appeared from one of storerooms below the upper balcony, bearing two cups on a tray. Emrys waved her away but she shook her head and brought them anyway. By that and by her bronze ear drops and bangles and gown of good wool, Faustus thought her to be the chieftain's wife or daughter.

"Sit," Emrys said to Faustus, "and show me with what gift your governor thinks to fashion me a slave collar."

Faustus offered the leather box again and this time Emrys took it and undid the catch. The woman caught her breath as he unwrapped the linen covering. Bowl and spoon were lovely, the work of skilled silversmiths, and a luxury such as she had probably never owned. After a moment though, her gaze grew thoughtful and she raised her eyes to Emrys's for an instant. If he could have read their thoughts, Faustus was reasonably sure he would have found them calculating how much the silver bowl might buy in iron weapons.

"Thank your governor for us," Emrys said. "If he comes to visit we will serve his soup in it."

"I will convey your gratitude," Faustus said. "Just now the governor is concerned with reports of raids from the north on our outposts and your outlying villages. Those closest to us have been hardest hit."

"Those men are Cornovii," Emrys said, "as you and the governor both know. Those who raid Caledone holdings will regret that, but attacks on your forts are the governor's problem."

"Are they only Cornovii?" Faustus took a sip from his cup. "This is excellent beer. Are you certain that this upheaval will not spread to your own clans?" He noted the woman sitting now, listening silently as they talked. Apparently Emrys valued her counsel.

"That we will settle between us," Emrys snapped. "I pay Rome taxes! Our councils are held under the prying noses of your magistrates. Our walls are pulled to rubble. But nothing in the peace we made says that I must ally with you to fight the Cornovii. The Cornovii also made treaty with you. Go and enforce that yourselves."

Faustus looked at the woman and could see no urge to disagreement in her face. None but discontented outliers like Piran would ally with the Cornovii, and Emrys seemed to think he could handle Piran. The Cornovii would only be an actual threat to Emrys if Rome left and set the highland clans free to resume their former habits of warring with each other. Emrys clearly intended to let Rome rid him of the Cornovii before that happened. After that his loyalty would grow uncertain.

XV. THE DOGS CAME WHEN I CALLED THEM

Faustus sent his report to the governor and detachments to help repair three villages that had been raided and their thatch set afire in apparent retaliation for refusal to send men of their own to the war band said to be gathering in the north.

"They know who's responsible, but they won't say," Indus reported.

"I know too," Faustus said. "It's Piran. And from what I understand, his headman should have dispossessed him for that."

"That would be Rhion," Indus said. "Who is brother to Calgacos's widow."

"You seem remarkably well informed." Indus was better than a ferret.

"I had a little chat with the blacksmith in exchange for a bit of coin and not noticing the sword blade he hid in the straw; thought I should mention that to you. Anyway, he says that before we came, Rhion's people and Emrys's were at war, or at least raiding each other all the time, but since the peace they've let Emrys give the orders because Calgacos's widow brought Emrys Calgacos's sword. He doesn't think that's going to last forever though, there's a lot of old bad blood. So Rhion is letting Piran run on a long leash on Emrys's orders, but probably because he feels about us the same way Emrys does."

"An excellent assessment," Faustus said. "They hate each other but are united in loathing us even more."

"I can't say I blame them, sir," Indus said. "All in all."

"Nor do I. But their wishes remain secondary to the good of the Empire. Thus we will keep our eye on Piran."

"It seems he's been courting Calgacos's widow," Indus said.

"Surely she's not going to have him?"

"It could put him in line to be headman since she's Rhion's sister. And he might be betting if she marries him she'll follow his lead and speak for rebellion, but the blacksmith says all he's done is annoy her."

Faustus thought of Aelwen and of Owain who had once been warlord of the Caledones. He had liked them both. Piran was a boil on everyone's backside and his impertinence set Faustus's teeth on edge. He would be happy to dispose of Piran if he got the chance, but maintaining peace in the north precluded simply snatching him and putting his head on a pole.

His report, duly delivered to the governor in Eburacum, brought an answer he had not expected: as a gesture of goodwill to stabilize matters in the north, Governor Lucullus intended to return the hostages taken by Governor Agricola.

"Well, he's lost his mind," Ansgarius said. "That's the only hold we have on them."

"The governor is counting on their gratitude," Faustus said, tight-lipped. He read the dispatch again, unhappily. The governor would send a senior tribune to deliver the former hostages to their homes, and since Prefect Valerianus had met the Caledone leaders previously at their surrender, he was to come to Eburacum to accompany the tribune as translator and guide to native customs.

"Which means stop him from insulting anyone by accident," Faustus said to Eirian while he packed dress uniform and the governor's orders into his kit.

"And what will those children be when they go back?"

"I don't know. The governor thinks their return will inspire the Caledones to fend off the Cornovii rebels out of gratitude." Faustus added the parade harness with his medals and two clean scarves. "Either that or he thinks they will be so thoroughly civilized by this time that they will convince their elders that alliance with Rome is to their advantage."

"They may," Eirian said thoughtfully. "They may rip their clans apart with it, poor things."

"The governor hopes to establish the Caledones as a client kingdom to be a buffer against the Cornovii, and collect their taxes without having to occupy their territory."

"Doesn't that only work if he has the men to occupy them again if they don't?"

"I assume he is hoping they won't notice that we don't." Faustus added the parade greaves that he never otherwise wore, newly polished by Paullus. "It's risky to send them back. I didn't like stealing children to start with, but—"

"Perhaps they will be like that god of yours, the one that looks two ways at once."

"Janus." The god of beginnings and doorways. And endings of course.

"Yes. They will see more than they would have otherwise, but they may see something entirely new. I don't think either your governor nor Emrys knows what it will be."

"Neither do I." He put his arm around her and kissed her. She and Silvia had been treating the Praetorium for the fleas that always hatched with the slightest warming of the weather, and she smelled of fleabane and mint, a not unpleasant scent. He thought longingly of bed, and then that they were going to have to make some decision soon. This was not a magical interlude in an ethereal archipelago at the top of the world, foreordained to end with the spring. This was something solid and whatever they did now would be a commitment. Eirian was no doubt thinking the same thing, but what she said was, "We need a loom. May I ask Ansgarius if your men can make one for us? It will save you money, not paying to have cloth woven."

He laughed at that, suddenly cheered by the domesticity of the request. "Yes, but promise him you will supervise and not Silvia. She will drive them mad."

"She's only afraid," Eirian said. "It comes out in a managing sort of way."

"Very well, Most Wise. I will remember that." He put his helmet on and knotted the chin strap as Paullus came, with Argos at his heel, to see to the baggage, and Lucius appeared with his mother to say farewell.

"Bring me a present?" Lucius suggested hopefully.

He would bring everyone presents, Faustus decided. Something to brighten the damp dreariness of the frontier. He would get Lucius a toy and Constantia would know what to take the rest of his oddly assorted household. The word *paterfamilias* crossed his mind and he winced.

In Eburacum he went to visit Constantia as soon as he had reported to Governor Lucullus and Tribune Caecilius, who would accompany them north with the children. Messages had been sent to Rhion and Emrys with news of the governor's gracious decision. Faustus had no idea how those had been received.

"Suspiciously," Constantia said.

"No doubt."

"We are glad to see you, however. Come and speak to Diulius."

In the bedchamber, Diulius put out a skeletal hand to take Faustus's and Faustus was startled at the change in him, despite Constantia's earlier letter. The housekeeper bustled about the room protectively, and shooed them out a few minutes later.

"You see," Constantia said, and he did. A sadness overlay the household that belied her affectionate greeting and Silus's welcome. Silus disappeared quickly into the clinic again, his status in the house awkward now, despite what Faustus saw was his and Constantia's obvious determination to do things properly.

Silus did not come to dinner. Heledd brought Constantia and Faustus a supper of fish and bread and watered wine and retired to the kitchen to play tabula with Paullus. Night had fallen, earlier now as autumn came in, and the shifting light of the oil lamps made the painted gods on the dining room walls look mysterious and knowing.

Constantia put her chin on her hand and looked at Faustus on the opposite couch over the rim of her mother's silver cup. "What will you do about that girl?"

"What will you do about Silus?"

"That is not something that Silus and I talk about," she said firmly.

"That's loyal of you. But I have known you a very long time and I have never seen you look at anyone the way you do Silus."

"No," Constantia said. "I know. I'm quite startled. But I won't start off on the wrong foot and neither will he. What is hindering you? Your sister?"

"Partly. How could I give attention to a family of my own when I have Silvia and Lucius in my hair? And what happens when she sees me fighting her own people?"

"As I understand it, the Orcades set themselves apart from the mainlanders, and she has no reason to love the mainland Cornovii just now."

"True. But later?" Faustus felt stubbornly determined to unearth any reason that he was a fool and the thing would not work. "Eirian has said that we will try it for a time and see if we wear on each other. She is more suited to the army than Silvia," he admitted. "If she could bear Castra Borea she could make do with any other posting."

"The question then is whether she can bear you, in the long term," Constantia said, laughing.

"Brat."

"You're very presentable when you're clean. I expect she will." Constantia smiled at him, more cheerful now. "I'm serious, Faustus. Do what you want to do. You haven't got parents to please. Even if Silvia doesn't like it, she hasn't a say. You're the head of your house."

Technically, Faustus thought as the most recent visitation by his father came to mind. Then, *Yes, and the old bastard hasn't got a say either.* He said, "You flatter me. In the meantime, I have presents to buy and a tribune and a band of children to deliver to the Caledones. Tell me what to get Silvia and Eirian and then tell me about Calgacos's daughter."

"You can't go wrong with scent," Silvia said. "Eburacum isn't Londinium but there's a perfume dealer on the north side next to the wool sellers who gets his goods from Egypt. Or so he says. And Calgacos's daughter is…" She spread her hands, looking for the right word. "Governor Lucullus might as well have made Emrys a present of a strung catapult and there is no telling who it's going to go off at, if you want my opinion."

–

Fifty children from the Caledones and the tribes that had allied with them against Rome filed on board the transport ship of the Fleet that docked at Eburacum harbor, attended by the servants who would now give them over to the care of Faustus, Tribune Caecilius, and a military escort from the Ninth Legion. They ranged in age from five to seventeen, mainly tall and fair like most of their people, clothed in their Roman tunics and gowns, their small bags of possessions following behind them on a cart.

Ceridwen was easy to identify, clearly their leader. Even the boys deferred to her. She was fifteen now, with barley-colored hair like her father's, tall and long-legged, with an unmistakable resemblance.

"You will put a guard outside our quarters while we are aboard ship," she informed Faustus in excellent Latin. A younger girl clung to her side. "And explain to the captain that we are not cargo. I do not trust sailors." Eburacum was a river port. Ceridwen would no doubt have seen enough crews on shore leave to have an informed opinion.

"Of course, lady." Faustus wondered what Caecilius thought of her. The tribune was a broad-stripe appointee from Rome, putting in his year in the army on the way up a promising political ladder. He was a pleasant man but inclined to think of the Britons as some sort of exotic species, uncivilized and disdainful of the benefits offered by the Empire – so Constantia said, and she generally knew things. The journey should be eye-opening.

"That one's a terror," was what Caecilius said as the ship made its way downriver on a morning tide. "You would think the little beasts would be grateful. I ventured to say how nice it must be, going home to her people, and she said I was a fool and actually quoted Seneca at me."

"Seneca?"

"Apparently they studied him during the education we wasted on them for the last three years."

"What did Seneca have to say?"

"'Do not ask for what you will wish you had not got.' I don't know if she meant me or her or the governor."

"All of those, I expect," Faustus said, amused.

"Well, I give her happily into your charge, Prefect. Governor Lucullus says you understand these people. A bit of native blood, isn't it?"

"More than a bit," Faustus said, now mildly annoyed. "My mother was Silure."

"Oh, sorry. No offense meant." Caecilius looked interested. "You don't look it."

"My father was a provincial citizen from Gallia Narbonensis. Our ancestors invested in land there when it first came into the Empire." Faustus wasn't quite sure why he felt the need to prove his pedigree to Caecilius. "Over two centuries ago, when southern Gaul was the frontier."

"Of course, of course. Excellent old families in Narbo Martius. War captive, was she?"

"Yes."

"Excellent, excellent. New blood refreshes old bloodlines, good idea every now and then."

"No doubt." Faustus gave Tribune Caecilius an appraising look. "We're going to need to take these children to their home clans," he told him. "We can't just dump them all on the nearest headman. It's going to take some time, and most of it on horse-back. My horse dislikes boats in a very emphatic way so I left him at Vacomagorum, but I have a chit for the horsemaster at the Tamia cavalry barracks."

Caecilius said, "As it happens, Prefect, I can handle a horse."

"That's good then." Faustus was dubious. Many Romans of the tribune's class disliked riding and the Tamia horsemaster would undoubtedly provide them with his most unprepossessing speci-mens. If the tribune was lying, he could always ride in the wagons with their charges.

–

The tribune proved to have an excellent seat, and Faustus suppressed his disappointment. There really wasn't anything wrong with Tribune Caecilius except for a privileged background that Faustus didn't share. The sort of background that his father Silvius Valerianus had had only contempt for: *political ambition and greed, always grasping for more power and honors, and like as not have to fall on their swords at the end when they come afoul of the emperor's cronies.* Faustus could hear his father saying so, self-righteous and assured of his moral superiority. He watched Tribune Caecilius lift an eyebrow at the horrifying dun nag presented him by the Tamia horsemaster, mount as it protested and tried to bite him, and then proceed to put it through its paces. He revised his opinion of the tribune upward a notch.

Faustus himself had been allotted a sorrel mare with a jolting trot like a cart with a loose wheel. They made an oddly assorted column. Paullus and Caecilius's slave were given charge of the baggage cart, and the children settled in a string of ox-drawn wagons. The escort from the Ninth Legion marched with them under the Ninth's red and gold vexillum and the governor's personal banner, with Argos trotting at their heels like an unoffi-cial rear guard. Faustus and Caecilius both attempted conversation with the children when they could, Caecilius awkwardly but with plain concern. The littlest ones would remember almost nothing of the homes they were being sent to; the older ones were having their lives overturned for the second time.

On the first day they took a handful of children south to the Venicone villages and delivered them with official platitudes to their parents. One of the youngest shrieked at being put in his mother's arms and howled for his nurse back in Eburacum.

"I expected to feel kindly and virtuous about this errand," Caecilius said as they rode away. "I don't. I feel like a beast."

"I do, too," Faustus muttered. It felt somehow more beastly to give them back than to have taken them in the first place. "The young are resilient," he added, hoping it was true.

They turned north again and camped for the night within a temporary ring of ditch and wall. The hostage children were valuable and a raid by the bands that had been harassing allied villages was more than possible. Faustus found Ceridwen standing atop the turf wall, looking up the glens that led to the holds around Bryn Caledon. Her mantle was pulled over her head against the evening chill and in its shadow the gold drops in her ears caught a faint flash of light from the watchfires as she turned to him. A parting gift from the governor.

"We will be there on the overmorrow," he said. "We have sent to tell your mother and your uncle that you are coming home."

He thought she was going to snap at him but her expression softened to doubt. "How do you know they will want me back? The ones who sent me away?" She looked younger now by moon and firelight than she had sitting imperiously in her wagon.

"They had little choice," Faustus said. "*We* saw to that. Could your mother have held your name back when they drew lots and still kept your people to the peace that was made?"

"No," Ceridwen said. "I am not needing you to tell me that. When I was sent south, I prayed to the Great Mother to take me home again, but I knew she would not. I might as well have been a cow. The sacrifice is not permitted to get up and walk from the knife."

"I think you have paid the Great Mother and your own mother both what you owe them," Faustus said gently. "Now come away from the wall before you worry our escort."

When he had seen her to her tent, he sat outside his own while Paullus and Argos snored inside, and wondered uneasily how the governor's decision might change the tenuous stability of the north. Governor Lucullus was offering what amounted to a bribe for good behavior. Beyond Bryn Caledon, the other Caledone villages were scattered through the mountains, a loosely tethered group of holds connected by blood and intermarriage. The clan headmen were chosen from among them through convoluted and often subtle politics in which Cuno and Rotri had given Faustus a lesson which he still had not entirely untangled. Rhion had been elected headman after Calgacos, but Aelwen had declined to move her house to Rhion's and so Bryn Caledon remained hers apparently, because no one was willing to challenge her for it.

According to Rotri, there had been mutterings about a woman holding Bryn Caledon – surely it should be Rhion, or at least some other man – but the Druids had ruled in her favor. The Druids who technically did not exist in Roman-occupied territory. Rotri had said that the old Druid at Bryn Caledon was half-mad, in his opinion. Cuno had said that Druids all lived with their heads in the sky so it was hard to tell, but he thought so too. Faustus was reluctant to pursue a mad old man and hoped fervently that he kept out of sight.

–

They took the Vacomagi children home next and pretended not to notice when two mothers holding screaming children spit at them as they rode away. An autumn chill was in the air now, with teeth sharper than the cold of summer rain. The track to Bryn Caledon lay beneath mountainsides turning red and brown on the heights, patched with the dark green of pine and juniper. On the lower slopes the wet summer had made the dying grass long and lush and the trees were still the dark emerald of late summer. The river that ran down the glen was full, over its banks in places, and fording it was complicated. The escort from the Ninth made a human weir downstream lest any of the small children tumble in. Caecilius's dun nag attempted to unseat him midriver and failed, increasing Faustus's appreciation for his horsemanship. The birds were thick in the autumn sky, migrating by unknown guidance, and a hare, startled from the long grass by Argos, was splotched brown and white, already half into its winter coat.

As they made their way higher, the glen narrowed and the jagged shoulders of the mountains lifted imposingly higher against a gray sky. Bryn Caledon sat four hundred feet above a long dark lake from which flowed the river they had followed. A cluster of crannog houses rose from its water to the west. They dug in a camp beside the lake for the vexillation of the Ninth and the children to be taken farther north to Emrys. The late afternoon sun was turning the water to crimson when they took the Caledone children up the switchback track to the ring-walled hold on the slope of the mountain from which it took its name.

Faustus rode beside Ceridwen's wagon but she didn't speak to him, only stared stiffly past the yoked oxen to the road ahead. The track was banked for chariot wheels but it was narrow and at intervals one side dropped sheer to the water below. The mazelike multiple gates on the western side and a portion of the wall on the east had been slighted on Agricola's orders, but Faustus thought that even so it would have been difficult to besiege it and even more difficult to take it unless the occupants were starved out.

Inside its walls, Bryn Caledon held a warren of byres and outbuildings, and clusters of round thatched houses. The yard outside the great hall was crowded with a throng from the outlying villages craning to see the faces on the wagon.

Aelwen came forward to meet them with Rhion beside her. Faustus nodded to him. Once, before the war, Rhion had translated for Calgacos at a doomed truce talk. And once before that, Rhion had been Calgacos's spy, posing as a trader himself, that perennial guise of spies. He had sold Pandora to Faustus. Next to Aelwen, Faustus saw the resemblance now and noted that his red hair, like hers, was going gray. He limped with the halting, purposeful stride of a man who has grown used to the damage. Faustus made a diplomatic speech, introduced Tribune Caecilius as the envoy of the governor, and began to help the children down, itching to finish the task and be gone.

"We will do that!" A sandy-haired man, whom Faustus also remembered as the one who had translated for Emrys at the peace-making, shouldered him aside and held his arms up to the children in the wagon. He lifted two of them down to be caught up by joyful, weeping mothers and grim-faced fathers, and then gave his hand to Ceridwen.

"Thank you, Coran Harper." She put her hand in his and stepped down carefully, looking around her.

The crowd moved back respectfully, amid a murmur of speculation. Ceridwen's pale hair was still pinned atop her head in a Roman knot, although untidily arranged with no maid to dress it for her, and the gold drops in her ears were finer than anything her people owned now. But she was Calgacos's daughter, child of a man who in his death was fast becoming legend, and as close to a royal woman as the Caledones acknowledged.

Aelwen came toward her, hands out. Ceridwen hesitated a moment before she took them, and then she was in her mother's arms.

Faustus found himself letting his breath out. Caecilius, beside him, murmured, "I was worried how that might go." He paused. "The governor has a question for her mother. It may be awkward."

"A question?"

"I'm afraid so. He seems to feel that this gesture will buy him the answer."

Faustus sighed, suspicious now of anything the governor considered a good idea. "I'll do my best."

He watched as Aelwen and Ceridwen stood with their arms around each other, Aelwen's flaming hair against Ceridwen's pale barley, the color of her father's. He noted again the growing streaks of gray in the red braids and the fact that the two women were of a height now.

Rhion appeared at his elbow. Faustus noted the scar down his calf and how it had tightened the muscle so that he stood unevenly, one hip higher than the other. "If you require further speech with us, Prefect," Rhion said, "the time for it is not now. You may come to Council, when we conduct our affairs before your magistrates." It was clear that they wished him to go away and also that the council was a sore point. The adherence that Rhion gave to the treaty was only because he didn't think he could win if he rescinded it. It had nothing to do with goodwill toward Rome.

No more than he wanted to be gone, Faustus thought grimly. "We will take our leave shortly, headman. We would bid farewell to your sister first."

"That is unnecessary," Rhion said, but Aelwen whispered to Ceridwen and Ceridwen stood back a few paces to let Faustus and Tribune Caecilius approach her mother again.

"Tribune Caecilius wishes speech with you before we depart," Faustus said formally to Aelwen.

Aelwen said, "The tribune may tell the governor that we are pleased to have our children returned to us. Nothing else is needed."

Caecilius spoke to her in Latin and Faustus translated uneasily. "The governor hopes that you can see that your children have received good care in his charge, even with parting gifts to show Rome's appreciation of the peace." They wore good new woolen clothing and each had a silver arm ring with the governor's personal sigil. Faustus paused and the tribune nodded at him impatiently to go on. Faustus had not been expecting the next part and it made the back of his neck itch. He said, reluctantly, "Now the governor would know where the warlord Calgacos is laid to rest."

There was an angry murmur at that.

"I do not know," Aelwen said. "He went with the Old Ones when he was dying."

"The Old Ones?" Caecilius repeated Faustus's translation, puzzled.

"The little hill people," Faustus said.

"I thought they weren't real."

"They are real," Faustus hissed. "The governor is going to have to take her word." He desperately wanted out of this conversation.

"Where did these Old Ones take him?" Caecilius persisted.

"Into the hills," Aelwen said flatly. "They did not tell me where. I took his sword to Emrys to show that he was dead."

Caecilius clearly wanted to keep prodding. Aelwen's expression said that would be futile.

"If there is nothing else you wish to discuss, Prefect," she told Faustus, "please tell the tribune that he should be on the road before dark falls. The way down the mountain is steep. I would not like to learn that you had fallen from the cliff into the lake."

Faustus was reasonably sure that she would be delighted to hear that. When they were out of earshot, retreating with the empty wagon, he demanded, "Why didn't you tell me you were going to ask that?"

"Should I have?" Caecilius's expression was mildly contrite but also said: *I outrank you.*

"You could have warned me." Faustus was aware there was no obvious reason for Caecilius to have done so. "*I* could have warned *you,*" he added, "that she wouldn't tell you."

"We'll have to find out somehow," Caecilius said. "Who else would know?"

"Nobody," Faustus said with certainty. "Why does it matter? Is this a bee in the governor's helmet or yours?"

"Both. We've been hearing rumors: he's not actually dead, he's sleeping with the Druids in some cave and he'll return when the time is right. That sort of thing."

"Those have been circulating since the last battle," Faustus said. Cuno and Rotri had heard them in Lyn Emrys. "It's only a bard's tale, a little bone to throw to the people who thought he could drive us out for them."

"The governor doesn't like it. He's worried about a cult forming. Those things are dangerous."

Faustus shrugged. "What's one more native god? If they want to deify him, let them. He's not coming back."

"Some cult out of Judaea thinks their leader came back from the dead and his people are refusing the state gods," Caecilius said.

"Don't we give the Jews some leeway on that anyway, to keep the peace over there?"

"These aren't Jews, not exactly, and Judaea revolts every time someone looks at them sideways, so the governor is leery of cults, particularly when we're losing troop strength here."

It was impossible to tell the tribune the truth, that Calgacos was neither dead nor coming back. It was likely that not even Aelwen was certain of that.

A bird flew up from a tree on the slope below and the dun nag bucked hysterically as it went past his ears. When Caecilius had prevented him from leaping off the roadway, he said, "Has anyone questioned these 'Old Ones'?"

Faustus thought of shying a rock at the dun in the hope that it would take Caecilius over the cliff this time. "If you can find them, Tribune, you can do that."

"How does one find them?"

Faustus considered the truth, saying, *Go find an oak grove, preferably one with a spring. Take off any iron and leave it outside. Put a small gift in the spring water – they like silver – and wait a few days. If they like the look of you, they'll come.* He doubted that would be well received and so he didn't. He also doubted that they would come anyway. The tribune would smell wrong in some indefinable way. And in any case, Faustus didn't know where the sidhe of Bryn Dan was, although they would probably come near it at Emrys's hold. He just said, "They find you if they want you," because that was easier.

"That is not a help, Prefect," Caecilius said.

"I know," Faustus said.

Caecilius gave him a suspicious look. "Could *you* find them?"

"I might," Faustus said evenly. "But they will not tell me a thing like that. That much I do know."

Caecilius looked doubtful, but he didn't argue further at the moment. He handed the dun horse to his slave as the oxcart rattled to the bottom of the track. Like the others, the empty wagon would be sent back to Tamia in the morning. Then they would take the rest of the children to Emrys, along with the handful who had come from Cornovii holds. Emrys could decide what to do with those.

The detachment from the Ninth was cooking dinner in field ovens for themselves and the last of the children. Faustus saw the girl who had clung to Ceridwen since Eburacum sitting well away from them. A soldier had tried to rape her there in the summer, Ceridwen had said, and she was frightened of men, even though they had let her watch him being beaten for it. Faustus cursed both the soldier and the idiots who had had her watch him beaten, and thought he would have a word with Emrys's wife if he could. The girl was of Emrys's house. And how had he come to feel responsible for them all? Julius Agricola had taken the hostages. Sallustius Lucullus had returned them. But he knew the answer. Their troubles were Rome's doing, which made them his.

When it was full dark, he made the rounds of the little camp, although with Bryn Caledon looming over them he thought any attack unlikely. Coming full circle, he found a seat on a rock just outside the gate and watched the moon silver the waters of the lake and silhouette the crannogs in the distance. The shape of a hunting owl flew silently overhead and his eyes followed it into the trees on the far side. There was no point in trying to find the sidhe of Bryn Dan because even if he did, he already knew where Calgacos was, and also if he did, the little dark people would probably sense that or know it already and that would further tangle matters. What they might feel was necessary to maintain the balance might not be to his liking.

The weather had been mostly fair but now a depressing drizzle of rain began, and through its curtain a familiar figure materialized.

"Go away," Faustus said wearily.

"All would have been different if you had given as much thought to your obligations to your family as to barbarian children and strangers."

"Also get out of my head."

Silvius Valerianus was almost as transparent as the rain. Over the last year Faustus had thought he might be losing his determination to hound his son, and then he would reappear again, querulous and stubborn, driven somehow to achieve what he had wanted in life and not got. Faustus had no more ability to grant him that than he had to answer Governor Lucullus's question. He stood and headed back to his tent. The silvery form drifted after him and he turned around and snapped at it. "Why in Persephone's name are you here? You can't change anything. I won't do what you want. It's too late. If I stop believing in you, will you go away?"

Argos stuck his nose from the tent at the sound of voices, ears lifted.

"I'm not imaginary," Silvius Valerianus retorted. "Your dog can see me. This is the old one's son, isn't it?" A translucent hand scratched the gray ears and Argos gave a pleased rumble.

Faustus glared at his father's shade, anger twisting his gut. "You were always kinder to the dogs than to us."

"I liked dogs."

Faustus didn't remember that, although he supposed the old man wouldn't have shown it. "And you didn't like us."

A tremor crossed his father's face. That had struck home. "I was afraid you would be like your mother. The dogs always came when I called them, and loved me when I fed them."

A soft conversation drifted from the gate, where the sentries were changing shift. Faustus turned his head toward it, biting his lip. He was prefect of a milliary cohort and commander in the north of Britain. He was not going to weep at words that came from a ghost. When he turned back, his father's shade was gone.

XVI. A SILVER ARM RING

Living in Bryn Caledon after the children came home was like living in a cauldron on the boil, the air thick with mingled joy and anger and misunderstanding, the parents nearly as volatile as their reunited children.

It would be a wonder if no one came to blows over something, Aelwen thought, practically anything. Ceridwen, for instance, who stalked about Bryn Caledon like a disgruntled kestrel, resentful of both the expectation that she would return naturally to her people's ways, and the suspicion that she was now irretrievably alien, bearing the foreign taint of Rome. She was willing to sink her beak into anyone who hinted at either.

Or Old Vellaunos raging at the sight of the Romans and at Coran Harper for having locked him in his hut so he would not come out and try to kill the tribune with his staff, driven by whatever madness had engulfed him. Or Piran at having been likewise forbidden entry to Bryn Caledon because Rhion, on the verge of dispossessing him, was still, like Emrys, unwilling to give him to the Romans. Or Rhion himself, because Aelwen stubbornly refused to agree to dispossession and Piran's hold was a smallhold of Bryn Caledon and so she had the last word.

"It will look as if you did it because I was unwilling to refuse him," she said when Rhion brought it up again. "I will not have that said."

"Nor will I have it said that I back him in his ill-judged incitement to rebellion," Rhion said. "The Cornovii hunting runs are far away to the north. *They* can strike Rome here and run north again. We cannot."

"He will fight you, and you are not young." Her gaze went to his stiffened leg and the memory came to both of them of Calgacos who had dispossessed a man for disloyalty. Idris had fought back and Calgacos had won but it had been a near thing. And Calgacos had not had a lame leg.

"I can beat Piran," Rhion said.

Aelwen bit back the retort that likely he could not. "If you do, or even if he does not fight you over it, where will he go?" A man dispossessed had no clan, and ill luck riding his back besides, and such a man could do a great deal of harm. It was why dispossession was a last resort.

"To the Cornovii," Rhion said. "Our alliance with them has not outlasted the war; he has seen to that. He is in too many places at once, like mold in grain. And Idgual follows his lead. I have to do something about him."

"You said you would let Rome do it," Aelwen pointed out. "Let them. I will not have it said that you dispossessed him because otherwise I would marry him. It is not my pride only, Rhion. It is being whispered that Calgacos will come back. That is what the Roman tribune was getting at. And that is likely to bring Rome down on us no matter, if they think there is truth in it."

"Piran is likely to bring Rome down on us no matter," Rhion said disgustedly. "Whether for tolerating his rebellion, or the rumor that I dispossessed him to keep you from remarrying. Take another man for a husband, Aelwen. Put that tale to rest, and I can rid us of him. There are better men than Piran."

Aelwen gave him a baleful glare. She should, she knew it, for the sake of the clan, and yet she could not bring herself to it. "I will think on it," she said, which meant that she would not. "I have enough to try me just now with Ceridwen."

Rhion gave it up for the moment, to her relief. And where was Ceridwen now, whom she had not seen all morning since the girl had flung herself from the kitchen in a temper because she couldn't remember the word, in her own language, for turnips?

Aelwen found her in the weaving house pulling angrily at the tangled warp threads of a just-begun length of red and blue cloth.

"They keep coming untied, or the thread breaks," Ceridwen said, exasperated. Her pale hair fell in braids over her shoulders now and she had taken off the fine woolen folds of her Roman-made gown and overgown and packed them away. The gold drops still hung in her ears.

Aelwen set her distaff and spindle aside and knelt in front of the loom. "Here. Your weights are too light for that thread." She began to unfasten them and retie another set from the baskets that lined the walls. "Where are the rest of the women who should be here?" It was a sunny day and so the light from the door and the gaps below the roof line was bright. There were not many days like these and nearly every woman in Bryn Caledon should have been here making use of it.

"They don't like me," Ceridwen said.

"That is not sufficient reason to neglect their work," Aelwen said, "and they will find that out. But what did you say to them?"

"I didn't. They said my speech sounds foreign."

"And you said?"

"I said theirs sounds like pigs."

Aelwen abandoned the loom weights. She pulled a stool from the corner and pointed at it. Ceridwen sat while Aelwen brought another and sat facing her. "It is not easy to come home, is it?"

"No," Ceridwen sniffled. "I didn't ask to."

"Would you go back if you could?"

"No." Ceridwen scrubbed at her face with her hand. "Not really. I didn't belong there either, but at least I was used to it."

"Can you grow used to us again?" Aelwen asked gently. "It will be easier for you if you can."

"I haven't a choice this time either," Ceridwen said pointedly.

"Do you remember that I loved you?" Aelwen asked. "Before?"

Ceridwen nodded.

"Can you believe that I still do?"

"I know you would not have chosen me if you could have helped it," Ceridwen said miserably. "I made myself remember that when the governor made a pet of me, more than the others, because I was Calgacos's daughter. I don't remember him very well now though. Do you?"

Aelwen nodded.

"I can read Latin," Ceridwen said. "And write it. I thought that might be useful to us sometime and I was practicing my letters before one of the stupid women said it was a spell and then they all made the sign of horns at me. After that they said I was a Roman spy."

"And that was when you said they talked like pigs?"

Ceridwen nodded. "Then they said I was a Roman whore and no one will marry me."

Aelwen clicked her teeth, exasperated. She would have to do something about the women, and the rumors, and the tale-telling. But what to do about Ceridwen she had no idea.

"I will talk to them," she said. "And you take those drops out of your ears."

Ceridwen looked rebellious.

"If you don't want to be called a Roman whore, take them out. When the rest of your people have gold again, you may wear them."

—

In the meantime, there was the autumn cattle drive down from the higher pastures, and the slaughter of fattened pigs and of any other beasts that would not keep over the coming winter, and that kept Ceridwen and her mother working side by side with little time for argument. The drive and slaughter came at the equinox, when day and night hung in balance between Lughnasa and Samhain, between summer plenty and winter hunger. The outlying holders gathered before dawn at Rhion's hall, a half day westward from Bryn Caledon, above the lakes strung like beads along the river. Aelwen took Ceridwen and the Bryn Caledon women to help Rhion's wife Efa with the slaughter.

With Aelwen present, none of the Bryn Caledon women spent their time rumormongering and Ceridwen settled to the work she had known since childhood. It came back, she found, a muscle memory not overlain by three years in Eburacum or by Latin lessons and Greek poetry and foreign gods. She tied an apron over her oldest dress, one left from her childhood with the hem halfway to her knees, and a kerchief over her coiled braids, and scraped the scalded hides beside her mother and Efa. Ceridwen knew that her mother hated butchering pigs but did it because it ill-suited her to shirk the work when Efa had her arms in the scalding tub. Ceridwen put her back into the scraping and saw Aelwen nod approvingly. Her apron and kerchief, arms and feet were splotched with blood; the smell of blood and offal hung in a miasma in the air. The boys who had not gone to bring the cattle down heaved the scraped carcasses up to hang from a rack and gutted them while the little ones chased the dogs away.

At day's end the men brought the cattle in to tally and sort each smallholder's herd while a whole pig roasted on a spit to feed them. Because official tribal councils must be held before the Roman magistrate at Tamia, Rhion had called for a private council the next morning to settle matters that he considered not Rome's business. When night fell and Rhion's slaves brought jars to fill and refill cups in the great hall, cases began to be argued ahead of time across the table. A smallholder from the west pounded his fist over a missing pig, bellowing into old Vellaunos's deaf ear while Vellaunos dribbled meat juices down his gown, attended by Swyddog who had been his pupil.

Ceridwen remembered Vellaunos as a great power, a terrifying old man who spoke to the gods. If the war with Rome had made this of him, it seemed to her a warning. She had been barely old enough to attend a feast before she had been sent to the Romans, but with the other children had helped the slaves in the kitchen and listened while great quantities of beer and mead were drunk, marriages arranged, and inevitably feuds begun that would need sorting out by the headman and the Druids later on. Now she sat at the table to her mother's right, still somehow on the outside, listening as if to one of the plays that a traveling troupe had brought to Eburacum. The governor had bought them all tickets and they had watched from seats at the edge of a clearing while the actors shouted and expostulated at one another, turning to the audience to demand their support. She nearly laughed now when old Mouric staggered to his feet and shouted at the hall.

"And a fine thing when a man's own wife won't feed him and sends him off with nought but a barley cake! And his sons not defending him!"

"Sit down, Da," one of the sons said, pulling at his arm. "You shouldn't have hit her then."

"She defied me and you did nothing. I'll have justice! And you'll have nothing when I'm gone! Like as not, you're not mine!"

His son stood too and shouted in his face. "Likely I'm not!"

"Sit down, both of you!" Rhion pounded his own fist on the table. "Inheritance is a matter for council, and your family is a thorn in my backside, always. Make peace between you or I'll dispossess you all!"

He would not, Ceridwen knew; dispossession was serious. They subsided anyway.

Ceridwen saw a young man with a sleek cap of dark hair watching her. He had a pleasant face under a thick dark mustache and he grinned and gave her a look of sympathetic amusement. The man next to him was plainer, with brushy red-blond hair, his face just slightly crooked, his mustache less luxuriant, but his blue eyes cast a watchful gaze over the room. A man who noticed things, Ceridwen thought. She saw her mother's gaze go to the dark-haired man and felt the glare that Aelwen gave him like a hot coal going past her ear. The dark-haired man grinned again and said something to the one next to him, and the other laughed but there was something dubious in the look he gave his companion. Spear brothers and not much older than she was, Ceridwen thought, remembering them now. Piran and Idgual, fostered together in the household of Celyn who had been killed in the war.

That night, crawling into bed with her mother in the women's rooms at Rhion's house, she waited for Aelwen to speak about Piran, but she didn't. It had only been a black look, Ceridwen thought. Maybe she had been wrong, maybe it had been aimed at someone else.

In the morning Piran found Ceridwen sitting on the stone wall outside the dairy and sat down beside her. Idgual was with him.

"And why are you not at my uncle's council?" she asked them.

"Because we are not missing any pigs and did not get a big head and try to kill anyone last night," Piran said.

"Nor do we wish to marry or take fosterlings," Idgual said. Both were things that required the headman's permission.

"Also," Piran said, with an air of confession, "because your uncle does not like us."

"And why is that?" Ceridwen asked. *My mother doesn't like you either*, she thought, convinced now, but kept that to herself.

"Disagreement over the treaty that has made us vassals of Rome," Piran said. "You were their captive, everyone knows how ill you were used in their hands."

"We were well cared for," Ceridwen said carefully. "The mistreatment lay in keeping us from our homes."

"You are young and female. I do not believe you were not mishandled."

"One girl was," Ceridwen admitted. "Not by the governor's order. I was not."

"It is understandable if you wish not to admit it, from shame," Piran said. "We will avenge you when we drive the Romans out."

Ceridwen considered him. He sat lordly-wise on the wall like a perching hawk in a fine checkered cloak and a silver armband. "How will you do that?"

"It is coming," Piran said. "Like a wave it is coming from the north in the spring. If your uncle is too cowardly to join us then, the wave will roll over him too."

"No wonder my uncle barred you from council," Ceridwen said.

"When he is no longer headman, that will matter little."

"You cannot beat the Romans," she said flatly to them both.

"We can if enough of our people gather their courage," Piran said. "You are Calgacos's daughter. They will listen to Calgacos's daughter when the time is right."

"And why should I listen to you?"

"For the reason that all women listen to their men, who know more than they."

Idgual looked uncomfortable at that, Ceridwen noticed. Spear brothers always had a bond and the partnership of warrior and driver was an intimate one, but she didn't think this one was physical. She thought Idgual was worried.

"What makes you think I would have you?" she asked Piran.

Piran laughed, "And have I asked you?"

"You will," Ceridwen said. "You are ambitious."

"And you may find it hard to get another husband. Idgual and I have heard the talk, have we not?"

"Some," Idgual admitted. He looked reluctant to pursue the subject.

"I am tainted by Rome," Ceridwen said acidly. "I have heard it too. And you have no idea what you are fighting. Even my father didn't."

"Tell us then," Idgual said.

"They are many. Their empire covers half the world, maybe more than that. No one knows exactly what is beyond their borders. If they wish to, they can send men with great siege weapons to break even Bryn Caledon open like an egg. I have seen these machines at practice. They throw stones large enough to smash your walls."

Piran was scornful. "Then why have they not?"

"Because peace was made."

"We are raiding their forts and villages and no great machines have come for us. Why not?"

"I don't know," Ceridwen said. "I know only that they can. I have seen pictures of wheeled towers tall enough to send men over the walls of any fortress."

"And we wait, fearful, just in case they do? Those are not words your father would have spoken."

Ceridwen thought that Idgual looked uncomfortable at that as well, but he didn't speak. "My mother will be looking for me," she said and hopped off the wall. "I am to help Efa with the cheese."

—

"Why have we not told them?" Idgual said uneasily as he set the ponies on the track toward Piran's hold. Piran's men had gone ahead, driving Piran's cattle, and the track was churned to mud already so that the ponies' hooves threw up clods that spattered the chariot and its occupants. "Pah! It's going to rain again before we are home. Something is wrong with the weather."

"It always rains," Piran said.

"Not this much. And why have we not told them?"

"Because useful information is only useful if you keep it to yourself," Piran said. "It's a coin you can only spend once. Are you thinking that his women would listen to us if they knew?"

"I'm thinking you had better make up your mind which one you are courting," Idgual said and grinned.

"Women grow unreasonable as they get old," Piran said. He looked irritated. "I brought her a gift of a silver arm ring and she refused it."

"I told you she might not have you."

"On the other hand, her daughter is sister's daughter to the headman. And young. I will give it to her."

Idgual nodded. He could see that Ceridwen's husband would be a candidate for headman when it was time to elect the next one. "Rhion is not old," he said.

"And may not get older, when the war comes, if he refuses to follow me."

"What of the little dark people?" Idgual asked because there was no point in arguing about Piran's courtship. "The little beasts

280

can't ever be trusted. It was their doing that we lost the Roman spies."

"Rhion has let them run tame instead of hunting them like game, which is the proper thing to do," Piran said. "When we have driven the Romans out, we will wipe that matter clean too. Iron collars make them mend their ways."

"Have you had word yet from Matauc?"

"I expect his man to be waiting for us. They will move south now to be ready and we will spread the word quietly over the winter. There are more who have come over to us than Rhion knows."

His certainty heartened Idgual. Idgual followed Piran. He always had. He would follow him in this too.

Still, he said, "If you wed that child you had best treat her well. She's like her father, I think."

"She's a child."

"She will come into it," Idgual said. "You'd best be faithful."

"When I am headman, I will find *you* a wife, Idgual, and *you* can be faithful."

Idgual shook his head. "You will see." The sky ahead of them was dark and there were no birds in it. "It's going to be filthy before we get back."

—

Idgual was right about the rain. It rained and now it kept raining. The hay spoiled before it could dry. Small streams turned to rivers and rivers to torrents that overflowed their banks and drowned the last of the uncut grain. In all the holds and their outlying villages people dug turnips from fields so wet that they sank into the earth with every step. The bogs overran their edges so that it was hard to tell where was solid ground covered by water and where was hidden bog ready to suck down the unwary. Sheep and cattle huddled miserably in their fields and byres, and dozens sickened with the same lung sickness that the humans got. The water washed away roosts and burrows, and creatures wild and tame invaded every dry place.

It was still raining at Samhain and there was no place at Rhion's hold to light the need-fire where the tinder could spark, let alone burn. The need-fire must be lit outdoors where spirits wandering the spectral paths that opened at Samhain could see it and be warned away. In other years in that rainy country the fire had been kindled under makeshift shelters, although it was considered ill luck, but now Vellaunos pronounced it an omen of death for everyone. Coran Harper hustled him away and fed him and gave him a cup of beer, to give Swyddog a chance to mend that if it could be mended. The younger man was effectively Chief Druid now, although he would never claim that title while Vellaunos, however mad, still lived.

Swyddog consulted the patterns in the water that flowed past his feet in the courtyard of Rhion's hold, and spoke. Vellaunos was a venerable man and great in his wisdom, Swyddog said, but he grew old, as came to every man, and had misinterpreted the omens. He slept now, he added, and would rest while lesser men built a shelter for the fire.

Ceridwen thought it most likely that Coran Harper had given Vellaunos something to ensure that.

Swyddog and Rhion built the shelter under the canopy of an old oak. Its branches, not yet leafless, gave further protection from the lashing rain overhead, and they coaxed a tiny flame into grass that had been hung by the hall fire to dry. Carefully dried wood, brought wrapped in oiled leather, was laid on it and it stayed alight long enough for each household to take a bit of ember in a clay pot and try to get it home still burning.

Piran stood at Ceridwen's shoulder watching the flames shiver in the wet wind. "Old Vellaunos was half right," he said quietly. "It is because we have let the Romans bide in our mountains."

"The Romans are getting rained on too," Ceridwen pointed out. "Lorn Trader said so. He is settled here in my uncle's hold for the winter but he said the Romans are no better off than we. Also, what you talk about you call down, on Samhain."

"True. It is not a night to be arguing about Romans. And you are wet." Piran tucked the folds of his checkered cloak around them both. "How have you fared since we spoke at the cattle drive?"

Ceridwen made a move to push him away and then changed her mind. She was wet and his cloak was fine thick wool, far better than hers. "Barring that my mother's women make the sign of horns at me when I pass, I have fared well enough."

"That is because you have power and they fear you," Piran said. "Remember whose daughter you are. If you lead, they will follow."

"I am daughter, not son," Ceridwen said. "My brother Bleddin should have been the one to follow but he died at Pap of the Mother. Also likely he would have had more sense than to listen to you."

"Women have led war bands before," Piran insisted. "The Queen of the Iceni in the south defeated a legion and burned their city."

A small boy ducked past them into the makeshift shelter, picked embers from the fire with tongs, and hurried away with them shielded in his pot. She said, "I learned of the Queen of the Iceni at the governor's school in Eburacum and of what happened to her afterward. They made sure of that. And we were not to argue about the Romans tonight, you said."

"No," Piran agreed. He smiled at her, teeth friendly in the firelight under his thick mustache. He felt in the pouch at his belt. "I have brought you something."

She cocked her head at him, interested, and he held out the silver armband she had seen him wearing the morning after the cattle drive. It was fine work with a trio of running horses forming the band and carnelians set between them.

"Will you wear it? From me?"

Ceridwen turned it over in her hand. "And if I do, what bargain have I made?"

"None just yet," Piran assured her. "It is only that I want you to know that I think of you."

Ceridwen put it on. It glimmered in the glow of the need-fire. Somewhere above the rain clouds there was a full moon and it shone through enough to wash the wet woods with a veil like milk. There was no doubt that he was handsome. She suspected the gift would cost her a kiss and she was willing to go that far. Farther maybe, her body said, and she told it to be quiet. Calgacos's daughter could not afford idle impulses that might have consequences. After he kissed her she pushed him away. It took some effort.

—

Aelwen grabbed her daughter by the wrist and pulled her sleeve back so that the arm ring shone in the circle that the oil lamp cast across the bed. "Where did you get that?"

Ceridwen pulled her arm away. "It was a gift."

"From Piran?"

Ceridwen shrugged her shoulders, an annoying gesture that was meant to be so.

Aelwen got a grip on her temper. "Sit down." She pointed at the bed and Ceridwen sat, warily. Aelwen sat down on the piled furs beside her. "I know it is from Piran," she said, "because Piran tried to give it to me the day we brought the cattle down."

"To you?"

"Piran has suggested that I should marry him. He has been suggesting it for over a year."

Ceridwen looked revolted and Aelwen resisted the urge to slap her.

"I am not in the grave yet, nor am I past pleasing a man. I will marry again if I choose."

"He is younger than Bleddin was!"

"I have told him no, and you are even more foolish than he!"

"I know things you do not," Ceridwen said, stung. "I can read and write, in Latin and even a little in Greek."

"That may be useful," Aelwen said. "Don't lose it, no matter who makes the sign of horns at you, but knowledge is not wisdom."

"I am wise enough to see that no man of our people will want to marry *me*," Ceridwen snapped. "Piran said so."

"Was that before or after he suggested he should marry you himself?"

Ceridwen was silent.

"Look you, child, do you know why he wants you?"

Ceridwen said grudgingly, "I am not as foolish as you think."

"I hope not, but I will tell you a thing. He wants you for the same reason he wanted me, because he thinks he can be what your father was, and you or I could bring others to his side. And he will fight the Romans again and lose again. Ceridwen, you must see that!"

"I do see that," Ceridwen said. "I will not give him my voice, but I am lonely, and he kissed me."

"Then pick another boy." Aelwen brushed her hand over her daughter's rebellious face. "It doesn't matter how many rumors there are, your husband will have some claim to be Rhion's heir. Piran knows that. Three men have come to Rhion already but he has told them you are too young, and you are. When you know who you want, then we will settle it."

Ceridwen looked dubious. "In Eburacum I knew that the governor would sell me to buy alliance where he needed it. So I never thought about what I wanted. How do I know who I want?"

"Try them out," Aelwen said with a small smile. "Go to the heather a few times."

"And drown," Ceridwen said as thunder boomed overhead.

"Or the pony shed. I will show you ways to be careful. Just not with Piran."

"Is that what you have done?" Ceridwen said suspiciously. "Gone to the heather?"

"I am not looking for a husband."

"That isn't what I asked."

"Maybe," Aelwen said. "It's not your business." She tapped a finger on the silver armband and the galloping ponies that circled it. "Wear it if you want to. I won't make you give it back. Just don't give him anything else for it."

Lightning cracked outside and the rain intensified. The drip from the roof became a splatter where the downpour had worked its way through the thatch. On the outer walls the stone ran wet with condensation; on the woven reeds that separated the sleeping chambers a dark mold was beginning to grow.

Ceridwen looked up fearfully. "Vellaunos says this storm has death in it."

"Vellaunos wanders in his mind," Aelwen said, "in some country we can't see. He'll step away into it soon. Still, I wouldn't be out in this alone. Take off that wet gown and get into bed. Do you remember the song I used to sing you when you were small?"

She helped Ceridwen pull off her sodden gown and called for a slave to hang it by the re-lit fire in the great hall below. Then she wrapped both of them in the same blanket and pulled the furs up, soft and alive-feeling. She began to sing quietly, a lullaby from a time they both barely remembered.

Sunset falls on living water
And the river's wet wild daughter
Comes to tell the evening news,
How the wind smelled when it blew,
Where the crow went when he flew.

Hidden from the wind and weather,
Drowsing deep among the heather,
Children of the hills and lakes,
Whisper soft for Mother's sake,
Sleep you, child, till daylight wakes...

Ceridwen pulled her knees up so that her mother's could fit in their hollow and took the hand that Aelwen draped across her shoulders. Outside the wind picked up and the water kept falling.

XVII. ALL THE WATERS OF THE EARTH

At Vacomagorum the drains overflowed. The wooden roofs leaked. Silvia found a badger in the Praetorium latrine. The garden became a swamp. Even the Batavians, who came from the marshy delta of the Rhenus where it was always wet, began to grumble and pick fights out of boredom. Only the native entrepreneurs who clustered around any fort, even one this far along the frontier, were undeterred. They roofed their wagons with oiled leather and carried on with the sale of beer and fleecing soldiers at dice.

Faustus, making his soggy rounds of the fort, encountered Indus with two of his cohort in tow, their armor mud-covered and their fox-fur caps looking like wet rats. One had what appeared to be a broken nose. They shied when they saw him and tried to hide behind Indus.

Faustus cocked his head at Indus, vine staff prominently displayed. "Should I take notice of this?"

"No need to worry yourself, sir," Indus said, with the earnestness of the reformed troublemaker. "They are very sorry, sir, and will be sorrier yet, but I have it in hand."

One of them attempted a salute and nearly fell into a puddle.

"Well, the drains need mucking out as soon as they can stand up. I'll leave it to you, Watch Commander."

"See now?" he heard Indus say as he led them away. "You're lucky it wasn't worse. I've had commanders who would've…"

His voice trailed away as they squelched off and Faustus decided that he had best schedule a long march as soon as he thought they wouldn't lose anyone in a bog. They were reckless with boredom. A commander had to stand for a certain amount of foolishness when things were precarious; too free a hand with the vine staff could set off mutiny in those circumstances. He remembered telling Tuathal that, in the days when they had both marched with Agricola. He also remembered telling him that the trick was in knowing how much.

Vacomagorum was high enough to afford protection from the overflowing rivers but Faustus watched uneasily as the face of the headland to the north of the fort fissured with the constant deluge, uprooting trees and cutting channels down to the riverbed below.

Lascius ordered that no one use the baths, which were fed from a tributary of the river, and no one drink water from anything but rain barrels. When the cohort protested, he said, "Floodwater carries disease. Strip and stand in the street if you want a bath, you'll get clean soon enough."

When they gathered at the standards to pray in the pouring rain, Faustus offered an extra prayer to Jupiter Best and Greatest, who ruled the clouds, to Neptune, god of floods, and to Mithras in his temple. Water ran down the flooded streets and under the doors of every building. Even the faint sight he caught of his father's shade looked damp, hovering beside the niche where the household gods lived.

"Your sister has decided that there is a curse on this place," Eirian said, mop in hand.

"She may be right," Faustus said.

"The badger upset her. And it's hard to keep Lucius out of the water."

"There is a resupply train due, assuming it can get here. Should I send her south with it?"

Eirian shook her head. "She won't go."

"I can make her," Faustus said grimly.

"No. You're her only anchor in the world right now. It will be worse if you do that. Let her stay and learn that she can weather more than she thinks she can."

"Very well, Most Wise." It struck Faustus how easily, and without his quite noticing, she had become confidant and advisor as well as lover. Her pale brown hair was tied up under a kerchief and her gown was mud-spattered and soaked at the hem. She was barefoot, he noted, a pragmatic measure to save shoes. He remembered that the deities of her islands dwelled in lakes and under the waters of the firth. "Your people's gods are all water born," he suggested. "Pray them to let the supply train through." It seemed as useful an action as any.

"I don't know that they care about the mainland," Eirian said seriously. "But I will ask them."

The supply train arrived at Vacomagorum on Samhain, its drivers dripping and anxious to be out of the wild on that night. They brought grain, oil, and wine that drew cheers from the sopping troops unloading it, and a letter from Constantia.

> *My friend Faustus,*
>
> *Diulius is gone. It was not as bad at the end as I feared. He slept mostly and woke enough to be sure I knew where his will was, and then left us. He has freed Heledd, and given her some money to start a shop with, but she is still here. She is too used to looking after people and now her eye has lit on Silus. When his leg pains him she wraps it in something that smells like a goat fell into a bog, but it does seem to help. Silus and I have married, as you suspected we would, and the clinic goes on as before. I think about those children and hope the governor was not as big a fool as I suspect to send them back. It felt to me like a desperate move for some reason, but I am not sure why. When you have leave, come and see us.*

He would, he thought, and take Eirian with him if she would go. Constantia's letter was punctuated by her usual afterthought: *What have you done about that girl?*

The rain was still coming down and he heard thunder booming and the sharp crack of lightning.

"Prefect!" Ansgarius stood dripping in the office doorway. "The headland has started to slide. Half a patrol went down with it!"

"Mithras!" Faustus snatched up his cloak.

"I've sent men down to the river to see what can be done." Ansgarius flinched at another crack of lightning. Thunderstorms were a rarity here and argued some direct action by the gods.

"Sandbags too," Faustus said. "Shore up that embankment before more of it slides. Paullus! Go back to the Praetorium and find the women. Tell them they're to stay put. I don't want to be worrying about where they are."

Outside, the rain that had drizzled all night was now coming down in sheets. A straggling line of refugees flooded out of low-lying villages crowded through the fort gates, their possessions on their backs or loaded on to carts. Faustus made his way cautiously down the muddy track to the river valley below. The path was slick with rain, and water pouring down had cut deep runnels across it. Below, swift-flowing water had already risen over the banks to lap against the cliff edge.

Men were digging frantically in the mud and uprooted trees below the spot where the headland had given way, their feet already ankle-deep in water. Trees, their roots upended, rose like jagged hands, and it looked as if the Underworld had risen up to pull the living back down with it.

He saw Indus, mud-smeared, trying to scrape the earth away from a still, half-buried figure while the water swirled around him, washing it back again. Faustus knelt and together they worked their hands under the ring-mail hauberk and heaved. The mud-encrusted mail was heavy as stone but they staggered back toward the path and laid him down to see if he lived. Faustus pried his mouth open and pulled mud from it. The man didn't move. They sat him up and untied his helmet. Indus pounded his back and but his head only slumped down to his chest.

Faustus put his ear to the mud-covered mouth and felt nothing. The mangled face was unrecognizable beneath the mud. "Who is it?"

Indus pulled the man's sodden scarf off and washed his face gently with the dark water that rushed past them. "Crispus," he said.

Faustus bowed his head for a moment. "Help me get him where the water won't take him."

They left Crispus's body partway up the path and went back to the men digging out their buried comrades. A cheer went up when one was pulled from the mud alive, but most were still by the time they were found. At the top of the bluff, Faustus could see Ansgarius ordering sandbags into position. The rain was still sheeting down and one bag slid over the edge as he watched. "Farther back!" he shouted over the rain. "Farther back! Let the water have what's already eroded."

He turned back to the men digging through the mud, wearily aware that by now they would be pulling only corpses out. By Indus's count, nineteen men had gone over. They had pulled three out alive, and twelve dead. The river was rising further and he saw one of the diggers swept into the current. Hands reached out downstream and the man grasped them, floundering ashore. As he did, another went in and was tangled in a wash of debris swept from upriver.

"Verax!" His comrades reached for him but he was gone into the water. Tree roots and branches, the broken wheel of a cart, and half a bedframe carried him into the current. He floundered, buffeted by the debris, then began to sink.

Faustus pulled off his cloak and ran for the water. He was the only one of them not wearing a coat of ring mail. Batavians could swim like otters but the mail would slow them and the current was taking Verax farther down each moment. And Verax didn't appear to be trying to swim.

The river was even colder than the rain and clogged with everything washed into it upstream. Faustus swam with the current, angling toward Verax. Something wrapped around his ankle and he kicked free of it frantically. Verax was caught in an eddy of lumber and the wreckage of a tent. The rushing water pushed him under. Faustus grasped him by the arm and Verax thrashed in his grip. He began to pull Faustus under too.

Faustus surfaced gasping and spat out a mouthful of water, "Stop that and swim!"

"Can't." Verax's voice was barely louder than the sound of the current. "Arm."

Faustus could feel where it swayed loose above the elbow, and the sharp point of bone through the skin. Broken likely by the tumbling debris. He got his arm around Verax's shoulders instead. Verax fought him again in a hysteria of pain and fear. He was heavy, weighed down by his ring mail. "Be still if you can't swim, curse you, or I'll drown you myself!"

He eyed the shore. They were nearer the far bank but if they climbed out there, they would never get back across. He turned them into the current and kicked off against the tangle of lumber, towing Verax. The water was cold. Colder than ice, and stinking. Faustus caught a mouthful and coughed it up again. Verax struggled as they bumped against another patch of debris, this one coalesced around the drowned body of a cow. Faustus felt something else snake across his ankles. There would be fishing nets in the water, and coils of rope, and other things to wrap around a man and pull him under. He saw a flash of lightning illuminate the sky. *Jupiter Thunderer, pity us.* His arms were beginning to spasm and his legs felt like stone. Another few feet toward the bank and another hundred down it. He swam desperately now. They would come soon to the confluence with the larger river and be lost in its roiling waters. He could see men following them through the floodwaters that covered the far bank. It was hard to tell through the rain where the bank was, but it must be the line of half-drowned trees. Verax's head went under the water again and Faustus heaved him up, trying to keep them both afloat. Verax's mail hauberk tugged them down. What Faustus thought was another piece of debris rose in front of him and he tried to push it away.

"Prefect!"

Indus and two more were on the other end of a sapling pine, its crown still brushy with needles. Faustus grasped it with his free hand. Verax's head was barely above the water. He had stilled, thank Mithras, but now Faustus was afraid he was dead.

Indus and the others pulled them cautiously landward, still in a foot of water but out of the strongest current. Faustus staggered upright. The men grasped Verax.

"Careful! His arm's broken."

"Is he alive?"

"I don't know. Get him out of the water."

They clambered through the trees and laid Verax on the first dry ground. Dry only in the sense that the river wasn't flowing over it. The rain was still sheeting down. Faustus lay down in the muddy grass and heaved up river water, propping himself on his elbows until he quit retching.

He heard Verax gag and vomit, an encouraging sound. He stood, somewhat unsteadily, and looked back upriver. The water was still rising, his men still stubbornly digging.

"That's enough! Get to high ground!"

Those still missing were bound to be dead. Rome didn't leave her dead, but he wouldn't risk losing more men. He would send a search party out again when the flood subsided. He looked at the sky, lit by a crack of lightning. If it did. He wondered if the land itself were trying to wash them away, out of Britain entirely.

Despite its perch on the headland, the fort too was awash when they stumbled up the river path, sliding in the slick mud. The tributary that fed the camp had overflowed its own banks and sent sheets of water everywhere until it poured around the sandbags and off the eroded cliff like a waterfall. The defensive ditches were filled with debris carried on the flood and caught against the trench wall.

The supply train's officer had ordered the empty carts driven into the granary and the grain sacks heaved back onto them in hope of keeping them dry, while the swarm of civilians in search of shelter huddled miserably under every roof and overhang, half-drowned and despondent. Faustus found Eirian sorting them out in the armorer's shed, assisted by Paullus.

Her eyes widened when she saw him, coated with black slime and weaving on his feet.

"Didn't I tell Paullus to have you stay inside?" he demanded. Her fur boots were sodden and skirts wet to the knee, her hair dark with water, plastered to her face.

Paullus gave him a look that said he had done that, for what it had been worth.

"You will get lung sickness out here."

"And you." Eirian stared at him. "Where have you been?"

"The prefect went in the river to pull Verax out," Indus said. "We thought we'd lost them both."

"Get out of those clothes," Eirian said. "And drink some wine to dilute whatever you swallowed out of that river. Lascius is right. Floodwater is evil."

"It nearly had the prefect," Indus volunteered.

Eirian closed her eyes for a moment. It was the first time Faustus had seen her look frightened.

"Will you go back in the Praetorium?" he asked her.

"You need someone to deal with these people." She turned back to a woman holding two children by the hand. "Go with him." She pointed to Paullus. "Give him your man's name and if he comes we will send him to you." She looked back to Faustus. "I am thinking the workshops will hold most of them. I told Ansgarius to move everything he can to clear space, and find any blankets in the storerooms. Lascius can take some of them into the hospital. They will need to be fed, too. They've lost everything. I told Gwladus to make as much porridge as she can find pots for."

Faustus gave up. A pair of Batavians passed them carrying another mud-covered body.

Eirian winced. "Have you seen Gwladus's man?"

"He's stacking sandbags," Indus said.

"Thank the Mother. Gwladus wanted to go down the cliff to look for him and finally Paullus set Argos to watch her and keep her in the house."

"I note that didn't work on you," Faustus said.

"Argos and I have an understanding."

A man leading a goat on a frayed rope came to the head of the line, looking as if he had no idea how he had got there. His breeches were torn down one leg and he had a bloody gash along his cheek. Eirian turned her attention to him.

"Go and get a count of the missing," Faustus told Indus wearily, "and bring it to my office."

Silvia and Lucius met him in the Praetorium portico.

"What is happening?" Silvia was white, her eyes wide and frightened. Lucius clung to her skirts.

"Flood. I've never seen anything like it. Stay inside. You could pray," he added.

Faustus informed Gwladus of her man's safety, called off Argos, and shucked off his mud-soaked clothing. Taking Lascius at his word, he stood shivering in the Praetorium garden until the rain washed the rest of him clean. If Gwladus saw him, no doubt she had seen worse. His hands and various other parts of him were scraped raw, and when he was dressed, an orderly from the hospital appeared to say that Surgeon Lascius required the prefect's presence.

"I've set Verax's arm," the surgeon said, inspecting Faustus as he spoke. "As well as I can. He'll likely not be fit for duty even if it heals. And everyone who was pulled out alive is still alive, so far." He held his hand out and the orderly put a pot of vinegar in it. "Hold still."

Lascius washed the scrapes on his arms and legs with vinegar while Faustus gritted his teeth.

"Hold your hands over the basin."

Faustus obeyed and Lascius poured vinegar over them too.

"Have you broken the skin anywhere else in that water?"

Faustus lifted his tunic and undertunic and Lascius washed his ribs. Faustus said, "Every cursed thing was in that water. Lumber, rope. I saw a dead cow. Apparently Jupiter has decided to drown the world again."

"Everyone who went in needs to wash themselves or come see me. With vinegar, mind."

Faustus nodded and went back out to give that order. And then to see to the refugees, now his responsibility. Conquest by Rome meant the protection of Rome afterward.

By the morning after Samhain the need-fire shelter beneath the oak at Rhion's hold had washed away. The boom of thunder through the night had frightened the visitors' teams in the pony shed and half of them had broken their tethers and scattered. Households who had taken coals home the night before came straggling back as their houses slid from under them, timber footings unearthed by the rushing water. Lords who had slept the Samhain night in Rhion's hall found themselves marooned from their own holdings. Swyddog consulted the gods, the leaden rain-filled sky, and the overflowing waters, and received no answer.

Rhion's hold was only half a day's ride from Bryn Caledon but it might as well have been on the other side of the ocean. The chariot tracks were washed half away, sheds and byres swept off their footings, crannog houses nearly submerged. It was as if all the waters of the earth had been sucked up into the sky to pour down on them here. Aelwen swept mud from Rhion's hall while the water kept coming down and the men drove the animals to high ground, crowding the courtyard around the hall with every beast from the low-lying villages: pigs, cows and sheep, bedraggled chickens, goats and ponies and plow oxen. As at Vacomagorum, the wild sought shelter too. Aelwen found a vixen denning in the dairy and hadn't the heart to drive her off. The cows and fully-grown pigs served to keep the wolves away but Aelwen saw a pair sitting on the roof of a drowned crannog. She fretted over what was happening at Bryn Caledon and tested the surface of the track and the depth of the river so often that Rhion shouted at her that she did not have a household of fools and they could no doubt come out of the rain. Everyone was wet and bad-tempered and almost every household was missing someone.

Rhion sent as many rivercraft as were not wrecked in the flood out onto the water to search for the missing while the rain pelted down. He went first, because he was headman, sitting in the bow, the hood of his cloak over his head, Coran Harper behind him. Aelwen watched with her hand over her mouth as they launched the boat into the roiling current. Three others launched behind him, Idgual and Piran in one, and she stopped herself from the ill luck of hoping that Piran drowned. Wishes like that could turn back on the source.

—

The current was tricky and it was difficult enough to stay on the edges of the lake that now covered the pastureland of the nearest village, and not be tumbled into the swiftest flow. Once into the main body of the water the only direction to go would be downstream, possibly forever. No boat could have fought its way upriver. Piran gave all this his attention but nevertheless the thought circled in his head that some use could be made of the circumstances. There was always some use to be made of things.

"This will have hit the Roman forts," he grunted, pulling at his oar. "Now is the time to catch them unprepared."

"Now is the time to not drown ourselves," Idgual said. "And we are in the same state as they."

"This storm will not have hit the Cornovii country, not unless the gods are trying to drown Britain entirely."

Idgual wondered if that might be so, but he kept it to himself.

"Matauc's war band and the men from Inis Fáil may come down from the north while the Romans are still digging out."

"The men from Inis Fáil are not coming until spring," Idgual pointed out.

"And with Matauc we may harry the Romans until then and keep them from regrouping. This is from the gods, look you. This is fated. Emrys and Rhion will see that now."

Idgual pulled at his oar. Piran never dealt only with the day at hand, he arranged the day ahead and the day after. That was no doubt what made Piran the leader of them, and Idgual his spear brother to follow.

"Ahead," Idgual said. He pointed through the rain.

An ancient standing stone that had been the center of a village when the water lay peaceable within its banks now jutted like a tooth from the current with a shape crouched atop it. The rising flood had left it and the disintegrating peaks of a few houses were the only things above water. As they came closer, Idgual could see that the shape was a child in a mud-soaked tattered shirt and the shreds of breeches.

They edged the boat alongside and Idgual kept it from drifting while Piran lifted his arms to the child on the stone. The child leaned down and Piran pulled him into the boat.

"Where is your mother?"

"Gone in the water," the child whispered.

"And your father?"

"He went to see to the pigs." The boy began to sob.

"We'll take you to Rhion's hold," Idgual said. "Maybe he will be there." It was unlikely; the stranded child was the first live soul they had seen.

A drowned body floated by, face down, hair spread like seawrack in the current, and the boy screamed and lunged for the side of the boat.

"Da!"

"No!" Piran grabbed him by the shirt. The child struggled and overbalanced. The boat rocked dangerously and he went into the black water.

"Taranis take you!" Piran plunged after him.

Idgual watched, heart pounding, as both sank into the water. There was no knowing where they would surface, if they did. He took up the other oar and backed into the current, trying to keep his place and watch the water. The boat bumped against the stone's upriver side as he scanned the floodwaters and the swifter current farther out. A head, or something, surfaced, and Idgual hesitated, trying to see clearly through the rain. An arm rose from the water and he pointed the boat toward it. The head and arm sank again and rose. A hand grasped the side and Piran shoved the child at Idgual. Idgual pulled him in and tried to steady the boat as Piran pulled himself over the side after him. The little boat rocked dangerously and Piran threw himself down flat between the thwarts, spitting up water.

The child in Idgual's arms was still. Idgual laid him over his knees and pounded his back while the boat drifted with the current toward the center of the lake.

Piran sat and snatched up an oar. "You'll drown us!" He brought the boat around and began to paddle. "Is he alive?" He coughed and spat up more.

"I think so," Idgual said. The child moved a little and coughed up filthy water.

"He had best be," Piran said grimly. "I nearly drowned finding the little beast."

"It's the Mother of Waters' own miracle you did," Idgual said. He sat the child upright. "There now, you're alive. What did you do that for?"

"Da," the child whimpered.

"That wasn't your da," Piran said. "That came from upriver. Your da is over the falls by now."

The child began to sob.

Idgual put him in the bottom of the boat and took an oar from Piran.

–

Below Rhion's hold, other boats were drawn up above the rising waterline, tethered to trees to keep them from the current. Some had brought in survivors, others had found nothing or nothing but bodies. Idgual carried the child up the washed-out track to Rhion's hall, wondering what to do with him. Having saved him from the water, Piran had only shrugged when asked.

Rhion and Coran Harper had come back with a girl found clinging to the top of her crannog, a chicken perched on her shoulders. They had brought the chicken too, a wet, bedraggled thing with stinking mud in its feathers. Now the girl stood clutching it to her chest, clearly the only thing left of her home.

"Here." Idgual set the child down in front of her. "This one needs looking after."

The girl looked blank.

"He's lost his people too," Idgual said softly.

The girl's eyes focused on the child. She nodded and held out her hand. The chicken fluttered down.

Rhion's wife Efa was sorting through the rescued.

"Piran went into the water after him," Idgual said to her as the child took the girl's hand. "I thought he wasn't coming back up."

"I'm sure Piran will tell us the tale," Efa said. "Several times." She paused, wiping water out of her eyes. "I'm sorry, Idgual. I am tired. I know he's your spear brother. That was well done of him."

"Of course he'll tell it," Idgual said, unoffended. Perhaps embellish it a bit. Piran didn't lack for courage and he would make use of that too. Idgual could see him now, speaking to Ceridwen, who was ladling hot soup from a cauldron under the pony shed roof. Idgual suspected that Ceridwen made Piran ill at ease in some way, despite his determination to wed her since making no headway with her mother. In Piran's mind a woman should not be able to write things down, making marks that no one else could decipher, including her husband.

Piran was planning to send a messenger north to Matauc as soon as the way was clear; if the message was written down, Idgual thought, it could not be changed, either from intent or mere stupidity. However, Matauc couldn't read it if it was, so Idgual supposed that didn't matter. Piran believed the old ways were the true ones, and when he was warlord he would bring them back. That sounded like a rightful thing to Idgual. Living under the Romans' shadow was shameful. Perhaps, as Piran said, the flood would convince Emrys and Rhion.

Piran drank his soup and handed the bowl back to Ceridwen with a smile.

The soup smelled good and Idgual went to the pony shed for his own bowl. "I think the rain is slacking," he said as she handed it to him. "The water is going to keep rising for a while though. That is what Swyddog has said anyway, and I suppose he knows about water."

"I barely remember a time when I was not wet," Ceridwen said, "but I think you are right." She peered into the drizzle.

"It feels as if the whole world is drowned."

"And afterward," she said, ladling soup, "there is a world made new, if you believe that tale."

"What tale is that?" Idgual drank while she handed bowls to the people huddled under the pony shed and took back the empty ones. Piran had gone off somewhere.

"A poet belonging to the Romans tells of it. I read it in the school at Eburacum."

"They have written it down?" The Druids held that to write a thing was to weaken it and make it vulnerable. Stories of gods and chieftains were learned by recitation. It could take the Druids twenty years or more to learn them all.

"Romans write everything down," Ceridwen said. "It is a wonder they are not buried in their writings. There are buildings in Rome with too many scrolls to count, all the stories of the world."

"What are scrolls?" She had used the Latin word. There was nothing similar in their language or experience.

"They are lengths of skin, or of papyrus, which is a plant that grows on the other side of the world in Egypt."

And she had read these, Idgual thought. He noted that she was wearing the silver arm ring. If she married Piran, she would always know more things than he did. Piran wouldn't like that.

"Go and dry off," she said, not unkindly. "I have more people to feed. Then if you want to help, you can chop the turnips in that basket that your spear brother is too important for."

—

Two days after Samhain the rain stopped, as if the sky was a cistern at last run dry. There were toadstools on the barracks floors and the horses' hooves were developing thrush. Faustus brought them into the Praetorium storeroom in search of a dry floor, and worried over Silvia's state of mind when she was too dispirited to protest.

Eirian joined him as he stood on the edge of the sandbagged headland and watched the brown waters below, still well over their banks, and the piles of debris deposited above the falling waterline. The landscape stretched out like a gray-green blanket smeared with the raw earth of washed-out houses and upended trees. The carrion birds, housekeepers of the wild, had settled on the corpses of drowned animals and Faustus had sent a detail to make sure there were no human bodies among them. The last of the men buried in the mudslide had been found and given proper prayers.

"What of the little dark people?" Eirian asked, looking at the devastation below. "What will this water have done to their houses?"

Faustus thought of collapsed rooms, buried in mud. But also of men drowned in the bog that the little dark people had led his legion into four years before. The same ones likely. It had been near here.

"They will be starving," Eirian said. "They live always on the edge of hunger already and many of my kind spoil their gardens when they find them."

"Why?" Faustus asked.

"For sport. For fear."

"You are afraid of them?"

"I am not. Maybe. They are old, far older than we are."

Faustus thought of Curlew at Llanmelin. And the ones who had guided Cuno and Rotri out of Cornovii country with Eirian, after betraying them. The little dark people made his head ache. "All right," he said. "Will you come with me? Likely they will know you. They are like crows, they tell each other things."

Faustus took the advice he would have given Tribune Caecilius and rode into the woods beyond the river until he found a likely looking grove of old oaks. Eirian rode with him on his spare horse, a small muscular figure with pale brown hair hanging loose down her back. Both of them were stripped of any iron and were followed by an escort armed to the teeth and two pack mules laden with bags of grain.

"We can ill spare that," the supply officer had protested.

"Think of it as an investment," Faustus said.

He halted the escort on the edge of the grove, dismounted and took the pack horses' leads. A cleared space and a flat stone at the center made him think the hill people would know this one, even if it wasn't theirs particularly. Oaks were sacred and groves all had some connection to the Mother as well as to the Sun Lord and whatever local deity lived in them.

Eirian went ahead of him and put her hand on the stone, palm down, for a moment. She spoke to it, then pulled a lock of her hair taut and cut a hand's width off with a small bronze blade. Faustus stood back until she had laid it on the stone and weighted it with a copper coin.

Then together they lifted the bags off the pack saddles and set them on the stone to keep them from the mud that was still everywhere. The lock of hair rested beneath, a message that proper respect had been given.

As they rode away Faustus listened for any sounds from the grove or the trees around it. They had gone half a mile when he heard it, an owl unaccountably awake in the daylight like a restless spirit. Any encounter with the little dark ones always made him feel as if he had stepped one foot precariously into another plane, some coexisting world that overlaid his own, and from which he suspected it might be hard to emerge if one went in entirely. The timber walls of Vacomagorum on the hill were a tether line of sorts, back out of a legendary world into the true one. He said so to Eirian and she snorted.

"They are not legend. You told me you had a grandmother from among them."

"Great-grandmother," Faustus said. "Or something."

The sky stayed clear and he forgot the little dark ones as he set himself to oversee the cleanup of the fort and the digging out and rebuilding of the neighboring villages, a task undertaken by Roman garrisons all along the drowned frontier.

Lucius had grown so restless in his confinement that Faustus took him down to the river to see the reconfigured land and marvel at the things the water had unearthed.

Lucius pulled a little flint arrowhead from the muck and held it up proudly. "Whose was this?"

"The oldest people," Faustus said. "Maybe the ones who set the standing stones."

Lucius laid it on his palm and prodded it with the fingers of his other hand. "Is it magic?"

"I don't think so."

Lucius tucked it in his tunic. "I will keep it anyway. You never know."

"Look there." Faustus pointed to a beaver cutting across the water with a branch in its mouth. "The river's engineers. They're already rebuilding their own houses."

"They'll make a pond," Lucius said, balancing on one leg on the riverbank. "Can I swim in it?"

The air went white for a moment and Faustus stood on the edge of another pond. His brother capered on the rock above it. "*I am Horatius Cocles on the Pons Sublicius and all the world belongs to me!*" Faustus blinked and the vision vanished. His hand shot out and caught Lucius by the tunic, jerking him away from the water.

Lucius looked up at him, startled. "What did I do?"

"Nothing." Faustus let his breath out. Where had that vision come from? Out of the water, he supposed, or his father's agonized presence shimmering like a cobweb in the corner of his eye. He put his arm around Lucius. "I'm sorry. You were so close to the edge."

"Mother doesn't like me to swim either," Lucius said. "I'm tired of things I can't do."

Faustus saw Marcus again for a moment as he dove through the shimmering air – the brother who should have inherited, the brother who was everything their father wanted. The brother

Faustus and Silvia had both loved, the shining, perfect son. The brother who broke his neck diving into a shallow pool.

He sat down on a flat stone above where the beavers were working and motioned Lucius down beside him. "Do you know why your mother doesn't like you to swim?"

Lucius sighed loudly. "My other uncle, Marcus, who drowned."

"Well, don't you see how she would worry?"

"She doesn't want me to watch the soldiers drill either," Lucius said. "She's afraid I'll be like you. She says I have to learn my sums and be an accountant." He picked up a stone and threw it in the water.

"She says what?"

"So I can buy another farm for us to live on."

Lucius might have been Faustus himself, after Marcus's death, weighed down with parental expectations and no more suited to them than Faustus had been. He looked at Lucius with growing affection. "We'll see what we can do about that," he promised.

"Can I join the army?"

How right was it to encourage the boy when Silvia was so against it? When if anything happened to Lucius it would probably kill her too? "The army's a hard life. And you're only eight. It will be ten years before you can do that."

"Can you make Mother change her mind before then?"

"I'm the *paterfamilias*," Faustus said. Enough people had told him so.

Lucius looked cheered.

"I'll take you to swim in the beaver pond when they've built it, if you promise to do as I say." Faustus pushed away the image of Marcus diving forever into those shallow depths. He would defy Silvia about that at least, before she pushed Lucius to something more dangerous, and unsupervised.

XVIII. THE COUNCIL

Ten days later the first raid swept through the newly repaired villages and tore them apart again.

Half a century of Batavians were in the village nearest Vacomagorum, helping dig paths clear of debris and cut timber for rebuilding ruined houses, and they fought off the raiders beside men of the village armed with axes and hunting spears. The invaders were long gone by the time a patrol from Vacomagorum came after them, and while Vacomagorum was undermanned, they struck the fort.

Faustus had come to the Praetorium to eat the afternoon meal and play latrunculi with Lucius, who was developing an unnerving knack for it, when shouts from the sentries on the walls were followed by a flight of arrows and a rush at the dexter gate.

Silvia jumped from her chair, plate and spoon clattering on the stone floor, hands to her mouth. Now they could smell smoke.

"Stay inside!" There was no time to say anything else. Faustus jammed his helmet back on his head and disappeared into the street.

Eirian pulled Silvia and Lucius into the storeroom at the back of the house while Paullus barred all the doors.

"Stay in here with Lucius," Eirian told Silvia. She took Faustus's hunting spear from its place in the corner. "The walls here are thickest. Bar the door and don't let anyone in unless it's us." She didn't wait for an answer, which in any case Silvia looked incapable of giving.

Gwladus was already closing the shutters. She had a kitchen knife stuck through her belt. Paullus had finished barring the

outer doors and had his own hunting spear in his hand and Argos
at his heel. They stood by the door and listened to the chaos in
the street.

–

The Via Praetoria swarmed with running men as Faustus headed
for the gate. A fire arrow stuck in the barracks roof and a soldier
climbed up and yanked it free. While they fought off the raiders
at the gate, more swarmed over the wall. The defenders picked
most of them off as they dropped and scattered. Faustus pushed
his way to the head of the men defending the gate and the cohort
signifer saw him and followed.

The Batavians were pushing outward now, driving the
attackers back through the narrow curved passage of the gate.
They followed Faustus and the signifer, the silver standard above
their heads. It was impossible to recognize faces under liberally
applied blue war paint – more than the Caledones customarily
wore into battle, Faustus realized, with the part of his mind that
was not occupied with swinging his sword at a blue-faced invader.

Abruptly the men who had made their way into the fort
scrambled back over the walls and the attackers at the gate fell
further back. The smell of smoke intensified. Someone had
poured oil across the granary doorway and set it alight. Three
soldiers were beating at it with their cloaks and Indus came with
three more and a bag of sand. More fires flared up throughout the
fort; everywhere the invaders had been little flames were licking
up from pools of oil.

"Pursuit, sir?" The first century trumpeter was at Faustus's
elbow, Ansgarius beside him, waiting for orders.

"No," Faustus decided, looking at all the angles. There seemed
to be too many. "They weren't trying to take the fort, just lure us
out of it. That and burn it. I want a dead one though."

There were two dead inside the walls, and they dragged them
before the prefect.

"Strip them and scrub their faces."

They looked at him oddly, but they did it. He stood a long while looking at the corpses, bloody in the mud, clan marks on their bare skin clear now: intricate patterns that covered face, torso, and arms. He told Ansgarius, "Ask Lady Eirian to come."

When she did, she knelt beside the corpses and inspected them dispassionately while Faustus waited for her to be sure. "Cornovii," she said at last.

"I thought so," Faustus said grimly. "In Caledone lands."

–

From then on the raiders struck every ten-day or so, staying just ahead of the Roman garrisons along the frontier line, tearing down rebuilt houses, looting what little was left, setting fire to anything not still too wet to burn.

Faustus sent a furious message to Rhion and another north to Emrys, and both replied politely that they had nothing to do with the raids, and no doubt these were men from outside Caledone lands as the prefect suspected. They appreciated the prefect's defense of Caledone villages and would send men of their own to help if the prefect would guarantee that he could tell them apart.

Faustus didn't reply. Rhion and Emrys would be doing what suited them about the raiders, no doubt including arming their own villages with weapons they were not supposed to have. He felt as if someone – the gods no doubt, they were good at that and easily amused – had enmeshed the entire frontier in a complex strategy game in which everyone became both allies and adversaries of everyone else. If there were rules, they appeared to be capricious.

He thought again of sending Silvia and Lucius to Eburacum. Eirian would not go, and had said so, not even to escort Silvia, suspecting him, rightly, of using that as a ruse to get her off the frontier as well. Neither would Gwladus go, because her man was in Vacomagorum.

"If he's killed and she's in Eburacum, what becomes of her then?" Eirian asked Faustus when he grumbled over it. "They aren't legally married, you said so yourself. You would see her taken care of, but who in Eburacum would? Her people are in the south."

Silvia appeared to have settled herself in a world of her own devising since the flood and the attack on the fort. In it chaos had no place. She prayed ritually and lengthily to the household gods each morning and evening, taught Lucius his lessons, and reclaimed the ruined garden. She spun. She wove Lucius a new cloak on the loom that Faustus had had built. She was never still, always frantically at some task, as if she would make the world orderly again with her own exacting orderliness. Faustus supposed it was possible that might work. He knew, although guiltily, that he had not the luxury of thinking about it overly much.

He instituted regular patrols in coordination with the other frontier garrisons and information from the scouts, trying to stay ahead of the intermittent raids, while never leaving a fort under-manned by enough to be dangerous. The scouts could tell him where the Cornovii raiders were camped but they never stayed more than a night in one place. There was movement among Rhion's men and sometimes Emrys's, but whether to deter the raiders or to assist them, the scouts were unsure. Deterrence was their guess. And Rhion had called a council but they didn't know why.

In the meantime, a sentry came to Faustus gingerly carrying a strange token left outside the decumana gate: a small oak twig still feathered with brown leaves. Its stem was wrapped in red thread and a piece of what looked like an army grain sack. He looked relieved when Faustus took it out of his hand. "I don't like the look of that."

"It's not an adder," Faustus said.

"Might turn into one for all I know," the sentry said. "Some kind of magic, the centurion thinks."

"In its way," Faustus said. "Tell your centurion I thank him for his observation but I don't think he need worry."

He took a small escort with him back to the oak grove, not only for form's sake but because it didn't do to go about alone just now, particularly with no sword and hauberk, for reasons having nothing to do with magic. He also went on foot because it was a good thing now and then to march alongside your men and let them see you do it.

He left them at the edge of the grove and squatted down beside the stone to wait. He almost sat on it to keep his backside out of the wet brown grass under the trees, but it was likely an altar of sorts, and he thought better of it.

He was used to the little dark people appearing in a whisper of movement, abruptly just *there* where they had not been before. This time he saw a flicker in the trees before the man was at his side. He was dressed in wolfskins and a belt of fox tails, his hair braided with small red beads, and he carried a spear with a leaf-shaped bronze tip.

"You are the commander at the fort yonder who left us grain," the man said. He spoke the dialect of the local Britons but with a soft accent that said it was not his own tongue.

"I am," Faustus said. "I am Prefect Faustus Silvius Valerianus," he added, because to give someone your name was accounted a politeness and a sign of trust among the people of the hills.

The little man nodded. "I am Starling," he offered.

Faustus stayed on his haunches so he would not tower over him. He had to look up, but not by much. "We found this by our gate." He gestured to the twig tucked into his belt.

"We thought you would come if you saw that," Starling said.

"And so I have." He waited for Starling to tell him why.

"You gave us grain when it was greatly needed. We pay our debts."

"I did not expect payment," Faustus said.

"Not that kind, no. But there is a debt all the same and so I have a thing to tell you in exchange, so that there is balance."

Faustus was aware that to Starling's people, balance meant that while the Romans and Caledones fought each other, they left the little dark ones alone. "What is the thing you would tell me?"

"Men from the island to the west," Starling said. "From Inis Fáil. Gaels. They will come here in the spring to fight."

"How do you know this?"

"My people speak to each other, from sidhe to sidhe. Do you doubt me?"

"No," Faustus said. *And may Neptune Seafather drown them all on the way.* He also doubted that Tuathal Techtmar was able to stop them or he would have done so already. "What else does the balance of things require of you?" he asked Starling. "Will you aid them?"

"No."

"Will you aid us?"

"Not that either. We do not care greatly which Sun People rule the others, you or the Caledones or the men of Inis Fáil. We thought once that the Caledones could stop you, and that might have been better because Romans never stop wanting more, but we saw that they cannot. Better that you fight each other and leave us alone."

"My mother was British. And my foremother was a woman out of a sidhe," Faustus said experimentally, to see if that made a difference. It didn't.

"Long ago and far away to the south." Starling was scornful. "We have heard that, but you smell of iron."

"I am grateful for your knowledge," Faustus told him. "If there is other aid you need, I will try to give it."

"We are building our houses anew," Starling said, "where the hillside has collapsed or washed away. It is too late to replant the gardens that the water took from us. Any food is useful."

"Are there foods you cannot eat? Or meat?" Faustus asked. It wouldn't do to bring them something that was forbidden.

Starling considered. "We do not eat men," he said finally. "I cannot think of anything else."

That had not occurred to Faustus but he found the specific denial reassuring. "I will try to bring something more. And I will warn my men to be careful if they come on your houses, to let

312

them be." The dwellings of the little dark people were almost invisible to someone who didn't know what to look for, but it was possible to stumble on one by accident. Now that he knew they were nearby he would see that they were not made sport of.

The sun was falling into the late November dusk when Faustus marched back to Vacomagorum with his escort, all of whom bristled with curiosity. He could hear the faint murmur of voices above the tramp of marching feet.

"That wasn't human if you ask me."

"Well then, what was it?"

"I've heard of them. They're what leads you off into a bog at night."

Faustus snapped his head around. "Is this a school outing? The next man who opens his mouth will regret it. March!"

They subsided. The prefect wasn't a terror like some, but he meant what he said, and a few of them had the marks of his vine staff to prove it.

Faustus sent a message to the governor, hoping he was at Eburacum and not on the coast designing baths for his villa. The message informed him of the raids by Cornovii fighters, and of intelligence of a war band from Hibernia in the spring. Faustus let it sound as if that too came from the frontier scouts, seeing no reason to involve the little dark people, particularly since Governor Lucullus was not inclined to believe in them anyway.

It was past the solstice by the time they got the governor's reply. The governor had indeed been in the south, but was due back before deep winter would make travel difficult. The legate of the Ninth at Eburacum, who had sent a courier in pursuit, had been forced to wait for an answer until his return since the governor did not seem to find the situation an emergency.

"The governor thanks me for my intelligence," Faustus growled to Ansgarius, reading it, "and is certain that it is too late in the season for a war band to form, but trusts me to keep an eye on the situation in the spring and let him know if we see any Hibernians about."

The governor added that his own excellent diplomatic relations with the High King should forestall any such attack, which made Faustus roll his eyes up into his helmet. "Unbroken ponies, that lot," was how Agricola's scouts had described the Gaels to him, and it wasn't far off. Tuathal might refuse to sanction an official invasion but he couldn't keep his subjects from raiding Britain when raiding Britain had been a Hibernian pastime for centuries.

"And the raids on villages here?" Ansgarius asked while Faustus glared at the governor's tablet.

"The governor suggests that those will slack off with the winter weather," Faustus said, "and stopping that sort of thing is why we're posted here, so we're to get on with it."

"I'd like to get on with it with a few more men," Ansgarius said. "Here's the Fit for Duty list."

Faustus looked at it and winced. "No replacements coming, I suppose. I asked for a hundred men and even that would leave us under strength by another fifty."

"No, sir," Ansgarius said. "They did send five hundred cavalry horses to Tamia though. Our courier came north with them. He said now they have twice as many horses as men to ride them, since the border cavalry can't get replacements either. He doesn't know what they're going to do with them but they'll be eating their heads off. The cavalry prefect was raging."

Faustus put the Fit for Duty list down. "Why do I feel that Governor Lucullus's estate breeds horses?"

Ansgarius grinned. "That new villa's got to be paid for somehow."

Faustus didn't ask how he had heard about that. Army gossip traveled on the wind. The thought crossed his mind again that governors who gave themselves too many regal airs sometimes regretted it, but so did subordinates who speculated about them, so he dropped the subject. "Best we confer with the other northern commanders then," he said, "and let them know we're on our own until spring." As the senior officer on the border he was in at least nominal command if the governor didn't intend to take a hand.

It would be full winter soon enough, although it didn't look like being the horror that the last one had been. The sky seemed to have wrung itself out with the final downpour and there had been only scattered snow. The raiders so far were more a nuisance than a serious threat, striking and retreating before a patrol, cautious of ambush, could catch them, but their presence unnerved everyone in both the villages and the forts and they managed to destroy nearly half of what had been rebuilt. Faustus sent messengers to Rhion and Emrys again, and again both replied flatly that the raids were none of their doing.

The information that came to Faustus had come to Rhion as well through his own channels, and Rhion, in a fury he had not exhibited in his message to Faustus, had called a council over it. It was the second council since Samhain, and the Kindred and other holders came grumbling through the mountain passes along rutted, icy tracks that were still clogged in places with flood debris and fanged with unearthed stones that shattered chariot wheels.

Rhion's hall was almost overheated between the hearth fire and the press of bodies steaming in its warmth. Iron firedogs capped with fanged beasts' heads radiated their heat into the room, pushing back the wintry wind as the last arrivals strode through the doorway, shaking snow from their cloaks and stamping their feet.

"Likely we'll all die of an ague," Mouric said, glaring at Rhion.

"You are too bad-tempered for an ague to take hold of you," Swyddog said. "Take off that wet cloak and sit by the fire and you will live to be a trial to your family for another year."

Aelwen had arrived the day before and sat at Council beside her brother. A certain number of looks still went her way over the issue of a woman as holder of Bryn Caledon but Aelwen had been born of the Kindred, the inner council of the clan, and no one was quite willing to pursue the issue. She had brought Ceridwen with her, simply saying that she thought it best that Ceridwen not be alone in Bryn Caledon just now, now that her uncle had made up his mind. What he had made it up to, Ceridwen did not know.

Mouric and Piran and the rest of the holders sat in a half ring around the fire. All of them were young except for Mouric and Maldwyn; much younger than holders would have been but for the war. They looked uneasy and angry at being summoned by Rhion yet again. Their drivers leaned against the walls, listening, sensing something weighty in the air.

Rhion sat silently a long while, watching them, until most began to fidget. Then he said, "Are you remembering what was said at Council when you came here last?"

"That the headman would drive the Cornovii raiders off our villages," Maldwyn grumbled. "Which he has not done."

"Those villages treat with Rome," Piran said. Piran looked around the room, gathering them to him. He wore finer clothing than the rest, a good shirt of blue and yellow wool and a twisted gold torque. Gold was still rare among the clans.

Rhion stared at Piran. "You are not headman. Nor likely to be," he added pointedly.

"We argued the matter of joining with the Cornovii against Rome," Piran said. "And you refused it for the clan, but let us decide each for ourselves."

"That was not a blessing given to raid our own people. Or even Emrys's. You knew that."

There was more general grumbling.

"We culled Emrys's cattle long before Rome came. You did yourself."

"We have heeded that thief long enough."

"When they treat with Rome, they are not ours. Happen that Piran is right in that."

Piran nodded at Rhion, satisfied.

"I forbade it," Rhion said. "And now you have done worse. You should have been quieter about your doings, Piran."

"I spoke openly that we should ally with the Cornovii to drive Rome out," Piran said. "You knew this and it was my right to speak so."

"It was not your right to go to Inis Fáil when both Emrys and I forbade it."

"If we had allied with the new High King there we would have had a base to strike Rome! I said that too. That was also my right."

Rhion stood, balancing carefully on his bad leg. "You had not the right to invite men of Inis Fáil to come here without my leave."

There was a stirring throughout the hall at that. To them the Gaels meant raiders in swift boats who beached in the coastal inlets and left again with loot and slaves.

Piran appeared to be deciding whether to deny it.

Rhion said, "Anyone who invites them in will not be rid of them again. They will be a worse danger than the Romans and will push us aside in our own lands. I will not have it and you are dispossessed. You have five days to leave your hold."

Another stirring and an indrawn hiss of breath came from the lords and everyone else in the room.

"That ruling is not yours to make!" Piran said. "My hold descends from Bryn Caledon." He looked at Aelwen.

Aelwen said, "I have given my agreement."

"There has been enough of wars we cannot win," Rhion said. "We are weary with it. We will not be led into another by a child just out of the egg." He spat on the floor.

Piran put his hand on his belt knife. "I will challenge you for this." He looked pointedly at Rhion's lame leg.

Idgual took up Piran's spear where it leaned against the wall by the door.

"No," Mouric said abruptly. "The Gaels have raided our coast time out of memory. You will not bring them to Caledone lands. I will back the headman in this. You are a fool."

Maldwyn stood too. "And I. Give them a foothold and they will never go away again."

317

"And I." Coran Harper stood.

One by one they stood.

Drust, Aelwen's driver, just that autumn come to his spear taking.

Cadr, holder of land that had been his foster father's before the last war.

Brychan, who was too old to fight even in that war, leaning on his stick.

Even Seiorgi, newly married to Piran's cousin.

Idgual thought he saw more figures rise behind them, made of smoke that wreathed around the firedogs' teeth:

Celyn of the Kindred.

Bleddin, son to Aelwen and foster son to Rhion.

Selisoc and Ula, spear brothers in life and death.

All the dead of the war rose again in the hearth fire's smoke, ranged behind the living lords and Rhion.

Piran glared at them. Idgual didn't know whether he could see the figures in the smoke or not.

"Bring them to the Cornovii's holds if you will," Rhion said, "and let the Cornovii regret they listened to you. I will have neither you nor men of Inis Fáil on Caledone land. Five days."

Piran looked as if he might fight anyway, even with the Council ranged behind Rhion. Then he shrugged his shoulders and said, "I will go. And return, with a war band that you will be shamed you did not lead. Will you at least give me shelter for the night, or do you turn me out roofless in the dark?" He pointed at the fading light that came through the shutters. The room was growing dimmer, lit only by tallow lights and the hearth fire.

"For the night," Rhion said, "you may sleep in the guesthouse. After that, any of our people who have followed you in this had best go with you."

Piran pushed his way through a gathering crowd of women, young hounds, and slaves from the kitchen, all drawn by whispers of something momentous between the headman and Piran. He took his spear from Idgual and stood balancing it in his grip for a moment, while the Council lords tensed, hands on knives. Then he stalked from the hall.

Idgual followed. He was surprised to see Ceridwen slip after them, but it was his own arm she caught at, not Piran's.

"Do not go with him."

Piran turned to her, his face flushed with anger. "Come with us. Come and be queen of the Caledones when we have driven Rome from here."

"The Caledones acknowledge no king or queen," Ceridwen said, "nor will they. You are a bigger fool than I thought. What did you think my uncle was going to do when he found out?"

"Your uncle becomes fearful since his leg was ruined," Piran spat. "It is no wonder he does not want a whole man here to challenge him. Maiming drains the courage from more than a man's limbs. You'll find that out."

"And why is it then that the Council backed him?" That was almost never done. If a headman dispossessed a holder and the holder made challenge, it was expected they would fight for it. That the Council had forestalled that meant something.

Ceridwen turned away from Piran when he didn't answer her, and Piran snapped, "Are you still a child to follow your mother and cling to her skirts with your thumb in your mouth?"

She was aware that her uncle was watching them from the hall door and so were half the Council. They would watch Piran until he left and then someone would follow him to be sure he kept going. Five days was not much time to return to his hold and take what he could with him. They would harry him north, maybe letting him drive his cattle with him and maybe not. She ignored Piran, instead studying Idgual's slightly crooked face under the brush of red-blond hair. His blue eyes were worried.

"Come with us," Piran said again, demanding her attention. "Take the place that your mother passed by."

"You do not understand Romans," Ceridwen said, still speaking to Idgual. "I have lived with the Romans. They will not go away because you bring men from Inis Fáil. They will not

319

go away unless they decide to, if it takes too many men to hold the highlands for what we are worth to them. They may do that. They have only so many men to spread across their empire. But they *won't* do it because we rebel against them."

"How else may a free people shake off thieves?" Piran demanded.

"They will defeat us first to make their point," Ceridwen said, still to Idgual. "And then go away. If they wish to. And even if they do, the Cornovii will be left with the Gaels in their holds."

The Council lords started from the hall doorway toward them and Piran spun on his heel. "I will be in the guesthouse," he said to Idgual. "Do you come with me?"

"I had best see to him," Idgual said uneasily.

"Don't go with him," Ceridwen said again.

He didn't answer, just turned unhappily toward the guest-house. Ceridwen watched him slow as he reached the door but he went in. He had heard her, she thought, but he had followed Piran's lead for so long that it might not be a habit he could break.

—

With the sunrise, Idgual was up and hitching the ponies to their yoke. It had snowed lightly overnight and the ground was rimed with frost. A thin sun glinted on it and on the skein of ice across the well mouth. Piran came out from the guesthouse yawning and angry because no one had sent them food.

Idgual pointed to a bag on the chariot floor. "I begged this from the kitchen for you."

Piran's hunting spear was already lashed to the chariot's side. Piran had brought Idgual's and began to fasten it to the other.

"No." Idgual put a hand on his arm.

Piran turned to him, spear still in his hand.

"I'm not going," Idgual said gently.

Piran let the spear fall. "We are spear brothers," he said as if that meant everything. It almost did.

"I know." Idgual looked miserably at the ground. "I have followed you because I love you."

"And you love me no longer?" Piran's eyes narrowed angrily.

"I love you still, but you are wrong in this. I cannot do it. Ceridwen is right."

Piran glared at him. "She is as foolish as her mother!"

"No. She is right, and Rhion is right, and we have been wrong. I just could not see it until now."

While they stood facing each other a kite soared overhead, its shadow passing across them like a hand. Its shrill call hung in the air like an accusation or a cry of parting.

Piran's shoulders sagged. He stepped into the chariot and took the ponies' reins. He didn't speak to Idgual again and Idgual watched him until the chariot was out of sight down the track that would take him to his own hold, and north after that, with the ill luck of the dispossessed riding on his shoulders. Some of the men who had followed him would go north with him, Idgual thought, but not all of them, not now.

Idgual turned away and went back to the guesthouse. He sat down by the remains of last night's fire and put his head in his hands.

—

Ceridwen found him there when the other Council lords and their drivers had gone. The silent figure looked small and miserable. She sat down by him.

"My uncle sends me to say you are to stay in his household for now until you find another lord you wish to swear to. If it is not him, he will understand."

"He was right," Idgual said. "I am the one in the wrong. I let him do it."

Ceridwen snorted. "You let him? When did anyone let Piran do anything? Piran does as he will. Would he have stopped if you had said, 'Brother, this is a bad idea'?"

"No," Idgual admitted. He had done that from time to time, and no, Piran had not stopped or even heeded him.

"Very well then. Come into the hall and get some more bread and cheese. I know you gave him what you had."

Idgual stood. He ran his hands through the brush of his hair, making it stand further on end. "I couldn't let him go hungry," he said, "and I don't think they would have fed him."

Ceridwen prodded him toward the door and he went obediently. He would mourn for Piran, she thought, but he was already beginning to emerge from Piran's shadow. Men like Piran cast suffocating shadows if you were foolish enough to love them.

She looked across the sweep of hills in the distance, the lake below them, the snow-covered mountain meadows. It was cold for wandering in the heather, she thought, but spring would come and with it the merciful fading of memory.

—

Piran's hold had been stripped of everything he could put on wagons and he was nearly to Lyn Emrys now, with gold and cattle to buy his welcome, and Rhion's malcontents behind him. It was bad weather for travel and they lost some of the cattle and ate some of the rest, but he knew now where to spend the coin that was the secret of Calgacos. Rhion might well have been glad to hear that the old warlord still lived. Emrys would not.

Emrys was suspicious enough at their arrival to make Piran's followers stay outside the walls, winter or no. Piran alone was allowed inside and Emrys gave him a long look, waiting for Piran to break the silence. Piran did not, confident of the upper hand now.

Finally Emrys said, "What is your business here so far north of your hold?"

Piran put his hands to the fire. "I have left Rhion's service to come to you with a gift that Rhion has not earned."

"He has dispossessed you," Emrys said flatly.

There was no point in denying it. Piran said, "That time was coming and I would not fight a lame man. Better to have those who are loyal behind me than Rhion's tame dogs."

"And join the Cornovii? To raid *my* holds?"

"To join you. And then with the Cornovii and men from Inis Fáil who are coming in the spring, to wipe the Romans from Britain. To be free men again."

Emrys snorted. "And left with Gaels from Inis Fáil in our land. I heard that you had done this. I should have given you to the Romans."

"That would have been a mistake," Piran told him.

"I can still do it. You have not so many men with you that I cannot do it."

"You do not know the gift I offer you," Piran said. "I know a thing that you do not. A thing you will wish me to tell no one else."

Emrys's mouth tightened. The old scar on his face tightened with it and he looked dangerous. "Do you threaten me?"

Piran looked around the hall. "Send your men away. And her." He gestured at Hafren.

Hafren rose. Emrys met her gaze. Then she tucked her sewing under her arm and beckoned to the handful of men who were fitting spearpoints to new shafts across the hearth.

When they had gone, Emrys waited.

"The old warlord still lives," Piran said.

"Is that your great secret? That has been said since the last battle, a nursery tale for old men and babies. Pah. Tell that story where you will."

"He is alive in Inis Fáil in the court of the new High King. I have seen him myself and spoken to him." Piran watched Emrys's face. That had hit home. "If he should return, where will you be then? Where will be your command over the highland clans, when it was for Calgacos that the Druids spoke? Will you wager that even your own men will follow you then?"

Emrys narrowed his eyes. "*If* that is true, *if* he was going to return, he would have. Aelwen told me of the wound he took.

Why would I bet on so foolish a venture as yours in fear of a man so maimed?"

"Ah," Piran said, "that is my point, you see. He does not have to return. It only has to be known that he lives to undermine your position. And also to send Rome back with an army so great you will be forced to fight them. They were in Rhion's hold asking where he was buried because they fear his power even dead. If he returned alive they would come to hunt him down. Better you fight them now with us while their numbers make them vulnerable. Do you see?"

Piran could see Emrys thinking it over, conceding his point no doubt. He grinned at Emrys. "And why have you not offered me anything to drink? It was cold and thirsty on the road."

Emrys smiled back at him. The smile didn't reach his eyes. "I am touched that you trust me not to poison you."

"If you were to poison me, it would not be within your own hall," Piran said, more confident now. "That would be too great a shame to you, to kill a guest under your roof."

"You are not a guest," Emrys said. "You are a most unwelcome ally."

"Then we are agreed."

"You may not winter here. I'll not have Gaels in my land or the sweepings of Rhion's pigsties. Take your men on the road again north to your Cornovii allies."

"And in the spring?"

"In the spring I will come north to meet you."

XIX. THE GAELS

SPRING, 841 ab urbe condita

The land began to green again, a slow sweep of new life, pale unfurling fronds of bracken and yellow-flowered gorse covering over the scarred hillsides and meadows, masking the white bones that lay scattered where the water had been. The curlews began to come back to their nesting grounds, their calls a bright silvery note in the warming air.

At Bryn Caledon where Idgual had come to bring Aelwen a message from her brother, and Ceridwen a handful of spring violets he had picked along the way, it seemed like the world made new that Ceridwen's Roman poet had spoken of.

At Vacomagorum, Eirian and Gwladus busied themselves with turning out all the winter bedding and washing it in a vat in the Praetorium courtyard and then washed the dog for good measure. The sky stayed blue. A supply train arrived laden with wine, oil and grain, dried meat and apples. Faustus and Eirian took a sack of grain and another of apples to the oak grove. They took Lucius to the river to swim in the beaver pond and observe the family of otters who were carving out a den below some willow trees in the newly altered structure of the bank. When Silvia objected, Faustus said bluntly, "Marcus didn't drown, he broke his neck."

"He's a child!"

"He's not a baby." Lucius had outgrown his tunic and breeches again. His legs stuck out below their hem like saplings.

"Come with us," Eirian said. "You'll see."

Silvia came reluctantly, but as they watched the otters shooting down their mud slide, a comical contrast to the businesslike engineering of the beavers, she softened. When Eirian stripped to her shift and took Lucius for a careful paddle to the other bank and back, she said, "I suppose it's best he learn to swim well. I am not an idiot, Faustus."

He patted her hand. "I never thought so."

The raids on border garrisons and villages had ceased despite a mild winter, and in the homely pleasure of watching otters with his oddly assorted family, Faustus began to wonder if Starling had been wrong in his warning.

—

The curlews could have told him the peace was fleeting. They had seen boats being fitted on the coast of Inis Fáil on their flight to their inland breeding grounds, but those were matters for men. Spring was for making eggs; the men shouting at each other around the boats drawn up on the sand at Inber Domnann were no business of theirs.

The High King's anger radiated around him like a forge fire and he would burn you if you touched him, Baine thought. He had already burned Riderch, but it wasn't going to matter. Riderch could not back down now even if the High King would. And he wouldn't. Even Owain had not been able to convince Tuathal that he could not force the fianna to his will. Now Fiachra stood between them before knives came out.

"I told you that if you went to make war in Britain you could not return," Tuathal said. He pushed past Fiachra to tower over the shorter man, tall and full of a dark fury, but Riderch stood his ground. "You have put your boats in the surf and so you are banished from Inis Fáil."

"We have always raided Britain," one of Riderch's fian protested. He was young, with the urge to earn a name for himself. That and gold. There were nearly five hundred of them on the shore, spearpoints glinting in the sun.

"You are not going to raid, as well you know, and I know, and the gods know, so do not twist the matter," Tuathal said.

"And why should we not make war in Britain?" Elwyn asked. "Does the High King fear the Romans so greatly? They have never come here, nor will they."

"And if they should, we will drive them away like driving cattle," one of Elwyn's men added.

"As you drove *my* army away?" Tuathal asked. His voice was level and dangerous, more dangerous than the men shouting at him. "Mine was trained by a Roman and we swept across Elim mac Conrach and his spearmen like the tide. Between you, you lead fifteen separate bands, and none answering to any but their captain. My old general in Britain, Julius Agricola, said that he could take Inis Fáil with one legion. He was recalled to Rome before he could prove it."

"And never could have!" Elwyn shouted.

"No," Tuathal conceded. "It would have taken two." He raised his hand. "I want the Druids."

Baine watched as Aíbinn and Sechnal came forward. Tuathal had already tried to convince the Druids to forbid the fianna. Druids had the power to stop a war if they wished, but they rarely exercised it, and this one they had refused out of hatred for the Romans. Nevertheless, they had come with him when he rode to Inber Domnann, because whatever happened on the shore would be a great matter. Baine had come too, at Fiachra's urging, because she was one of the few who could speak to the High King when his temper overflowed.

Now Tuathal said to Aíbinn and Sechnal, "Witness that I have commanded these men that they are not to go to Britain to make war."

There was an angry murmuring among the fianna. "A geas cannot not be cast across the sea!"

"That is established," Tuathal said. "Witness also that they defy me, and thus I put a geas that they may not set foot on Inis Fáil once they have left it. That I may do."

A rising tide of angry voices came from the men on the shore. Tuathal ignored it.

327

Sechnal thumped his staff on the ground and Aíbinn murmured, "We witness."

Baine thought they didn't like that it had come to this, despite that they had refused to intervene. The brehons had also declared the matter outside their purview.

"May it turn on you, High King!" someone shouted.

Tuathal stood silently while the fianna waded to the boats. The sky was clear with only a few clouds moving across, fair sailing weather. A flock of seagulls squabbled along the sand for scraps from last night's camp.

Baine wondered how Tuathal's Roman, now commander in the north of Britain, would like having the fianna's troublesome remnants permanently in his territory, unable to come home again. The Cornovii, who had invited them, she thought, would regret it.

The boats moved out into the channel on the tide and Baine laid a hand on Tuathal's arm as he stood watching them. The Druids had gone back to their carriage, pointedly leaving the High King alone on the beach except for his driver and a few of his household hounds.

"Are you certain you have done the right thing?" No one else could ask him that, not even Owain or Fiachra, so she might as well.

"I am culling the fools," Tuathal said.

"And what of the Epidii? The fianna will make landfall there and they are your mother's people."

Tuathal looked stubborn, as stubborn as Elwyn and Riderch. "The Epidii are half-Gael already. That is why my father took a wife from among them. Cadman will give them safe passage, not fight them." Cadman's relationship with Rome was tenuous and only a formality. The Epidii traded regularly with raiders from Inis Fáil and were often willing to give them harbor for a price. "Don't try to change my mind, Baine. This must be done and I must do it."

Tuathal had wanted to be High King. It was all he had wanted since he was old enough to understand what had been stolen from him. Now that he was, she suspected he was finding it less than satisfactory. The boats were beyond Reachra now, past calling back. "What would your General Agricola have done?" she asked him.

"Agricola commanded an army, not a country of mad poets. He would have ordered them flogged, and possibly crucified."

Baine smiled. "No. I see. You can't do that."

"I would like to. Aside from not wishing to attract the attention of Rome, I owe Faustus Valerianus a debt, and I am loath to send these fools into his territory."

–

Starling had been right; the beacons flaming to the southwest told Faustus all he needed to know of ships in the channel. The scouts sent to watch the north came in to say a war band was also massing on the edge of the Great Firth. Most likely they would come south through the glens while the boats from Inis Fáil swept up the coastal inlets in the west to catch the border forts between them. Dispatches were sent to the governor in Eburacum and word came back that he would bring the Ninth Legion north to meet them. The border forts were to hold until then.

"Agricola would have been on the border already," Faustus said furiously, "not sitting in Eburacum three hundred miles away! We told him last autumn. That's fifteen days at forced march. Ten maybe, if he can get the Fleet under sail."

"Not so much now," Ansgarius said. "Assuming he set out when he sent the dispatch north."

"Assuming he didn't have to have his hair cut first, or order new boots," Faustus said. He took a breath and got a grip on his temper. "All right. Until the Ninth gets here, the border garrisons are all we have."

"That isn't going to be enough if the Caledones join in."

"I think they won't." He hoped to Pluto they didn't. "But it isn't enough anyway. Get me a map."

Ansgarius produced their copy of the map Agricola's cartographer had drawn and Faustus studied it. The line of border forts ran southwest through Castra Pinnata to Tamia and down to Alauna. Castra Pinnata was not yet occupied by the legion for which it was intended, and work had slowed as more and more cohorts were drawn off to the point that Faustus was beginning to doubt it would be.

Ansgarius looked over his shoulder. "Do we take the cohort south to Tamia and pull the southern garrisons north to meet us and get caught between the Hibernians and the Cornovii? Or split with not enough men to fight either?"

"Pull them all together at Tamia, and hope the Ninth is in time," Faustus said. And hope it was enough. The Ninth was understrength with detachments still serving on the Rhenus and not likely to be sent back. And without them, he had only enough men, barely, to hold off the Cornovii, but not Hibernian raiders too.

Faustus rolled up the map. "I want to meet with Rhion on the way."

The Caledones might not be willing to fight on Rome's side, but they wouldn't like having their land trampled over and eaten bare by Cornovii, let alone Gaels from Hibernia. There might be something to be done besides arming the Caledones, even if they had been willing. Faustus knew arming the Caledones, particularly if they were willing, would be a bad idea.

–

Rhion considered the Roman commander sitting beside his hearth, drinking the beer that Efa had brought him. He said, "It was part of the peace we made, that Rome would defend us if we handed over our weapons. Does Rome say now that it cannot?"

"Rome abides by the treaty," Faustus said. "But considerable damage could be done to your fields and herds before the governor can arrive with a legion to support us."

Rhion stretched his bad leg out, easing a cramp in the torn muscle. "Your governor is short-sighted. We both knew the Cornovii were going to rebel. And we both knew about the men from Inis Fáil."

Faustus didn't ask how Rhion knew. Or how he thought Faustus knew. It was entirely possible that they had the same source. "Since they were invited here by one of your clan, headman, it may be said that *you* have broken the treaty terms."

"The man responsible for that has been dispossessed of his holding and is exiled."

"I regret that we did not find him first."

"I would not worry, Prefect. He has ill luck riding on his back now. I have considerable faith in Rome's capacity for revenge."

"That is true," Faustus admitted. "In fact, I can practically guarantee it. But if we cannot hold them off until Rome arrives, neither you nor I may be able to appreciate that."

"They are hunting you, Prefect, not me."

"For now." Rhion's clan would mend their walls, close their gates, and settle in until the fighting was over. "On the other hand, headman, you cannot take every sheep and cow from your pastures into defensible holds, nor can you guard your plowed fields if you are waiting out the war in Bryn Caledon. There will be very little left to you after the war band has passed by."

"We will not fight for Rome," Rhion said flatly.

"No," Faustus agreed. "Nor would I wish to arm your people, to be frank." Other than the arms that he suspected they had already reacquired.

"Then why have you come to me? For surety that we will not attack your rear?"

"Not entirely. There is the matter of the Hibernians. They have no grievance against Rome, they are adventuring, and will attack what is in their path."

The Gaels had raided the western coast for decades, always driven out again, always returning like starlings to a roosting place to be driven out once more. One day they would stay and if they got a foothold, they would keep coming.

Rhion weighed that.

"They are hungry," Faustus said.

"What do you want of me then?"

–

Fog wreathed the tree canopy, shrouding the newly greening branches, masking the shapes of horses and riders on the edge of the hillside. Below in Clota Mouth they could see the ships, dim shapes with masts jutting through the mist, almost invisible but there, deadly wraiths on the water. As Faustus had feared, their Epidii kin had given them safe passage.

The sketchy garrisons that manned the Agricolan forts south of the Clota had gone to strengthen the ranks of the border forts massing to drive the Cornovii back. Until the Ninth came from Eburacum, the horsemen on the hillside were nearly all there was to halt the men from Inis Fáil: five hundred false cavalry on the spare remounts from Tamia. Adults and twelve-year-olds, anyone who could sit a horse, carrying hunting spears, broken chariot poles, even trimmed saplings. Anything that would look like a spear to the men on the ships.

The first century of Faustus's Batavian cohort was interspersed among them in the trees; the fourth century waited in the woods below, near where the ships would beach, silent and unmoving enough that the flock of crows that had risen up at their coming had settled back to their roosts. Faustus had left Ansgarius to command the rest and given command of the combined border troops to the prefect at Tamia because, as that prefect said, the only one insane enough to command Faustus's imaginary army was Faustus.

He slipped among the riders on foot now, speaking quietly. "You are not to engage, remember that." Even armed with broom handles, the Caledones' instinct was going to be to fight, particularly against the Gaels. "You are to stay on the hillside until they come after you. Then you disperse and run."

"That will leave your men to be swallowed up," a rider said, and Faustus recognized Ceridwen, Calgacos's daughter, with a rake handle topped with a makeshift blade that had once been a belt knife. She wore breeches and a dark shirt and her hair was plaited into a braid down her back.

"That was my bargain with your uncle," he said. "You will not fight for Rome. You are not armed and half of you are children. You are to make them think we are more than we are. That is all. If they decide to attack anyway, then you run."

"We are not all children," she said stubbornly.

Mars save him from a people who would fight just because they could, past caring that it was on Rome's side. "No!"

If he couldn't control the situation and they were killed, it would set the whole border in flames. That was another risk, aside from the risk of trying to frighten off the Gaels with two centuries and an ala of illusory cavalry.

A man in a helmet and ring mail sidled his horse next to Ceridwen's. "Leave be," he told her. "I listened to you, do you listen to him and to Rhion. We will frighten the Gaels and come away with good horses for it."

Faustus ignored that since he had no illusions about getting the horses back afterward. If they did what he hoped, the horses would be worth it. Someone would try to dock him for it, he supposed. That would be something to worry about if he got back alive. He was aware of the likelihood that he wouldn't. And he had left his household at Vacomagorum, with most of the garrison leaving to meet the Cornovii. He should have sent Paullus to take them south no matter what when he still could, and now the terror of seeing Vacomagorum burned and empty gnawed at him.

"Retreat when you hear the call," he said again. "If they start up the hill, we will hold them as long as we can. Retreat and don't look back. If all we do is delay them it may still be enough."

The ships were close now and would have spotted the riders on the hillside. The mist was lifting, the sun glinting here and there

333

on spearpoint and helmet. Rome was rich in iron; her cavalry wore helmets. At this distance the Gaels wouldn't see that some of them were cook pots. Faustus raised his hand and the riders moved forward, their mounts recognizable by their size as Roman troop horses, not the smaller ponies of the highland clans. The riders with hunting spears and armor formed the front line, the false weapons and helmets farther back, silhouettes in the trees' shadow.

The men from Inis Fáil hauled their ships from the water above the tide line, leaping from them onto the rocky shore and gathering in small bands under what Faustus suspected were numerous commanders. They looked upward at the riders that blocked their path inland.

"That's given them to think now," Indus, beside him, said with satisfaction. "And bugger the lot."

Faustus pulled a leafy branch from a sapling birch and strode out to stand in front of the massed riders. The morning sun threw his shadow down the hillside. He waved the branch.

Six different commanders appeared to confer. Faustus waited, and wondered if he knew any of them. That might help, or it might not. Two men came forward from the rest, spoke to another man, and watched him march up the hillside. When the messenger was halfway up, he called out in halting Latin, "Lord Elwyn permits you into his camp to speak with him, and guarantees you safe passage. I am to translate."

Elwyn. Faustus remembered him, one of the men recruited under Tuathal's banner. An adventurer by nature.

"Don't you trust them, Prefect," Indus protested.

"If there is one thing I can trust them for, it's to keep a truce," Faustus said. "Nothing else, mind you, but they respect that." He started down the slope carrying the green branch. "I don't need you," he said to the messenger in his own language.

Elwyn. And Riderch. He saw their eyes widen a bit as they recognized him. "You are not welcome," Faustus said when he stood before them.

"We have not asked your leave," Elwyn said truculently. He balanced on the balls of his feet, rocking back and forth, eager to fight something.

"If the High King gave you leave, he made a mistake," Faustus said. "And so have the men who invited you here. There is a Roman legion on the way to prove that to you."

"We do not need the High King's leave," Riderch spat. "We are free men."

"Then you are free to go again to Inis Fáil," Faustus said.

They were silent a moment. Then, "Men of Laigin do not turn from battle," Riderch growled.

"I have withdrawn the service pledged to Tuathal Techtmar," Elwyn said. "I will go where I will," he added pointedly.

They had not had the king's blessing for this invasion, Faustus was positive. It was likely that as payment for defying him he would not take them back afterward. Faustus couldn't blame Tuathal for that, not really. The High King's throne was slippery enough. He had sent Rome his own troublemakers to be rid of them, a tactic not unlike Rhion's.

Faustus counted their ranks in his head, and compared them to the century hidden in the woods to their left, and the one in the trees on the hillside. Five to one, nearly. And no sign from the watchtowers on the hills to the east that would signal the approach of the Ninth.

"You would do better to go to the ones who asked you here," he suggested. "Sail north where you will be welcome." He actually doubted that. Matauc would not care to have them permanently in his country either.

"We are promised land here," Riderch said. "When Rome has gone."

"Matauc of the Cornovii makes dangerously free with other people's land," Faustus said. "That may come around to bite him. And you will be dust in a barrow when Rome has gone. Look up, Riderch."

Riderch and Elwyn both raised their eyes to the riders on the hilltop.

"There may be more that you cannot see," Faustus suggested.

"I do not believe that!" Elwyn said.

"You fought under my command. You should. Fight me and see. Or go north. I will give you a day to think on it."

"We will give *you* a day to pull back!" Riderch snapped.

Faustus lifted the green branch in mock salute. "Sail north, while Matauc's men are away from home."

He set out up the hill again. He had bought a day. Even though the undefended Cornovii holds might be tempting, likely the fianna had sworn an oath to Matauc and they would abide by that, for now. But they would argue over whether to sail by a different route before Faustus could march to cut them off, setting the shame of avoiding a fight against the practicality of joining the Cornovii at full strength. Ultimately they would decide to fight him, but they would quarrel over it first, each fian commander with a different and competing idea of how to do it.

Faustus ordered the first century to dig a camp on the hilltop, with the Caledone civilians at the center lest Elwyn and Riderch send spies up the slope in the night. The fourth century in the woods below would camp where they hid, uncomfortably and without fire, but Faustus wanted them kept for a surprise.

At dusk, to give the look of greater numbers, they lit multiple fires on the hilltop. Faustus patrolled the camp, listening to the night with the sentries on the perimeter, looking east to the watchtowers again, stopping to speak to his Batavians and to the Caledone civilians. He saw Ceridwen at a fire with the man who had ridden beside her earlier. His name was Idgual, Faustus remembered, and now the name echoed in his memory: one of those who had gone to Tuathal at Tara looking for alliance. So Idgual had abandoned Piran, and likely that was what he had meant by listening to Ceridwen. He had his arm about her shoulders now. Her father came to Faustus's mind again, the uneasy presence of something he shouldn't know. He felt it every time he saw Aelwen, and now her daughter, who gave every sign of being much like him. Idgual had gone to Inis Fáil with Piran.

He must know. Had he told her? Did he wrestle with the same dilemma? And what exactly would happen if Rome got word that Calgacos was alive, not to mention that the officer they had lent to Tuathal knew it and hadn't spoken?

The mist came down again overnight, and in the early dawn, Faustus's scouts said that the Gaels were breaking their camp. Faustus squinted his eyes at the hills to the east.

"Nothing yet, Prefect," the scout said.

"Form them up. The likeliest-looking to the front, and our men before them." He hadn't named a commander among the civilians. They seemed to gather about Ceridwen in the way that the hostage children had, so he went to her. "You know the trumpet call. I've played it for you. When you hear it, run."

She nodded, realistic now. They would be slaughtered if they fought the Gaels. That or taken for slaves. "We know," she said. "Prefect—"

He could see movement near the ships, like ghosts in the fog. "They are coming. They may halt when we hit their rear. They may not."

"I have asked the Mother to watch over you."

"That is kind of you," he said, startled.

"It is not easy, having a foot in two worlds. I know."

"I expect you do. But mine are planted firmly in Rome. On her border at any rate."

"I was told you are half-Silure. You are one pace into another world whether you will or no."

"Maybe," Faustus conceded. He could feel the blue stone where it lay against his chest under his tunic. He touched it with a fingertip, tightened his helmet strap, and signaled to Indus and the trumpeter. The cohort standard, which followed its prefect, rose over their heads, milky in the fog.

A wild howl came from the men at the ships, and a chanted taunt, over and over: the prefect of Rome and his men and his horses would all go down in a fine red tide of blood. The men of Inis Fáil would strip their bodies bare and leave them for the carrion crows.

337

The Batavians stirred, murmuring angrily. The Gaels' chant made the hair rise on their arms. They didn't need to understand it.

"Ignore them," Faustus said. "No one was ever slain yet by bad poetry."

"Is that what it is then?" Indus said. "I thought it was pigs being slaughtered."

A ripple of laughter that was half bravado ran down the line. "Batavians!" someone shouted and they all picked it up. "Batavians!"

"We'll catch them between us and they'll sing another song," Faustus shouted back. He cast one desperate look to the east. Nothing. The men of Inis Fáil rushed the slope screaming. Riderch was at their head with an axe in his hand, blade gray and deadly as the mist that made it hard to sort one face from another.

Faustus signaled the trumpeter. The *Advance* sang out and the century waiting in the woods below burst from the trees. "On the second call," Faustus said to the men beside him. "Let them engage first."

The fourth century peppered the Gaels' rear with pila and slingstones and then formed a wedge and drove it into them as their war band swarmed up the slope. The Gaels stumbled backward and the Batavians opened up their wedge to let them fall through and spitted them with spears. Shouted orders, some conflicting, came from the leaders, but those in the rear turned around to meet the attackers.

"Now!" The trumpet sounded the *Advance* again and the first century braced itself to meet the men coming up out of the mist. A flight of pila caught the first rank and some went down, but they were many and the century was stretched thin. They battered the Gaels with their shields, pushed them down and back into their own ranks, drove deadly short swords up under their guard at close quarters, but they kept coming. At the rear, the fourth century had snarled the advance but half the Gaels had turned on them

338

now, pushing them back toward the sea. The century split and tried to make their way around the flanks of the war band and the band's rear coalesced again, moving uphill now unhindered.

Faustus struggled to take the first century forward and hold the line as the Gaels swarmed at them. Another ten paces or so and they would see his fraudulent cavalry for what they were. He had left Arion at Vacomagorum. He would fight this battle on the ground with his men. Riderch was at the front of the Inis Fáil line and Faustus lunged at him, catching the blade of Riderch's axe on his shield edge, yanking it toward him, trying to pull it from his hand. Taking out the Inis Fáil commanders would do more good than anything. Each fian followed its own lord and if he fell it was not easy to bring them under another's orders.

Riderch wrenched his axe away and stumbled back a pace, changing his grip. He swung it at Faustus's head. Faustus blocked the blow again, staggering at the force of it, and tried to go under Riderch's defenses with his sword, holding his shield high. Riderch pulled back and feinted, looking for an opening, and another sword struck Riderch's axe handle broadside. It missed his knuckles but Riderch's arm bent backward with the blow and he lost his grip. Faustus saw Indus in his peripheral vision as he caught up the axe and threw it at a man advancing on him, then he was lost in the chaos. Riderch drew his sword and Faustus went after him. The axe was Riderch's weapon and he was clumsy with a sword; Faustus had watched him fight in Inis Fáil. Faustus closed in on him.

He had only time for a glancing blow at Riderch's ribs, splitting the ring-mail hauberk open a few inches, before he felt the momentum of the battle shifting, rushing uphill like a living siege tower now, driving the first century backward and scattering the fourth. They weren't going to hold them.

"*Cavalry Pull Back*," Faustus gasped to the trumpeter and he blew the call once and then again. Faustus looked to the east again. Nothing.

Ceridwen and her people turned their mounts at the call and scattered through the forest, making for the rendezvous spot that

Faustus had shown them. Making for that and then for home, staying ahead of whatever would be chasing them as soon as the Batavians fell.

The Batavians fought their way back into the trees, into the shadows, keeping the Gaels in pursuit of them, away from the direction the riders had taken. Faustus had lost sight of Riderch in the chaos of screaming spearmen. The fianna were well armed, some with long swords, most with axes and spears. Their formation was nonexistent, which gave the Batavians a slight advantage as they made a shield wall and backed up behind it, but they were too badly outnumbered to hold for long.

"Pull back!" Faustus shouted. The trumpeter sounded the call and the Batavians fell back all at once into the deeper forest and the heavy understory. The Gaels hesitated, afraid of ambush, and he signaled the trumpeter again: the cavalry *Advance*, a call many of them would recognize from his days of command in Inis Fáil. It would take them a while to realize that no cavalry answered it. They didn't hesitate long. When no horsemen appeared, they hurled themselves howling after the retreating Romans.

Faustus kept his men in the heavy woodlands, tents and gear abandoned, staying clear of the native tracks that crossed through them or the leveled dirt road that ran north toward Alauna. They had practiced this last desperate drill on the way, knowing it might mean life or death. Pull into the trees, make yourself hard to find before you sling a lead bullet out of nowhere to strike head or chest or break a knee. Always pulling back, always under cover, watching to see that the enemy does not come around your flank. Faustus sent a lead stone flying into a helmetless head and saw his target drop and tangle another man in his legs and spear shaft. He fitted another into the sling, stumbling over the body of the fourth century's commander who had bled and died as he ran.

The Gaels chased them doggedly, wary of the stones and of where the cavalry might still be, Riderch convinced there was an ambush waiting, Elwyn arguing, the other fian commanders siding with one or the other.

All day Faustus's men stumbled through the trees, gasping and picking stones from the ground now, their lead ammunition long gone, armed with short swords and the few spears that hadn't yet gone into the enemy. When dark came they halted exhausted as the howl of the pursuing band quieted with the nightfall. They too would be too tired to move until morning. Faustus's weary, bloodied stragglers shared out the little left of their provisions and tied up each other's injuries because the field medics attached to each century were both dead. Of the hundred and thirty he had set out with, there were eighty-five in the camp with him now. He thought they had killed at least that number of the Gaels, but the odds grew worse not better with each death. Before they slept he paraded them before the cohort standard and said the prayers for the slain. Eventually they would go back – or someone would – and burn the bodies and bring their ashes home. He set a rotating watch and lay down to sleep an exhausted sleep not even dreams could penetrate.

–

At the meeting place Ceridwen counted heads in the failing light, as Rhion or her father would have done. Rhion had given leave for anyone who wanted to play the prefect's game to go with him, and they had bought their people time to gather the rest of the clan into Bryn Caledon and shore up its walls. The Cornovii would attack the Roman forts first, but if they overran them, they would turn to the Caledone villages next. The highland clans had always raided each other; only the alliance against the Romans had united them and that was unraveling now, setting clan against clan in the old way.

It would be four days' hard ride to Bryn Caledon and Ceridwen was grateful for the Roman cavalry mounts. Idgual was right about that, although it was a shame there weren't more mares. She watched him organizing the band, some to ride ahead to scout the way home, others to hunt game along the way, the youngest and oldest in the middle. He was still in Rhion's house, both of them seeming content to let matters stay that way, and out from under Piran's thumb Idgual had become someone new. She looked over her shoulder for the beacon that the Roman prefect had said would show when the governor's legion from Eburacum was sighted. Nothing. She caught Idgual's eye and pointed at the nothing and he nodded. They had best move on at first light. When the Gaels had killed the prefect's men they would come on their own trail.

–

At Clota Mouth at dusk a dozen small figures crept out of the trees where the ships from Inis Fáil were beached. They halted to make sure there was no one left on board and when they were certain they climbed everywhere, stripping cordage and canvas sailcloth, timber, and bronze fittings, packing it into neat bundles that could be carried by one or two men. When they had finished their harvest, Starling thought for a moment and then bade them drive several holes into the hull of each ship for good measure – because of the apples, he said. Then they picked up their bundles and set off into the hills. They saw the camps of the Gaels and of the Roman prefect's men but neither saw them as they went by. In the morning, also because of the apples, the guts of a dead pine marten were fouling the water where the Gaels were camped.

Riderch rose in a temper because of that, and because they were hungry too, and the fianna commanders were still arguing. He shouted them into silence with the promise of bread and meat from the first village, and loot, and more when they caught the fleeing Romans. They were nearly on their quarry when a wisp of smoke rose in the hills to the east and a faint flame flowered beneath it.

XX. THE GRASS CROWN

Faustus saw the smoke too, the signal they had hoped for: the Ninth Legion, still miles away. It was likely he and his men wouldn't make it that far but the Ninth would be in time to defend the border forts, and to avenge their losses on the Gaels. They had struggled to hold the Gaels back. Now they could lead them into the teeth of the legion.

"Run!" he shouted wearily. "Run!"

If the Gaels recognized the significance of the beacon, they did not slow their pursuit. They hunted Faustus and his remaining men through the tangled forest, picking them off singly as they caught them, losing their own ranks to the slingstones and the swords of men who took someone with them as they died.

Starving, bleeding from wounds tied up with scraps of neck scarf or tunic, the Batavian detachment aimed for the beacon and then for the next one in the line of signal towers. Those manning the towers saw them stumble past but there was nothing that one or two more could do against the tide of the Gaels. When the Gaels realized the meaning of the beacons they swarmed up the towers anyway and left their keepers' bodies in the ashes.

Faustus kept them moving through some force of will he hadn't known he possessed. As dark fell they fed the gnawing hunger in their bellies with what they could catch, hares and birds brought down with stones, plantain leaves, and unripe berries. Afterward they slept the sleep of the half-dead and in the morning they ran again. If nothing else, they would lead the Gaels into the pila of the legion.

Slowly the numbers fell from eighty-five to seventy to sixty to forty-five, the shreds of what had been two centuries. Indus was still among them, with six dead Gaels to his credit and a gash down one calf that he staunched with a handful of plantain and tied up in his scarf.

"Do you think the governor is leading the Ninth himself?" he asked Faustus, because they were both on watch and if you didn't talk, you fell asleep on your feet, dragged down by the bone-weary despair of the hunted.

"I hope not," Faustus said. The night bred candor and what would have been impolitic to say in Vacomagorum wasn't a sentiment likely to get back to the governor, since they weren't either.

"They've a new legate since last year," Indus said. "He's accounted to be an old war horse."

Faustus had heard the same, and Indus's information was generally good. "That's hopeful then."

"Is it all for nothing, Prefect?" Indus asked. "I don't mean us, poor bastards. But what General Agricola did? Is that all going to slide into the Styx? Leave little bits of ditch and wall, a few spare pilum points, where we used to be? I was proud to be part of that. It would make up for a lot if I thought it would last."

Night and weariness and a longing for those he knew he wouldn't see again brought honesty. "I don't know."

–

In the morning they were on the run again. The cohort standard still led them. The signifer was limping and had lost his fox-skin hood but the standard would be brought home even if there was only one man left to carry it. Faustus praised them, cajoled them, led them on, clawing their way through the forest and the wild growth under the canopy, taking careful aim with slingstones when the hunters got too close. Then over the noise of their movement they heard another distant sound, the rumble of wagon wheels and thousands of mailed sandals, the drumming hooves of heavy cavalry. If they stopped running for a moment, they could feel it in the ground.

344

"Come on you bastards!" Indus shouted at the Gaels behind them. "Come and get a pilum down your throat and another up your ass! Batavians!"

"*Batavians!*"

"*Batavians! Rome!*"

They gathered the last strength they had and ran.

–

The Ninth Legion, even understrength, was a scarlet sea spread out across the scrub and grassland along the Alauna road under its great gold Eagle; five cohorts had already engaged the Cornovii along with the auxiliaries of the border forts who had held them off for two days. The legion's catapults were positioned on a rise overlooking the valley; their bolts screamed over the Roman line to land in the midst of the Cornovii war band, shattering chariots, horses, and foot fighters. The Ninth's legate watched from a hill behind them, calculating when to throw the balance of the legion in.

The First Batavians were on the western end of the line and Ansgarius saw their missing centuries before anyone else but the legate did. "Open ranks! Pull them in!"

The Gaels on their heels ran almost onto the Roman line as the last of their prey staggered through the Batavians' shield wall.

"Get them to the rear," Faustus told Indus, gasping for breath.

Ansgarius said, "You too, sir! Mother of All, how did you get back?"

"I don't know. How long have you—"

"Been fighting off these demons? Since the day before yesterday. We couldn't make a dent in them but we kept them stoppered. Barely. It was Tyr's own gift to see the Ninth."

Faustus took the cohort standard from the signifer and handed it to the first man he saw. "Now! Batavians! To me!" Miraculously, he had done what he set out to. Now the battle was the legate's to command. His own task was just to be seen, keep his cohort together, and drive it into the Cornovii ranks.

Ansgarius looked ready to protest. Faustus said, "You're a fine commander but they need to see me." The second wind that fear and fury gave would last him for a while. They needed to see him on his feet. The cohort cheered and surged forward behind him, their standard bright against the sky.

—

Riderch and Elwyn reordered their ranks, pressing their men against the legion's front line beside the Cornovii spearmen. A rider from Matauc ordered them to come around the Roman left flank where the defenses were weakest. They ignored him. Battle honors belonged to those in the forefront.

"They will fight as they are accustomed," Piran said to Matauc when his rider returned with that news. "Just be glad I have brought them to you."

"You did little enough and I am warlord," Matauc said. "Do you bring them to heel."

"As you say, you are warlord, so you may command them," Piran said. The Gaels would be dangerous afterward. He had no intention of allowing them to stay in his own territory once he was headman.

"And where are the allies who were to have joined us? Where are Emrys's men? Did you lie to me?"

"They are coming," Piran said. But they hadn't.

The battle swelled around them, and they left arguing to shout at their banner bearers, urging their men forward to howl for blood, for death to the Roman invaders, for the Morrigan to aid them, bringing the wealth that the Romans had siphoned off back to her own people. The Cornovii numbered in the thousands, swelled by the malcontents of Rhion's clan, but of Emrys there was no sign. Emrys would be sorry for that, Piran decided, when he turned the Gaels on Emrys's holds.

—

Faustus gripped his battered shield and sword. He had a three-day-old gash in his sword arm and his head was swimming. The Cornovii and the Gaels were hammering at the front shield line, but the auxiliaries and the fresh strength of the legion held them and pushed back. Faustus slotted himself into his cohort's front rank, in the old familiar place at the end of the shield wall, the familiar one step forward and then another, stab upward with the deadly short sword, ignore the pain in his arm, take another step. When a man fell, the man behind him moved forward and the wall closed up.

On Faustus's other side, a cohort of the Ninth was driving back the Cornovii, now intermingled with the Gaels in the chaos of their charge. A Cornovii warrior, red-bearded, face painted with the same blue that overlaid the clan marks on his arms, came at him, spear leveled, and Faustus swung up his shield to block it, wedging his sword up under the blow. The blade glanced off the man's leather shirt, turned by thick padding. Faustus stabbed again while the spearpoint wedged in the shield of the second century man beside him, tangling them together. The sword went through the leather hauberk this time and the Cornovii staggered and fell. As he went down, Faustus sheathed his sword to wrench the spear free. Another came at him and he thrust the Cornovii spear past the man's own shield into his chest. He pulled it loose again, drove it at another fighter in a ring-mail hauberk and lost it as the man slammed his shield into the spear shaft, an axe in his other hand. Faustus drew his sword again and went after him, and saw that it was Riderch. Riderch buried the edge of his axe blade into the shield wall and pulled the damaged shield from the auxiliaryman beside Faustus. Another came up from the second rank and took his place while Faustus held Riderch off. Riderch swung his axe and a legionary of the Ninth move sideways into the gap and drove his short sword up under Riderch's guard hard enough to split the ring mail where Faustus had notched it in the battle at Clota Mouth. The axe blade skimmed Faustus's helmet as Riderch dropped, blood bubbling through his mail.

"Thank you, friend," Faustus gasped.

"We saw you come in with them on your tail," the legionary said. "Couldn't let them have you now."

-

The legate of the Ninth watched the line from his vantage point on the hill. He took note of the prefect who had waylaid the Gaels until the legion could come up. He was the one who had sent a warning in the autumn and been ignored by Sallustius Lucullus. The legate thought now that Lucullus had had other things on his mind. There had been messages back and forth between Eburacum and Germany from people with whom the legate had no wish to be associated, including Antonius Saturninus, the governor of Upper Germany, who was dangerously ambitious, and Lartius Marena, who was simply dangerous. When Lucullus had ordered him north with the legion rather than lead it himself, the legate hadn't known if that argued that the governor did not expect this battle to be important enough to burnish his reputation, or if there were other matters involved. He decided that he would be careful in his dealings with Lucullus when he returned to Eburacum.

The legate raised his hand and a courier trotted over. "Bring the rest of the legion forward and send the reserve cavalry around the left flank. Drive the Gaels, assuming that's what they are, into the Britons and let them tangle each other." The border auxiliaries needed rest but he couldn't spare them yet.

-

A battle was always a few square feet to either side and a few before and behind. There was no way to see past that, only to feel the tide shifting when it did, forward momentum or pressure back. Either might hang on the cliff's edge for a moment and then break. This time, Faustus felt the push from the enemy slacken and stop as the reserves of the Ninth came into the line. And then they were moving forward, faster, as the war band's front line broke, cohorts formed into wedge-shaped formations that split them, funneled them backward into the Roman lines, cut them down and moved over them.

Another series of scorpion bolts flew over. Scorpions had to be carefully recalibrated when the target moved and Faustus said a quick prayer to the shade of Archimedes before the bolt landed solidly in the war band as it began to pull back. Another bolt shot over and then another, while the war band's lords shouted conflicting orders. Some pulled back; others charged the Roman pursuers with a howl. Among the Britons and Gaels, men who died in battle went to the best part of the afterlife, borne on the wings of the Morrigan herself. It made them resistant to retreat, and reckless in defeat.

The legate signaled his trumpeter: the auxiliaries to retire, the legion to open up on the wings and let the Cornovii and their allies run. It would cost fewer casualties to hunt them down that way than penned in and desperate.

Faustus's vision had begun to blur with exhaustion. The Gael came at him out of nowhere, out of the retreat, screaming, swinging his axe, ready to die in a fine red battle fury if he could take Faustus with him. Faustus had time only to glimpse a white face barely old enough for its straggling mustache before he raised his shield to defend himself. The axe thudded into the shield, splintering it. Faustus braced himself and pulled the shield free, felt Ansgarius come up on his other side.

"Back off, you fool!" Faustus shouted at the boy. Let the Morrigan take someone else.

The Gael swung his axe again and Ansgarius blocked it with his own shield while Faustus drove his sword into the boy's chest, armored only with a leather shirt. Just a boy who had been barely old enough to take his spear when Faustus had seen him in Inis Fáil.

Faustus stood over him in a black fury – at the dead boy, at all the adventurous boys, led by men old enough to know other and better ways to slake their boredom, who had cost him so many of his own; one of them Gwladus's man who had only wanted to serve out his twenty-five years and retire to a farm on the Rhenus.

"Do you know you're bleeding?" Ansgarius asked him.

"Where?"

"Pretty much everywhere unless it's someone else's. Some of it is, I think, but there's a slice out of your arm."

Faustus looked at his sword arm, tied up with a filthy strip torn from his undertunic. "I thought it had stopped. Opened up again, I guess." He swayed on his feet.

Ansgarius put his shoulder under Faustus's other arm. "Hospital."

The hospital tent was at the rear of the camp where the Ninth had joined the border garrisons. There the combined surgical staffs of the Ninth and the frontier forts were treating a steady stream of wounded.

Faustus blinked in the dimmer light of the tent, but what he had assumed to be an apparition born of longing continued to look back at him: Eirian with a bloody apron over her gown. She was washing vinegar into a festering arm. She closed her eyes for a moment when she saw him, lips offering a silent thanksgiving.

"I told you he was still with us," her patient, one of the shreds of the fourth century, said through gritted teeth.

"You did," she said. "I was afraid you were raving. Now be still. This is dangerously infected and Lascius says to wash it in vinegar and so we shall."

"Sit down, Prefect," Lascius said. He finished wrapping the end of a bandage around a clean ten inches of an otherwise filthy leg, and turned to Faustus. "Apparently you are immortal." He inspected Faustus's arm. "Did you clean this yourself?"

"With water," Faustus said.

"Well Aesculapius knows what was in the water, so we'll do it again." He held out his hand and an orderly put a sponge and a pot of vinegar in it. "And please don't order your lady out of here, she's been a godsend, along with your sister."

"My *sister*?" Faustus looked around wildly and saw, of all people, Silvia, ducking under the tent door with a pair of water jugs. "What are they *doing* here?"

Eirian rebandaged her patient's arm and came to stand beside him. "We attached ourselves to the column," she said quietly. "To know what was happening the soonest. It seemed to calm Silvia. Paullus found us a tent."

"Where?" Faustus asked. His own tent was long gone, abandoned in flight and scavenged no doubt by the Gaels, but Paullus was an expert at acquisition through dubious channels.

"He said it was reissued."

Reissued meant *don't ask where it came from*.

"And Lascius has let us make ourselves useful."

"It was like to be safer than the fort," Ansgarius said, joining Eirian's earnest explanation. "I gave them leave to come. I thought..." He broke off but it was clear what he had thought. When the prefect didn't come back he could try to see them to safety.

"Thank you," Faustus said, shaking now. "I see." Silvia had joined them. "I am all right," he told her. "Where is my nephew?"

"With Paullus and Gwladus, keeping him from getting underfoot." Silvia wore an apron as bloody as Eirian's.

Faustus closed his eyes for a moment. "Gwladus. I couldn't bring her man back."

"She didn't think you would," Silvia said. "I have promised we will take care of her."

He blinked at her. "How did you think to?" *When you thought I would be gone too. When I told you I probably would.* Something startling had happened to Silvia.

"I knew you would come back," Silvia said firmly. "I just did." She glanced at Eirian. "Both of us did."

He looked at Eirian. Eirian hadn't, he could tell. No one with any sense would have.

"I gave the Mother my gold armband," Eirian said. "I put it in the well for her." Water was always the link to the gods of the Orcades.

Perhaps that had saved him. One never knew. Not every man could say he was bought with a gold armband. He winced as Lascius set to cleaning the gash in his arm and smeared it with honey and a salve that smelled of garlic.

Eirian and Silvia took him to the reissued tent, let Lucius see him to prove he was alive, and left him to Paullus to put to bed. He heard Gwladus weeping but he hadn't the strength to speak to her. He didn't wake until morning, when trumpets blasted him from sleep and Paullus said the cohort was forming up and the legate of the Ninth had said that Faustus had best be with it. He growled and dressed, clenched his teeth, and let Paullus pull his ring mail back over his injured arm.

The legate paraded the legion and auxiliaries and spoke of their courage, the glory of Rome, and the favor of the gods. And then he summoned Faustus before him and picked up a wreath of dried grasses interwoven with sedge and yellow broom and the tiny white flowers of bedstraw.

Faustus gaped.

"Close your mouth, Prefect, and take your helmet off."

Faustus bent his bare head and the legate set it on his hair. "This comes not from me but was voted to you by the men of the border and of the Ninth Hispana."

The grass crown, woven from plants growing on the battle-field. Given rarely, and only to an officer who had saved an army. Its stems and leaves whispered in the breeze.

"Call up the men who came back with you."

Faustus turned to the ragged remnants of the first and fourth centuries. Ansgarius prodded them forward to stand under the silver spear of the cohort standard. The legate nodded to his optio and the optio wrote orders for six silver phalerae each as Faustus named them, his voice shaking. He thought he saw the dead ones paraded beside them. They saluted him and the legate and dissipated with the mist that was still burning off.

–

The Ninth and the border auxiliaries broke camp the next day. The war band had been hunted down and the few who had not been caught were no further danger. The Caledones would likely hound those out of their glens. Paullus dug up a box for the wreath of grasses and Eirian said, "If I pack it in sand it will keep."

"It's ephemeral," Faustus said. "It's supposed to be."

The army's other awards were silver or gold, but the grass crown, the most important of them, was fleeting. The emperor might, if he felt like it, send him a version in gold, but the thing itself would reduce to dry leaves as a reminder to its recipient that he too was mortal. Which was precisely what was on his mind.

"I spoke to the legate," he said, "and he will witness for us before the legion leaves."

"Witness what?"

"A marriage. Now. Today. Ansgarius and Lascius too, but I want the legate, the higher the rank of the witnesses the better."

Eirian set the wreath in the box. She looked at him uneasily. "Faustus, we were to wait and see."

"We waited too long," he said. "I will never do that again and take the chance you'll be left with nothing, like Gwladus, if I'm killed."

"Poor Gwladus. Her man would have married her if he'd been allowed."

"I'm allowed." He pulled her to him and she laid her head on his chest. He said, "If you hadn't wanted me, you wouldn't have followed the column." It wasn't a question.

"No," she admitted.

"Are you worried where we might go next?" The north was crumbling despite their victory. He could be posted anywhere.

"Silvia says that officers' wives are expected to advance their careers. I don't know quite what she means. Be suitable, I think."

"Silvia didn't want me in the army in the first place and I haven't the background or connections to go much higher than I have. Silvia should mind her own spinning." He would have a word with Silvia.

"Don't scold her," Eirian said, reading that thought with unnerving accuracy. "She never thinks before she says things."

"Forget Silvia. I never thought to see you again after we sailed from the Orcades," he whispered into her hair. "Nor again when we marched ten days ago. If the gods have given you back to me twice, or me to you, that's something not to be refused."

—

A marriage might be embellished with priests and sacrifices but all that was actually required was a statement by the couple that they intended to live as husband and wife, witnessed by parties of established character. Faustus and Eirian stood before the legate on the camp parade ground where he had been given the grass crown and swore to their intent before the gods.

The legate signed the document, written by his own scribe in a finer hand than Faustus could have produced, and stamped it with his seal. It was a small kindness that the legate found satisfying to confer before he took the Ninth south again. The border was stabilized for the time being but they couldn't afford another campaign in the highlands. He couldn't leave the Brigantes around Eburacum unwatched with the Second Adiutrix pulled from Britain; the Brigantes' pacification was tenuous and always had been. Agricola had intended the Ninth to occupy Castra Pinnata as the primary military bastion of the north, but work there had almost ceased from lack of supplies and men. The border auxiliaries under Prefect Valerianus would have to hold the frontier. Officers' wives there were a hindrance or an asset, depending on the wife. This girl from the Orcades had nerves of iron; the legate had seen her in the hospital helping the Batavians' surgeon take a man's leg off.

Ansgarius and Lascius signed the document as well, and Faustus tucked it in his belt. That was what they would find a strongbox for, not the crown of grass.

—

They spent the afternoon in bed while the cohort drank the prefect's health.

"Once for my coming back alive," Faustus said, panting, his left hand on her breast and his right propped on a pillow to ease the pressure on his healing arm. "And twice for the marriage." He began to kiss her again and she wrapped her arms around his back. The clan markings on her breasts were dappled and indistinct in the dim light, like a seal's coat. Once he had wondered if she might actually turn to one in his arms, but that had been in the islands, when she had seemed to him a creature of water and magic. This woman was solid, her true form warm and inviting, pulling him down into her again.

Afterward, her head propped on his shoulder, he said, "When I have leave, when the north is not coming apart, I will take you to Londinium or Aquae Sulis. Even to Rome."

"Silvia says there are great wonders in Rome."

"She is right for once. There are even greater ones in Egypt. When I retire we will go to see the pyramids."

"What are those?" She pulled the blankets closer about them.

"Tombs of ancient kings, older even than Rome, thousands of years old. More than four hundred feet high. They are one of the seven wonders of the world, with the Pharos at Alexandria and the gardens of Babylon."

"Have you seen all those?" The world outside of Britain, beyond the highlands even, seemed vast and inconceivable to her.

"Only in paintings. My father had scenes from the Nile painted on our dining room walls." The crocodile had been the subject of his childhood nightmares.

"Who were these kings?" Eirian asked him.

"The old lords of Egypt. They were buried with great treasures for the afterlife so the tombs have mostly been robbed."

That struck Eirian as a dangerous undertaking; the treasures must have been great indeed. She sat up, practical-minded now. "I will go see about supper. I think Argos caught a hare if Paullus hasn't let him eat it himself. Sleep if you can. That arm will heal best if you rest it."

She disappeared into the front of the tent and Faustus wondered again where it had come from. It was an officer's tent, red leather, with three rooms and a wooden floor, better than his old one. He yawned. He was still bone weary and making love to Eirian had been soporific. He would give Paullus a present for what he had done, he thought sleepily. He could give him his freedom but Paullus had enough money to buy it himself and didn't seem to want to. Faustus had freed Paullus in his will but until that came about Paullus appeared to like the army. He took like a seagull to the craft of procuring things that were technically unavailable; the tent had a rug that Faustus had never seen before.

"One day she will look for her skin as your mother did," a voice said, and Faustus jerked awake again. His father's shade was hovering over the bedside.

Faustus sat up. "She isn't a selkie and neither was Mother. Go away."

"She might as well have been," the shade said fretfully.

"How old was she when you bought her?" Faustus had never asked his mother her age. She was just Mother. Mothers didn't have an age in their children's eyes, as if they were never children themselves. But she had been.

"Fifteen," the shade said. "I waited until she was seventeen to marry her."

Fifteen to be caught by strangers and taken to a slave market.

"And you couldn't figure out why she didn't love you?" Faustus asked acidly.

"I gave her a good life. Far better than she would have had with most men who might buy her."

"You saved her from a brothel or a life hoeing onions. She should have fallen down and kissed your feet. I can't think why she didn't."

"Your tone is disrespectful."

"Your presence is unwelcome."

Silvius Valerianus looked affronted. "I only wish to keep you from the errors that I made."

"You've already done that," Faustus snapped. "When in doubt, I think 'What would Father do?' and then I do the other thing." He lay down and turned his back on the old man.

"Deliberate disrespect."

"It's served me well so far," Faustus said.

"You risked your sister's life bringing her to this place!"

Faustus sat up again. His father's accusations had an unhappy habit of mirroring his own secret worries. "*You* married her to Manlius!"

"If you hadn't sold the farm that had been in our family for *two hundred years* she could have come to live with you there. *You* are responsible now, for whatever happens to her. *And* your wife, *and* the men who follow you." The shade gave the box with the grass crown a scornful look as if he could see through the wood to the wreath of grasses that Faustus's living men had gathered from among the dead.

"I do not need you to haunt me," Faustus whispered. "I have them."

–

The fleeing remnants of the war band made an attempt to find safety in Caledone villages and found Rhion's men waiting to harry them north instead. Rhion added to his acquisition of five hundred good Roman horses loot from the retreating Cornovii before sending them on their way.

The Gaels they hounded north as well, while Elwyn's survivors and Riderch's quarreled with each other and the lesser fian commanders swayed any argument from one side to the other like trees in a high wind.

"Cuckoo eggs in Matauc's nest," Rhion said with satisfaction.

"Matauc is more than likely dead," Idgual said.

"If he isn't he'll not trouble us for a generation at least."

Neither mentioned Piran, who would trouble no one anymore either, except perhaps in Idgual's memory of two boys who had taken their spears together.

Piran fled north with the survivors but they gave him a wide berth, exiling from their companionship the one who had convinced Matauc to take his tribe against Rome, convinced the restless among the Caledones to follow, promised an alliance with Emrys that had never come. Stumbling at last into their own lands, they came to empty villages and found that Emrys's men had been before them. So far from joining the war band, Emrys's raiders had looted the undefended holds as soon as the Cornovii marched south. Emrys had placed his wager with Rome.

A track fit for goats narrowed along a cliff, rising steeply over a lake where a cluster of crannogs huddled. Smoke still rose from the charred thatch of their roofs and even from here Piran could see the broken walls, the pilings fractured where an axe had cut nearly through them. The sky was a rare clear blue. Across it a flock of crows flapped overhead to settle in a stand of pines above him. It was the kind of summer day that showed the world clearly, almost too bright to keep his eyes on. He stared at the sky, bewildered. Nothing had unfolded as he had imagined it. He would never be the avenging warlord of a free people, the hero who drove the hated Romans back across the water out of Britain. The omens had seemed so clear, bright as the sky, and yet neither Aelwen nor Ceridwen had wed him, he was not headman of the Caledones, and even Idgual had left him. The Romans had won. The Cornovii were unlikely to give him shelter. He looked over his shoulder at the crows and knew who sent them. It was a long drop to the lake, long enough to be deadly. Piran balanced on the cliff edge and the outcropping rocks. He thought he saw black wings around him as he fell but they did not bear him up.

XXI. AT THE HINGES OF THE YEAR

LATE WINTER, 842 ab urbe condita

The courier arrived on a lathered horse and Ansgarius brought the sealed tablet to Faustus in the Praetorium. "It looked important enough to hunt you up," he said. "Coming through bad weather to get here."

Faustus broke the seal. Anything that came in on the heels of a snowstorm was important, but this widened his eyes as he read. "Mithras," he whispered.

Ansgarius looked at him, expectant and uneasy.

"Lucullus is gone."

"He's been recalled?"

"His head has."

Ansgarius looked green.

"They've sent a procurator to be in charge in the interim, not another governor. It doesn't say what the interim is going to be."

The rest of the story came shortly after, by official proclamation and word of mouth. Antonius Saturninus, governor of Upper Germany, had staged a failed revolt with the two legions under his command and a tribe of Germans who had abandoned him at the last moment. A great many heads had rolled, including his own and those of the other senators suspected of being in on it. Sallustius Lucullus had been one of them. So had Lartius Marena and his son. Like most of Rome, the emperor had owed Marena money. Whether the Marenas had actually been involved in the conspiracy or not, it had provided the emperor with an opportunity to cancel the debt. The position of *amicus* to the emperor was not one to overstep.

Faustus absorbed all this along with the information from the horsemaster at Tamia that those five hundred horses had not been paid for before the governor's death and so their expense was unofficially off the books, in case the prefect was worrying about that. The prefect had been, but he also knew there would be no replacements for his lost men. That was clear.

The occupation of the north was over. Six years with Julius Agricola for his successor to lose it all in four. The emperor wouldn't trust another military governor with Britain for years. The disposal of Lartius Marena seemed almost unimportant in comparison, although Faustus thought briefly of the curse he had paid for with his phalera. Ceridwen had quoted Seneca to Tribune Caecilius: *Do not ask for what you will wish you had not got.* Faustus would have traded a permanent posting to the icy halls of Castra Borea to preserve the borders his general had achieved.

–

At Beltane, as a gesture of peaceable intentions, Rhion invited the Roman commander to the feasting that followed the marriage of Ceridwen, the old warlord's daughter, and Idgual, new lord of Piran's old holding. Faustus bought a bronze cook pot for a wedding present and made a decision.

It took some maneuvering to find Aelwen by herself while the celebration in the courtyard of Bryn Caledon grew merrier and louder. Eirian was watching Ceridwen and Idgual, both crowned with heather, dance around the Beltane fire to the increasingly rowdy cheers of the guests. Aelwen stood to one side, half smiling and wistful, and her face made up Faustus's mind for him.

"There is something I have thought for a long while on whether to say to you, lady," Faustus said.

She looked at him suspiciously. "You sent our people back alive as you promised when my brother let them follow you, so I must listen, but it had best not be to trust you with my daughter or any others again."

"I commanded Tuathal Techtmar's army when he took the High King's throne in Inis Fáil," Faustus said carefully. "There were some of your clan among them, men who fought in the war against Rome."

Aelwen's expression shifted. "Dai?" she asked carefully. "We have not known where he went."

"Dai and one other."

The cheering around the fire grew louder. She rocked on her feet a little and put out a hand as if she would take his arm to steady herself, then pulled it back. He could barely hear her whisper, "Tell me."

"He is Owain now," Faustus said as quietly. "He has land and a good holding in Inis Fáil that the High King has given him."

"His arm?"

"He has little use of it but he is very dangerous with the other one." He could see her swallowing that information. Whether it was a bitter drink or not he couldn't tell.

"And you have not told your governor? The new one or the other?"

"No." *Mithras, no.* Not unless he had a death wish.

"And yet you tell me. Why?"

"Because I do not know how long we can keep the emperor's peace in the north," Faustus said. "We may become enemies again. I tell you now to be sure that I can."

Aelwen stared at the fire and the dancing figures. "He will have found another woman by now."

"He has not."

"Then why has he not sent for me?"

"Likely he thinks you are better off without him."

"Why do men decide what women want without asking them?" She was angry now, whether at him or at Owain he wasn't certain. Both probably.

"Mostly because we are fools," Faustus said. "He won't come back," he added. "He was asked to and he refused. Because of that I saw no need to tell the governor. You will have to go to him."

"I will think on that," Aelwen said. "It may be too late. Nevertheless, thank you for telling me. And for keeping his secret. That was dangerous for you to do."

"It was."

"What would happen if your new governor found out?"

"Nothing good for me."

"And for him? Would they hunt him down?"

"The governor's arm doesn't reach to Inis Fáil. But his name alone is sufficient to set the frontier in flames, whether he comes back or no. You have enough hotheads left for that." He hesitated. "There is one other thing. Piran knew and Idgual knows."

"I will speak to Idgual," Aelwen said. "And we will have words about why he did not tell me. But Idgual is not a fool."

Nor was Aelwen, Faustus thought. He had as good as told her that Rome's grip on the north was sliding. All that Agricola had gained would be gone again soon enough. It wasn't strictly for Owain's sake that he had sought the chance to speak to her and slip that sideways into the talk. All her brother Rhion need do was outwait them. Attrition would accomplish what war had not, with no more lives lost for nothing, Mithras willing. Mars Ultor was war's god but Mithras was the soldiers' god.

―

There were always ghosts at Samhain. Owain watched them drift through the bare trees, clustering beyond the need-fire. Ghosts of the men he had killed, of the men who had held this land before him, of the one that the High King had slain only yesterday.

Tuathal and a cavalcade of lords had been on their way to Cruachan for Samhain, quarreling as they went because the High King would not rescind his order that no man who had gone to Britain might come back. Matters had come to a head as they halted for the night at Owain's hold. Word had come of the defeat in Britain and lords with sons in the fianna began to argue to take them back again. The argument had spiraled into a direct challenge to the High King and ended with one lord dead and the rest grumbling but acquiescent. No one else had pulled a knife but Cassan and Dai had looked ready to if it had gone on longer. The whole quarrelsome lot had ridden the next day for Cruachan, taking the dead lord with them.

Here at the hinge of the year Owain felt double-bodied, two men on different sides of a doorway. It was probably time to close that door, to belong where he lived now. If the fianna could not go home, neither could he.

It was full dark and his people had scattered to their homes, taking their bits of fire to light the village hearths, when the rider came up the track from the sea road to Drumanagh. Another wandering ghost, he thought, and nodded to it. There was not much left in this world or the next for him to fear.

Then a horse in his stable whickered and the ghost horse whickered back. The rider put the hood back from their cloak. Owain sat up and then stood. There was still enough red in her hair to burn like a fox's pelt in the firelight.

–

Faustus and Eirian stood on the sentry walk of Vacomagorum to watch the fire being lit in the village below. It was the last Samhain they would spend in the north. The tablet with his orders sat on his desk in the Principia.

"Do you think she went to him?"

"Rhion said she went to live with the holy women on Mona," Faustus said. He remembered the holy mother there. She had been young but, like Curlew, still imbued with some old deep power he would not have wanted to cross. Neither had General Agricola.

"It is a long journey," Eirian said. "But I hope she did."

"Isca's a long way from your islands," Faustus said. The First Batavians were being pulled out to shore up the Danuvius but he was posted south. Back to Isca Silurum, back to his old legion, with a substantial promotion. He and the Ninth Hispana's legate had until the next spring to supervise the evacuation of the north and the decommissioning of the incomplete fort at Castra Pinnata.

"I will go where you go," Eirian said quietly. "I gave the Mother my gold armband for you."

He hadn't said that the legate of the Second Augusta had asked for him not strictly for his mad heroics on the border but because he was half-Silure. *There is something brewing here that I don't like*, the legate had written in a letter that accompanied the official posting.

Even Silvia approved of the posting. Isca had become greatly more attractive after the northern border. Lucius could go to a proper school, and Gwladus would be back among her own people. Faustus owed her that at least. His father's shade would no doubt trail behind them, an aggrieved presence just out of sight. He had appeared just once since the battle, to hover over the Augusta legate's letter like candle smoke and advise dolefully, "Do not go to your mother's people. They will bind you as they did her."

The wooden fire drill began to smoke and suddenly flames rose in the kindling. Faustus put his arm around Eirian and they watched as the village came to take burning brands from it, running toward their darkened houses, sparks streaming behind them. The things that preyed on his mind lifted and dissipated in the river of sparks. For now there was a new fire, a new posting, a marriage still relatively new and still a source of wonder and gratitude. His father's shade and whatever the Silures were up to could look after themselves for the night. He kissed his wife and made a rude gesture behind his back when the sentries on the walkway hooted at them and cheered.

Author's Note

On Language, History, and Myth

The language spoken in Britain at this time would have been dialects of Brythonic. The Gaels of Ireland had not yet come to what is now Scotland, and the language of the Caledones would instead have been similar to that of the southern tribes. The only remnants of Brythonic now are in the languages of Wales, Cornwall, and Brittany, and so when choosing names for my Caledones and their hillforts I have looked more to names from Welsh sources than to Gaelic ones. The exceptions are Tuathal Techtmar and Calgacos of the Caledones, who live at the edges of history where it often crosses into myth.

The only source for the existence of Calgacos is the Roman historian Cornelius Tacitus and he may have simply made up a war leader on whom to hang an eloquent pre-battle speech. At any rate, Calgacos is never heard of afterward and Tacitus says nothing about what happened to him after the final battle with Agricola's forces, a circumstance which is too much for any writer to resist.

Tuathal Techtmar is a legendary High King of Ireland, son of a deposed ruler who came back from exile in Britain to reclaim his father's throne. The first accounts of him appear in medieval sources but it is thought that he actually existed, and historians put his exile and return in the first or second century, ranging from the time of the Flavian emperors through the reign of Hadrian. One theory stems from Tacitus's mention of an exiled Irish prince who was to be Agricola's pretext for an invasion of Hibernia, and there is a possibility that he may have been given unofficial Roman support. Because this fits my purposes nicely, I have chosen to adopt it.

The written history of Ireland begins in the ninth century with the *Historia Brittonum* of Nennius, which is highly suspect, as is Gerald of Wales's twelfth-century *Topographia Hibernica* and the eleventh-century *Lebor Gabála Érenn*. In other words, nobody really knows what was going on in the first century. So my first-century Irish are composed mainly of myth and guesswork, with Tuathal's battles for the High Kingship based largely on the *Lebor Gabála Érenn*. As to their language, Primitive Irish is thought to have been very close to Gaulish. Maybe.

No one really knows what was going on in Britain after Agricola was recalled either. Sallustius Lucullus may have been the next governor, followed by someone uncertain, or vice versa. Little is known about Lucullus other than that Domitian had him executed in either 89 or 93. Suetonius attributes his downfall to naming a fancy new kind of lance after himself, and at least one modern historian thinks he may have been the owner, or one of them, of Fishbourne Roman Palace near Chichester, Britain's largest Roman palace. The theory that he may have been involved in the rebellion of Antonius Saturninus in Germany offers a more serious possibility.

We have no real confirmation of Roman permanent forts in the highlands north of Stracathro (which I have named Vacomagorum since we don't know its actual Roman name), let alone as far north as I have put Castra Borea. But Agricola would certainly have meant to incorporate the highlands into the Empire after investing a six-year campaign in conquering them, so he must have intended some of his temporary camps to become permanent, as there would be very little chance of maintaining that without a military presence. I have sited fictional Roman camps such as Castra Borea in places where there have been found at least a few Roman artefacts, and fictional Celtic ones where there is evidence of Iron Age habitation. Guesswork based on possibility is the work of the historical novelist.

Where I cross most definitely into the territory of myth is with the Old Ones, the little dark people of the hills. There was indeed a small, dark, probably blue-eyed, race who lived in Britain before the tall fair Celts, and whose DNA still appears in Britons of today. "Cheddar Man," the Mesolithic body dated to 7150 BCE and found in Somerset, provided the DNA evidence for dark skin and pale eyes. He also, with more advanced testing, proved to have a living relative, a Somerset history teacher who shares his mitochondrial DNA, indicating a common maternal ancestor. These folk flourished at least 6,000 years before the Celts first came, and their descendants were no doubt absorbed into the dominant populace long before the date of this novel, even if they did not entirely vanish, making their continued presence as a distinct people unlikely.

Mythologically speaking, however, they are still a presence and their echoes may be heard even today in folklore, in the tales of small folk inhabiting the hollow hills, the Neolithic burial chambers that dot the land, seldom encountered and often vengeful and dangerous when they are. As each new wave of invaders flows across Britain these old ones fade ever further into the background, living on the edges of the newcomers' settlements, hunting with the flint and bronze weapons that the newcomers' iron blades so easily defeat; remnants who eventually achieve the status of the fae of fireside stories, for whom it is still advisable to put out a saucer of milk now and then. For that reason they inhabit this series.

And Gratitude

I owe grateful thanks as always to my husband, Tony Neuron, for general moral support, map-making, and a librarian's eye for fact-checking (do wolves have dew claws?); to Kit Nevile, who is a peerless editor; and to Kate Berens, an equally peerless copy editor. All three have saved me from errors large and small.

And to my brother-in-law Michael Neuron for the story of José de la Guerra and the false cavalry.

Place Names

368

Eburacum York
Great Firth* Moray Firth
Isca Silurum Caerleon
Lyn Emrys* New Kinord
Nall's hold Beinn Freiceadain
Orcades The Orkneys
Tamia Bertha, north of Perth
Tarvo Dubron Thurso
Trimontium Eildon
Tuesis (camp) Bellie
Tuesis (river) Spey
Vacomagorum* Stracathro
Venta Silurum Caerwent

Elsewhere

Aeaea mythical Greek island inhabited by the sorceress Circe
Narbo Martius Narbonne, France

Glossary

Annwn Celtic land of the dead

amicus a personal friend

Archimedes Greek mathematician, considered the father of modern mathematics

Bellona Roman goddess of war

Boreas personification of the North Wind

brehons Irish judges who dealt with all matters of law

Brigid Celtic goddess of poetry and art

bulla protective amulet worn by Roman boys until adulthood

century eighty men

Ceres goddess of the harvest and also doorwarden of the portal between life and death

cohort six centuries; ten cohorts make a legion

coryza a cold

crannog a lake dwelling built on pilings over the water

Dagda the good god, chief god of Ireland

decumana gate rear gate

dexter gate right hand gate

Dobunni British tribe centered roughly in Gloucestershire

Druids ancient Celtic priesthood

the Eagles the Roman army; from the eagle standards of the legions

Epona Celtic goddess of horses and guide to the afterlife

fian band of young fighting men in Ireland; plural *fianna*

fascinus amulet embodying the divine phallus; generally a penis with wings

fine Irish family group of five generations

Gaia among the most common of Roman names, thus a generic name for any woman

geas a taboo that may not be broken; breaking a geas results in death

genius loci the spirit or god of a place

the Goddess Earth Mother in any of her many forms

gorgon monstrous woman with snakes for hair whose gaze turns people to stone

gladius Roman short sword

greaves lower leg armor

hauberk shirt of ring mail or scale

Hyperborea mythical land north of the known world

Janus Roman god of change and time; two-faced, he could see both past and future

Juno chief Roman goddess and wife of Jupiter

Jupiter chief of the Roman pantheon

Lares household gods

latrunculi Roman board game of strategy

Lleu Welsh name of Lugh

lorica armor made of segmented plates

Lugh Celtic god of the sun and harvest

Manannan mac Lir Celtic god of the sea

Manes spirits of revered ancestors representing the divine dead

Mithras Persian savior god adopted by Roman soldiers

paterfamilias head of a Roman household

phalera medal for bravery, a disk of gold or silver

poppy tears painkiller made from the opium poppy

Praetorian Gate main gate in a Roman camp

Praetorium commander's house in a fort or camp

Principia headquarters in a fort or camp

Rosaliae signorum in the Roman army, the garlanding of the standards

sidhe in Celtic legend, the hollow hills of faery; here a dwelling of an older race

spoon "spoon of Diocles," an instrument for pulling arrows and spearpoints

tabula Roman board game, ancestor of backgammon

Taranis Celtic god of thunder

tribune military officer, either political appointee or career man. Political appointees wore a broad purple stripe on their tunic, career men a narrow stripe.

tuath cluster of families that made up an Irish kingdom

Tyr Germanic god of war

Venus Roman goddess of love and of gardens and growing things

Vercingetorix Gaulish chieftain who led a rebellion against Julius Caesar

vicus civilian village surrounding a Roman fort

Vesta Roman goddess of home and family

Wisdom Celtic board game